SOULJAH

John R Gordon lives and works in London, England. He is the author of five other novels, *Black Butterflies*, (GMP 1993), for which he won a New London Writers' Award; *Skin Deep*, (GMP 1997); and *Warriors & Outlaws* (GMP 2001), both of which have been taught on graduate and post-graduate courses on Race & Sexuality in Literature in the United States; *Faggamuffin* (Team Angelica 2012); and *Colour Scheme* (Team Angelica 2013). He script-edited and wrote for the world's first black gay television show, Patrik-Ian Polk's *Noah's Arc* (2005-6). In 2007 he wrote the autobiography of America's most famous black gay porn-star from taped interviews he conducted, *My Life in Porn: the Bobby Blake Story*, (Perseus 2008). In 2008 he co-wrote the screenplay for the GLAAD Award-winning *Noah's Arc* feature-film, *Jumping the Broom* (Logo) for which he received an NAACP Image Award nomination. That same year his short film *Souljah* (directed by Rikki Beadle-Blair) won the Soho Rushes Award for Best Film.

As well as mentoring and encouraging young gay and lesbian and racially-diverse writers, he also paints, cartoons and does film and theatre design; and he is a student of Vodoun.

www.johnrgordon.com

SOULJAH

JOHN R GORDON

TEAM
ANGELICA

Published September 2014 by Team Angelica Publishing,
an imprint of Angelica Entertainments Ltd

Team Angelica Publishing
51 Coningham Road
London W12 8BS

TEAM
ANGELICA

www.teamangelica.com

A CIP catalogue record for this book is available from the
British Library

ISBN 978-0-9569719-5-1

Printed and bound by Lightning Source

For Rikki and Diriye, two soldiers;
For Isabel, my mother, and
Peter, my father

Bi o s'enia, imale o si
If humanity were not, the gods would not be

(Yoruba proverb)

Chapter One

The youth pulled aside the pinned piece of fabric that served for a curtain and looked out across the estate. Towerblocks named for the points of the compass rose up at its corners like prison watch-towers.

The flat the youth and his mother had been allocated was on the fifteenth floor of the westernmost of these, Cardinal One. It looked inwards, into the estate, not out across the city. They had been there four months now.

Between the Cardinals interconnected low-rises, grey, pebble-dashed and small-windowed, sprawled in a monochrome maze. Those in the middle of the estate rose up on ferroconcrete struts above a sunken central area of lock-ups and disused parking-spaces the residents called the rat-run and avoided. From the walkways that crisscrossed the space above the rat-run bin-bags of used nappies were flung, fridges, sofas and chairs were tipped, and analogue television sets dropped to smash plosively among the burnt-out, TWOCd motors that rusted below.

The walkways radiated out through the low-rises and ran down to the edges of the estate. There, and only there, in a narrow outermost ring, could be found trees and grass. The trees struggled and were scrawny, and the grass was poisoned by dog-urine and by carbon monoxide from the urban dual carriageways that cut the estate off from its neighbours. This isolation didn't spare it the violence that scarred the rest of the area, however: split by administrative chance into three different postcodes, it was plagued by battles for territory between gangs of local youths.

Beyond all that, and on this particular day hazy under a dull sky, was the city the African youth had dreamed of: the London of Dickens and Shakespeare, Fashion Week and Carnaby Street, Savile Row and the King's Road; the London of the romantic past that was also a city of the shining future, all glinting skyscrapers; its lighthouse-tipped Canary Wharf, curving, gleaming Gherkin and jutting Shard as unreachable to him as that city of centuries past, despite being not so far away in miles from where he lived.

No, from where he had been put. Where they had all been put.

Looking out, the youth ignored what was further off. Today he was concerned only with what was near: the twice-daily gauntlet he had to run to get off and on the estate.

First, of course, came the lift, if the lift was working. If it wasn't working you started your day trudging down fifteen flights of stairs knowing you would probably have to struggle back up them later, but at least you had a good chance of not being bothered for most of your descent: the jackals, as his mother called the drug-dealing youths of the estate, were too lazy to climb more than a few floors to carry out their transactions, as were their customers. One time he had found a used syringe as high as the twelfth floor, along with a random spray of blood up the wall from where some junkie had cleaned out his or her needle before injecting, but that was a one-off.

The advantage of the stairs over the lift was you were moving. If the jackals were down there, so long as they were distracted by a customer or by some other resident who had the bad luck to be passing up or down ahead of you, you had a good chance of getting by them with only words being hurled at you.

The lift, which stank so persistently of urine that to begin with he had imagined it was the presence of some mechani-cal lubricant that just happened to smell exactly like urine, did work sometimes, and that was a relief. But every time it stopped there was a danger one or more of *them* would get in, and you would be trapped for the long, slow ascent or descent, to be spat at, menaced, toyed with or aggressively ignored, as it pleased their mood.

Once you were outside, then came the playground. Its swings, slide and climbing-frame were gaily-painted in yellows, blues and reds, yet surrounded by fifteen-foot railings it felt like a prison yard. Sometimes the jackals did their business there, but mostly they preferred the underpass. This lay down a flight of steps just beyond the play-ground and, unless you were prepared to take a lengthy detour, was the only way off the estate on its western side: the only way you could reach the bus-stops, local shops and the school the youth attended. Its fluorescent lights were perpetually broken, dimmed or flickering, and going down there felt like a descent into the underworld.

At its centre, in a gap between the lanes of the dual-carriageway above, was a space open to the sky.

There the jackals waited, predatory and bored; and there, in tunnels that owing to poor drainage had in their centres rancid pools of rainwater, rotting leaves and trash, their customers loitered, zombie-like, disconcerting, but generally harmless as long as they had had their hit.

And finally, beyond that, just a few streets further along, although to him this morning it felt impossibly far off, was the boy's goal: a run-down secondary school from which, owing to government cutbacks, a rebuilding grant had just been withdrawn. It was, nonetheless, a sanctuary for the quiet and studious young African, who turned away from the window with a sigh, letting the make-do curtain fall back into place.

Every day began this way for him, as it did for his mother, with dread.

The youth was short and slightly built. He had a shaved head and a face that was sculpted like a Benin bronze. His full features were pretty rather than handsome, and his skinny frame was delicately articulated. A feyness in his manner that he couldn't conceal drew hostility towards him from other boys, and sometimes from girls too. He was seventeen years old, though the papers granting him leave to remain in the United Kingdom said he was fifteen, and his name was Stanlake. He and his mother had been in the U.K. for nine months now, in London for four. They were asylum-seekers.

Stanlake experienced his existence in the U.K. within a corruption of words. 'Asylum', once an old-fashioned word for safety, was now permanently fused in his mind with 'Centre', and carried with it an undertow of 'lunatic', both associations suggesting forcible confinement. The word 'refugee' had been split from its root, 'refuge', and had acquired ugly connotations: uneducated, unwanted, resourceless, dirty, idle – words that once flung stuck and burned like phosphorus. Yet those words lied. Stanlake studied hard and learned while the other students at his school seemed concerned only with gaining experience of sex-acts and deranging the senses with drink and drugs; and his mother worked at jobs the parents of his fellow pupils scorned to do, preferring for the state to pay them to be idle. The idea of relying on the state for one's livelihood was utterly alien to Stanlake, as it was to his mother. How are we parasites, he would wonder as he passed yet another vicious newspaper headline: surely to pick up and make use of what was discarded and unwanted was a good thing?

It seemed he had passed through forests only to arrive at further forests.

First there had been the forest of his childhood, filled with spirits, a magical, sometimes frightening place of songs and stories and wonder. Then the war forest, terrible and awful, that had been his home for three hallucinatory years, until he fled it and ran back to his village and his mother and escaped with her. Then came the forest of bureaucracy through which they had had to fight their way when they arrived at Dover penniless, friendless, under-dressed and bitterly cold. And now there was this: urban jungle, with human beasts round every corner.

A fistful of jewels and a diamond tiara had got them onto the ship, all that Stanlake had taken with him when he and his fellow-soldiers deserted the roadblock as the war exploded around them. His mother had looked at him as he pushed the glittering tangle into the man's hand, and she had not asked him how he came by it any more than she had asked him about the tiara he had been wearing on his head when he emerged from the forest, weaponless and ragged, concave-bellied and dull-eyed, staggering like one already dead, crowned like an ancestor, to reclaim her from the plunging chaos of the war.

'Most of these are worthless,' the man had said dismissively as he cast an eye over the tangle of pendants, chains and bangles. He was the deputy harbourmaster, a short, stocky man with a gut that thrust against the front of his freshly-pressed, short-sleeved shirt like a two-year pregnancy. A gold sovereign-ring with a ruby in it glinted on his right little finger. His round face was shiny with sweat. The three of them were huddled in the shadow of a shipping container, out of the sight of the others. He twisted the tiara so it sparkled and flashed in the low light. 'Worthless,' he repeated.

'So give me back the ones that are worthless and keep the ones of value for yourself,' said Stanlake, keeping his eyes on the deputy harbourmaster's.

The man grinned. 'Okay, okay,' he said. 'Since I can see you are very desperate I will help you.' He pocketed the gleaming tangle of chains and pendants and the tiara too, and for a second Stanlake regretted giving it to him. Now I have nothing, he thought. The man glanced back along the dock. 'Come with me,' he said. 'Quickly-o.'

Stanlake and his mother, their few other possessions in a knotted bundle on her head, followed him across the dock and, at his indication, joined a line of people waiting to make their way up a narrow gang-plank to the brightly-lit deck of a cargo-ship that was otherwise unreachable some twenty feet above their heads. Below, invisible in the dark, the waves slapped flatly metallic against the rising side of the ship. There were fifteen or twenty people ahead of Stanlake and his mother in the line, men and women, all carrying bags and bundles, some even with suitcases. Coming to this place was the first time Stanlake had ever seen the sea. By day the blank, featureless horizon had made him uneasy; concealed in darkness it was worse. Strange, it struck him later, how the unknown can terrify you however great the terrors you are running from.

The deputy harbourmaster approached a tall, boney-faced man with gold-braided epaulettes on his shoulders who seemed to be checking names off a clipboard, though he wasn't asking anyone for identity papers or travel docu-ments. The two men spoke and the deputy harbourmaster pointed to Stanlake and his mother. The man with the clipboard looked annoyed and made a dismissive gesture. The deputy harbourmaster looked offended. Discussion between the two became heated, though they kept their voices low so their actual words were inaudible.

The man with the clipboard glanced at his watch and gestured to a tall man in an orange tee-shirt who was standing at the head of the line that he could board. Steadying the bundle on his head with one hand, the man stepped cautiously onto the gangplank. His weight made it bow a little and set the links of the handrail-chains clinking. The other passengers followed him. Stanlake and his mother shuffled forward. The argument between the deputy harbourmaster and the other man was still going on. The clipboard man wasn't looking at them. Could they sneak onto the ship unnoticed? Surely not. If they weren't let on, would the deputy harbourmaster betray them? Take the jewels and turn them away? If he did, there would be nothing Stanlake could do about it. Not here. In the forest he would have acted without hesitation, as the bullet does not hesitate when the hammer strikes its base. But here he had no status, no Kalash.

Still, the deputy harbourmaster was from his tribe. Surely even in these times where everything had been turned upside-down and torn inside-out that still counted for something? Yet equally surely this man must be a government lackey to be holding such a prestigious post. Stanlake had fought against the government, had fought for – what? He couldn't remember, and it didn't matter.

Now he and his mother were at the foot of the gang-plank. The last.

He glanced round at the town, a low dark mass beyond the dazzle of the harbour-lights. Only a few lights showed out there, in the windows of those lucky ones whose generators had neither been looted by rebels nor requisitioned by government troops, and who could afford the bribes for fuel. The lights were mostly clustered round the army barracks. This was a long, low building, formerly a hospital, that Stanlake and Poppy had had no option but to pass when, with bowed heads and downcast eyes, they had entered the town a week ago. It had been mid-afternoon, the sun derangingly hot, and the soldiers had watched from the shade with bored contempt as these two broken figures crept forward beneath its pitiless glare, at that hour the only people on the road.

Before, with its market and bars, its buses, cars, motor-bikes, businesses, churches and schools, its dock, its fishermen's boats and container ships, its whitewashed homes and satellite dishes and well-tended gardens ablaze with amyrillis and bird-of-paradise, the town would have impressed Stanlake. His father had worked here when he was a young man, and it had once been somewhere for Stanlake to aspire to, a place where life might be lived and not just put up with. Now it was a half-deserted heap of rubble to pass through and leave behind. There were no longer any flowers in the gardens.

He and his mother had walked for ten days to get there, the cranes on the dock slowly rising up ahead keeping them going, beacons of hope.

He looked round at the man with the clipboard and hesitated: without some clear signal from him they couldn't ascend. The man noticed, pursed his lips, looked down at his papers and shook his head, but then gestured with the top of his pen that they could board. Without acknowledging the gesture in any way, as if to do so might break some spell, Stanlake stepped onto the gangplank. His mother followed him. The plank sagged slightly under their combined weight and Stanlake put out a hand for the safety chain. It was heavy, curiously supple and clammy to the touch. The smell of decaying seaweed wafted up from the black water below as they climbed, cut with the tang of salt and the metallic odour of diesel.

Now they were on the ship. The gang-plank was still down, they could still be removed, but it was something.

With a grunt Poppy tipped her bundle onto the deck under an awning beneath which the other passengers were huddled, and mother and son sank down onto it, glad of a chance to rest legs and backs and feet that still ached from what had felt like endless days of walking. An old woman squatting on her haunches nearby was setting up a little stove. She produced a small bundle of charcoal from the bag she had carried the stove in.

'No fires on deck,' a passing sailor warned her. The old

woman looked up at him blankly. 'Do you want the ship to burn up, enh? This is wood.' He squatted down and tapped the deck. 'Wood burns. You want the ship to burn up?' Grudgingly the woman returned the charcoal to the bag. 'Ignorant,' the man said, shaking his head. 'These people are ignorant. They should not be travelling. Who gave them documents, enh? You do not know the rules, you should not travel-o.'

The man went off along the deck muttering to himself. Stanlake stared at the gangplank. Pull it up, he thought. Cut us off from the land. Neither he nor Poppy could even begin to feel safe until it was raised and the ship was on its way.

But I *am* safe, he thought. No-one here knows I was a rebel. No-one who would recognise me is still alive.

As the land began to release its heat into the sweaty night it pulled in the cooler air that was massed over the ocean. Stanlake shivered, and for the first time worried whether his tee-shirt and shorts would be enough clothing for the journey. Both England and Holland were cold, he knew, though at that time he had no understanding of what cold meant: that you could be alive and yet chilled all the way through like the dead; that your fingers could be frozen rigid as corpse-fingers by the bitter air; that they could be icy to the touch, and numb, and yet burn inside at the same time.

There was nothing to do now but sit. There were no plans to make, no decisions. What would come would come. It was almost a relief. How do the ancestors travel, he wondered. What do they take with them? He had thrown away his rifle before returning to his mother. It had run out of bullets anyway. He had discarded his rebel uniform one ripped piece at a time as they walked, and now he had given over the last things he had brought with him from the forest: the tiara he had worn on his head as he wandered, and the single handful of jewellery he had kept against just the emergency it had been needed for. He had nothing now but the few clothes he wore, the rubber sandals on his feet. No passport, no papers, no money. He hated the powerlessness of it but he was glad to be rid of the jewels: they had burned and vibrated in his pocket like the manifestation of a curse, like a spirit dragging him back towards what he was fleeing from.

Well, they were gone. And they had paid for his mother's passage as well as his own, and that, perhaps, was the beginning of an atonement, if such a thing was possible, which he did not believe. Sometimes he couldn't bear the fear and hate he caught in Poppy's eyes when she looked at him. Was this how God had intended things? If so, to what end?

From the direction of the town came the roar of an approaching vehicle, and his stomach clenched as a jeep filled with government soldiers slewed onto the quay. Its initially rapid progress turned erratic as the driver was forced to negotiate potholes made in the cement by recent mortar-fire, but still it came on slalom-fast. The other passengers on the deck shifted uneasily. Stanlake glanced about him, looking for places where it might be possible to hide, realising he knew nothing of the layout of ships, knowing it would be hopeless if the soldiers were really coming for him, the rebel, the deserter.

Laughing, drunk and probably high, the soldiers in the back of the jeep yelled and gestured wildly with their rifles and fired random shots into the air. Stanlake and his fellow-passengers pressed themselves back into the shadows under the awning, crouching low, keeping as out of sight as possible. The jeep was heading straight for them. Theirs was the one lit ship. Not now, he thought, not when we are so close.

With a lengthy screech of flabby tyres the jeep skidded round in an arc, almost flinging out several of its gun-toting passengers, who bellowed hoarsely at the driver in anger and alarm, and passed out of sight behind a row of rust-red shipping containers. These containers, Stanlake knew, were piled high with bananas, bananas that had gone from bright, pert yellow-green to sagging, fly-covered stinking black in the dull, dead days he and Poppy had spent on the dock waiting for a way forward. The two of them had felt as marooned and powerless as the putrefying bananas as they watched the ships load and unload their cargo and the trucks come and go with their produce, trying to understand how the port worked, what possibilities it could offer them, who they could approach about obtaining passage. And with each passing day the anxiety had grown on them that there might be a rebel advance, that the town might once more become a war-zone, that the port would be closed.

Accelerating, the jeep barreled up the quay the way it had come and headed back into the town. Its headlights cut cones of white into the blackness of the unlit streets. Then its one working tail-light flared red as the driver stepped on the brake, it turned a corner and was gone.

A hooter sounded overhead and as the arms of the cranes swung away crewmen bustled about, casting off cables and winching up the gang-plank. The passengers shifted, starting to shed a little of their tension. The journey really was about to begin. Having parted with their money they weren't going to be thrown off at the last moment. The odd murmured remark passed between them. There was even soft laughter.

With a juicy rattle the anchor-chain began to wind in and the ship's turbines started to turn, making the deck vibrate. We cannot go back, Stanlake thought as slowly and without fanfare the ship began to move away from its berth, and he felt a little fear and a little sadness. But with that thought came its corollary: there is nothing to go back to. Not for me. His father's face came into his mind then, but it was unbearable and he pushed it away. He looked over at his mother. She was gazing back at the town and the land beyond that she could not see, sunk as it was in darkness, and at that angle only the outline of her cheek was visible, the corded stretch of her neck. She drew in a deep, shuddering breath, as if she was taking with her what she could of the air and the scents of home. So Stanlake thought then. Later he came to believe that she had been looking back into a void filled only with horror, and had been fighting down not a sigh but a sob.

At a leisurely pace the ship rotated in the harbour, the water churning at the back of it, offering as it turned a panorama of nothing distinguishable topped by a billion stars. There was no moon. The wind sharpened. It was odd not to hear the sound of insects. Stanlake and Poppy stood at the rail for a while watching, then went and sat back down.

Night passed into day into night into day. At first there was the ocean on one side and a low line of coast on the other, against which the sails of small fishing-boats were sometimes visible. Then they must have headed further out to sea because there was no coast, just water on every side, with occasionally what Stanlake assumed to be another cargo ship passing in the distance. The engines turned relentlessly, but in an expanse without markers it felt to him that the ship was barely moving at all. This illusion of stasis was challenged only by the slow but relentless draining of warmth from the air, and the more rapid depletion of the small amount of food they had brought with them, though the ship's crew, who otherwise ignored them, at least gave them plastic cans of water when they asked. The water had a bitter aftertaste. He began to think they would all die on this journey, as if that was the necessary price for the possibility of rebirth somewhere else as someone else.

They talked little with their fellow passengers. All were fleeing the horrors of war and a collapsing state: what need to share the details of what each had suffered? What use? It would relieve them of nothing, and whose hands in those bloody times of coups and counter-coups and shifting allegiances were so clean that he or she did not have some secret it was better to conceal? What talk there was was mostly speculation about what lay ahead. The ship, it seemed, was to stop at Dover first, then go on to Rotterdam, which was in the Netherlands. One woman claimed to have family in the Netherlands and so was set on getting there. The man in the orange tee-shirt wondered aloud why, if that was so, she had not been sent for and travelled legitimately, but since his observation all too sharply reminded the rest of them that they were not wanted by anyone in the prosperous places of the world, he was not encouraged to pursue his thought.

Stanlake knew nothing about the Netherlands except that its language was Dutch, which he could not speak. England he knew something about, and he knew English, so to him that seemed a better option. In any case, wherever they hoped to get to, they would most likely be kicked off the ship at the first port where they put in, and that was Dover. He shivered and pulled his blanket closer around him. The vibration of the engines made his cramped stomach pulse, and his bones ached.

*

It was some nine days later, Stanlake reckoned, that they
finally reached Dover. His clothes were sodden and glistening with sea-mist, and he was feverish and trembling with
cold. The ship's hooter blared above his head, announcing
their approach. It made him want to stand, but he was so ill
that his mother, though she was weakened and exhausted
herself, had to help him struggle to his feet. Bracing themselves up on the rail, side by side they looked out at a wall of
white cliffs above which a grey sky lowered. In a gap in the
wall the port sprawled, bleak and incomprehensible, its
concrete arms flung out into the choppy, dull-green water.
Devoid of trees, flowers, animals or market-vendors, it
seemed a place of inhumanity.

As they drew nearer Stanlake saw lorries drawn up in
serried rows. Across the way, next to blocks of administrative
buildings, dozens of containers were stacked two or three
high, and ships like the one he and Poppy were on were
unloading their cargo. Stanlake watched the swivelling
armatures of the dockside cranes – each of them two or three
times the height of the ones back home – as they swung their
gibs into position above the ships' holds and stevedores
caught the swaying cables and hooked them onto the
containers within. A small white boat, for passengers rather
than freight, Stanlake guessed from its numerous portholes
and prominent observation deck, slid smoothly backwards
from its berth, wheeled round and headed out into the open
ocean. Gulls cried and flapped, buffeted by the biting wind.
The cold squeezed tears from the corners of Stanlake's eyes.
Needing to miss nothing, he blinked them away.

After a half-hour wait during which nothing seemed to be
happening their ship moved forward and docked. Before he
or his fellow-passengers could think what to do, uniformed
officials, all of them white, came on board. They looked at
Stanlake and the others and seemed neither surprised nor
angry. 'Papers?' one of them asked. When nobody produced
any they asked for passports. When none were offered they
talked quietly among themselves. Eventually one of them
said, 'Come with us.' Wordlessly Stanlake and his fellow-
passengers gathered up their possessions and followed them
down the gangplank. It felt odd to have solid, unmoving

ground beneath his feet again.

That day Stanlake learned of the particular strength and courage of women, of mothers. He had been in a war. He had learned to fire many weapons. He had killed enemies and he had lost comrades. He had been strong and he had been ruthless. But he was also just a boy, a boy who had been lost in the forest, and for this new battle he had no resources. It was Poppy who dealt with the relentless questionings of the port authorities and the immigration authorities, and later on the assessment officers, the case-workers and the administrators, while Stanlake sat beside her in a state of near-catatonia, pretending he could speak no English. He listened as well as he could, but he found the accents difficult, and much of what they were saying incomprehensible.

Because they came from a war-zone, and because he appeared to be a minor, he and Poppy weren't turned away, but they weren't let in either. After three hours of waiting and an hour of interrogation his mother was given some sort of papers on behalf of the two of them. Then they were led, thirsty and hungry and by then wanting the toilet but afraid to ask for it, to a waiting minivan. They were locked in the minivan along with other people from other countries. All of them had brown skin. No-one said anything. They waited. More people were brought until the minivan was full. Then they were driven through damp green fields to what was called an asylum centre but was in reality a prison, and were put in separate rooms in separate blocks in dormitories segregated by sex.

There they were kept, shivering in the perpetual cold, staring out through chain-link fences topped with razor-wire at fields of cabbages and sprouts, at grey skies and rain. There Stanlake was spoken to by counsellors and eventually a psychiatrist, and was unable to answer any of their questions, even had he wanted to. Truthfully he couldn't speak about what had happened to him or what he had done, and in any case playing the idiot seemed safer. After a month he was given pills, antidepressants they said, which he pretended to take but did not. It was the world, not the chemical balance of his brain, which was depressing him, and to take drugs to deny that fact would only make him vulnerable.

He and his mother ate little, for the food was off-puttingly unfamiliar. It was flavourless and stodgy and also, as the grumbles of the other inmates and sometimes even the staff of the centre made clear, badly-prepared even by its own standards. He was constantly constipated and felt distorted inside.

People came and people went. A few got to move forward into the U.K., but most were sent back. A boy from Iraq hanged himself. A girl from Sierre Leone with a persistent hacking cough turned out to have tubercolosis and died of a haemorrhage, or so the rumours said when she didn't come back from the hospital to which she had eventually grudgingly been sent. Two men from Uganda escaped. They were caught a day later and brought back, muddy and defeated. But most days nothing happened.

Out of boredom Stanlake began to read. At first, because he had not read anything for more than three years, it was difficult. Concentrating was hard, and the fluorescent strip-lights gave him a headache. But he found he had an appetite for it. He read whatever was lying around, newspapers, magazines, the occasional book, and in his mind he assembled a collage of this new country in which he found himself: how it saw itself, and, between the lines, how it really was. Too, he listened to the stories of his fellow inmates. They came mostly from other parts of Africa, the Middle East, India, Pakistan and Bangladesh. He began to understand that his situation was determined by forces as far beyond his control as tides made by the Moon.

As well as reading, like most of the inmates he spent a lot of time watching the TV that blared constantly in the day-room, trying to make sense of what it told him. So much was contradictory. The U.K. seemed violent and fearful of violence, and yet violence was rare enough that individual victims of it would be named on the national news. It was at war on several fronts, but the war was far away, and individual soldiers who died were named, and footage of their funerals shown. They were not left to rot by the roadside, tipped into ditches or buried in mass graves.

Sex it seemed was everywhere, aimless and brazen and

often allied with drunkenness, which apparently was destroying the nation's health and was a big problem. Yet alcohol was advertised constantly, drunkenness was a commonplace subject of humour, and to not 'drink' was to be an outsider. There was frequent talk of immigration damaging British values but no-one ever said what these values were, however carefully he listened. Old people seemed little respected and the entire continent of Africa was rarely mentioned at all. Occasionally impoverished people were shown in refugee camps in dusty locations, inert or imploring in the face of calamity. It was not a representation he recognised.

Though people in the U.K. had a vast array of material comforts they often seemed to consider themselves poor and hard done by, and were constantly worried about running short of money and not having enough things. Children were apparently a burden to take on only uneasily, and often so late in life that women had trouble conceiving through old age and needed technology to help them. Or else children came too early and with the assumption that the state would provide for them, even though both father and mother were capable of work but chose not to bother. Women were too thin, and seemed to want clearly artificial-looking breasts that were too large for their frames; or they were too fat from a very young age due to sitting about too much. Women were obsessed with shoes; men with football and alcohol. Sanitary products were advertised. Men did not want to lead their households. Small amounts of corruption could topple big men in power, and there were women in many positions of power too. Religion was little mentioned.

Most viscerally compelling to Stanlake was the issue of gays. In his village they had rarely been spoken of except by visiting Christian preachers, who said they were abominations who were somehow destroying the entire world with their acts, though quite how was never made clear. They were also somehow things that had been brought over from Europe and America. In the forest any youth who fell short in any way had been called a faggot or a cocksucker, meaning he was the lowest of the low, lower even than a beast because unnatural. Yet Stanlake remembered hugging Big Gun in the cabin by the roadblock, and they had been more than comrades that afternoon, and neither abominations nor faggots but just themselves.

The word 'gay' had never spoken to him then, not as a word that might describe him. There it had been a word of attack, of condemnation. In the U.K. it was different. Here gays were people who had rights, who could be shown in newspapers and on television as if they were human beings just as good as others. People – most often the loudly religious – spoke against them, it was true, and were violent against them, but they were not allowed to drive them from public life as they would have done at home. They did not print their faces in the newspapers for others to attack them. Here gay people could even have families, and he had seen photographs in a Sunday newspaper of two men with a baby, their baby, held in one of the men's arms, though he did not understand the mechanics of how such a thing could happen. A woman was mentioned as a 'surrogate', but he did not understand the word, and there was no-one he could ask about it. The tone of the article was congratulatory, but this was not always so, as Stanlake was reminded one drab afternoon while watching the news in the day-room with Peyman, a scrawny Iranian.

'It's disgusting,' grumbled Peyman, in reference to an item about a Christian woman who had been dismissed from her job for refusing to perform a marriage between two men on the grounds of her religious beliefs. The marriage was called a commitment ceremony, but everyone knew it meant marriage. The woman had appealed but had lost her appeal. 'This country is a sewer of filth,' Peyman said, 'and it will soon be destroyed.'

'How do you know?' Stanlake asked.

Peyman shrugged.

'So why did you come here, then?'

'Holland is worse,' Peyman said. 'There it is perverts all over. Whores sit in shop-windows selling themselves and drugs are legal. And I could not stay in France.'

'Then why not go to a Muslim country?' Stanlake asked. By now he knew of Iraq, Iran, Saudi Arabia, Pakistan and Afghanistan from the news, though none of them sounded like countries where anyone would choose to live if they were given a choice. But Peyman talked so often and so passionately about the Umma and the unity of Muslims throughout the world, their love for and support of each other, the greatness of the Prophet and the all-encompassing truths of Islam and the justness of Sharia law, that surely, Stanlake thought, he would rather go and live in a Muslim country. In fact when he first heard Peyman holding forth Stanlake had assumed he was in the asylum centre on transit to one of those countries that so fully embodied his vision of the ideal way of life. But here he still was, months later, filling in forms like the rest of them, sitting around in the day-room hoping for indefinite leave to remain in the despicable, kufar Islamophobic United Kingdom.

'Here you can operate,' Peyman said.

'Operate?'

Peyman seemed like he was about to say more, but changed his mind and fell silent. Stanlake suspected the Iranian liked to give the impression of being in possession of superior knowledge about things. Most of the time Stanlake thought what Peyman said was bullshit. Now he was making out he was on some spiritual-political mission rather than looking for the soft life like the rest of them. Stanlake also believed Peyman despised him for being a heathen, not even a Christian. He often muttered about kufars.

'The religions of the sand people,' Stanlake's father Pacific had called Christianity and Islam. 'They were forced on us and they do not fit us,' he said to Stanlake one day. 'They are not African.' Poppy had left the room angrily shaking her head, and gone to pound foofoo.

There was another Iranian in the dormitory, a shy, nervous youth with thick spectacles not much older than Stanlake. His name was Mohammed, which Stanlake knew was the most Islamic name of all, but he drank alcohol and played cards, and Peyman wouldn't speak to him, wouldn't even acknowledge him as a fellow Iranian. Perhaps back home they were at war, Stanlake thought, wondering, if that was so, who most oppressed who?

As on the ship people were reluctant to tell much about themselves; and even had they wanted to, many of them had little English. Also there was a general belief that the officials running the centre planted spies among the inmates, and that a word from one of these spies could get you sent back.

When asked about himself Stanlake would say only, 'Our village was massacred. We fled from war. We came here because that is where the boat came.'

Every so often people would be called to the administration block and sometimes they didn't come back. Whether they had received permission to stay and been released, or had been transferred to some other location to await deportation was often not discoverable. Rumours of violent removals and unfriendly changes of policy circulated constantly, and the more the authorities denied them the more they were believed. Everyone knew the administration was hostile. Everyone felt victimised by the perverse randomness of its decisions. And all of them came to see the asylum centre as emblematic of the hostility of both the British state and the British people, who shouted so loudly and relentlessly in the media about overcrowding and scarce resources.

Mohammed left, then a week later Peyman. In or out? Stanlake didn't know.

Stanlake mostly sat with the other African men. Back home he would have felt remote from them: they would have been foreigners from countries he had never been to, with whom he had nothing in common, tribe, language or religion. But here, among these other faces and races, they seemed like family, sharing an understanding of each other that was, in one way, a great relief. Yet in another way it made them wary of each other, for that same understanding could expose bullshitting and stratagems built on lies; and since the corollary of intimacy was betrayal they remained guarded with each other. Still, they were company, and as English was the one language they all had in common, Stanlake found himself speaking it with increasing fluidity and confidence.

It was only with his fellow Africans that he was talkative. To the authorities he was careful at all times to appear as dull-witted and passive as possible. So ingrained had this habit become that even when he and Poppy were eventually brought to the administrator's office, five months after they had arrived, to be told they had been granted indefinite leave to remain, he barely reacted. Only once he was in the corridor outside did he begin to shake and tremble so violently that he was almost sick.

He and Poppy were assigned a case-worker, Ms. McKenzie, who told them they would be allocated a two-bedroom flat in a high-rise apartment block in South London. 'On the fifteenth floor. You'll probably have views of the Eye and Big Ben,' Ms. McKenzie enthused. Stanlake and Poppy nodded politely. Stanlake hadn't heard of the Eye. He had heard of Big Ben, but couldn't remember what – or even who – that was. Evidently they were good things to be able to see, judging from Ms. McKenzie's tone of voice, and so he and Poppy did their best to look pleased. The state, she told them, would pay their rent. Poppy signed more forms.

A week later they found themselves on a National Express coach to London, Victoria, with various residency documents in their pockets, thirty pounds in cash, food vouchers worth sixty-two pounds, a hardship voucher for furniture, a front-door key and a spare front-door key, and a hard-to-follow set of instructions for how to make their way from the coach station to the estate that was to be their new home.

It was fortunate they had so few possessions as the lift hadn't been working the day they arrived.

Chapter Two

Stanlake looked at his reflection and straightened his tie. It was silky to the touch, with diagonal silver and ultramarine stripes, and was the one part of the school uniform he liked. The rest – white shirt, black trousers, charcoal jacket – he found drab and constraining. He wandered through to the kitchen and fixed himself a bowl of cornflakes. It was six a.m. and he was alone in the flat. His mother had left for work an hour earlier. He had got up with her as he did every morning, at 4.45, and made her a mug of tea. Wordlessly he had offered it to her and wordlessly she had drunk it, hunched over the small table in their narrow galley kitchen, eyes downcast as if in prayer, a large orange and blue headscarf knotted round her coiled and braided hair, her one indulgence.

Once she had finished her tea Poppy slipped out of her flip-flops and wiggled her feet into the trainers she had got for five pounds off a stall in East Street Market. She put a Tupperware of lunch into a pink-and-white-striped carrier-bag, pulled her coat on over her blue nylon cleaner's overalls, and left the flat. Stanlake washed up her mug, then got out his schoolbooks and sat at the same small table where she had been sitting, and studied.

Away from the classroom things were clearer to him: the black words stood out crisply on the cool white page instead of being obscured by the heavy accents of the teachers, whose voices were in any case often drowned out by the other pupils, who seemed to feel no obligation to keep quiet. Back in the flat the words could take their own time.

His first day of school in the U.K. had been filled with the perversity of dream-logic, where you witness craziness but everyone around you acts as if it is all perfectly reasonable. What was that book his father had had on the shelf with the strange drawings? *Alice in Wonderland*. It had been like that, except not magical.

Instead of at desks in rows facing the teacher so he or she could teach them, pupils sat around tables in groups. This meant that at all times at least a quarter of them had their backs to the teacher, who rather than teaching trailed between the tables speaking quietly to individual students who had problems while the others chatted, squabbled, texted and even shouted and threw things at each other. They seemed to have no fear of the teacher, who never used the cane Stanlake at first assumed she must have hidden somewhere in the room, and who never took charge. No-one stood for the teacher when she arrived, and rudeness was commonplace. When the deputy head-teacher introduced Stanlake to the class few of the students even bothered to look his way, and no-one took any interest in him or asked any questions. The deputy head-teacher, a dumpy, bespectacled white woman in very flat shoes and a rumpled blouse, seemed unsurprised, as if this was normal. She handed him over to the form teacher, another white woman, this one with straight brown hair and a tired face, and left.

Stanlake was assigned to a table with three shy Asian boys, a bold-faced black girl with her hair in cups-and-saucers who texted constantly, and a thin white girl with straight yellow hair and a hunched posture. Behind the Asian boys sat a middle-aged Asian lady in a sari and cardigan who whispered to them throughout the lesson. Her hair was pulled back in a bun, she wore gold-rimmed spectacles and had a red bindi spot on her forehead.

'Is she their auntie?' Stanlake asked the white girl.

'Nah, she's like a assistant or whatever.'

'Assistant?'

'Cos they ain't got no English, though.' The girl twirled her hair. She chewed gum like a cow, with her mouth open. 'D'you like my bracelet?'

She held up her arm to display it, turning it to show the blue veins running up the inside of her pale wrist. The bracelet was pretty: amber blocks linked by gold wire. Stanlake imagined it on his own wrist; how the translucent orangey-brown of the blocks would tone with his smooth, dark-brown skin. 'I like it,' he said.

'Primark,' she said. He knew that was a shop.

'Was it costly?'

She shrugged. 'Yeah, but I snatched it though. What's your name?'

'I am Stanlake.'

'I'm Shelley,' she said. 'And that's Yvonne.' She indicated the texting black girl.

'Why are they in the same room as us?' Stanlake asked quietly, nodding in the direction of the three Asian boys.

'Don't you like Asians?' Shelley asked loudly. The motherly woman raised her head and gave Shelley and Stanlake a dirty look.

'No, I mean, wouldn't they be less distracted?'

'Mixed ability, innit,' Shelley shrugged.

The form teacher handed Stanlake a worksheet and a blunt pencil and told him to do his best. It was prose comprehension followed by multiple choice questions. He found it hard to concentrate because of the noise the other students were making in the echoey classroom, but the prose, a couple of paragraphs about a boy playing football, was simple and the questions were easy. Others seemed to struggle. He supposed it was because he was older than them – they were barely fifteen – or because in some cases they did not know the language.

Stanlake put his hand up to let the teacher know he had finished. Yvonne elbowed him in the ribs.

'Why you sucking up for, man?' she hissed.

'I have finished.'

'What, you think you're better than us just cos you're a African?'

He didn't know how to reply to this. In the forest he would probably have shot her.

A bell rang. The students immediately started shovelling things into bags as the teacher shouted homework instructions in a strained voice. In the din Stanlake missed most of what she was saying, but he took the textbooks and workbooks she offered him as he passed her desk.

The school was, compared to what he had known, vast: a city of thousands of children from every corner of the world. At his school they had all known each other their whole lives, and known each others' families. They had been each others' whole world. Until war came.

The war here was inside the school, and it was between groups – gangs of boys and sometimes girls. Their differences were defined partly by race or nationality but more decisively by what postcode they lived in. Stanlake couldn't understand it. They thought they fought for honour, or so it seemed to him: the honour of their streets, their ends. And they fought with their fists, their feet, their little knives. But to him it was honour without content, a pointless attempt to delineate territories that had no natural edges, that marked no difference of religion or political system or tribe; territories, moreover, that were won or lost by children only, as regardless of which side triumphed in each small skirmish the newly-established borders could be, and were, crossed with impunity by adults, by the police, by buses, cars and bicycles. No serious attempt was made to invade or occupy new territory. No barriers were set up to stop traffic and extort money from travellers to let them pass through.

No roadblocks.

It was on their fourth day walking the road, during all of which time they hadn't met a soul, that, parched and hungry and footsore, Stanlake and his mother saw up ahead something strung between two thorn-trees, barring their way. At that distance they couldn't make out what it was. It seemed to be a dirty length of damp cloth that had been twisted to wring the water out of it then stretched between the trees to dry, so that it only accidentally made a barrier.

Closer to, it was clear.

On either side of the road, into the branches of the dry, dusty thorn-trees, had been hoisted the torso of a man. The men's lower halves had been hacked off at the waist, and their eyes had rotted out or been pecked away by crows. Flies crawled over them in an iridescent black mass, greedy for moisture. Their intestines had been pulled out from under their ribcages, stretched across the road, and knotted together in the middle where they met. And there they hung, pinky-black and dessicating, blocking the way at waist-height.

The torsos had been stripped of clothing but both men

had been in their thirties, therefore most likely in the military, so this had been a rebel roadblock, not a government one. Fortunately those guarding it had run, and some time ago, Stanlake reckoned: the torsos were dried out enough to not stink too badly despite the feasting of the flies. As he watched, maggots dropped from their cavities to the ground, where they squirmed, cooking and dying in the hot dust. His mother crossed herself. He touched the charm around his neck. Discarded rifle-shells glinted like strewn gold, the gods' payments, or men's. No vehicle had come this way for many days, or the barrier would have been broken: its strength was only in horror. Why had no dogs eaten it? Mother and son went around it, and continued on their way.

Stanlake pushed the memory from his mind and wondered how much of the little money his mother had left him he should take to school today, how much he could afford to lose. It wasn't the petty extortion that went on within the school that worried him: only the younger children were victims of that, not older teenagers like him. No, those who threatened him were the ones beyond the school gates: the expelled, discarded, unemployed and unemployable youths of the area. The thugs and dealers who set up shop along the route he had to take every time he wanted to pass in or out of the estate.

From the coins stacked on the shelf in the hall he counted off three pounds fifty, pocketed it, then put the Tupperware lunchbox Poppy had left him in his school-bag. The bag was brown leather and had a pretty clasp in the shape of a butterfly, a girl's bag, probably, but he didn't care. He wound a black, grey and blue wool scarf round his thin neck, took his key from the hook on the back of the front door and left the flat. He had exams today. Mocks.

He pressed the button that called the lift. It lit up, so the lift was probably working. Somewhere below a door sighed shut. Then came the almost-melodic clanging of the cables slapping against each other as it rose towards him. Stanlake wasn't too worried about encountering the jackals as they were rarely up this early. Still, he was relieved when the lift arrived empty. He pressed 'lobby' and it descended without stopping at any other floor.

He crossed the deserted playground and made his way down into the underpass. The tunnel ahead was unlit. In the middle of it, in a puddle of water, sat an abandoned supermarket trolley loaded with disturbingly-bulging black bin-liners. He slipped past it, taking a jump over the puddle to keep his only pair of trainers dry. Rush-hour traffic rumbled overhead, reverberating ominously.

Up ahead was a hexagon of pale light: the central area, off which the other tunnels radiated, and which was open to the sky. At this hour it was deserted, as he had hoped it would be. In the middle of it, on a circular brick dais, was a lumpen abstract concrete sculpture. On this locally-unloved, graffiti-tagged artwork the dealers habitually perched. A small brass plaque gave its name as *Genius Loci*, offering below the translation, 'Spirit of Place'. A sudden gust of wind sent a waxed KFC cup clattering emptily across the ground in front of it, and a flimsy corner-shop plastic bag and a handful of dead leaves went whirling upwards in a chilly vortex.

Stanlake hurried past the sculpture and down the tunnel opposite. It too was unlit; it too was unoccupied. He climbed the steps on the other side and was off the estate. A small relief. Ahead was a parade of shops where other students from his school were stopping off to buy crisps, sweets, pop and cigarettes from sharp-eyed, half-resentful shopkeepers. He passed the shops and turned onto a long, poplar-lined street. It ran through a small estate of houses rather than tower-blocks, and led right up to the school gates. Students were converging on it from the surrounding sidestreets, a few in a hurry, the majority drifting along in chattering groups not much concerned with punctuality, a handful arriving by car.

Stanlake walked alone. He had no friends here and wasn't sure he wanted any, not yet. Nothing about this place gave him any sense of belonging, so how could he trust anyone? He only felt at home when he was back in the flat with his mother, though the atmosphere there was often thick with unspoken resentment. The other students took no interest in him, but if they had he would have found it difficult to respond to, because always at the back of his mind was the thought, If they knew what I have done they would hate me. They would put me out of this country. I would be sent back and I would be killed. So he kept to himself and did his best to study and move his life on inside his head.

I do not need friends, he thought. My friends are within me. And I find new friends every day in books.

His parents had always valued learning. Like everyone in the village they understood that schooling was both a privilege and a liberation, and passed that understanding on to their son. Stanlake, along with his three best friends, Matthew, Robert and Patrick, thought nothing of the four miles they walked to school each morning, or the same four miles they walked back afterwards. Instead they thanked God for the dew on the grass by the roadside, in which they could cool their feet as they set out in the predawn light, and for the good meal that would be waiting for them when they got home sweaty beneath the sun late in the afternoon.

The school was on the outskirts of the town, and as they lived in the outermost part of the district they had to pass through two other villages to get there. Other students might join them on the way, and they would walk together, sometimes kicking a football along, exchanging their news and views on life as they walked. Their form-teacher, Mr Abimbola, was strict, and demanded his students work hard, and beat them if they did not. But he was also progressive, and would bring in all sorts of unusual books and magazines to give the boys and girls he taught a wider perspective on things. Most often these focused on aspects of science or technology or geography. Sometimes they had religious content. Sometimes they were cultural and historical. One time he brought in a book titled African Women of Achievement, and scolded the boys for laughing at it.

Occasionally Mr Abimbola would also bring in fashion magazines from Italy, France, Britain and America. Stanlake found the images that crowded their pages oddly exciting, and the traces of scent that lingered on the slick, shiny surface of the paper intoxicating. He had to fight the girls in his class over who got to look at them first. The girls found his passion for the magazines hilarious, and so did the boys, but Stanlake didn't care: he had found love, and couldn't be ashamed.

The models on the catwalks of that faraway and immeasurably wealthy world fascinated him. He took note of them, and soon enough he knew their names – Kendra, Naomi, Anna Jagodzinska, and his own personal favourite, Alex Wek, whose espresso-dark skin, proudly African features and effortless glamour delighted him – as well as the names of the designers whose styles they so elegantly embodied: Tom Ford, Alexander McQueen, Karl Lagerfeld, John Galliano, Dolce & Gabbana, Jean Paul Gaultier. In his mind he built a shrine to honour these spirits of beauty who dwelt in forests of fabric.

After school he and his friends would walk home together, and often, before tackling the afternoon's chores, they would go to Stanlake's family's compound and sit for a while on the bench in front of his parents' hut. There they would enjoy the shade of the banana trees, drink Fanta, and share their dreams.

Robert, Patrick, Matthew and Stanlake were particularly close because they had been initiated into manhood together. Their induction into the local men's society, the Society of Masks, had been an arduous ordeal. All of them had shivered as at its conclusion they sat naked on the ground, waiting with legs spread, the older men's hands on their shoulders, reassuring and intimidating in equal measure. Their eyes had been wide with fear, but not one of them had flinched as the drums pounded and the men of the village chanted the names of the ancestors back and back to the beginning and the knife drew icy and burning across their foreskins, though their penises shrank back like cut worms before being quickly bound red and bloody in rolls of white cotton to heal. Not one of them had cried out and shamed himself before his peers: if you cried out you could never fully be a man.

It had been a frightening, exhilarating, magical time, a man's time from which women were excluded, a bonding of sons with fathers and grandfathers and the ancestral dead, with the spirits of the forest and the natural world. Below their feet were the bones of the first men, sent by Olodumare unguessable years ago to found the three villages; and when the men of today wore the masks that for the rest of the year slept in the hut on the edge of the village that no woman was permitted to enter, and came dancing through the lanes and went whirling out into the forest, their forms strange, their heads extended beyond the height of any man by tall grasses, they were no longer men but spirits, transmitting wisdom down the generations through dance and song.

Wholly other in their outline-concealing costumes of shoots and spears, no longer older brothers, uncles, fathers and grandfathers, they clapped and chanted and compelled Stanlake and the other still-healing boys to whirl and dance around the low, domed altar in the sacred grove until at last, exhausted and light-headed, they entered a state of dizzy ecstasy and fell convulsing to the ground, and the spirits of the forest entered them. Then all for a while was blank. Stanlake was at once both elsewhere and present, and there was for a length of time that felt both short and endless no division between himself and the secret life of the forest.

Then the patiently waiting bullock was dragged forward and its throat was cut. The head was hacked off swiftly and dextrously, and the body convulsed as the boys had con-vulsed on the ground, and the blood first sprayed, then pumped out more slowly onto the altar-stone, feeding it life and power. Lines of energy converged, then radiated out-wards. The men had brought the boys to this secret place late the night before, waking them unexpectedly and leading them by unfamiliar paths that none of them would have been able to retrace on his own, spirit paths they had walked for many hours. Only on their return, once the ancestors had accepted them, would these becoming-men be shown the faster, straighter way from the village to the grove.

The bullock twitched, then stilled. At a gesture from one of the elders, Stanlake, Matthew, Patrick and Robert knelt.

Each of them in turn sipped warm iron blood from the shallow wooden dish held to his lips by one of the Masks. Each had a cross of white paste thumbed on his forehead by a second Mask, the movement made first down, then across, for they had been brought to the place within themselves where the worlds of the dead and the living meet: the crossroads. Each youth bowed his head and a charm was hung around his neck on a rope of plaited grass. Each felt the small cloth bag rest strange and heavy on his breast-bone; and as he passed along the line in which they knelt, to each in turn the lead Mask said, 'Now you are a man,' raising the youth to be greeted for the first time in his life as a man by the other men of the Society of which he was now a part, and Stanlake was the last.

'Now you are a man,' the lead Mask said, raising him up too, and only at that moment did Stanlake recognise the voice as his father's voice, strange as it seemed to think back on it. But perhaps not strange at all: for up until that point it had been a spirit talking, and not his father.

Before that night Stanlake had not known that his father was not only a respected man in the village but also the head of the Society of Masks. Perhaps the knowledge had been kept from him because his mother, a committed Christian, did not approve of close contact with the spirits and the ancestors. Nor, as he was to discover later, was she willing to support anything that exacerbated the differences between the sexes, sure in her mind that such differentiation tended to work to women's detriment, whatever Pacific and the other men might claim. And so Pacific, who respected his wife and valued harmony in the home, spoke of such things to his son less than he might otherwise have done.

Stanlake returned to the village that morning aware that his childhood had ended, that he was now at the beginning of being a man, and that he would have many adult responsibilities to take on, even if what those responsibilities actually were was as yet hazy in his mind. He stood more upright nonetheless, and began for the first time to think of the future.

Though now officially a man of the village, Stanlake was still only thirteen, and slightly built, and in fact his parents didn't expect him to do much more around the compound or in the fields than he had been doing already, and he and the other young Masks still found time to share a bench in the shade of the banana-trees and talk of hopes and plans and dreams and schemes, as they were doing one afternoon just a few weeks, although of course they didn't know it then, before the soldiers came.

On the other side of the compound the girls were

pounding millet and washing clothes. Occasionally they would cast eyes at the boys and giggle. Before, they would have ignored the boys completely, but now that Stanlake and his friends were initiated, and so at least spiritually men, they were worthy of a little attention. Sometimes the boys would discuss which girls they found attractive, which girls found them attractive, who they might marry and so on. These conversations had become increasingly common with the passing of time but never felt real to Stanlake. At the time he had assumed that the others felt the same way towards girls as he did: friendly, but fundamentally indifferent. Any talk of the relative merits of this girl or that girl on the part of his friends he took to be a lightweight matter, and he assumed that like him they saw marriage as a looming and unwelcome obligation, and thought that nothing could be more pleasant than continuing on as they were, in the easy society of their fellows.

On this particular day, however, they were talking not of girls but of career-plans.

'A doctor,' Patrick was saying. 'Or a lawyer.' He was taller than the others, and had a large overbite and a winning smile. 'But a doctor is better for people. Both are well-paid, but with a lawyer he is more for himself.'

The others nodded. 'For me it is accounting,' said Robert, the chubbiest of the four. 'Or perhaps engineering. I have a good head for figures.'

'So does Stanlake,' Matthew said. 'When we are tested it is always between the two of you.' He was slender, the same height as Stanlake, and wore glasses with round gold frames. People sometimes took them for brothers.

'I am better,' Robert said, pushing out his chest pugnaciously and looking very young.

Stanlake shook his head. 'Robert, you are not,' he said, smiling. 'Just louder.'

'Still, though, all this studying is expensive,' Matthew said. 'We cannot just assume our parents can afford it, even though it will repay them in the end.'

This was a common theme in their discussions. They knew they were far from the centre of things, and that any progression in life is difficult where money is scarce and connections are lacking.

'Teacher said there may be scholarships or bursaries for good students,' Patrick said. 'And we all study hard and are able, so perhaps we will be assisted. What about you, Stanlake? What do you want to study? Accounting?'

Stanlake shook his head. 'Fashion design,' he said.

The others laughed and shook their heads. 'Your father will not pay for such a foolish choice-o,' Robert said.

'He will if I show I have talent,' Stanlake said confidently, though it was hard to imagine Pacific approving of such a vague, ambitious and costly plan.

'Anyway he could not afford it,' Matthew said. 'And there are no scholarships for fashion.'

'He *could* afford it,' Stanlake said, and perhaps he was right. His father owned the largest amount of land around the village and ran a small stationery business in town, while his mother worked as a community midwife: by local standards they were well-off. Also Stanlake, unusually, and unlike the others, was an only child. His birth had been complicated, his mother had been in hospital for three weeks afterwards, and even though the bad spirits had repeatedly been driven away she had failed to conceive again. His father, out of loyalty to her, and despite being the head of the Society of Masks, had refused to take a second wife, and so Stanlake had remained without siblings.

It was after that difficult time that his mother had decided to train as a nurse.

Her experience in the hospital had strengthened Poppy in her Christian faith, and, once she had trained, she found that stressing her Christianity enabled her to side-step the problem of people refusing her care due to suspicions that her own health problems had been the result of a curse having been put on her, which would, in their eyes, make her an unlucky person to have looking after them. Also, and putting things the other way about, her piety helped allay suspicions that she had had a spell put on her husband in order to keep him from remarrying once he realised she would be unable to bear him any more children. As a devout Christian wife she did not wear charms; nor did she go to the witch-doctor to have curses put on others.

It took time for her demonstrations of piety to bear fruit, but now Poppy was a highly-respected woman in the village. Pacific did not share her faith, but he understood her strategy, and was proud of her intelligence and industry. And so he contented himself with having just one son.

'What do you know about fashion anyway?' Robert said. 'This' – he gestured at the smoothly-swept, brick-red earth of the compound – 'is not a catwalk. It is dirt. And our girls have breasts. And buttocks.' The others smiled and nodded.

'I could go to study in Paris,' Stanlake said, waving his hand vaguely skywards. 'Or Milan. Or London.'

'You could not even find those places on a map, my brother,' Patrick said.

'I do not need to know where they are,' Stanlake replied haughtily. 'All I need is a plane ticket.'

Patrick laughed at his boldness, and the four of them clinked their Fanta bottles together, toasting the future.

And now here Stanlake was in London, and Patrick and Robert and Matthew were dead. He carried them with him in his heart, and spoke to them, sometimes in dreams, sometimes in the mirror, where they stood behind him just beyond the corner of his eye, and he would share things with them as he had done when they were alive; and around his wrist he wore a leather thong on which were three cowries, one for each of his Mask brothers who now dwelt in the realm of the ancestors, and who sometimes came to meet him and tell him news at the crossroads.

The bell began to ring as Stanlake and his class-mates made their way to the sports hall where the exams were being held. Individual desks and chairs were lined up in rows, facing forward in what he still thought of as the appropriate way for a schoolroom to be laid out. These weren't the final GCSE exams, they were interim tests, but were still considered important as a guide to how well each student was performing. Stanlake was sitting two exams today. In the morning was Foundational Chemistry, in the afternoon Foundational Human Biology. The exams were multiple choice, which Stanlake, like every student before him, preferred because it meant that even if you didn't know the answer you could guess and still maybe pick up the mark.

Neither was his favourite subject, which was art. Of the two he preferred biology to chemistry because it was less abstract, more human. Sometimes, though, with its clinical descriptions of the mechanical functions of the human body, it took him back to bad places. In one lesson the teacher told the class that if you unrolled the human digestive tract it would be over seven metres long, and some of the other pupils had laughed in surprise. Stanlake had not.

Chemistry was more impersonal, but he found in the emotionless world of minerals and their properties a curious relief. It could be strange and magical if you let yourself respond to it. But it too could tell disquieting stories. Under pressure and time, for instance, dead trees became coal became diamonds became beauty became wars became death, and the dead went back into the ground where their bones would one day become stone, or had their ashes compressed into new diamonds to be worn on the fingers of wealthy widows.

'You may begin,' the invigilator said.

Stanlake turned his paper over and began to tick boxes confidently.

In the lunch-break he didn't go to the canteen. Instead he sat on the playground steps, eating with a plastic canteen fork rice and fish stew from the Tupperware Poppy had left out for him that morning. Yvonne, the girl with the cups-and-saucers hair with whom he shared a table in Ms. Powell's class, was holding forth to some friends nearby.

'What I'm gonna need any of this shit for?' she asked of the exams. 'Sums, science, whatever. I'm gonna be a singer, innit.'

'You better do maths, then,' said the girl next to her. Her hair was braided, her skin dark and flawless, and she breathed through her nose as she rooted in a family-sized KFC bucket with plump fingers for scraps of discarded coating.

'Why, though?'

The other girl rolled her eyes as she shovelled bits of batter into her mouth. 'So you don't get ripped off, gal, that's why.'

Yvonne kissed her teeth. 'I'm a free spirit, though,' she

said. 'Easy come, easy go, that's me.'

'Whatever,' the other girl said. 'But you won't be so easy when it's gone, though.' A Lethal Bizzle track began to play muffledly inside Yvonne's bag. 'That your new phone, then?' her friend asked as Yvonne fished out her mobile. 'Zat a Curve? Let's see, then.'

Yvonne held up a warning finger as she answered it. 'Trevone. Finally. So where's this party at, then?' She cocked her head and listened. 'So when you gonna come collect me? Nah, not then, though, that's too early. Come like nine, yeah. Cos I gotta eat, don't I? My mum, yeah. Cos you can't afford no Nando's, that's why. What?' She listened again. 'For real? She's pregnant *again*? She better get a app for that!' She laughed exaggeratedly.

Stanlake found Yvonne's manner tiring and unfeminine, but he could see it was the world that made her what she was, the same world that beat his mother down, that obscured her beauty beneath ugly, utilitarian clothing, allotted her a badly-paid job that was below her level of education and barely legal, and gave her little reason to hold her head high.

It began to spot with rain.

The afternoon exam, human biology, went well enough, though afterwards he realised that on one of the questions he'd muddled up radius and ulna with tibia and fibula. Afterwards, having nothing else to do, and not yet wanting to brave getting back onto the estate, he found himself wandering the streets. His chest tightened as he thought of the inevitable persecution to come.

Still, his feet took him in the direction of home: he had, after all, nowhere else to go. He dawdled along the little parade of shops that led back to the underpass, coming to a stop in front of a chemist's. A Jack Russell terrier in a tartan coat was tied up outside. It looked in anxiously through the glass door with a cocked ear and shivered, and he felt a spasm of sympathy for the little creature, and contempt for its uselessness.

In the window of the chemist's was a dusty card-mounted display. It featured a blown-up photograph of a beautiful, smiling black woman, and advertised products for darker skin-tones. The woman's tawny, straightened hair was tossed back, her café-au-lait skin was Photoshop-flawless, and her green eyeshadow and eye-catchingly full red lips were glossy and lush. Somehow Stanlake felt she would be American. He moved his face close to the glass, turning his head until the ghostly reflection of his three-quarters profile was mapped exactly onto hers. A thrill of excitement ran through him: yes, today he would go in. The bell above the door jumped and clanged springily as he entered.

The shop wasn't large and there were only two aisles. One was for medical things, sanitary products and things for babies; the other was for hair-care products, razors, deodorant, perfume, sunblock and make-up. The make-up display was underlit in flattering pink neon, and its scalloped white plastic shelves offered lipsticks, mascara, blushers, eyebrow-pencils, eyeshadow, nail-varnish, false eyelashes, and various instruments for tweezering and plucking one's eyebrows. In the centre was a small mirror. Beneath the mirror a row of testers sat invitingly on a shelf, along with cotton wool balls for the use of customers.

Stanlake studied at his face in the mirror. It was smooth, free at the moment from spots or blemishes, and was, he considered, elegant. He had high cheekbones and sculptural, felinely-slanting eyelids. His lips were large, strongly defined and sensual, and his nose, flat though it was, was at least straight and symmetrical.

He glanced round at the counter. A portly, bearded Asian man in a navy-blue turban and a white coat that was slightly too small for him was showing an elderly Asian woman bottles of pills that he took from a glass-fronted cabinet behind him. Silver bangles glinted on his fleshy, hairy wrist. The woman examined the contents-list on each bottle he handed her with the obsessive minuteness of the desperately understimulated. Next to her an old white woman in a buttoned-up, mud-coloured coat and woolly purple beret sat waiting on a chair, a prescription-slip in her veiny, arthritis-slanted hand. She was staring blankly at the sad dog through the glass door of the shop. It met her gaze and its silky ears twitched and drooped and it let out a sharp bark to which she didn't respond.

No, not purple, Stanlake thought. The colour of the woman's beret was cerise. He dipped the tip of his forefinger into a sampler of eyeshadow called Carnival Gold. Just the name was exciting. It felt slippery in a cool, granular way. Hesitantly he brought his fingertip up to his right eye and, closing it, stroked from his nose out towards his cheek, coating the tremulous lid in gold. He did the same with the left, then rubbed the little that remained over his lips. Looking at himself in the mirror, glittering, androgynous, at the beginning of a journey to somewhere where who knew what might be possible, eyelids veiling secrets, lips inviting kisses, his heart began to pound so hard his chest heaved. He moved in closer, to examine his new face in minuter detail.

It was as he was nearing the smeary glass of the mirror, half-wanting to kiss his own reflection, that he realised the shopkeeper was watching him, a smirk on his plump, bearded face.

Embarrassment tore through Stanlake. He jerked his head back, and with a series of rapid movements rubbed the back of his hand over his lips, then his eyelids. That mostly only smeared the gold around, so he took one of the cotton wool balls and fumblingly wiped the eyeshadow off as best he could without the aid of cleanser or make-up remover. He looked at himself in the mirror again. Now he was just mutedly glittery. He glanced back at the shopkeeper and was relieved to find he had turned back to his customer, who was still fussing over her pill-bottles.

A pretty young Asian woman in a white coat came out from a back room then, with a packet for the old white woman in the beret. The old woman struggled to her feet, thrusting her prescription-slip out aggressively as if she was having to force her way through a crowd to get the young woman's attention.

This wasn't the first time that Stanlake had been in the shop and looked with longing at the make-up display, though it was the first time he had found the nerve to actually try one of the testers. When he had come in today he had thought he might buy a lipstick and some eye-shadow – which, perhaps, was what he had really had in mind when he wavered over how much money to bring out with him that morning – but now he was too embarrassed to take anything make-up-related to the till.

In any case all the money he had with him wasn't enough to buy what he really wanted, a glittery gold gift-bag that hung next to the display and contained – as he knew from previous visits – some very red lipsticks, green and gold eyeshadow, an eyeliner pencil, foundation, mascara, and other intriguing things such as shimmering cleavage enhancer. It was priced at nine pounds and he had coveted it for weeks.

At the counter the man and the woman were still busy with their respective customers. His need strong in him, with a praying-mantis snap Stanlake took the gift-bag from the rack, shoved it inside his jacket, and moved quickly to the door.

The bell jangled noisily as he exited. He didn't look back. His heart thudded as he hurried away along the pavement in odd, pecking steps. Strange that this was bringing him so much fear, he who had fought running gun-battles and survived. It was down to shame, of course. Back then there had been no room for shame. Either you lived or you died, and that was it: no more worries.

The tear-streaked face of a young girl came into his mind then. What had her name been? Florence. That night he had been ashamed, though he could not have done other than he did, and was less culpable, perhaps, than the others. Or was that merely because of his nature, and therefore no credit to him? Regardless, they were dead and he was alive, and so he had their burden to bear, for the contrition of the dead can have no meaning, and the duty of restitution falls to the living.

Now he had his prize he was eager to get home. When he reached the top of the steps that led down into the underpass, though, he hesitated. This, again.

Two skinny, hunch-shouldered youths in hoodies bundled past him. One was white, with lank, greasy hair shoved forward messily, the other mixed-race with skin like a rash. They disappeared down into the darkness as if on a mission. Good: they would distract the jackals, who, though they were often bored and always full of undischarged aggression, were also primarily entrepreneurs, and would put business before the pleasure of tormenting him. But it also meant the jackals would definitely be there.

They weren't always there. Every so often – twice in the months since Stanlake and Poppy had been moved onto the estate – the police, in response to complaints from local residents, would send pairs of special constables to patrol the underpass every couple of hours. This would go on for a few days, during which time the jackals would relocate to the nearby playground, or, if driven from there, would loiter on the walkways round the rat-run or in the stairwells of the Cardinals, and the dealing would continue almost uninterrupted. Then the patrols would fizzle out and the jackals would return to the underpass, by which time the residents would feel almost relieved, because down there the trouble they caused was at least geographically contained. Better to have junkies shooting up in the transient zone of the underpass than find them needle-armed in the lobby, or twitching in the lift into which you've just wheeled your baby, your fortnight's benefits money in the handbag you've slung so snatchably from the handle of the pushchair.

It helped that the dealers understood there was a tipping-point. Too many incidents of threatening behaviour, too much verbal abuse of passers-by, or actual violence or robbing; too much spillover petty theft from cars parked nearby, too many burglaries committed by their clients, and they knew the authorities would be forced to come down on them. So they were to a degree self-policing. But always there was a tension between them and the local community because they fed degradation, and what you feed grows, and they drew to the area the damaged and lost; the discarded ones, the ones nobody wanted near them.

Last time the police intervened it was because crack whores had been attempting to ply their trade in broad daylight along the parade of shops on the way to Stanlake's school, pitiful in their lack of curves, abject in their nervy desperation. The breaking-point had come when one of them had wandered up and down in the middle of the road, rambling to herself as she exposed her flat breasts and prominent ribcage to passing motorists and offered them a good fuck.

A leaflet had been pushed through the letterbox of every flat in the block petitioning the council to seal up the under-pass and replace it with a bridge. The leaflet featured an artist's impression of an elegant ribbon of concrete and steel arching cleanly over the busy carriageways. Poppy studied the leaflet approvingly but didn't sign the petition attached to it. She didn't want her name associated with any sort of conflict with the authorities, for fear it would somehow rebound on her or her son.

The following week a council newsletter came round, telling residents that in a time of financial belt-tightening there was no money for such a project, but informing them that the underpass had now been designated as an area in which the consumption of alcohol was illegal. It also headed off any idea of having CCTV cameras installed down there: that, the newsletter said, was also too expensive.

What was it about this place that filled so many with despair, Stanlake wondered, that drove so many to self-obliterating drugs? On the roadblock they had smoked cheeba, sure, and on a daily basis, but that was to numb themselves to the committing of acts of savage violence, to the ever-present threat of death. When they could get it they had snorted cocaine too, mixed in with gunpowder they tapped illicitly from carefully-split rifle-cartridges, but they had used it not for a kick at a party but in the same way you hammered spikes into a fetish: to fire it up, to anger it and give it the energy to do the terrible things that needed to be done. And he, Stanlake, had done terrible things, they had all done them, the boys on the roadblock with him, his com-rades, the Beasts, as their commander Makinde had called them. Beasts he had made of boys.

Stanlake thought of Florence again. He remembered Big Gun looking at him with hollowed eyes. 'It is good, Little Gun,' he had said tonelessly. 'It is fun.' Florence wore a tiara on her head, the same tiara he, Stanlake, was wearing when he came out of the forest alone.

Back in the asylum centre he had often thought about trying to get hold of some cheeba to mute his churning thoughts. But he knew that smoking not only deadened your head, it made you paranoid, and in the already paranoia-inducing bureaucratic maze of the asylum system that would have been disastrous: it was hard enough to tell reality from nightmare while fully lucid. Out on the roadblock there had been no such thing as paranoia. Paranoia was seeing things exactly as they were. You thought they were out to get you. They were. You feared betrayal. You were betrayed.

Here cheeba was called skunk, and the name was apt, expressing as it did the rankness that crouched behind the sweet-smelling smoke.

Walking alone in the forest after all the others were gone he had opened his heart and listened for the voices of the spirits. As the days passed and the drugs passed from his system, as he grew hungrier and more dehydrated, he heard them speak to him with increasing clarity. He promised them sacrifices if they would protect him from the animals of the forest, if they would guide his feet home. And they had protected him, and they had brought him home, but he had not had time to make a sacrifice; and they had brought him here, and still he had not made a sacrifice. He was in the gods' debt, and he knew it.

Here, though it was another sort of horror show, he had no desire for drugs: here he needed clarity, the clarity he had gained wandering lost in the forest.

Perhaps it was the weather that broke so many people: the numbing cold and draining greyness. Yet the people here were surely used to it as he was used to the seasons back home: that in and of itself shouldn't destroy them in such numbers.

Stanlake remained puzzled. But he had come to see two things that bore on the question. One was the low horizons of the lives around him, lives lacking any purpose beyond a quest for what could never resolve that lack: distraction as an end in itself. Getting 'off your face' or 'off your tits'. Emptily screwing 'mingers' while 'pissed'. Developing a capacity for pints and fights on a Saturday night. Playing video games for hours and hours; online gambling.

And then there was fame: the idea of being that curious, empty, childlike thing, a celebrity. He was struck by the gulf between the constricted lives around him and that glittering citadel where everyone was somehow important, regardless of whether they had achieved anything or not, or had any talent or not, and from whose lives all boring obligations had been forever lifted. Their failure to live lives like the ones reflected back at them on every TV screen, every magazine-cover, corroded people's spirits. For them, it seemed to Stanlake, no dream could ever be made to connect with reality: the chasm between the two was absolute. So why not snort or smoke or slide a needle in and free yourself from even having to try?

He was in the tunnel now. It smelt of urine: the marking-out of territory. Then he was through it and coming out into the open space beyond.

The jackals were there.

Three of them sat on the concrete sculpture, as still as if they were a part of it, hooded and hunched like vultures. On a child's bike a fourth made figure-eights in front of it, his movements repetitive as those of a caged animal. Evidently a transaction had just been completed: the two junkies who had shoved past Stanlake earlier were now hurrying back towards him, eager to get away and consume their purchases. He moved aside to avoid being barged into.

'And don't even think of smoking it round here!' the youth at the sculpture's apex shouted after them. He was small, not much taller than Stanlake, but his elevated position and manner proclaimed he was the don. His eyes were hidden by the shadow of his hoodie but Stanlake could see he was black, a little older than himself, and had a full-lipped, disdainful mouth in which a gold tooth flashed. He wore a black-and-gold limited edition Adidas Mohamed Ali tracksuit, tight black gloves with skeleton-bone motifs on their backs, and old skool hi-top trainers with pumps on the tongues.

Of the pair perching below him one was taller, heavier-set and also black. The other was short, stocky and East Asian. The boy on the bike, who was white, was broadly-built, and gold glinted on his thick, pale fingers.

All of them wore black or white or grey tracksuits, Nike swooshes or Adidas strips the only touches of colour; and their eyes were shadowed by their hoods. Empty KFC and Mickey D containers were strewn about the base of the sculpture, along with gnawed chicken-bones and used paper napkins.

Trying to keep his pace easy yet purposive Stanlake came forward. As he did so, in a bored, unemphatic tone, and without even seeming to glance at him, the heavier-set black youth said, 'Queer alert,' and in near-perfect unison the others turned their heads to follow his progress. He avoided meeting their eyes, but knowing they were watching him magnified the swish in his step, the effeminacy that normally he could forget was there, that he would have hidden if he could, but could not.

From one of the three on the sculpture, Stanlake couldn't be sure which because he was looking at them only obliquely, nor did it in any case matter, came the challenge-word, the slur that any man must respond to if he is a man, or any youth who dares to assert that he thinks he is a man, the word curled with relish in the mouth then spat out with disdain: 'Battyboy.'

Stanlake tried to keep going but now the youth on the bike rolled round in front of him and blocked his way. 'Didn't you hear what he said, mate?' Stanlake looked at his mouth so as not to meet his eyes and trigger conflict. His lips were red, his teeth crowded. From below his lower lip a strip of light-brown hair ran vertically down. His mouth was wide, almost sensual. If Stanlake looked him in the eye the youth might see the terrible things he was capable of, and what then? Better to be thought a cissy. Safer. Stanlake did not want to be a soldier again.

'He called you a battyboy,' the youth said, jabbing at Stanlake's non-responsiveness. 'You know what that is, right?'

Stanlake didn't say anything, made no gestures. The others dropped down from the sculpture and, moving easily like the predators they were, they came towards him. As a child he had watched jackals take a dying cow at sunset: the movements were the same.

'A battyboy is a cocksucker who likes it up the arse,' the white boy said. Stanlake twitched a shrug. 'You like it up the arse? I bet you do. I bet you'd like to suck all our cocks right now.' He hefted his crotch with his sovereign-ringed hand.

Stanlake stood motionless as they moved into position around him, points of a malign compass, all of them, it turned out, taller than him, and heavier, except for the click's leader, who positioned himself directly behind Stanlake and leaned in close. 'Battyboy,' he said softly, his lips almost brushing Stanlake's ear.

The larger black youth reached out and took hold of Stanlake's bag and yanked it off his shoulder, pushing him off-balance. One end of the strap tore away from the body of the bag. Stanlake staggered, regained his balance. He was both present and absent.

The youth fumbled the bag open and inverted it, dumping Stanlake's schoolbooks out onto the damp, dirty ground. As if what was happening was some impersonal process Stanlake bent over to pick them up. As he did so the glittery gold make-up bag fell out from where he had shoved it down the front of his jacket earlier. He snatched it up before his assailants had noticed what it was and pushed it back into its hiding-place, then squatted down and grubbed up his books as quickly as he could, hunching his body in anticipation of some random kick or punch. While he was doing this the bigger black youth held up his bag and the Chinese youth gave it a kick, sending it flying across the open space, and a glance told Stanlake the pretty golden butterfly clasp was broken now as well as the strap. He got to his feet, cradling his scuffed, dirt-marked textbooks and exercise-books awkwardly in his arms.

Now he did look at them. They looked back at him. He knew they needed him to react in order to grant them further license: there was that barrier in them still. They had not yet reached that place of pure cruelty. Without a word he turned away from them. They didn't react. He began to walk away, slowly for the first few steps, then faster as he entered the tunnel that led home.

'Chichi na fight,' he heard one of them say to the others as he narrowly avoided colliding with the binbag-laden supermarket trolley in the dark.

They didn't follow him.

Why do they do this, he asked himself angrily as he climbed the steps at the far end of the tunnel. Why do they want to drag me back into the past? Is this my punishment? I do not want to be a soldier again. I want to be me.

But who was 'me'?

He shifted his books into the crook of his arm and reached inside his jacket: yes, his prize was still there. He imagined cleavage enhancer glittering between his flat pectorals and felt excited.

Someone had left the block's security-door propped open with a brick. This often happened, despite a strongly-worded notice pinned up on the community noticeboard about burglaries. The lift was out of order. A note said that an engineer had been called. Stanlake began the weary climb to the fifteenth floor.

Though he couldn't see them he could hear other people in the stairwell making their slow way up or down. He thought of his mother and the pain she had suffered ever since the asylum centre in her wrists and knees, and life seemed suddenly unbearable. Why could he protect her from nothing? Was he not a man after all, as the jackals said, and had just now tried to prove with their petty humiliations?

What could it mean to be a man here? He paused for breath on the fourth floor.

Eleven to go.

Chapter Three

Everil James Evans, a.k.a. Evill, don of the Blows Crew, woke groggily from his usual bad night's sleep, mind and spirit deadened by the vodka and skunk he had chugged and blazed the night before, hitting his bed only as dawn began to redden the rims of the sky. Residual toxins still pulsed through his torpid lymph system, keeping him poisoned and depleted. He was nineteen years old, his system hadn't had a day free from some sort of stimulant or intoxicant for eight years, and crashing serotonin levels were his daily reality.

He fumbled for his mobile to check the time, squinting at the screen in the dim light. 11.20 a.m. That was early for him, but he didn't want to sleep any more. Had he had a nightmare? He thought so: there was something inside his head, some sense of a shape or a movement that had made his skin crawl, but he couldn't remember what it was. Feeling dissatisfied, as he did most mornings, he reached for the blunt in the ashtray by the bed, put it to his lips and sparked it into life. A seed cracked and popped as he dragged and fell from the glowing tip onto the duvet, where it threatened to smoulder. He brushed it away irritably, swung out of bed with a grunt and put his bare feet on the floorboards.

He sat for a while facing the window. The blind was down. Muted whiteness glowed around its edges. Leaning forward he levered two of the slats apart and looked out. Terraced and semi-detached houses with neat, well-tended front gardens met his eyes, houses which contained, he supposed, mostly respectable inhabitants with respectable lives. He had inherited his mother's tenancy. She hadn't been respectable.

He took the ashtray with him to the bathroom and left the joint smouldering on its lip while he showered. The mould on the shower-curtain was getting worse, he noticed. He wondered if you could get rid of it. Probably, he supposed, but he didn't know what with. Bleach? Or he could get a new shower-curtain from Poundland. Even that seemed somehow difficult.

He wiped the steam from the mirror over the sink and studied his face without much liking what he saw. He might have been handsome once – he knew from a photograph his mother had taken of him when he was a little kid, dressed up for a party in a white tuxedo and red bow-tie, that he'd looked cute back then – but he doubted anything of that boy was left in the face that met his stare now. Nerves kept the skin taut over the skull, and his brow was gouged with what seemed permanent furrows of hostility. His eyes were bloodshot and cold, and his freshly-razored shaven head looked brutal and pornographic.

He bared his teeth. The gold in his mouth shone. His dick rose, its engorging head bumping the chill white ceramic underside of the sink. Staring into his angry reflection Evill gripped its shaft and began to move his fist on it. There were no images in his mind. Less than a minute later the sinews tensed across his bare, lean chest and vascular right arm and, lifting himself up on the balls of his feet, he ejaculated into the sink.

He felt nothing.

After rinsing the pearly ropes away and deoderising he went back to his bedroom to dress. It was a bare, impersonal room. There were no framed photographs on the dusty shelves, no pictures or posters on the dun-coloured walls. Only his clothes and footwear mattered. These he kept immaculate: the trainers on crepe paper in their boxes; the teeshirts, tracksuits, hoodies and underwear folded with shop-display neatness in the chest-of-drawers. Sovereign-rings and gold ropes lay in a glass dish on the bedside table. He put the rings on, pulled on black Calvin trunks, white sports socks, a white vest, and his black and gold tracksuit. Around his neck he hung one of the ropes. Then he pushed his feet into his favourite old skool hi-tops. He pumped them till they gripped, stood, struck a pose in front of the ward-robe mirror, and nodded at what he saw reflected back at him.

The externals he could control.

Kneeling in the gap between the bed and the window, he levered up a short length of floorboard. In the space between the joists sat several half-filled carrier-bags and an eighteen-inch hunting knife. The knife had a serrated blade and a black vulcanised rubber handle: for certainty of grip even when wet, the website had said. Evill delved into one of the carrier-bags and pulled out a roll of grubby banknotes. He peeled off as much as he reckoned he would need that day and returned the rest of the roll to the bag. He replaced the board, trod it into place, and went downstairs.

The morning's post lay on the mat. Bills, shit from the council, shit from the hospital, shit from estate agents, leaflets from Polish cleaners and pizza flyers. Kissing his teeth Evill shuffled it together, piled it on the shelf by the front door, and left the house. The day's work waited, as dull in prospect, almost, as any legitimate job.

Once it had felt like freedom. Like a gesture of defiance against the slavery machine, the nigger factory that exists purely to produce submissive units to service the wants of the overlords. Dealing had seemed to be a way of, if not escaping, at least side-stepping that machine. But the reality was it was no different: you had to put in the hours, shift the product, feed the supply chain. Those higher up made the big money; those at the bottom were expendable, and had poor promotional prospects. And it ran on fear. Evill wasn't at the bottom but he wasn't far from it, and each day brought an intensifying horror at his predicament, an increasingly unbearable sense of entrapment with a diminishing chance to kick against it, to be in any way free. He sucked on his asthma inhaler and felt his breathing passages, which had been damaged in the womb, expand. Each hit he took reminded him: he had never really had a chance, not in the normal, healthy world most people took for granted. He couldn't even breathe their air.

He stopped off at the cornershop for cigarettes, papers and rolling tobacco. The front pages of the newspapers were blaring another M.P. corruption scandal, another footballer caught up in a sex-scandal.

All that cash and still ruled by gash, he thought, glancing at the headlines. If I had millions I wouldn't let no bitch within a mile of me. He paid and left the shop. Ahead of him was the underpass. His turf. His manor. Behind him was the school he had intermittently attended for seven years. Was this it? Was this as wide as his world was going to get?

My ends, he thought. My end.

He remembered a history lesson about medieval peasants, how ninety-nine percent of them spent their whole lives not going more than five miles from where they had been born. It had sounded so pathetic, but wasn't that him? Sure, he had been to Benidorm and Aya Napa, but that had been to get pissed and slob about in the sun, not to see or do anything new. To do what he normally did, but in the sun. Nothing about it had widened his life. The travel had been nothing: the box of the tube followed by the box of the airport then the box of the plane, boring, enclosed, administrative, at every turn keeping you so far under manners you resented it. And then it had seemed like everyone in Spain was English, or spoke English, anyway, so you hardly felt you were abroad at all: only there was something in the air that was different. But the actual Spanish were like extras in a film: pure background, to be ignored. And then you came home and carried on exactly where you had left off.

Where he had left off was a filthy underpass that junkies pissed in, sometimes even shat in. And even that hole in the ground was territory that had to be fought for. It was why they called each other 'souljah' as well as 'blood' and 'fam': because this life was a battlefield.

The four exits from the underpass corresponded to points on the compass, and like in a children's story each one led to a different postcode run by a rival crew. To the north were the Somali Boyz, to the west the P.P., the Piranha Posse, to the south the Stab Up Crew.

Bits of newspaper came blowing along the street. A full-page advertisement recruiting for Starbucks – *Do you have what it takes to be a barrista?* – tumbled by in slow motion, then wrapped itself round a lamp-post. It didn't, he noticed, mention pay or conditions.

He had read somewhere about how Starbucks worked, and it had stayed with him because of the ruthlessness of it. The chain moved into an area in force, setting up lots of outlets, licensing out franchises to anyone who wanted them. It sold cheap, even at a loss, driving prices down and crowding out and bankrupting any similar-type businesses that were already there. It set up so many outlets that they went into competition with each other as well as with everyone else. It was a war of all against all and the big bosses didn't give a fuck; in fact it even suited them because it sorted out the soldiers from the faggots. Some branches brought in the dollars, others went to the wall and that was the end of them: they were collateral damage. It was war as much as, or even more than, business, and wasn't that exactly the war that he was in? Wasn't it a fact that the same connections who supplied his click, the Blows Crew, also supplied the Somali Boyz, the P.P. and the Stab Up Crew? The situation was pure fuckeries, and only a stone-cold killer could get out from under it, if his soul could stand it.

Evill hadn't offed anyone, not yet, but he could feel his time was coming, his trial by ordeal, the something he had never dealt with that would make him into a man, that would make him real in the world. Everything else was just running to stand still. Maybe that was why he was tired the whole time. He went down the steps and rolled through the tunnel, building his swagger.

The others were already there, he was pleased to see. Good soldiers. Not too smart, but loyal. Solid, Cuts and Pit-Bull. The core members of the Blows Crew and his lieutenants, mates since time: family from when blood-ties were choked off.

Solid was the tallest and heaviest-set of them. His flat face seemed almost bovine, but he took shit in without seeming to notice. He came up in care never knowing his biological parents. All he knew was that his birth-mother was Nigerian, that she had been too young when she had him, and that she had gone back to Nigeria shortly afterwards, erasing him, he supposed, from her history. His father was a total blank: black, he knew from looking at his face in the mirror, and that was it. Solid had been an angry boy, sullen and uncommunicative, ignored by teachers, sent first to a pupil referral unit, then excluded from school altogether. Foster placements never took, and he spent most of his time up until the age of seventeen in one residential home or another. Then his birthday came round and they kicked him out. Not quite onto the streets, though: the social set him up in a flat on the estate, in Cardinal Three, gave him a fifty-pound voucher for furniture, and closed the file on him.

Cuts' father was Chinese, his mother white. When his father walked out on them his mother blamed it on Cuts being a difficult baby. So difficult, it turned out, that he drove her to drink and drugs and partying: from a young age she would leave him home alone for days and nights together. The social never caught her, and he never told: you don't grass up your mum.

When she took up with a new man, a white man, he soon made it clear that he didn't want no mixed-race pickney dirtying up his yard, and after one ruck too many Cuts walked out on the fucked-up situation. He was fourteen then. Theoretically he stayed with an aunt, his father's sister, but he mostly couched at Solid's, sleeping in the lounge on the outsize leather sofa that was Solid's prize possession.

Unlike the others Pit-Bull still lived with his parents. They were second-generation-unemployed heavy drinkers who never backed off from a fight, and nor did their son. Their unloved, grey-pebble-dashed maisonette was in one of the low-rise blocks that overlooked the rat-run. Pit-Bull's father had a S[t] George flag tattooed on one bulging, flabby bicep and a bulldog in a Union Jack vest on the other. His mother had been on the sick with stress and depression since the age of eighteen, and had picked up the term 'self-medication' to describe and justify her relentless consumption of alcohol. Both of them voted BNP on the grounds that immigrants were taking all the jobs, and couldn't fathom why their son preferred to hang around with niggers and chinks dealing drugs rather than respectable white people like the ones his parents knew; why he didn't love his culture. Pit-Bull would laugh when the black kids talked about licks: he knew what licks were, alright. But then a look of something near envy would show on his face when they stitched their tales of violent attention into talk of strictness, boundaries, sobriety, aspirations, church.

Perhaps that was why of all the crew Evill was closest to

Pit-Bull: because Evill, though black, though of Jamaican descent, had missed out on that upbringing too; he shared that lack at his centre. His grandparents had thrown his mum out when she was fifteen for having him, and had barely spoken to her – or to him – since. They said she would become a whore, she told him when she thought he was old enough to deal with it. Or more likely she didn't think at all, just found that on some random evening she couldn't keep it inside her another moment. 'A whore. So I did what they said. I thought that'd show them and they'd be sorry.' And she had clawed at her wrists between nervy drags on a cigarette like she always did when her need was on her. He had been seven years old then and had understood her child-like reasoning, her petulant emotionality, if not its consequences.

He looked like her: he saw it every time he studied his face in the mirror. His mouth, his eyes, even the shape of his jaw was hers. There was no feature of which he could say definitely, 'That's not hers, that's got to be my father's.' It was as if he had come into being through parthenogenesis; or as if, out of some act of will or rage on his mother's part, or indifference on his father's, one half of his genetic heritage had withdrawn itself like a dick retracting in the cold.

Still, he had wanted to know what his father was like.

'He raped me,' his mother said the first time he pushed her on the subject, or so he remembered it, though perhaps it was just the first time she had replaced her habit of evasion with attack. She had said it intentionally punitively, wanting to wound him, the product of that miserable event, as if causing him pain would somehow alleviate her own. Then, catching the look of slain innocence that must have shown on his ten-year-old face, she had tried to pull back. 'Well, not rape exactly. It was more like I was young and so was he, and he wanted what he wanted and I thought I did too, so I made out like I was up for it, but when we got to it I didn't really wanna do it cos I was only fourteen. But I only knew that for real once we'd got started, and you can't tell a man halfway-through, can you? He's gonna finish, isn't he?'

She had put the stem of the little glass pipe to her lips and run her lighter under the bowl, and repeated, 'He was young too,' as the glass blackened.

Those things you didn't share with your mates, or not explicitly, but you knew they got it. Their attitude to everything else in this world told you: that disconnection and hostility others couldn't understand, or at least didn't want to, out of fear, perhaps, of what it might reveal about themselves.

He bumped fists with Pit-Bull, then Solid and Cuts, and scrambled up onto the sculpture, which they called the Rock, and took his place high up.

'Dere been any trouble?' he asked.

There was a general shaking of heads. 'Not much business though either, fam,' Pit-Bull said, rubbing his buzz-cut head. It began to spit with rain and he flicked his hood up.

'Go get us some eats, blood,' Evill said, peeling a twenty off his roll and passing it to him.

'Aiight.'

Pit-Bull dropped down from the Rock and rolled off down West Tunnel. The snack-run was low-status but the concrete was cold and damp to sit on and no customers were around, so Evill knew he wouldn't mind. He shivered. *Maaga*, his aunt Esther called him, and it was true, he had always been skinny. Sometimes he hated food, and his body.

Solid was playing a game on his phone, seemingly oblivious to his surroundings. Cuts flicked a cigarette-butt away, jumped down and wandered off up North Tunnel to take a piss.

An officey-looking white woman in a puffa jacket and a grey pencil skirt came hurrying towards them out of South Tunnel, the echo of her court-shoes preceding her. She had thick legs in semi-opaque white tights and big hips, and was talking officiously on her mobile. She shot Evill and Solid a look as she passed them and tightened her elbow against her side, pinning her Louis Vuitton knock-off shoulder bag awkwardly against her upper body. Evill kissed his teeth. The woman heard him and picked up her pace, flinching as Cuts emerged from North Tunnel in front of her but keeping going past him into the dark, not looking back.

'You do that?' Solid asked, as she vanished from sight.

Before Evill could reply he answered himself: 'I'd do that.'

'Don't women feel it though?' Evill said.

'What?' Cuts clambered back up onto the Rock.

'The cold. On their legs. Ain't they got nerves?'

'Fat,' Cuts said.

'It ain't fat, blood,' Solid said. 'Not all birds got fat legs, is it? In fact most gyal what show dem legs got skinny legs, innit.'

'So what then, blood?'

'It's a trade-off for dick,' Solid said. 'They don't show no legs or arse, they don't get no dick.'

'So why come mans-dem don't show their chest or arms, then?' Cuts said.

'They do sometimes,' Solid said.

'Not so often, though,' Cuts said.

'Cos mans is at the top of the pile,' Evill said. 'So gash gotta please a man more'n a man got to please dem.'

'What about alla dat bout puttin' 'em on a pedestal an' shit, though?' Cuts said.

'What they want,' Solid agreed.

'You can do that if you want, fam,' Evill said. 'Me, I want 'em to have low expectations from day one, you get me? Cos I mean there just ain't no advantage to a demanding-type bitch. Before you know it she won't even give you none 'less you buy her shit and take her places. And that's just wrong, blood. Like, if you're gonna end up in a pimp-whore situation you gotta make sure it's you what's pimping, you get me? Otherwise she's pimping you, and that just ain't right, blood. It ain't natural.'

'I'd still do a tick chick,' Solid said.

'Any hole is a goal, bruv,' Cuts said.

'Suit up, though,' said Solid.

'She get up the duff, though, so what?'

'Fuck 'up the duff',' Solid said. 'There's chlamydia. Gonnorhea, herpes, syphilis. AIDS. They aint no joke.'

Cuts nodded. 'Suit up,' he agreed. He and Solid brushed knuckles languidly. Solid went back to his game. Evill's stomach rumbled and his chest cramped. He took a hit on his inhaler. It didn't help much.

'Business,' Solid said, not looking up.

A pair of skinny, hunch-shouldered youths were coming forward, postures already suppliant. Oily and Stats, two of the Crew's regulars. They had all been at school together back in the day. Then Oily had been Olly, the posh white boy with the greasy hair in the wrong catchment area because of his parents' divorce, and Stats had been standout good at maths, with a 'fro that made him look like he must be in a band.

They had been the hopefuls, the ones you took for granted would get on up and out of it, the ones who didn't spend half the term excluded. Intelligent and likeable and uninterested in pointless beefs, they had been popular with the girls, a party-going double-act with nothing but good things ahead of them. Now they were here at the foot of the Rock and Evill was up top like Simba in *the Lion King*.

It almost felt good.

He had never disliked them but now he despised them, and that was a relief. Their charm and amiability and popularity had got them nowhere, had got them here, its corollary some fundamental weakness of character, it seemed to him.

'Sup, Evill, man?' Oily said, shooting him a nervous smile, extending a bent arm in a gesture that was half a wave, half an invitation to high-five. Strange how crack had erased his middle-classness. Or perhaps not strange at all: becoming street from being on the streets. An inevitable transformation. A butterfly made out of dirt.

'Aiight,' Evill said. Then with the ghost of a nod to the other youth: 'Stats.'

'A wha gwaan, Evill, man?' Stats smiled to reveal a missing front tooth. The sight irritated Evill: such a blatant giveaway. Why didn't crackheads make the effort to cover it up? It was like obvious queers: why couldn't they at least try and man up and keep their shit private? Stats and Oily lived together. Evill wondered if they ever fucked each other. He didn't think so. He wondered if they would fuck each other for crack, or sixty-nine. Probably they would. They looked up at him with appealing, desperate faces. He was sure they would.

He imagined making them do it, making them lie down

right there in front of him, in front of the Crew, on the cold ground, shove their grimy trousers and shitty underpants down and blow each other. He imagined telling them they would only get the stuff after they both came, no faking; whether they'd be able to; how they'd look at each other afterwards as they nodded out in the front room of what he assumed was the shithole they lived in. Maybe they wouldn't give that much of a fuck, not while they were high, anyway. Maybe they'd admit it was disgusting but it still beat getting a job or getting clean; maybe bumping down to the bottom of the sewer of degradation would be some sort of relief for them.

'You bitches Muslims?' he asked. The question was so unexpected Cuts and Solid looked round at him.

'You what?' said Stats.

'New rules,' Evill said. 'You wanna buy, you gotta be Muslim.'

'Like dem Somali Boyz,' Cuts chimed in.

'Course we are,' said Oily.

'Prove it.'

'How?'

Evill thought for a moment. He had begun this on a whim and was already almost bored of it. 'Say as-salaam alaikum.'

'Arsey slam,' Stats began. Then he tried again. 'An arsey lamb.'

'Slimy slam I like you,' finished Oily.

They looked up at Evill expectantly, grinning and squirming like little kids needing to take a shit. They seemed more confident now. He had wanted them to humiliate themselves, they had done so, now they were due their reward.

'Pathetic,' he said.

Stats and Oily looked to Solid and Cuts, who kept their expressions blank: the decision, as always, was Evill's.

Evill relented. 'So what you got for us, then?'

'This,' said Oily. Glancing about him theatrically, he pulled up the front of his hoodie to reveal, shoved into the waistband of his track-pants, a handgun.

Evill dropped from the Rock and moved close to Oily.

After double-checking that no-one was about he reached down and tugged the gun from Oily's waistband. Cuts and Solid huddled round him for cover. The gun, a matt-black carbon compact Glock, was heavy in his hand, and even through his gloves Evill could feel it was warm from the heat of Oily's body.

'Where you get this, bruv?' A gun was an asset, but a dirty gun that could see you fitted up for someone else's b.s. was a liability.

'I ripped it off,' Oily said.

'Yeah?' Evill snapped back the housing and looked the gun over. It seemed in decent working order. He was careful to keep his finger off the trigger. Glocks, he knew, were designed with no safety-catch: instead the trigger needed a double-pull to discharge. That was good because it meant they couldn't go off if you dropped them like a regular gun could if you had the safety off, but you didn't want to toy with them or get itchy fingers. The weight felt good in his hand. He hadn't heard of any shootings in the area in the last six weeks or so. 'So who you rip it off from, fam?' he asked. Oily shrugged. 'And they know it was you what took it?'

Oily shrugged again. 'I don't reckon. It was just like laying around.'

'Cos we don't want no beefs over this,' Evill said. 'We don't need no blowback.'

Oily nodded.

With a press of his thumb Evill ejected the clip from the Glock's grip and looked it over. A bullet gleamed dully at the top of it. He tried to push the bullet down but couldn't: the clip was full. He pocketed it. Now he'd removed the clip he could safely check the trigger-mechanism.

On the first double-pull nothing happened. Frowning, he tried again. This time it clicked as it was supposed to. Suspiciously he pulled the trigger a third time: again it clicked. Okay. He got the clip out of his pocket and rammed it back into place. It slid up inside the grip smoothly enough but there was no sense of it locking properly into place at the top of the slot. He tried to eject it. This time it didn't slide out, just stayed stuck where it was. Giving Oily a look Evill bumped the base of the clip with the heel of his hand. Now there was a click, as of it locking into place, but muffled. He pressed the button to eject it. It dropped out easily. He slid the clip up into the grip a third time. This time the click was clear. He replaced the base-plate then pulled the slide back. The topmost bullet in the clip rose up into the breech. Evill pushed it back down, making the weapon safe again.

'It's a piece of shit,' he said.

'You don't want it, then?'

Evill looked away from Oily, taking his time. 'Aiight,' he said. 'Four wraps.' Before Oily or Stats could try to bargain he turned to Cuts and said, 'Give 'em the stuff, bruv.'

Cuts nodded and rolled off down South Tunnel. During business hours the Crew kept a bag of wraps shoved behind the translucent plastic cover of one of the permanently-broken striplights that lined the tunnel walls at head height. To the casual eye the cover looked firmly fixed in place, but in fact it could easily be slid sideways for quick access. No-one peering into the darkness of the tunnel could see exactly where Cuts went or what he was doing down there, and it was just far enough away from the Rock that the Crew could deny it had anything to do with them if the feds found it. He was back inside of thirty seconds.

Pit-Bull appeared from West Tunnel with a bulging bag of snacks he had got from one of the shops in the parade. 'What's that, fam?' he asked, shoving a whole Lion bar into his mouth: he had caught a glimpse of the bulky black object Evill was pocketing.

'Gat,' said Solid, as Cuts palmed the wraps to Oily and Stats.

As Evill had done, Pit-Bull shot a glance this way and that, then said, 'Let's see it, fam.'

Evill pulled the gun partway out of his pocket, flashing it to Pit-Bull. Pit-Bull looked excited. 'Come lemme handle it, blood,' he said. Behind him Stats and Oily were hurrying off with their stash.

'And don't even think of smoking it round here!' Evill called after them.

'Come, fam,' Pit-Bull said, reaching for the gun.

'Queer alert,' said Solid.

Evill shoved the Glock back into his pocket, making sure

it was pushed down deep enough to be wholly out of sight. As one he, Solid and Cuts slid back up onto the Rock, locking their eyes on the slight, shaven-headed African boy who had just emerged from the tunnel Oily and Stats had vanished down. He was wearing school uniform, and had a satchel-type brown leather bag slung girlishly over one shoulder.

Pit-Bull straddled his bike and pushed off in a lazy loop, turning through a figure eight, then another one, not exactly heading for the youth but moving enough in his direction to unsettle him. The youth avoided looking at him, at any of them, the same way everyone who wasn't looking for business did, as if hoping that what they didn't see couldn't see them, like kids.

This was a daily ritual, menacing this boy who attended the school they once went to, this boy who looked into a future that was dead to them. Sometimes they did nothing, just stared at him. Sometimes they were busy with customers so he managed to pass by unpunished. Other times they shouted shit or made kissy noises and watched his shoulders hunch in autonomic response however intently his averted face remained impassive.

He was only one of many, of course. Just more potentially entertaining than some.

Who did they think they were anyway, Evill thought, these immigrants who came here knowing nothing except that once they pitched they would get a ton of stuff off of the council for free?

The debate that dominated the agendas of politicians and newspaper headlines about the burden immigrants laid on taxpayers was an abstraction to Evill: he paid no tax and didn't give a fuck about politics. But the presence of the Somali Boyz as his rivals to the north was a concrete threat to him, and a more visceral one than whatever it was the bellyachers in the *Daily Mail* worried on about. Coming from a fucked-up country like Somalia those brers were tough: you had to respect that. Not that this youth was Somali: his features were too wide, too feline; he was too short. West African, Evill reckoned, like Solid. Not that Solid would cop to that. If he admitted to any identity it was 'Black British'.

Of course if it wasn't the Somali Boyz up in their grill it

would be some other crew, and whether they came from here, there or somewhere else made no odds. And this boy was nothing to do with any of that. But still Evill and the rest of the Blows Crew looked on him with hostile eyes.

And they were bored, hungry for something to happen that was, while still under their control, a break from the routine. Still, this wasn't some town centre on a Saturday night, where you could start a ruck with no repercussions beyond busted knuckles or bruk-up teeth or a beef with the feds. This was business. You couldn't cut and run. There was a balance to keep.

They would take their cue from Evill.

Sometimes violence was what he needed. Sometimes he had to start something just to relieve the pressure that built up constantly in his head; to achieve, albeit for only a few pathetic moments, some sense of clarity. It wasn't much more than the psychological equivalent of a good shit, but for a short time after some violent act he felt he could see the world for exactly what it was, without the chaos of his own subjectivity getting in the way. So sharp-edged then it was scary: absolutely real.

For that cleansing conversion of the potential into the kinetic those who weren't going to put up much of a fight were best. Not total victims: there was no lift to be got out of beating on them; no more thrill than you would get from kicking bags of rubbish around. And serious contenders might batter you back or shank you or even shot you, and Evill hated his life but he didn't want to die. Yet something about this youth drew from him a more complex, ambivalent response than his usual simple assessment as to which of the three categories he seemed to belong in, a fascination Evill didn't yet understand.

'Battyboy,' he said, almost without thinking. The youth's shoulders hunched as if a punch had landed between them but he kept on going. His face, though averted, seemed highlit, glittering, somehow golden. Evill imagined running his tongue up the side of the youth's shiny shaved head, the greasy smoothness and salt taste of it, and felt his dick kick in his track-pants.

By speaking he had given the others the permission they

needed. Now Pit-Bull blocked the boy's way, taunting him for being a dutty queer. The boy did nothing. What could he do against four of them, all older than him, bigger than him, street-smarter than him?

Solid, Cuts and Evill slid down off the Rock. Wordlessly the three of them moved to surround the youth. There was no plan or clear intention, just a desire to alleviate the boredom of the moment, and, on Evill's side, an inchoate desire to attempt a connection, in however perverse a manner.

Solid grabbed the conspicuously effeminate bag, breaking the strap as he wrenched it off the boy's shoulder. The boy turned to confront him, showing he had heart despite his feyness. Solid tipped his books out onto the dirty ground, focusing on defiling, perhaps, what he himself had long ago lost, and Evill stood watching as Solid held up the bag and Cuts kicked it into touch, and the boy squatted and grubbed about picking up his coursework as if it mattered, as if schoolwork could get him up out of this when all that mattered – all that ever mattered – was surviving the next five minutes.

The youth stood then, his dirtied-up books in his arms, and gave them a long look that was neither confrontational nor, it seemed to Evill, particularly afraid. Any other youth would be chaotic with surging adrenaline by this point, unable to repress the need to fight or flee. This youth was different, though Evill could not understand why, or in what way.

Without a word the young man turned from Evill. To get away he had to pass between Pit-Bull and Solid. Either of them could have blocked his way again, could have kept the game going, but today, randomly, they didn't. The predator in them, they discovered to their almost-surprise, had been sufficiently fed for now by the effeminate African boy's debasement.

'Chi-chi na fight,' Pit-Bull called after the boy as he walked away. He didn't look back, though he did step more quickly as he vanished down East Tunnel.

Another youth appeared then, from South Tunnel. He was scrawny, white, in a too-small grey hoodie and skin-tight jeans that constricted his crotch, and came skulking up to them fast, hands jammed into his pockets. They shifted their postures. Funtime was over: it was back to business.

Chapter Four

Poppy reached the bus-stop just after five a.m. The sky lacked any hint of the dawn to come: it still felt like the middle of the night. She was used to this now. Her friend Lucy was already there, along with five or six other early-hours workers, all of whom were black or Asian, and a pair of drained-looking white girls with stringy blonde hair, panda eyes and long, bare legs. The girls monopolised the seats in the shelter, smoking and staring ahead glazedly, late-night revellers only now on their way home. Poppy couldn't imagine such a life. It seemed both amazing and appalling. She greeted Lucy.

'It is cold this morning, enh,' said Lucy, slapping her woollen-gloved hands together. 'But they say it will be sunny later, praise Jesus.'

'Praise him,' said Poppy. One of the white girls flicked a glance at her.

'Will I see you at service this evening?' Lucy asked. She was a keen member of the Anointed Joy and Prosperity Mission, a shopfront church off the Walworth Road that Poppy had started attending since Lucy had befriended her.

'I will come,' Poppy said. 'This evening' meant around four p.m., tea-time for most people, but it felt like evening to her and Lucy because of the hours they worked. The lively services lifted Poppy's heart, and even though they were lengthy and at the end of a long day, the dancing and singing revived her body as well as her spirit.

'And your son?' Lucy asked.

'He has to study,' Poppy said evasively.

Lucy looked at her. 'There is room to study and to praise God,' she said.

'Please let us leave it,' Poppy said.

'Okay.'

The bus arrived. At that hour it wasn't crowded, and they

easily found seats together. Poppy was glad to have Lucy for a friend as well as a work-colleague. She was Poppy's one real friend in the U.K., the only person she ever tried to share anything personal with. It was through Lucy, who was Ghanaian, and the church, whose pastor and congregation were mostly Nigerian, and by going to the market, where several times a week she shopped at Mister Awolowo's stall and passed the time of day with him, that Poppy had built up a world she could understand and belong in: a network of arteries that threaded through the body of the larger white world in which she lived, but did not feel a part of.

Though 'white' was really not the right word for it: so many Londoners were not white, and so many of the white ones were not British, like Janina, the Polish woman she and Lucy worked with. And then many of the ones who clearly were Londoners, who had been born here but who were black or Asian or Chinese, lacked comprehensible English, speaking an opaque pidgin instead.

It was all very confusing.

Even at that hour there was a surprising amount of traffic on the roads, but the bus moved along briskly, passing one empty stop after another. Not like the return journey, which hit the beginning of the rush-hour and was always slow, unpleasantly crowded and tiring, even if you were lucky enough to get a seat, which often she was not. The bus sped down into the Rotherhithe Tunnel. It was strange to think of all that water overhead: the endless weight of it, always and forever wanting to rush in.

At first when they moved here Poppy had tried to get work as a nurse, but she had been unable to show papers proving she was qualified: like almost everything else they had been left behind when she fled. This job was all she could get. She didn't resent it.

The bus emerged from the tunnel. They were now north of the river. Beyond the still-lit street-lights the corners of the sky were beginning to pale. Although the weather here changed fast-fast many times a day, the dawns and dusks were long and slow.

So many things here were upside-down.

Soon the bus was passing ranks of apartment-blocks

that, despite their greyness and resemblance in general outline to the block where she lived, Poppy had been told were very costly and desirable. They faced the river and lined the way to the gleaming glass towers of Canary Wharf. At that distance the polished surfaces of those towers reflected the shifting sky and looked almost magical. Up close they did not.

It was in one of those towers that Poppy, Lucy, Janina and Paramjit worked as cleaners.

Poppy and Lucy got off at their stop and made their way along a sidestreet. The buildings there were old and mostly of dirt-blackened pinkish brick. Above their peeling pad-locked doors and shutters were painted the names of the businesses that had once traded there, now barely legible. Time had worn away patches of the tarmac too, exposing cobbles that were greasy to walk on.

A little way on they came to the plaza, which was not old but clean and new, not brick but steel and glass, and under-foot was marble. The absence of markers of some past of which she was ignorant made it more bearable to Poppy than the sidestreet, which filled her with vague anxiety. I did not choose to come here, she thought. I did not seek out this burden: to know about this.

She and Lucy crossed the plaza. At the glass wall of their block they held up their passes to Olu, the security guard on the reception desk. He came over and unlocked the door, which was a handleless glass panel within the wall of glass, and let them in. He knew them by sight, of course, but it was a matter of respect to show him their passes: he was Securi-ty.

'Good morning, brother,' said Lucy, bobbing her head and giving Olu a toothy smile. He was a tall, handsome man. 'Strapping,' Lucy called him, and she couldn't resist flirting with him, even though he was neither a regular churchgoer nor Ghanaian. 'He is single and I am twenty-nine this year,' Lucy said when Poppy teased her about it. 'That is getting on a bit.'

Olu muttered a good morning in reply, not meeting Lucy's eyes. His shortness with her was, Lucy was convinced, born out of his finding her attractive but not knowing how to go about doing anything about it. Poppy thought she was probably right.

Poppy, Lucy, Janina and Paramjit were one of ten cleaning teams in the tower and they had, between the four of them, five floors to attend to every morning. They mostly worked in pairs, though each pair could often see the other through the glass walls between the various office-spaces as they worked.

They had their routines.

One would empty wastepaper baskets, replacing the used liners with new ones, each new liner requiring a knot to be tied in its corner to hold it in place, while the other pushed the vacuum-cleaner around the main thoroughfares. Deeper vacuuming, getting into all the corners, was done quarterly. The interior glass had to be cleaned once a week; the out-sides were someone else's job. Surface areas of desks and computer-screens had also to be cleaned, though papers and personal items were never to be touched. This was done in rotation, one fifth section of each office's furniture and windows being wiped over each day. On each floor there were four offices, and in that way all the offices were entirely cleaned once a week. The principle was that things had to be cleaned before they looked dirty.

That part of the job had to be done by 7.30, because that was when the office-workers began to arrive. Even before then there were usually a few already at their desks, those who had shown up early to impress the boss, or to cover up mistakes they'd made the day before, or embezzle without witnesses. Or perhaps, Poppy thought, they were getting away from unhappy lives at home. Occasionally they even arrived for work at the same time as she, Lucy, Janina and Paramjit did. Once they had been let in by Olu these eager beavers would hurry on ahead, press the elevator button repeatedly, drum their fingers as the lift rose to their floor, and rush to log on to their computers as if what they were doing was a matter of life or death. Their furrowed-brow presence made Poppy and the others feel guilty for making a noise vacuuming, and self-conscious each time they acci-dentally clonked one of the metal wastepaper baskets against something. Sometimes Poppy liked to sing while she worked, hymns or childhood songs, but when there were office-workers there she felt she had to keep quiet.

Dawn broke even more slowly than usual, disclosing a grey, lightless sky that barely brightened as the shift wore on. Days like this made you feel like you were dead.

When it was sunny it was different. On sunny days the sheer glass walls gave a view of the city that could still amaze. The fundamental greyness of the buildings was lifted by coppers and soft greens and flashes of gold on domes and spires; by the flaring pink and silver-blue rim of the dawn catching glinting glass and shimmering on the river. It was a – what was the word? – a *panorama*.

Several times Poppy had stood at the walls of glass and tried to find the block where she and her son lived – the Cardinals were surely tall enough to stand out even at that distance – but had never succeeded. Her failure hadn't surprised her: the two buildings, after all, were barely in the same universe. She reproved herself for making the attempt: her desire to make the connection was, after all, a sort of vanity.

After the offices had been done, then came the public areas. The corridors were a straightforward vacuuming job with only a few bins to empty along the way. Next were the toilets. As well as being intrinsically unpleasant to deal with, these were made far more laborious to clean than necessary by the material used for the sink-surrounds, walls and floors. This was a black, silver-flecked and very shiny imitation stone that showed every smear and water-droplet, and had to be buffed completely dry by hand with paper towels or else it didn't look like it had been cleaned at all.

Once the toilets were done they usually broke for lunch. Most days this would be around 10.30. They were entitled to use any of the staff canteens in the building by showing their passes, but even with a 25% discount these were too expensive, so instead they ate food they had prepared at home and brought in themselves. They weren't allowed to eat their own food in the canteens, however, so, because it was too cold at that time of year to sit outside, they commandeered for themselves a small storeroom on Floor 26 where cleaning agents, photocopier parts and copy paper were kept. It was windowless and had unplastered breeze block walls, but it was private and felt like it was theirs, even if that was only because no-one else wanted it. There, over Tupperwares of food and thermoses of tea or coffee, they shared some of the troubles of their lives and offered each other what support they could.

Immigration issues loomed large for all of them. Though she was evasive – as they all were – about the exact details, Paramjit was currently the most worried about her situation. Her father, who lived back in India, had badgered her into using the relative of a family friend for a lawyer, and she was afraid he was bungling her case.

'I don't trust him,' she said. 'Yes, he is Punjabi and a second cousin once removed and all of that, but I don't even know if he is doing what he is supposed to be doing, never mind doing it well. But when I speak to my father about it he just says Sachveer's father is a good man and isn't Sachveer properly qualified and yes he is, so well, then.'

'But this is really too important for you to worry so much about your father's feelings,' Lucy said, offering a bottle of hot sauce to Poppy, who took it to shake on her rice and fish stew. 'If this friend mishandles your case he will be hurt much worse, and you will be in real difficulties.'

'But I can't go against my father's wishes when I don't know for certain that Sachveer is doing a bad job,' Paramjit said. 'And my stepmother just keeps right out of it.'

'I think you should find a better lawyer and just not tell your father until later on,' said Lucy. 'A good result will – '

'But I can't afford a better lawyer,' Paramjit said. 'That's how I ended up with Sachveer in the first place. And he is costing me money: he isn't for free. And on top of all that, now he is telling me it may hurt my case if I am found to be working!'

The others shook their heads. 'This country, enh?' said Lucy. 'They call you a parasite if you do not work, and then if you get a job they want to throw you out because you are not an asylum-seeker, you are an economic migrant, and that is a bad thing even though you pay a lot of taxes and do a job others refuse. I thank God I have my faith.'

'Anyway, it is all on my shoulders,' Paramjit said, and

sighed.

The others knew Paramjit's husband had left her, it seemed for a younger woman, shortly after they reached the U.K., leaving her with three young children to whose upkeep he failed to contribute, and on top of that Paramjit had no idea where he was living. And now for her to remain in the country the government needed this paper and that paper, none of which she had, and which she was worriedly starting to believe her husband had never correctly obtained in the first place.

'Surely your lawyer knows where your husband is?' asked Janina.

'He says he doesn't, but I don't know if I believe him.' Paramjit sighed again. 'What would you do, Poppy?'

'Well – ' Poppy began.

'Cheap you can afford is better than costly you cannot,' Janina interrupted.

'I don't agree,' said Poppy. 'I think it is best to do everything you can to get a good outcome now, then sort out the fallout later. Your father will forgive you for doing what you think is for the best. His pride will survive it. It might even be that this friend has been badgering him for you to give his son work, and he has never had much confidence in him. Get another lawyer who doesn't want too much money upfront on the table and see what happens. If you stop paying the lawyer you do not think is any good you can believe he will soon disappear out of your life.'

Lucy nodded in agreement.

Paramjit nodded too, but more hesitantly. 'I don't know. Changing lawyers now might make for even more of a mess,' she said. 'That is what Sachveer advised me when I told him I wasn't happy about what he is doing.' She rubbed her eyes tiredly. 'I just don't know. It's too important to make a mistake.' She fell silent. The others all guessed that, despite Poppy's advice, Paramjit would stick with a lawyer she didn't trust or even think was competent because he was someone she had a personal connection with, however tenuous, in a country of strangers, in the face of a hostile state.

Lucy glanced at her watch. 'Well,' she said, methodically pressing the lid back onto her Tupperware one corner at a

time, 'I suppose we had better get on.' She returned the
bottle of hot sauce to her bag. 'I'm sure it will get sorted out,
Paramjit. God moves in mysterious ways.'

Paramjit, Janina – who was a devout Catholic – and
Poppy all nodded, although today to Poppy the words
seemed mere conventional mouthings. Though her faith in
Jesus and His love for the world was strong, she lacked
Lucy's apparent utter certainty that whatever happened was
always what God intended. In the back of her mind, kept
present, perhaps, by the beliefs her husband had held and
that her son still held, was the suspicion that bad luck was
not God's will at all, but was engineered by angry spirits,
displeased ancestors or wicked individuals using witchcraft.
Or if not that, if she rejected that as superstition, then it was
blind chance. A tumour; a lost travel-pass; a random act of
selfish cruelty that benefited the perpetrator not at all: evil
things happened every day, regardless of God's overall plan.
That, Poppy was certain, was always for the best. Sometimes,
however, that certainty, that faith, was a matter less of the
passive acceptance of the revelation of God's grace than an
act of will on her part, consciously exercised, and that
troubled her.

'Tell me, Lucy,' she said later that afternoon, as they
mopped the floor of the now-deserted staff canteen on the
twenty-seventh floor, 'They say God is everywhere, don't
they?'

'Of course He is,' said Lucy.

'So even at the worst of times and in the worst of places,
He is there?'

'He is always there,' said Lucy.

'Watching?'

'Watching over us.'

'But not doing?'

'Waiting for us to reach out to Him in our prayers.'

'But not reaching out to us?'

'He sent us His only son to die for us, Poppy. That was a
great thing to give. Think of it,' Lucy said, and her eyes
brightened. 'His *son*.'

'That was a long time ago,' Poppy said. The death of
Jesus on the cross seemed suddenly unbearably remote to

her, too far away to be the balance. And men and boys were sent to war, to die, every day. Sons. Sons of sons and sons of mothers. And sometimes they died and sometimes they came back from the dead and you were afraid of them, of what you knew they had done, and you could not see God's hand in any of it.

'We must choose to come to God, Poppy,' Lucy said. 'It is not up to Him to prove Himself to us.'

Poppy nodded and wrung out her mop in the bucket. Her wrists ached, as they did every day when the weather was damp. A chemical smell billowed up from the grey, foamy water that made her eyes sting. 'Sometimes I think He takes days off,' she said tiredly.

To her surprise Lucy nodded agreement and said, 'The Bible tells us this: "On the seventh day He rested."'

'So who is running the show then?' Poppy asked. 'When God is resting?'

If she was hoping for an answer she didn't get one. 'When I am puzzled about things I pray,' Lucy said. 'I open my heart and I listen out for what God is telling me. He is like a radio station that is always broadcasting. You just have to turn the dial.' When Poppy didn't say anything she added, 'Ask Reverend Obasanjo for guidance after service tonight.'

'But he is so busy,' Poppy said. 'It makes it difficult.'

And that was true. But it was also true that she found the Reverend intimidating, in his expensively-cut suits and designer shoes, his silk shirts with the cuffs that folded back on themselves, French cuffs her son had told her they were called, pierced and pinned by gold-and-ruby cufflinks; the Rolex watch that glittered on his wrist; the gold cross gleaming plain and heavy on his chest, all these things intimidated her. It was only a little better when he dressed West African style, in cream silk embroidered in gold: a shade less remote, but still declaring he was a Big Man. And always he was as immaculately-groomed as a popular singer, his goatee close-clipped, his short hair in a flawless fade, his dark skin smooth and moisturised.

The Reverend even smelt expensive. When he worked himself up in front of the congregation, preaching the Word until his spit like mist made the microphone crackle with each exhortation of the faithful, and the sweat ran down his face and flew from his shining skin in glinting droplets and stained his clothing in blotted patches, then wafts of perfume, not sourness, came from him. And unlike some preachers whose churches Poppy had attended over the years Reverend Obasanjo wasn't fat: what bulk he carried under his well-cut suit was all muscle; and so that sweat was the result of the passionate activities of a fit man, not, as it was so often, the byproduct of corpulent, unhealthy over-exertion.

The Reverend was also comparatively young, in his mid-thirties, perhaps: no older than forty. But his eyes were penetrating: he had seen things, she could tell. The first time she had met his gaze, which was perhaps the third time she had attended a service at his church, he had locked his eyes onto hers and she knew she had been seen, and she felt as if she was looking into a mirror, and the mirror was looking into her, and it had been a relief and a terror.

The experience had been brief – just a few seconds in the middle of a lengthy and fervent service replete with hallelujahs, streaming tears and dramatic fallings-out – but it had unnerved her so much that she had avoided the next few services, giving Lucy vague, weak excuses for not attending. Then, feeling foolish at having been unnerved by so unclear a thing, and also feeling drawn in a way she couldn't really understand, she started going again. Although she wasn't wholly comfortable in this church it seemed to be God's plan that she go, and so she went. Also it got her out of the flat, and away from her son.

'He is a good boy,' she said to Lucy one lunchtime about a month earlier, trying to begin without beginning to share something of her difficulties, if not all at once the source of those difficulties. They had been eating sandwiches on a bench in the plaza, enjoying a day of rare sunshine and unexpected mildness. 'He studies hard, he does not go out drinking or taking drugs.'

'Any girlfriends?'

'No.'

'That is good,' Lucy said. 'You do not want him getting some girl pregnant and being distracted from his studies.

There is plenty of time for all that later, especially if you are a man. A successful man will be able to pick and choose.'

And Poppy didn't say, 'I do not think girls will come into the picture,' and she didn't say, 'Sometimes I am afraid of him,' the two thoughts uppermost in her mind. She just nodded, relieved after all that Lucy had not picked up on the things she was haltingly trying to reach towards saying, but couldn't get to without help. Sometimes she thought Lucy liked giving advice more than she liked listening. Sometimes Poppy thought God was like that too.

Perhaps Reverend Obasanjo could give her guidance, as Lucy suggested. But whenever Poppy considered trying to approach him she was put off by the thought of the inner circle, mostly female, who surrounded him and did their best to control access to him. How perverse it was that she, who had seen war and death and savage acts committed before her eyes, should be so intimidated by these pious women of good standing! But they did intimidate her. And who was she? Here at the Anointed Joy and Prosperity Mission she wasn't a qualified nurse with a good and moneyed husband, she was a refugee, a cleaner, a woman with a child and no husband who claimed to be a widow, while they were all either married to prosperous men or were businesswomen in their own right, or were young and pretty with good prospects.

She wondered how much of a hierarchy there was in Heaven, how it worked up there. Reverend Obasanjo was wealthy both spiritually and materially, so perhaps as above it was as below, though such an equivalence seemed wrong to her, for many of those who had wealth and status in this world were those who did wrong. Still, Poppy accepted that the Reverend's material wealth was God's benison, given to him by God as a reward for his hard work at spreading His word.

She remembered her son, going.

She remembered burying her husband, using the machete that had been used to hack his body in front of her because that was the only tool to hand.

It had been hard work. The machete was not good for digging, and the dry ground was like rock. It took her two days to make a hole deep and wide and long enough to take him.

At least they hadn't raped her.

Even so, she couldn't imagine ever being with a man again. In her head and her heart she was still married to Pacific.

A newspaper headline at a kiosk she and Lucy passed on the way to work that morning had denounced the latest round of 'fat cat bonuses' as 'an obscenity'. How easily people used such words!

Perhaps Pacific had been right in this: death draws you closer to the dead. When those around you die you find you have more in common with the ancestors than with the new strangers you meet in the world of the living. Normally such knowledge is reserved to the elders, but those had not been normal times.

She remembered when Stanlake told her he wanted to be a fashion designer. What a drama that had been! Her son, so good at his studies, so sensible and yet so fundamentally stubborn, coming up with such a hare-brained scheme.

'So we are sending you to school for this,' she had objected. 'So you can be a tailor?'

'Not a tailor,' he said earnestly. 'A *fashion designer*.'

'And what is that?'

'Someone who gives clothes a new shape that is wonderful, beautiful and amazing.'

'So that is why you have been snipping up and restitching my old clothes, enh?'

'And all the girls like what I have done very much.'

'You have been giving away my clothes to the girls? Stanlake, sometimes you are fool-fool.'

'No, I am good.'

'Cloth does not grow on trees.'

'Cotton does.'

And so the argument had gone on. Later Pacific had become involved, when Poppy had told him to talk some sense into his son. Pacific's response to her had been that fashion designers sometimes made very good money and became known all over the world; and his response to Stanlake was that it was unwise to gamble his life on a career he was so unlikely to succeed in, especially given that he had no personal connections in that arena, and that therefore he should train in something there would be a clear demand for, such as business or law or accounting, and practise fashion on the side. Both mother and son had turned away from him dissatisfied but, as Pacific had no doubt intended, no longer quarrelling with each other.

It was impossible now to recall how important all that had seemed at the time; impossible not to wonder why they had put so much passion into what were really such small disagreements. But that was back when they had had a future, or so it had seemed to them: a future where business-es could function and so businessmen were needed; where the rule of law stood for something and so lawyers were needed; where the government could demand proper accounting so as to raise revenue for the efficient administra-tion of the state for the benefit of its citizens. And if those citizens knew, as they surely did, that they hadn't yet reached that level of full democratic accountability, it was at least, they believed, where they were heading.

In reality, unseen by any of them, the sequence of events that would destroy that future had already begun to unfold: the interplay of history, ideology, economics, neo-colonialist realpolitik, personal greed and power-lust about which they knew as little as a fish knows of tides and the Moon, quotas, developments in factory-fishing or shifting fashions in *haute cuisine*. Yet in retrospect it seemed to her strange that she had felt no creeping chill, no latent anticipation, no dread in the curl of the leaves or the shrillness of the birdsong.

And now here she was in a country that valued the individual above all other associations. It was vanity, she thought, to imagine you could live your life somehow unaffected by what others were doing, folly to believe it was possible to do so, and wrong and selfish to believe such an attempt was good. That was the lesson of her life, if her life had a lesson, which she hoped it did. That, and the possibil-ity of endurance in the face of an adversity you would have thought would break you utterly.

Yet once she had been a girl, and had danced and clapped and sung and been happy. She had been rude to her mother sometimes, and competitive with her brothers to a degree that was judged unfeminine, and she had been ashamed when her menstruation began and irrevocably split her off from them, but those things she did not now remember: only the good things stayed with her. She knew it was nostalgia, but was it not still the truth, even if only a part of it? And she had grown to be a strong, good-looking young woman, and Pacific, who was handsome, and ambitious without being heartlessly so, had been a good match for her in every way, except in one big-small respect: he was only nominally a Christian. But that grain of disagreement between them had been the grit that made the pearl grow, the difference that taught them both forebearance and accommodation. Their marriage hadn't been perfect, and neither of them had expected it to be, but on a deep as well as a surface level it had worked well.

Pacific would sometimes talk of travel but Poppy had never been keen on the idea, preferring to be around people she knew and places she was familiar with. Gently he would mock her unadventurousness. Perhaps he had leaned towards Stanlake's designer dreams more than she had expected because the names Stanlake reeled off – Paris, New York, London, Milan – were places Pacific would love to have visited himself, but never did; or perhaps the son picked up the idea of globe-trotting from the father. And now here she was, in another country, on another continent, wondering if she could ever go home. But what was home, when the army and the rebels swept backwards and forwards over every inch of it like the sea, neither side standing for anything now, if indeed they ever had, jackals eating jackals, swine eating swine, dogs eating dogs, destroying everything they came across? What was that saying? 'Home is where the heart is'. But that was no answer.

Their working day ended at three. A different security guard was on the desk when Poppy and the others left the building, a heavy-set, youngish white man who never acknowledged them in any way. To him, which Poppy knew was how the managers wanted it to be, they were invisible, non-people. She said her goodbyes to Lucy and the others – Lucy was going straight to the mission to help get things ready for tonight's service – and headed to the bus-stop. A light rain was falling as she crossed the plaza but she was too tired to hurry. She felt the weight of her body as a burden, and thought of being lifted by angels.

Something made her look up then. High above the clouds were moving fast. For a brief moment and far off the sun broke through, sending down golden rays like bicycle-spokes. One time Poppy had found herself in the National Gallery, an intimidating porticoed edifice on Trafalgar Square, and had seen in hushed, dimly-lit rooms paintings of saints, and almost always in the backgrounds of those paintings were just such roiling clouds and golden spokes of sunshine, symbols or manifestations of the immanence of God and His grace. She had gone to the gallery to be inter-viewed for – inevitably – a cleaning job, and afterwards had wandered the sombre halls and high-ceilinged rooms, and had become unexpectedly involved in those paintings that seemed to interest the other gallery-goers least. In such art-works each gesture was symbolic: decodeable if you only knew the meaning. In them the haloes of the saints were perpetually visible. If only faith could be so simple! The attendants were almost all African, and she and they acknowledged each other with small nods as she passed from room to room.

She hadn't got the job.

The sun vanished behind the clouds as abruptly as if a louver had been twisted shut.

Several buses to other destinations came and went. Eventually the one she wanted pulled up and she got on. It was a small single-decker and all the seats were taken, so she had to stand. The route the bus took cut across the arteries leading in and out of the city. It wound its way through congested backstreets, eventually passing the bottom of East Street, off the Walworth Road, her destination. She had groceries and household things to buy in the market there before returning home to cook and change for church.

This was her routine, her life.

The day was sinking into dusk by the time Poppy reached the underpass, carrier-bags heavy in each hand, the stretched plastic of the thin handles slicing into the undersides of her fingers, cutting off the circulation. She said a little prayer that the jackals wouldn't be there but they were, sitting on that ugly concrete lump with their hoods up. Please Lord, she thought, let me get past them without trouble today.

They were bantering with a girl in a shiny black puffa-jacket, though Poppy didn't take in any of their actual words. The girl was skinny, mixed-race, and despite the cold she wore a provocatively short skirt. Her hair had been straightened and dyed honey-brown, and her too-thin brown legs were elongated by spike-heeled ankle-boots. An addict, Poppy didn't doubt, and most likely a prostitute too, and she knew it was selfish but she was glad the girl was there with her rotten life to distract them.

But no: the instant they noticed Poppy they dropped down from the concrete lump and came prowling up to her. Keeping her head down Poppy kept on going until the tallest of them, a barrel-chested black youth with West African features, physically blocked her way.

'Where you going?' he asked tonelessly.

She said nothing. She knew he didn't want a reply: this was just a game to him. She tried to move forward but he mirrored her movement, blocking her again, meaning she would have to physically push past him. But if she did so then she knew that this blank-faced young man would feel aggrieved, disrespected, and that that would justify in his mind some sort of retribution. So she just stood there: put all choices on him, and by implication all responsibility.

The stocky white youth joined the black youth, draping an arm around his shoulders and leaning in. 'You want to get by, you say excuse me,' he said in a tone that suggested the other boy's actions were reasonable, that this situation was reasonable.

The other two moved in close behind Poppy and one of them – the black one – brought his lips close to her ear. 'See, this ain't no African underpass,' he said softly. She didn't look round at him.

'It ain't no illegal immigrant underpass,' the Chinese-looking one added in her other ear, and as he moved his face close to hers Poppy could feel the radiant heat of his skin and smell the stale lager on his breath.

'Please,' she said.

Once she would have said, such a thing could never happen where I come from. There elders are respected, the young are guided by the whole village, discipline is strict, values are shared, orphans are taken in and cared for, and no child is left to grow wild and rude like this. But then the soldiers had come, and mostly they were youths or even boys, and they had shown no respect, and they had done terrible things and laughed and not cared at all. And they had taken her son and made him into – what?

An arm slid across her chest and crooked round her neck, dragging her sideways. The short black youth, choking her. He smelt rank and sweet. A knife flashed and the Chinese boy was holding it up in front of her face, close. Poppy's heart lurched.

'Brer likes knives,' the short black youth said, and he was grinning now, and gold flared in his mouth, and his face was shameless.

'I love 'em,' the Chinese youth said, his breath strong in her face. Poppy twisted her head away from him and saw the girl leaning against the concrete sculpture smoking a cigarette, neither watching nor not, bored.

'I wouldn't do that, though,' the white youth warned Poppy. 'He might think you don't like him. You might offend him. He's proper psycho like that.'

'But he likes you,' the short black youth said, still smiling, his arm tight round Poppy's neck.

Unable to bear another second of this torment, with a gasping cry Poppy wrenched herself free. One of her shopping bags tore and bargain moisturiser, toilet-paper and a bumper plastic bottle of wet wipes fell to the ground. The skinny black youth and the Chinese youth stepped back, putting up their hands as if to say this was just a joke, not a real threat, but no gesture could make the knife-blade in front of her eyes not real.

With no thought for her lost shopping Poppy rushed down the unlit tunnel that led to Cardinal One. Halfway along and at full tilt she crashed into the rubbish-laden supermarket trolley, banging her thigh and jarring her hip.

Her dress caught on one of the twisted broken wires that stuck out from the side of it and the material ripped audibly as in a panic she tore it loose.

Then she was stumbling up the steps on the other side. Safe. Like the animals they were she knew they wouldn't leave their hunting-ground. She stood for a moment at the top of the steps, cradling the bag of shopping she had managed to hold onto like a baby, short of breath and blinking back tears.

'Forgive them, Lord,' she said, needing to speak her prayer out loud because she knew she was asking Him to do what she could not. And wasn't that the point of God: to do and be better than us, and do what we cannot? Even to ask for forgiveness on behalf of the jackals gave her strength, and a minute later she was able to go forward with her head held high, her back straight and her heart no longer hammering in her chest.

Cardinal One loomed up before her, its windows lit but not welcoming: where she was but not home.

The lift was out of order. Her hip began to throb where she had banged it on the trolley. Perhaps she wouldn't go to church this evening after all. The prospect of struggling up fifteen flights of stairs, then down again, then up again after the service was over, made her feel exhausted. Getting to this country was supposed to have been the end of her ordeal, not a continuation of it by other means.

She wondered if Pacific would be waiting for her on the other side, if being dead would really be so bad; if hating your own life to the point where you sometimes wished it was over was really a crime against God's creation, as Reverend Obasanjo had once said. Wasn't Heaven a place you were supposed to want to get to?

With an effort she pushed the fire-door open and entered the stairwell. Above her the handrail rose and receded in endless black rectangles.

It was there to be climbed.

She could take her time.

Chapter Five

Stanlake sat before the mirror, adjusted the lamp, and studied the planes and contours of his face. On a square of sky-blue silk the contents of the gift-bag he had stolen earlier were laid out with the precision of a surgeon's tools. Around the mirror were collaged images he had cut from magazines: Naomi and Alex and Beyoncé and Rhianna looked down on him, flawless mocha inspirations in an arbour of sweet vanilla.

A hot bath had opened his pores. He cleansed, then applied a light moisturiser, then studied his face again, pulling the bedside lamp around to ensure that he had the best light possible for the operation ahead. Though they were naturally narrow and shapely, his eyebrows dissatisfied him. He picked up his mother's tweezers and, amidst winces, plucked out the few errant hairs that spoiled their silky arches or gestured towards connecting them in the middle. Each plucked hair had at the end that had been buried in the skin a tiny, bulbous white root he found slightly disgusting: they reminded him of fly-eggs.

He applied foundation. The textureless cream made his face blanker, more sculptural, less human, less his. A neutral base on which to paint a new persona. As he stared at himself there were no thoughts in his head: his face might as well have been a block of stone or wood, and that was a relief. He dabbed a little colour on his cheeks to bring out his cheekbones. Then came the application of eyeshadow. This always excited him. Today he chose carnival green. He had done this in secret a dozen times before, and his fingers moved deftly, spreading the smooth iridescence out across the curving cowrie-shells of his upper eyelids, blending it into his temples on either side. With a tiny brush he drew touches of gold in at the outer corners of his eyes, angling the strokes upwards to accentuate their feline shape. Then he blocked in his eyebrows, raising and extending their curves. That done, it was time for the eyeliner, so densely black and defining; then mascara to magnify and thicken his lashes, and with that his eyes were complete.

Next came the lipstick. He unscrewed the plastic-gold cylinder, pouted his large, full lips, and glided the soft, slippery, faintly-perfumed point around his mouth. Following guidance he had read in a magazine he made two strong arcs for the top lip then two for the bottom one, making sure always to move outwards from the centre to the corners. The result felt better than it looked, and he had to do some tidying up with a tissue to get the sharp-edged symmetricality he was aiming for. After he had sorted that out he couldn't resist painting on just a little gold, to further enhance his mouth's gleaming glossiness.

He pushed his chair back. Keeping his eyes on his reflection he moved his legs to one side, twisting his bare torso so it too was turned sideways-on, pushed out his chest, tipped his head back and gazed dreamily at himself over one shoulder. The being that returned his gaze was strange, but not a stranger: not him, but him. A mask that did not simply conceal but also possessed, like the masks in the hut of the Society of Masks; a mask that, once put on, transformed the innermost part of the wearer.

Stanlake flashed a Tyra Banks 'pop' at the mirror and smiled a wide, professional smile, as if for a photo shoot. 'Yes, people often do ask me what is the secret of my flawless skin,' he said, speaking out loud, adopting the style of an interviewee on a chat show, or, more precisely, the style of an infomercial for a beauty product that was being filmed to look like a chat-show. 'I always say detoxing is key. I have a healthy diet rich in goji berries and anti-oxidants, I drink plenty of water and – ' Stanlake held up a bottle of cheap generic cleanser his mother had bought in the Pound Shop as if displaying it for the camera. 'I always use Clarins deep-cleansing cream.' He flashed another smile. 'Being a super-model means never being afraid to demand the best.'

He returned the cleanser to the shelf. The smile left his face.

A supermodel would never have had to do the things he

had done.

He remembered Florence. Why her, who he had barely known, more than the others? Perhaps this new face was partly hers. She had looked a little like him, he thought now, though he had not thought so then. Was it true? If so, perhaps that was what kept her in his mind. Or was it being here, a stranger in an unfamiliar place filled with so many different faces, that drew him closer to her?

To the crossroads, to the surface of the mirror, where the living and the dead can meet and share their news.

The rebels had taken him, had taken all the young men of the village. Except for Patrick, who had tried to defend his mother: him they had shot in the face. Grotesquely he did not die all at once, but lay on his back in the dirt twitching and kicking, and he seemed to be wearing a mask of knotted red sisal with no features behind it. No eyes, no teeth: the former pulp, the latter scattered on the ground. Later, while they were being led into the forest to who knew what fate, Matthew had panicked and tried to run, but he had been quickly caught and brought back. One too-angry rifle-butt blow to his skull and he had gone down and not got up again. Robert Stanlake had not seen die, but he heard later that everyone in Robert's unit had been massacred by government forces, and he knew in his heart that this last of his Mask brothers was surely gone as well.

Though he too had been almost unbearably afraid, Stanlake had not run. Because where could he run to? There in the town square they had made him do a very terrible thing. With a single act they had made him into what they were, into them. From the very beginning they had done that, so there could be no running away. They were very smart.

He had saved his mother that day, at least that. Had he saved himself? The act he had committed put him on the bad side of the abyss that yawned between human beings and beasts, put him beyond salvation.

'My Beasts.'

That was what Makinde had christened Stanlake and the other young boys in the unit he commanded, and blood was their baptism. He was no hypocrite, Makinde: he led from the front and was the most bestial of them all. At the close of that first red day he marched them in a phalanx into the darkening forest. There he would recreate them in his image and fill them with his vision, and there right and wrong got lost, and only fear and rage and the instinct for survival remained.

Stanlake remembered little of those early days, just a forced march made worse by hunger, thirst, anxiety and exhaustion, with no sense of where they were going or how long it would take to get there. The march was accompanied by interminable ideological harangues from the older soldiers, and contempt and disdain from those soldiers Stanlake's age or younger who had been so long in the bush they were amazed he didn't even know how to set a rifle's safety-catch to 'off', never mind strip the weapon down and rebuild it. One of the younger soldiers, Big Gun, who was no older than thirteen, and small, with small hands, could place a pistol in a bag, put his hands in the bag and break the pistol down to its constituent parts without looking. He would then tip the parts out in front of Stanlake and the others, put them back in the bag in a jumble, shake them up, reach in and, again without being able to see what he was doing, reassemble the pistol. Then he would bark in his high, sharp voice, 'Time?'

'Two minutes and twenty seconds,' someone would shout back. 'A new record.'

And Big Gun would nod, his eyes dark in the firelight, and the expression on his face dared you to challenge him. He had killed many men, Stanlake was told, and he kept aloof from the others. On his chest were keloid scars caused by shrapnel from when a landmine blew up another boy next to him. He had been spattered with blood and shredded flesh, cut by shards of bone and metal and temporarily deafened, and had never fully come back from that experience, they said.

Yet he and Stanlake became friends. Not then but a year later, on the roadblock. One night when Stanlake was keeping watch Big Gun had sauntered out of the cabin to share some cheeba with him. They had smoked in silence for a while, sitting on old ammo-boxes and listening to the ceaseless sounds of the forest; and then, as if continuing a conversation they had not, in fact, been having, Big Gun said, 'At least you did not have to watch them rape your mother and your sister with objects before putting bullets in their heads.' He was staring out at the wall of darkness into which the road vanished, and his eyes were hard. Slinging his rifle over his shoulder, Stanlake had turned to him and hugged him awkwardly, and Big Gun had closed his eyes and let Stanlake hold him, and a tremor had passed through them.

In the forest they had drilled for hours every day and been trained in the use of weapons, in unarmed combat and in the techniques of guerrilla warfare. They were always hungry, always short of sleep, and always afraid, both of the as-yet-unencountered enemy forces and of their own commanders. All of them, even those as young as seven, smoked cheeba, and all of them snorted gunpowder and cocaine when the adult soldiers offered it to excite their spirits for some action. And all of them listened, and believed, when Makinde told them the government would like nothing better than to kill them; that the government perversely refused to make peace even though the demands of the rebels were reasonable; and that in the eyes of the rest of the world they, the rebels, were not freedom fighters, but wicked war criminals.

'If you are caught you will be put to death!' he barked. 'You will be tortured, tortured, tortured to inform on your comrades. And whether you break and inform or whether you do not, then you will be shot. They will begin aiming at your groin and work their way up to your chest to ensure you suffer before you die. So what must you do?' he demanded. 'What must you do, my Beasts?'

'Fight to the death, oga!' they chorused back.

'And when your last bullet is gone?'

'Fight with our knives and bayonets.'

'And when they are blunted or broken?'

'Fight with stones and sticks and fists.'

'And when they are gone and your fists are broken?'

'Fight with our teeth, oga!'

'And when your teeth are smashed?'

'We will be dead, oga!'

And he led them in songs and war-chants until there was nothing left inside them that belonged to them, and there was a terrible relief in that. There were forty, maybe as many as fifty boys at the camp out there in the forest, and every day some left and never came back, and others were brought there to train with them.

'The government is wicked and corrupt,' Makinde would lecture them nightly, red-eyed and harsh-voiced, striding back and forth in his neatly-ironed camouflage gear and always-gleaming boots, boots they, mostly in sneakers or even flipflops, looked at with envy as they sat on the ground cross-legged gazing up at him. And he seemed tall as a tree, as the sky, handsome and ugly, terrifying and marvellous. 'The government does not care for the people. It does not build for the future. What have any of you ever seen this government build? Anything?' He would point at one youth, then another, and all would shake their heads in agreement about the terribleness of the government. 'It is the slave of outside interests who loot our resources,' Makinde continued. 'Neo-colonialists! Faggot imperialists! They take our diamonds for their necklaces! They take our coltan for their mobile phones, their iPods and iPads! They even take our copper and our iron! And our so-called democratic government gives itself over to this. Like a cheap whore it lets itself be fucked up the arse for money. But we will stop this! We will strangle them with their diamond necklaces and choke them with their mobile phones! Death to the parasites!'

'Death to the parasites!' the young soldiers yelled back, and the ones who were most high, usually older youths standing about smoking at the back of the session, would spray bullets up into the sky, machine-tooled orgasms.

Those were their nights. By day they would train and go out on patrol. They raided whatever villages they came across that were still occupied, that still had anything left to take. Makinde instructed them that as these villages, unlike Stanlake's, were in a district under rebel protection, the inhabitants were not to be harmed unless they refused to give food to the hungry freedom fighters who suddenly appeared in their midst.

The fear on the faces of the villagers excited Stanlake,

excited them all as they stalked grim and silent among the
thatched huts and mud-walled compounds, rifles at the
ready. But it also filled them with shame and a shared,
barely-stifled rage at being seen not as who they had once
hoped to be, but as the Beasts they had been made into. And
that rage, which was the rage of children, made them cruel,
and their cruelty was capricious, set off by random associations, random moods and chance upsets. They were usually
high when out on patrol, and that added to their tendency to
explode in sudden violence.

'Don't look at my face!' Stanlake had snarled at one
kneeling man, a man resembling his father, who had done no
more than fearfully glance up at him, breaking the man's
nose with a blow from his rifle-butt.

Each act made other acts easier.

He stared into his reflection. Could this new face let him
be new? Could the new be both a way forward and a way
back to what was undamaged from before? Could this face be
found beautiful, be kissed, be loved?

Florence.

He lost track of how long they were in the forest and
gained little sense of the geography of the region they were
in. All he knew was that they moved many times, set many
camps, and passed through many villages. Increasingly the
villages were deserted, the crops neglected, dead in the
fields. It was the dry season, and the streams shrank then
turned to dusty slots, the riverbeds became crocodile-
skinned highways of cracked mud. The leaves passed from
yellow to brown, dessicated and surely dead forever this
time, and the branches of the trees turned the dirty white of
bones. They had several engagements with government
forces, but always at a distance, just half-hearted sniping,
and as the withering heat continued even those seemed to
drop off.

Perhaps the government was giving up.

They knew that behind the scenes strategies were being
discussed. The import of these discussions was never shared
with the younger soldiers: they were told to obey orders
without question, to fight without question, to die without
question; that the cause they were fighting for was just and

noble, and that that was all they needed to know. They barked out, 'Sir, yes, sir!' and took perverse pride in their submission and self-abnegation. And they marched and they made camp and they broke camp and they marched again and they waited, tired and hungry, and as they waited plans were made, policies were adjusted and strategies devised. Here there were advances, there withdrawals. Though rumours were rife concerning how the war was going, they were never told anything specific. But so it came about that, towards the end of the dry season and after a hurried two-day march, Stanlake and his unit found themselves split off from the others and assigned to man a blockade that Makinde told them was on a stretch of road crucial for the Revolutionary People's Party's supply-lines.

Among themselves Stanlake and the others agreed that this was potentially a sweet deal: they would be in one place, not constantly moving around, and would be kept supplied with food and ammunition by the passing convoys, who would be relying on them to keep the road open. It certainly sounded better than squatting starving by inches in the forest, or trudging wearily towards danger and death on the ever-shifting frontline. How dangerously situated the roadblock was they had no idea, but what difference did it make? They had no choice in the matter.

At first their luck was in: right next to the roadblock, which at some point had evidently been a checkpoint for the army, was a largish cabin, abandoned but structurally sound. It was single-storey, twenty-five feet long and ten feet wide, with the long side facing the road; had breeze block walls, a dirt floor, and an unpartitioned interior. The roof, which was pitched and made of corrugated iron, extended out into an awning, offering shade and shelter to whoever was outside on watch. Shutters of plaited grass dangled by threads in the unglazed windows, or lay torn on the ground. For furniture there was a table and some chairs and cots, along with a stove and other useful things – blankets, a broom, a can-opener – that had been left behind in a hurry. A layer of grit lay over everything, and that was reassuring: this place had been abandoned months ago; it hadn't been overrun just lately. Hopefully it was still some way from the frontline.

After months of misery and hardship in the forest it was like moving into a palace, and once they had swept out the dirt, along with several scorpions and snakes, stopped up rat-holes and repaired the shutters against mosquitoes and the night, it felt like a refuge.

The barrier had once had a proper striped arm, counter-weighted and mounted on a pole set into a concrete block, but the arm had been broken off and flung into a ditch on the other side of the road, and the way was blocked instead by a five-foot mound of blown-out car and truck tyres. This, the Beasts quickly saw, was the rough end of the deal: lugging enough of the tyres aside every time a truck came for it to get through, then reassembling the barrier afterwards, would be heavy, dirty, boring work, and would no doubt have to be done at the double. And they had no idea how many trucks might need to come through on any given day. Makinde, if he knew himself, refused to give them any information on that point, saying it was 'hush-hush'. Instead he stressed that they must constantly be on the alert, and ready to act at a moment's notice at any time of the day or night.

'Yes, oga!' they choroused.

There were four of them assigned to the roadblock: Stanlake, now known as Little Gun because his family name was Olusegun, and Big Gun was already Big Gun; his friend Big Gun; and two other youths, Blondie and Diamondz. Blondie and Diamondz were a couple of years older than Stanlake and Big Gun, and had fought in towns, and had looted. Blondie wore a blonde wig, taken from a mannequin in a department store, that became more and more crazy as the weeks went by and it stiffened with accumulated sweat and dirt. Diamondz wore dangling diamond earrings as well as his military beret, and diamond – or diamante – necklaces and bracelets as well as his camouflage fatigues.

No-one questioned this, for by then what standpoint was there from which they could make a judgement as to whether this or that behaviour was normal – or normal enough, at least, to be permissible? And in such a situation, who permitted? All of them had killed. All of them had done cruel things when ordered, and some of them had done those things when they had not been ordered. They witnessed each other's cruelties and covered each others' backs: they were a unit. That was what mattered, nothing else. Loyal devils were better than traitor saints. Beyond that you could do as you pleased, and there you found a freedom that was both dreadful and exhilarating, a freedom from all constraints whatsoever. It was as if when the state had collapsed so had their sense of themselves: they had become a mirror to chaos, inchoate and without boundaries.

None of them used their given names. The names they took and were known by – Big Gun, Little Gun, Diamondz, Blondie – were a way of othering themselves: performing people who could do what they did without it being the whole truth of them, hoping thereby to preserve, buried deep down inside, some spark or ember that might, one unimaginable day when this was all over, be blown back into life.

They were not yet dead all the way through: that was what the taking of names meant. But they knew a time would come when their new names were their real names. Then the war would never end, because it would be inside them, always.

The first day perhaps five trucks came. That night three more, pulling up at the roadblock at two-hourly intervals, sounding their horns, leaving their engines running, the officers yelling for the barrier to be taken down quickly-o, in a hurry to be on their way. The next day there were more, the day after less, then more again. Most of the trucks were filled with soldiers, usually grown men, and most headed in one direction only. From the weary aspect of the men, who often showed hastily-bandaged injuries, Stanlake assumed they were being driven away from the frontline, and from their numbers he guessed that things weren't going well. Trucks transporting supplies were less frequent, but passed in both directions, so it wasn't yet a rout. From the vehicles carrying soldiers the Beasts asked nothing, but from the drivers of the supply-trucks they demanded dash as they had no other way of procuring food and other supplies for themselves.

On their busiest, most exhausting day fifteen trucks came, one an hour or more, and several jeeps too, and their arms were almost torn from their sockets tugging down the mountain of tyres and rebuilding it once each vehicle had gone through. After that the numbers fell off sharply, as if some strategic withdrawal had taken place and left only a few stragglers or rearguarders behind. Or perhaps the focus of the war had moved elsewhere? The Beasts began to fear that soon it might reach where they were, and they would be caught up in a fire-fight they could never win at a post they didn't dare desert. They listened for the sound of distant gun- or mortar-fire, but heard nothing.

Then the rainy season began, and days went by with no traffic at all. Makinde was often the only one on the road. He passed by irregularly, arriving in his jeep at any hour of the day or night. Sometimes he was in a hurry, and would sound his horn and curse the Beasts for delaying him, but as often he would pull over, and he and any other soldiers he had with him would break their journey at the cabin. They would share cheeba and liquor and cigars and tobacco and tins of food and looted trinkets with the young Beasts, and play cards and gamble, sometimes until the sun came up. During such sessions there would be talk – always guarded – of how the war was going, which increasingly seemed to be: uncertainly. All talk of triumphal sweeps to victory had long since fallen away.

Of course during these sessions one of the Beasts would have to remain outside, to watch the road and watch over the commander's jeep.

The rain came down relentlessly.

At first it was a relief. When the dry season was at its height all the nearby streams had been baked to clay, and to get drinking water they had had to walk a trail through the forest for an hour each way just to get to a river through the centre of which a sluggish rivulet of potable water still ran. They would fill their cans from it then trudge back to the roadblock, knees buckling under the weight. The chore was made more tedious than it had to be because they dared spare only a single member of the unit to do it, as at any moment a truck might need to come through, and to dismantle the tyre-barrier speedily enough to avoid a reprimand took at least three of them.

Weeks had dragged by in this dusty, arduous way, so at first when the rains came, despite the stifling humidity the

Beasts were just glad that drinking-water was no longer a scarce resource. But the heaviness of the saturated air began quickly to send them all a little mad, sodden with sweat as they constantly were, and persecuted as they began to feel by the rain's relentless pounding on the corrugated-iron roof of the cabin, Shango drumming, drumming.

One night, after the rains had been falling for perhaps six weeks, Stanlake was outside keeping watch from beneath the awning when a pair of headlights came bouncing along the road, which was now more a raised, rutted red river than a functioning thoroughfare. Stanlake squinted through the beaded curtain of rain into the dazzle of the headlights and could make out it was a jeep. Putting the butt of his rifle to his shoulder, he set his sights on where he knew the driver's chest would be. (Always aim for the chest, he had been taught. Then if you are a little low it is the bowels; if a little high it is the head. Don't waste time being a marksman. Never try to be clever).

He tracked the jeep as it turned off the road towards him, jolting to a halt under some sodden, sagging banana trees about thirty feet from where he was standing. There was the sound of the handbrake being wrenched up and the head-lights went out.

'Who goes there?' Stanlake called, reaching up and punching the underside of the corrugated-iron roof twice, to alert the others inside that there was a potential situation.

A head thrust out from the driver's-side window, a black outline unreadable against the blackness of the night. 'Is that you, Little Gun?' a slurred voice demanded.

If Stanlake couldn't make out the face he knew the voice. 'Yes, oga!' he shouted, shouldering his rifle smartly and snapping to attention. 'Sorry I aimed my weapon at you, oga!'

'At ease, soldier,' Makinde said as he got out of the jeep. His movements were clumsy and Stanlake guessed he was drunk. Stanlake moved to the 'at ease' position but continued to hold himself rigidly upright, chest out, shoulders back, feet exactly eighteen inches apart: drunk or not, this was his commanding officer.

'I have brought something for you, Little Gun,' Makinde

said. 'A treat. For all my Beasts.' He leaned back into the jeep and said something to someone out of sight in the canvas-covered rear of the vehicle. Stanlake heard the words, 'Do not run. Or I will kill you.'

With the over-articulated movements of a drunk being careful Makinde straightened up, slammed the door shut, and crossed unsteadily to where Stanlake stood waiting. The rain had abruptly fallen off, and was at that moment only light and hazy. Chinks in the cabin's shutters let out shards of lamp-light that slid over Makinde's lower body as he came forward, glinting on the nearly-full bottle of whiskey he dangled, and on the rings on his fingers.

As Makinde neared him Stanlake held himself more rigidly still. It always felt like a privilege to be visited by the Unit Commander. Scary, because his moods were so change-able and his temper was so volatile, but exciting, because each visit was filled with the promise of secret lessons in strategy, politics, women and wealth. He would have been not more than thirty years old, now Stanlake looked back on it, but back then, surrounded by youths none of whom were even out of their teens, he was a Big Man. They feared him and in a terrible way they loved him too. Stanlake would have died for him. They all would have. Then.

Makinde was a head taller than Stanlake. He was broad-shouldered, lean and narrow-hipped. His movements, except when he was drunk, were economical and purposive. His hands were large and square. His forearms were corded with veins and sinews, as was his neck; and even his angular face had a sinewy look to it, the product of years of living hard in the forest. On his right wrist, stacked up his forearm, were three gold Rolexes, and in his wide mouth was the unlit butt of a cigar. There seemed to be no other soldiers with him today and Stanlake was pleased: these would often be the best visits, when he was on his own, because then he would confide in his young Beasts the most.

Makinde put a hand on Stanlake's shoulder to steady himself. 'How is it going, Little Gun?'

'It is going well, oga.'

Makinde nodded. Absent-mindedly he made the gestures of an officer checking a soldier's uniform on parade; tweaking the ragged collar of Stanlake's sodden khaki shirt as if to straighten it, brushing Stanlake's shoulders as if removing specks of dust from an otherwise-immaculate uniform. 'Good, good,' he said. 'Many trucks today?'

'Two, oga.'

Makinde pulled a face. Stanlake decided to risk a question: 'How is it going, oga?'

'Not good, Little Gun. But tonight we will forget all that for a while, enh?' Makinde swayed where he stood. 'I need to piss,' he said, and staggered off round the back of the cabin to relieve himself.

While he was gone the cabin door creaked open and Big Gun peeped out.

'Oga,' Stanlake said.

'Okay,' Big Gun said, and withdrew.

A minute later Makinde returned, clapped Stanlake on the shoulder once more and made like he was about to say something but didn't. Instead he went over to the cabin door, pulled it open and went in. Light sliced out and there was the sudden particular sound of soldiers jumping to attention. The door banged shut. Stanlake returned to his post, looking out along the road. There was nothing to see. It was late, and he stifled a yawn.

For no apparent reason there began to grow on him a sense that something was prowling about in the bushes on the far side of the road. He cocked his head and listened hard, but heard nothing beyond trickling rivulets, dripping leaves and the rasping of insects. He screwed up his eyes, but saw nothing. Probably it was just his imagination. Makinde's presence always did this to him: made him sense enemies whether they were out there or not. Partly it was the paranoia Makinde gave off like a stink – alertness, he called it – but also the Unit Commander's appearances were a reminder that they really were at war; that there was danger all around them, and that death might turn up at any moment. Out there on the roadblock, especially at night when no traffic came, it was as if the rest of the world had fallen away, and it was oddly easy to forget the war. At those times Stanlake would think of the spirits of the forest, and his Mask brothers, and feel sad and strange.

A burst of laughter came from inside the cabin. The squeak and clonk of chairs being pulled round the table and cots pushed back against the walls was followed by the clink of glasses being set down. Music began to play – Makinde must have brought batteries for their looted radio – and though the reception drifted in and out of an insectile fuzz it reminded Stanlake of happier times and made him think of dancing.

He didn't dance, though: just stood rigidly to attention.

Four more hours before he was relieved.

In the absence of any other distraction, the jeep began to draw his attention. It sat there under the banana trees, clicking and creaking as its engine cooled. No other sound or movement came from inside it, and Stanlake began to think he had imagined Makinde speaking to someone back there.

More laughter came from inside the cabin and there was the clinking of bottle on glass. Curiosity rising up in him, Stanlake decided he should check the jeep. If there was someone in there, he rationalised to himself, they might be in difficulties and need assistance. Due to his drinking the Unit Commander might have forgotten about them. Yes, he should check. Then he wavered: even though he hadn't been ordered not to look in the jeep it might make the Unit Commander angry if he did so. And to move even thirty feet from where he was standing monitoring the road might be considered a dereliction of duty.

He stayed where he was.

More time passed.

The rain was still no more than a soft gauze, as if tempting him to go over there, why not? It would only take a moment, after all, to go and peep in. There was a breathless shimmer to the air.

Stanlake gave in to his curiosity. With a glance back at the cabin, he crossed to the jeep in quick, pecking steps. Rifle held awkwardly at the ready in his right hand, with his left he reached for the driver's-side door handle and slowly and carefully lifted it. The door swung open with a soft creak. He smelt sweat and perfume and engine-oil. In the back, in the darkness, something stirred. With a single reflex movement Stanlake brought up his rifle, thumbed off the safety-catch and drew his sights on the shadowy shape. 'Come out of there!' he ordered, glancing back at the cabin again, keeping his voice low for fear of being overheard. The movement stopped. 'I said come out. Or I will shoot you.'

Nothing happened.

Stanlake noticed a torch Makinde had left lying on the passenger seat. Keeping the rifle trained as best he could on whatever it was back there he groped for the torch, got hold of it, and lined it up with the barrel of his rifle like a laser-sight. Then he clicked it on. It threw a weak circle of light into the back of the jeep that revealed hunched up there a skinny, scared-looking girl.

She was maybe fourteen, though it was hard to tell in those times when so many didn't get enough to eat, and so were under-developed. Her face was wide and pretty, and her eyes were full of fear. She had on too much make-up, clumsily applied in garish colours that made her look younger, a child playing dress-up, and she wore a red beaded party-dress that was both too big for her little girl's body and too short for decency. The beading on the dress was poorly-stitched: threads had broken, and the drab green grooved metal floor of the back of the jeep was littered with tiny red beads that glittered in the torchlight like fleeing exotic beetles. On the girl's immaculately spirally-braided head was perched a diamond tiara. Her mascara was smudged from where she had been crying, and as she looked up at Stanlake with her wide-apart eyes her lower lip trembled. On her bare upper arms were small half-moon bruises: fingermarks.

'Ah, Little Gun,' a voice said behind him.

Stanlake jerked back sharply, dropping the torch and banging his head on the roof of the jeep.

'I see you have found your present.'

Backlit by lamplight, the Unit Commander was standing in the cabin doorway, his shirt now unbuttoned to the waist, serrated belly arching forward. He held a pistol loosely in one hand.

'Yes, oga,' Stanlake said, discreetly exploring his head with the tips of his fingers to feel if his scalp had got cut on one of the metal flanges.

'Well, bring it then.'

'Yes, oga.'

Stanlake leaned back into the jeep, recovered the torch and shone it at the girl. 'Come,' he said.

She was staring at him fixedly, and he realised that she wasn't just fearful, a mental state in which reason and the calculation of advantage could still operate, but terrified, and so unable to follow even the most basic order. He reached in, grabbing for her thin wrist. 'Come,' he repeated. But she squirmed away from his grasping fingers and pushed herself into the far corner of the jeep, getting as far away from him as she could. A spasm of anger flared up in him: who did she think she was, this nobody girl? He leaned in further, caught hold of her wrist and yanked her forward. 'Didn't you hear me?' he snapped. 'I said come.'

But she was too afraid to control herself, even too afraid to do as she was told by an angry young soldier who had power of life and death over her, and he had to drag the whole weight of her up and over the front seats of the jeep. She was small – smaller than him, anyway – and yet how heavy she was in her unwillingness! Like a dead thing she said nothing and made no noise.

Annoyance surging through him, he slung his rifle over his shoulder, grabbed her under her arms, pulled her roughly out of the jeep, then dropped her face-down on the sodden ground. He felt curiously breathless as he did so. Perhaps it was the violent tremor that had run from her body into his as he lifted her. Perhaps it was the beat of her heart or the heat of her in his arms. She lay where he had deposited her, inert as a sack of maize. 'Get up,' he said. When she didn't react he swung his rifle round and aimed the muzzle at her bowed head. He wanted her to do what he said without having to touch her again. He thumbed the safety-catch on then off again.

She heard the click and looked up at him, and she must have seen in his eyes that he would kill her if she didn't obey him, because she got to her feet. Her face and the front of her dress were now ochre-spattered with mud. She kept her eyes on his, but not defiantly. He knew she was hoping he would see her as a person; that she had realised that was her best strategy for survival.

But my eyes are stones, he thought. Or lead, like bullets. And my heart too.

After what seemed like the longest time she turned away from him and looked over to where Makinde was waiting, but she didn't go to him. Shame and anger flared up in Stanlake. Why would she not obey orders? Did she want his commander to see that he, Little Gun, could not even control a girl?

To get her going he aimed a kick at her backside. His plimsoled foot connected with her buttocks, and the unexpectedness of it sent her stumbling onto her hands and knees. A moment later she was up again. Without looking round at him she took a few quick steps forward. Then, once she was out of his range, she hesitated, because before her was not a way out of this but Makinde. Defeat visibly overcame her. With eyes downcast and shoulders hunched she approached the Unit Commander. Smiling, he stood aside for her to enter the cabin. Head bowed, she did so. Jamming the butt of the cigar into his wide mouth Makinde turned to Stanlake.

'Do not worry, Little Gun. I will not forget you. You will have your turn.'

His face tight and burning, Stanlake nodded. Makinde turned and followed the girl inside. The cabin door banged shut.

There was nothing for Stanlake to do but return to his sentry duty. Suddenly he felt exhausted. Taking a seat on an empty ammunition-box that had been placed under the awning for that purpose, he set his rifle against the wall. Then he leant back until the base of his skull rested against the clammy breeze blocks and stared into the night. But his mind was in the room behind him, and his ears were attuned now not to the sounds of the forest but to the smallest sounds that came from within.

Over everything, like a wash, was the music, and its upbeatness, its pervasive, unstoppable pre-recorded optimism seemed frenzied, hysterical, almost an act of violence in itself. Makinde's voice ordered, 'Cut cards, cut cards!' Then came a pause, then laughter, then the thump of something being overturned followed by more laughter, the clinking of glasses, a slap, a gasp, a sob. Blondie's voice saying, 'No, no, Big Gun, aces are high. It is me first. You are last.' Material ripping. Muffled comments. Makinde's voice, irritated, taking charge: 'You first, then you, then you.' A pause. Then: 'She is a whore. She loves to do everything.'

The talk ceased, leaving just the music, joyous, innocent, awful. Soon it was interpolated by a low conversation the words of which Stanlake could not make out, though the tone was punctuated by verbal ejaculations of the sort made by those playing cards and cursing or exhorting their luck. Shortly he heard the stifled grunts and moans of sex. Stanlake's dick stirred as the sex-sounds went on, though at the same time he felt disgusted.

Perhaps half an hour crawled by. The humidity spiked scalp-crawlingly and a downpour began. A small scorpion came scuttling out of the rain, its carapace black, lacquered, almost beautiful. Stanlake watched it as it hurried towards the wall of the cabin, seeking shelter. After a moment he lifted the butt of his rifle and crushed it.

Makinde appeared in the doorway then, and Stanlake got to his feet. Makinde was now undressed to the waist, and his skin was as shiny as the scorpion's back had been. 'Here, Little Gun. Drink this,' he said, and he thrust a bottle of whiskey at Stanlake that was still a quarter full.

'Yes, oga.' Stanlake took the bottle and swigged. The spirit burned his throat, but it warmed his gut and deadened his head. He took another swig. Any fucker who came down the road tonight, he would shoot them.

'Finish it,' Makinde ordered.

'Yes, oga.'

The commander disappeared back inside. Stanlake sat back down. He drank, and drank again. Time stretched. He wore a watch, white gold with a delicate, girlish chain, but the battery had run down, and where could you get such a thing as a watch-battery in the middle of a war? Anyway, the time was what you were told it was. So it was that he had no idea how long it was between him being given the whiskey by Makinde and a sweaty, bloated-faced Blondie emerging bare-chested from the cabin, Kalash swinging at his waist, saying, 'Makinde says to go in. It is my watch now.'

Stanlake nodded, got to his feet and went in.

The air inside the cabin was warm as blood and smelt sharply of sweat, sex and cheeba. On the table in the middle of the room were strewn playing cards, glasses and bottles, jewellery that was being gambled for, wads of long-since-ludicrously-devalued bank-notes showing the now ex-president's face, a bayonet, several mobile phones, a Bowie knife and Makinde's pistol. Rifles leaned in a row against the wall by the door, ready for action at a moment's notice. Makinde and Diamondz sprawled on two of the cots, their backs resting against the bare breeze blocks, sharing a joint. In a far corner of the room blankets had been pinned up to screen a third cot from view. From behind these blankets Big Gun was emerging. Like the others he was stripped to the waist and slick and glossy with sweat, and he was attempting to button up his army trousers with fingers that trembled. He looked round at Stanlake.

'She is good,' he said tonelessly. 'It is fun, Little Gun. You will like it.'

Diamondz laughed, but there was a desolation in Big Gun's voice and eyes that filled Stanlake with pity and dread. Big Gun went and joined Diamondz on his cot. Diamondz offered him what was left of the joint. Eyes averted, Big Gun took it and toked.

Stanlake stood swaying in the middle of the room, extremely drunk he now realised. He looked vacantly about him, wanting a way out of this but unable to think of one, for once hoping a truck would come, because that would end it, because duty always comes before pleasure. His rifle was still slung over his shoulder as if he was on parade. He tilted his head back and tried to listen over the music for sounds outside. Makinde and Diamondz watched him, amused, puzzled. A little time passed but no truck came.

'Put your gun down, soldier,' Makinde ordered, when it became obvious to him that the younth would do nothing without external input. With a clunk Stanlake did so. 'Stand easy.'

'Yes, oga.'

'Are you drunk-o, Little Gun?' Diamondz asked playfully.

'Yes.'

'A real man is never too drunk to fuck,' Makinde said.

'Yes, oga.'

'You want weed?'

'No, oga.'

Feeling heavy-limbed and weary as an old man, Stanlake went over to where the pinned-up blankets hung and slipped round behind them. The girl was there, of course, waiting for him on the cot. Her dress was now pushed up to her waist, and she had no underwear on. She didn't attempt to pull the dress down. More glittering red beads were scattered over the grey blanket. One of the girl's cheeks was bruised and a spot of blood had coagulated under her left nostril. She still had the tiara on, but it was now at an angle, and where it had been forced down it had marked her skin and torn small tufts out of her braids. Stanlake could smell the sharp odour of semen. He pitied her. He wanted to be kind to her. But when he reached out to touch her she pulled back from him with such a blaze of hatred in her eyes that he withdrew his hand as if it had been burned.

He froze, not knowing what to do next, watching the expression on her face contort as, realising her life might well depend on pleasing him, she did her best to push that hatred down, to conceal it and let the need to live flood over it and drown it. To make herself if not alluring, because that was impossible under the circumstances, at least welcoming. It was a terrible, powerful thing to see. Almost, he admired her. But he could not bear her.

And so they stared at each other. Stanlake wanted to vomit from all the whiskey he had drunk.

'Are you up her yet, Little Gun?' Diamondz called from beyond the blanket, his voice creaky from smoking.

'She likes it if you bit her tits,' Makinde added, and Diamondz laughed and Stanlake struggled for breath and looked away from the girl as she tugged the front of her dress up to protect herself. She hardly had breasts.

'Do you want some help, Little Gun?' Diamondz called.

'No!' Stanlake called back thickly.

There was no way out. Resignedly he slid on top of the girl. She stiffened, then, fearing his violence, forced herself to become more pliant. Again, an incredible act of will. Now, limp as a dead body and as unresponsive as one, she waited for him to begin. But he didn't begin.

A puzzled expression appeared on the girl's face when she realised the youth on top of her was not unbuttoning his fly, a look shot through, Stanlake could tell, with fresh fears: if he does not do this will I be blamed? If he does not do this does it mean he wants to do something even worse?

'What is your name?' he asked, trying to will kindness into his eyes, to match that strength in her.

The girl swallowed. 'Florence,' she said.

'Florence, we will pretend.'

She nodded tightly. The why of it didn't matter to her. All that mattered was that this boy didn't want to hurt her, at least not for a little while; and that he wished to conceal his desire not to hurt her from the others.

Bracing himself above her so they didn't touch above the waist he began to move his hips against hers. The cot creaked with each movement, spurring laughter from Diamondz and Makinde on the other side of the screen of blankets. Stanlake's face burned. How could this arouse any man?

It was after that night that Big Gun had told Stanlake about his mother and sister.

It was after that night that one time they had kissed, and Big Gun had given Stanlake a charm he said could turn aside bullets.

'You two faggots,' Makinde had said, though he had only seen them embrace like comrades. 'You should get married.'

Big Gun in the forest in Florence's red dress, the tiara on his head.

Big Gun's skull open at the front, a white-and-red doorway through which a bullet had dug a dark, wet tunnel, a look of surprise on his face though by then each of them had been sure they were all going to die.

Stanlake moved his hips faster. The creaking of the cot was at least proof to the others that something was happening.

'Make some noise, please, Florence,' he said.

She nodded and started to make little gasps. More laughter came from beyond the blankets. His face burning with mortification, Stanlake began to make noises too, moans that paralleled hers, but deeper, huskier. He was fourteen, nearly fifteen, and he had never had sex, and if this was what sex was he knew he never would.

He bumped his hips against hers until his lower back began to burn. Bracing himself up over her in press-up position made his arms ache, and now they began to tremble, and cramp arced between his shoulderblades. He just wanted it to be over. Anger and frustration and loathing competed in his chest as his grunts and Florence's gasps built to what sounded like at least his climax, which was, after all, the only one that mattered. He shouted, loudly.

'Have you come?' Makinde called from beyond the blanket-wall.

'Yes, oga,' Stanlake called back. 'I am done.'

At once, like a magnet whose pole had been reversed, he slid backwards off Florence. 'No!' she gasped, and she reached for his hand, trying to prolong their time together, trying to strengthen their connection. But he only wanted to get away from her, and could not let her make herself his responsibility. She read this in him as he wriggled his hand away from hers, and something in her eyes went out.

He emerged from behind the blankets as Big Gun had done, slick with sweat and with, he knew though he did not see them, eyes as terrible, though his buttoning of his fly was only a mime. The air in the cabin was now heavy with cigar-smoke, sweet with dope-smoke. Makinde, his red-eyed monster-father, grinned. 'Now you are a man,' he said.

Stanlake remembered Pacific, masked in braided grass, in the grove in the forest, placing the charm over his son's bowed head. 'Now you are a man,' he too had said.

I did not need you to tell me this, Unit Commander, he thought.

The rain rose up with sudden intensity, rattling so heavily on the roof above their heads that it almost blotted out the music. Makinde toked, then heaved himself up from the cot. With a gesture almost of boredom he picked up his pistol from where it lay on the table and thumbed off the safety-catch. Then he tugged down the pinned-up blankets, exposing Florence. The red dress with the broken beading was still pushed up around her waist. She looked up at him

blankly. His eyes too were blank. Almost before she had time
to register her understanding of what he was about to do he
raised the pistol and, without any break in the movement,
shot her in the face. Drunk and stoned as the rest of them
were, the loud, flat sound still made them jump. A second
later, his chest heaving, his rifle at the ready, Blondie yanked
the cabin door open and looked in with a startled expression
on his face; but when he saw what had happened he went out
again.

Stanlake looked at the body, for that was what this
person who had once been a girl now was: just that. The
bullet had gone in below her right eye, where it had made a
small hole that looked more like a tattooed red disc than a
lethal wound; but blood spread out rapidly from the great
unseen wound in the back of her head, soaking into the
pillow, the blanket, the fabric of the cot. His cot, the one he
most often slept on. Her body had arched just a little at the
pistol's report, slumped back, and she was gone. The room
had an extra sour, metallic smell now. The rain hammered
down on the roof with even greater violence, and the sound
of water running down the grooves in the corrugated iron
and spattering onto the muddy ground below was like that of
many men pissing.

'Get rid of it,' Makinde said, indicating with a wave of his
hand that he meant that Diamondz and Big Gun should deal
with the body as he slid the pistol back into the holster at his
hip.

'Yes, oga,' they chorused, struggling stonedly to their feet
as he returned to the cot on which he had been lolling.
Stanlake stood watching as they tugged the blanket round
from under Florence's body and laid it over her, covering her
face but leaving her bare legs exposed. They took hold of the
corners of the cot and lifted it like a stretcher.

'Should we dig a hole, oga?' Big Gun asked.

'If you want to bother that is up to you,' Makinde said,
reaching for the whiskey-bottle on the table.

'It is too rainy,' Diamondz said. 'We can just throw her in
the ditch.'

Big Gun going backwards, they went out. The door
swung shut behind them. Makinde looked at Stanlake with

glazed eyes and snorted. What did he see? Stanlake felt not naked then but absent. As if he was a mirror, Makinde's mirror, and hidden behind that mirror was nothing. It was a sort of possession, this feeling. 'You did well, Little Gun,' Makinde said. Stanlake nodded.

A minute later Big Gun and Diamondz were back, soaked by the downpour and breathless, their glittering faces unexpectedly feral and excited. The tiara was wedged onto Diamondz' head, and Big Gun was carrying the now-sodden red bead dress.

The cot and the body were gone.

It was as if the girl had never existed.

'You put it downstream from where you drink?' Makinde said.

'Yes, oga,' Big Gun replied.

Stanlake stared at his flawlessly-painted face in the mirror. Of all the dead, why was it Florence he thought of most often? But the answer was simple: though he had failed to save her he had not harmed her, or had harmed her very little, and had tried to spare her pain. And the hand that took her life so casually had not been his.

Stanlake thought of his father then, but not on that last day: even now, three years later, to do so was unbearable. Instead he remembered another day, sitting with Pacific on the bench in front of their hut, drinking tea from enamel mugs. Nearby his mother was cooking, stirring stew in a pot suspended above glowing charcoal. At the other end of the compound the younger girls were washing clothes in plastic bowls, wringing them out and hanging them up to dry. Across the way Robert's father was showing him something under the bonnet of his truck and Robert was nodding. Painted in yellow and black on the rust-pocked side of the truck was the name of Robert's father's business, *Jesus Loves Bananas*. Nearer to, chickens pecked at the ground, their movements jerky as they foraged for seeds. In the compound obliquely opposite, Matthew's mother was sprinkling water from a basin so she could sweep without raising dust. Somewhere out of sight someone's pig let out a squeal and a grunt. The village generator chugged mutedly. Beyond the village bounds the land fell away gently, and Stanlake could see across the banana and palm-oil plantations the forest, the river glittering in the sunlight, and, further off, a sprawl of low lavender hills below a wide sky scudded with white clouds.

Pacific was watching Poppy as she cooked. Her movements were deft and economical. 'Women are a blessing, my son,' he said. One hand was resting on his belly, which had grown substantially in the last couple of years. 'They talk, but they work too. When men stop, women go on.'

'Talking?' Stanlake asked teasingly.

Pacific smiled. 'Working. Look at your mother,' he said. 'Now she is training as a midwife. She never stops. She is never idle.'

'Daddy?'

'Yes?'

'I was wondering if – ' Stanlake hesitated, searching for the right words, then went on, 'Some of my friends say the reason I have no brothers or sisters is because one time Mummy looked at the Masks when they came through the village.'

'It's true it's forbidden for girls and women,' Pacific said, 'and to peep can make a woman barren, but with your mother it was medical problems. Ovarian cysts.'

Stanlake nodded.

'I am very lucky with your mother,' Pacific said. 'I hope you will be as lucky in your marriage as I have been in mine.'

Ah, Daddy.

Stanlake stared at his reflection, lowered his glittering eyelids sensually. I am a man, he thought. Twice a man: once in good, once in evil. I kissed Big Gun in the cabin by the roadblock. And now I am here and I am this new person.

He thought of lacy underwear and silky camisoles and, imagining himself wearing them, became half-erect. He wanted them – no, more than that: he needed them – but how could he obtain such costly garments? And even if he did somehow manage to find the necessary money, how would he get up the nerve to buy them? The thought of asking for such things at one of the market stalls was unbearable, perhaps particularly because such stalls were almost always run by men; but then he couldn't imagine going into a proper shop either. There he would most likely be dealing with women, but that might be worse, because women were more perceptive than men, more likely to ask questions. To really laugh at him.

Also, a proper shop would certainly be more expensive.

He pictured himself in school uniform, wearing skimpy lace panties underneath, and the thought excited him. It would be my secret, he thought. My new self no-one else would even know existed. If they were as skimpy as I am imagining, he thought, then I would need to get a Brazilian.

Now he was fully erect.

He let the towel fall to the ground, moving further away from the mirror to take in his reflection from the top of his head to mid-thigh. His skin was smooth and dark, his slender body lean, narrow-hipped and sideways-on flat except for the muscled globes of his butt; and due to his eating so modestly his stomach-muscles were ridged. His dick jutted. I could give myself a Brazilian now, he thought. So I am ready for when I get some panties. I could even shave it all off. That was what some girls did, he knew from the magazines. Then they could wear even skimpier panties with full confidence.

With his erection wagging, he padded naked through to the kitchen and got the Wahl clippers from the drawer. Most of the time these were what he used to shave his head. Sometimes he needed the closeness of the razor, but, although he enjoyed the extremity of the smoothness, wary of ingrown hairs and the resultant bumps he avoided wet-shaving his head too often.

He decided to shave his armpits first, to get into it. There were only a few coils of hair there, and it was quickly done. The buzzing tickled him and made him wrinkle his nose. The flat underside of the clipper-head was cold against his skin and there was nothing particularly exciting about doing it beyond a slight sense of breaking some taboo.

Shaving his crotch was different: his chest heaved as he slowly worked the clippers down from the bump of his navel to the base of his now-rigid dick, sending coils of hair sliding softly to the floor, then speckles of stubble; and he thought he might come just from bending his pulsing, thrilling erection this way and that as he shaved the sides of it smooth. Holding the still-buzzing clippers he stood back and stared at himself in the mirror, turning and standing on tip-toe and arching his back to better evoke the stylisedly feminine. All the lines of his body were clean now, and as aerodynamic as the slick strokes of a fashion drawing. He returned the clippers to their drawer, swept up the fallen hair with the dustpan and brush and tipped it into the rubbish-bag.

Although the flat was well heated, the glow of the bath he had had earlier was passing from him, and he began to feel chilly. He reached for a red skinny-rib vest, lifting the neck-hole carefully over his fully made-up face, then pulled on a pair of plain white men's briefs from a multi-pack Poppy had bought at the market, and over them dull red track-pants. Finally he tied a red headscarf round his skull. He checked his reflection and felt a sudden longing for hoop earrings: though he hadn't yet had his ears pierced, they would give this compromised ensemble a lift, he thought: Seventies gypsy.

Suddenly, with a rush of excitement, he remembered the cleavage enhancer. He squeezed a glob of the glittering gel onto his fingertips and applied it between the flat plates of his pectorals, brushing it out along the curves of his clavicle. Once this was done he studied the results in the mirror with a critical, but not displeased eye.

The front door rattled: his mother letting herself in.

Chapter Six

Stanlake made no effort to conceal his appearance: just silently watched his mother in the mirror as she came in with a bag of shopping, breathing heavily from the long climb. Only after closing and locking the door behind her did she notice him sitting there in his bedroom with his back to her, and see reflected in the mirror his painted, glittering, watching eyes and glistening scarlet lips. She tensed visibly. Then, out of weariness, or resignation, or both, without a word she turned away from him and went into the kitchen. She had seen him wearing make-up and articles of feminine clothing before, and she both understood what he was attempting to do and did not. This was one of the many things she had wanted to talk to Lucy about, but had been too ashamed to. And too there was a complexity to it that was not easy to express, that could not be sorted out by prayer.

Stanlake listened to his mother banging things down on the work-surface: a tin, another tin, the clonk of a jar, the thud of a plastic bottle. After a moment he got up and went through to face her. Masked in make-up he felt no shame. He stood in the kitchen doorway and watched as she slammed a tin of Value tomatoes down next to a twin roll of toilet-paper and a sliced white loaf. Her face was shiny with sweat but he could feel the coldness of the air outside still radiating off her. Her face was set. There was a long tear in her dress, he noticed, and her coat had lost its lowest button. His face hardened: he could guess why.

Poppy balled up the empty carrier-bag and rammed it into a bag already strainingly full with similar carrier bags that hung from a cupboard doorhandle. Asserting its nature it at once began to expand, making furtive rustling noises as it did so.

'Take this through,' Poppy said, handing Stanlake the

pack of toilet rolls without looking at him. He took it from her but didn't go. 'Please.' Still he stood there watching her. She lifted a jar of honey to put away in the cupboard but seemed unable to decide which shelf it should go on. As she hesitated her hand began to tremble. Suddenly he thought she might cry. He took the honey from her and chose a shelf.

'It can go here.'

'Thank you,' she said in a small, husky voice. Why was this all so difficult, she wondered. Once she had been a strong woman who knew her mind, who made even tough decisions swiftly, who bore hardship readily. She should be able to put things behind her, get on with it, move on. But where had she moved to to move on from? Where was she?

Alone.

'They tore your dress,' Stanlake said.

She looked down and didn't answer. She was afraid of what acknowledging the attack might trigger in her son, this son who was, it seemed to her, beyond fear, who moved in this new, uncertain world with a certainty that could terrify her, who had come out of the forest with a tiara on his head, a head filled with death, and had led her away from the war. Who was extraordinary, and she didn't forget it, and that was not a mother's pride: when you had done what she knew he had done, and what else besides she did not want to know, of course you could no longer be ordinary. Better this, she thought, than what else was waiting to claim him: the skull-faced warrior with holes for eyes and a pit for a heart.

Better make-up than war-paint, oh, Jesus. Better pillowy crimson peace than scarlet war, praise the Lord.

She let Stanlake take her hands in his and turn her to him, though still she kept her eyes downcast. Gently he unbuttoned her coat and pushed it from her shoulders. Its weight sent it sliding down her arms, but he caught it before it could reach the floor, took it and hung it on a hook.

'Lift your arms,' he said, and she did so, and as he raised her torn dress above her head, leaving her in only her slip, she looked up at him for what felt like the first time in a long time. He looked beautiful, and she wished she could forgive him. Though he was only an inch or so taller than her, and skinny like a boy, she felt strangely like a little girl before a man.

'I will cook,' she said.

He nodded. 'I will study. Later I will mend this.'

He took her dress and returned to his room. Poppy went to her room, changed into a jumper and a denim skirt and went back to the kitchen. And there they were, doing the same things that everyone does everywhere, though here they often felt strange.

Stanlake had his final exams tomorrow – Geography and English – and it was also the last day before the half-term break. He alternated between reminding himself of the various parts of a glacier – snout, terminal moraine, zone of accumulation, zone of ablation – and re-reading the Pass Notes booklet on *Doctor Jeckyll and Mister Hyde* by Robert Louis Stevenson. It had taken him a while to see past the olden-times setting of the book and its difficult language, but then he had realised that its themes spoke to him as they seemed to speak to none of the other students, who apparently found it nothing but a chore. The revelation that Doctor Jeckyll was Mister Hyde had surprised him very much, and had put many thoughts into his head.

Still he found it hard to concentrate.

Mummy's dress.

The jackals, getting worse.

Teeth that rot do not repair themselves.

Something must be done.

Needing a break he put his studies aside, took up needle and thread, and with minute, fastidious stitches repaired the rip in his mother's dress. It took time and attention, but the result, when he held it up to the light, was a near-invisible mend. That done, he fetched her coat from its hook and sewed on a button he had found in the street a few days ago and for some reason kept, to replace the one that was gone. The replacement was grey and smaller than the others, but it was unobtrusive. He bent forward and bit through the thread.

The sounds and smells of cooking came floating through from the kitchen, and his stomach grumbled. To him this, familiar food and warmth and a locked door against the outside world – all of them things the asylum centre had not offered – had become, almost against its will, home.

In part this was because his heart was less tied than Poppy's to the village life they had had before the war, even though until the soldiers came it had been his whole world. Perhaps it was the adaptability of youth; or perhaps he had known from the very beginning that within his nature was something that would always have taken him away from that life. And after the harshness of the forest and the endlessness of the roadblock he had become used to accepting what was good in whatever was on offer: home was wherever you were, and that was that. You could only go forward, never back.

Sounds of a row breaking out in the flat below came up through the floor, and from elsewhere in the block different types of music competed with each other, beats against beats, dissonant, contradictory.

For both Stanlake and his mother it was disquieting to live so crowded in with strangers with whom you had nothing in common but an accident of address, and it created many small social difficulties. When the lift was working, for instance, it was always awkward because Stanlake never knew how to greet the other passengers, or even whether to greet them. Back home you greeted everyone as a matter of course. In the U.K. friendliness was often looked on as a ploy to take advantage, as the prelude to an imposition, or as a sign of outright craziness. And should you even greet the women in burqas? If he smiled at them they often looked away, as if his smile offended Allah, or perhaps their husbands or brothers or uncles. Maybe they would have smiled back if Stanlake was a woman, he didn't know. Perhaps they lacked English, and themselves feared social embarrassment and giving offence if they tried to make conversation. Sometimes there would be drug addicts or alcoholic near-derelicts in the lift who would ask for money with varying degrees of menace, and that too encouraged residents to keep their faces and their hearts closed.

At first Poppy used to greet other people waiting at the bus-stop just as she would have done back home. Stanlake had been with her in those innocent days, and had seen how the other people in the queue looked at her as if she was mad, or a beggar, or both. Soon she drew a curtain on that small window of human contact.

In the U.K., Stanlake thought, people seemed to find it difficult to be people.

The sound of a television suddenly turned up loud came from somewhere overhead: a stream of hectoring chat punctuated by hysterical laughter that was cut off with mechanical abruptness, then more chat. Stanlake knew Poppy was trying to put aside a little money each week to save up for a set. A friend of hers at church was supposedly asking about to see if one was going spare.

No luck so far.

Stanlake didn't much care about not having a television except that it was part of the glass wall between him and the other students at school, all of whom, however allegedly poor, had mobile phones, MP3 players and, he didn't doubt because they often said so, HD TVs, X-boxes and Sky at home; and if not all or even any of those, at least a washing-machine and more than one pair of trainers.

Over their evening meal, after Poppy had said grace and Stanlake had bowed his head and thought of the gods of the forest and the ancestors, they talked a little, their words as everyday as they could make them, and Poppy asked her son what plans he had for the holiday period.

'Read and study,' he said. 'I do not think there is any job I can get for just one week.'

Poppy nodded. It was true that in this administratively-complicated country it could be hard to work. Of course Lucy would have reminded her that there was always work to do at the church: Reverend Obasanjo was forever calling for help with various worthwhile projects in the community. But he wanted volunteers who didn't expect to get paid, and as she had no desire to make her son do work for its own sake, Poppy didn't mention volunteering directly. Instead she said, 'Perhaps next time I go to church you could come with me.'

Without the slightest pause for thought Stanlake replied, 'Daddy did not believe in the church, or the mosque, and neither do I. So no.'

Getting up, he took his empty plate to the sink and washed it. She looked at the outline of his shoulders, the lines of his neck. Like his father, and not. Like her, and not.

There was a tremor in his hand as he put the clean plate in the rack.

'Are you finished?' he asked, without looking round.

'Yes.'

He glanced back and took the plate she was offering him and washed that up too. Poppy rose from her chair with an effort – her back was aching and her calves were painfully tight now – and stood alongside him at the counter, filling two Tupperwares with leftovers for their lunches tomorrow. He put on the kettle and made them both tea. Then he went back to his room to study some more. As always he left his door open. She did the same. It was as if they feared to put any unnecessary barrier between them; as if each feared that, unseen, the other might disappear.

Poppy sat at the small kitchen table and, clasping her hands round the mug of tea, tried to relax. The flat had no living-room; or rather what should have been the living-room was being used as the second bedroom: under the new housing benefit regulations this was the only way they could afford the rent. She tried to be grateful.

Around eleven Stanlake went to bed. Only after his light had clicked out could Poppy go to her room. She was exhausted but knew that sleep wouldn't come easily. She hadn't slept well since she came to this country. The stars in the sky were different here, the sun and moon further away, and on some deep level she found that disquieting. Carefully she lowered herself to the floor and, supporting her elbows on the chair she kept by the mattress that served as her bed, on her knees she prayed.

I do not ask for much, Lord Jesus. I just pray that things don't get any worse. I pray for the strength to carry on. I pray for what I lack in my heart. Help me to want to forgive my son. And even though he does not believe in You please protect him from himself. Please do not let the past return. Thank you, Jesus.

Struggling to her feet, she took a photograph from a drawer in the dresser. It was behind glass in a tin frame she had found for three pounds in the market. The style of the frame was Art Nouveau, though she couldn't have named it: just, she had liked the elegant iris design the metal had been struck on. She had planned to display it on the shelf in the kitchen, or perhaps hang it on the wall, but once the picture was in there she found she couldn't bear to. Forcing the hasps round at the back of it she had cracked the glass. Another failure.

It was a family photograph, and the only personal thing she had managed to keep with her except for her wedding-ring. It showed her, Pacific and Stanlake standing smiling in front of their home, dressed in their smartest and most colourful clothes. The crack in the glass ran across Pacific's face. His cousin Solomon had taken it, making a great fuss about achieving a good composition and finding an angle where the sun was behind him but not dazzling them so they didn't have to squint unattractively. They had been on their way to a wedding. Helen, Solomon's niece by marriage, was marrying Chinua, her childhood sweetheart. Chinua had a bicycle-repair business, and would pedal between the villages with his tools in his basket and all manner of spare parts slung in a duffle-bag across his shoulders, keeping everyone's bikes working. So everyone knew Chinua. He worked hard and was well-liked, as was Helen, and it had looked set to be a lively and joyous day.

And it had been. Pacific had hired a taxi to ferry them and they had arrived in style. The wedding was lavish, the young couple clearly very much in love; and afterwards, once the vows had been exchanged and the books signed, the newly-weds and their guests had eaten and drunk and danced until the night was past and dawn was brightening the edges of the sky.

Poppy smiled sadly. My husband, what would you think of the fix we are in now? What would you think of your son and his antics? I do not think his wedding will be coming soon.

Though she had known him so well, better, she believed, than anyone else, Poppy did not know how Pacific would have answered her. Did Stanlake, who believed himself in constant communion with the ancestral spirits, know?

With a sigh she returned the photograph to its drawer and covered it with a folded teeshirt. It was impossible to believe the image was only three years old, such were the changes that had taken place since it was taken, so many were the deaths. Why had she kept it instead of her wedding photograph?

She knew the answer.

Because her son was in it.

She went through to the bathroom to wash her face. On the way back to her bedroom she looked in on him. Cleansed of make-up his sleeping face looked startlingly young, and as innocent, almost, as it did in the photograph. The thin duvet she had got him using the last of the social service vouchers was hunched to his shoulder.

Her dress was draped over the hardback chair that faced his desk and mirror, as if waiting for her to collect it. She crossed the threshold by just a single step, took it, and returned to her room. Examining it in the lamplight she couldn't find where the tear had been. The flawlessness of the mend seemed symbolic of something, and though she could not express the thought clearly to herself she was oddly moved by this small restorative act, and it helped her to put the unpleasantness of the day behind her.

After carefully wrapping her braided hair in the head-scarf she slept in, she slipped under her own equally thin duvet and switched off the light. Please Lord, she thought as she turned onto her side and closed her eyes, just let me sleep. But the unlined curtains were backlit by the reflected glow and latent dazzle of the city. Here it was never properly dark.

Stanlake woke abruptly in the small hours. Staring up at the ceiling, he realised he had decided what he was going to do. Both exams were in the afternoon. That would give him time. The jackals usually set up shop around eleven. That too would give him time. What he needed to do wouldn't take long, however it turned out. He closed his eyes, tried to make himself sleep. I will need my wits, my strength, my focus. From below came a further burst of an argument that seemed to have bubbled on for hours, more clearly audible now there was no background noise to muffle it. His bed-room seemed to be above their living-room, and his mattress was on a bare, lino-tiled floor.

'Ye fuckin' asshole,' the woman was shouting drunkenly. 'If youse was any kind of a man ye'd fuckin' stop talkin' an' do something about it!'

'Fuckin' do *you*!' the man bellowed in return. 'Ye dried-up fuckin' cunt! Ye fuckin' slag!'

There was the crash of some piece of furniture being turned over and glass smashing. A dog started barking. Someone from another flat yelled, 'Fucking shut up!'

'Fuck you!' the woman shouted in response. 'Mind yer own fucking business!'

'It's everyone's business at three a.m., love!'

'Don't you call me love, you fuckin' pervert!'

'I'm calling the police!'

'Fuck you!'

Doors slammed, things were muttered, then silence fell. Stanlake could feel the tension bleeding up through the floor. He considered masturbating but there were no images in his mind. He recited geographical terms in his head to try and dull his churning thoughts. Crevasses, basal slip, plastic flow. Fjörds. Hanging valleys. Endless cold in impersonal faraway places. Types of snow. Types of cloud. Nimbus, cumulonimbus, stratus, cirrostratus, cumulostratus.

Sleep drifted over him.

He woke with a start, confused, thinking he was late. Glancing at the clock, however, he saw it was just a few minutes before the usual time he got up: 4.55 a.m. Beyond the curtains it was still night. Without giving himself a chance to think about how tired and unrefreshed he was he rolled out of bed, pulled on his track-pants and vest, and went through to the kitchen to prepare tea and toast for his mother's breakfast. Once the kettle was on and the bread under the grill he went to the bathroom and washed his face and brushed his teeth. The sound of the toilet flushing woke Poppy just before her alarm was due to go off, and they passed each other in the hall as he returned to the kitchen to turn the toast and she went to wash.

Sitting opposite each other at the little table they ate without speaking. She had toast and strawberry jam, he had cereal, and they both drank tea. At ten past five Poppy put her things in the sink and got ready to leave the flat.

'Aren't you going to wish me good luck?' Stanlake said, as she reached the front door.

There was something in his voice that made her look at him but his expression was, at that moment, unreadable to her. 'Good luck,' she said. 'I will see you tonight, enh?' He nodded. She left the flat.

Stanlake went back to his cereal. He ate slowly. There were hours to go before he needed to do anything: it was almost still the night before. He would do this thing, this one last thing, and then he would be done with it. He would bury who he had been and move on. For himself he could have put up with worse, but the way they had treated his mother: no, that could not be left. He knew too well that those who push will push until they get pushed back.

He washed up the plates and mugs and sat quietly at the table, thinking. The building was still. Somewhere water trickled inside pipes. Appliances hummed. A muted clang and whir told him the lift was working again though he didn't think anyone had come to repair it. Perhaps it was Ogun, speeding him on his way.

Yes, he would wear red.

He took two candles from a drawer, placed them on the shelf above the fridge and lit them from the box of matches by the cooker. Threads of black smoke twisted up from the soft orange flames towards the ceiling and the broken fire-alarm.

'Big Gun, Diamondz, Blondie, help me,' he said. 'Patrick, Matthew, Robert, help me. My Masks, my Beasts, my brothers, guide me to do this thing right as it needs to be done, and for my mother's sake keep me from harm while I do it. Strengthen my arm to do what I must. I know I owe you sacrifices, and I know you will send me a way of making the sacrifice I owe.'

Something shifted, in him, in the surrounding air, and he felt the reassurance you feel when you know a loved one, though out of sight, is in another room. With two pats of his palm he extinguished the candles, put them back in the drawer, and returned to his bedroom to prepare.

First he put on his school uniform. Then he laid out the make-up as he had the day before. He would make himself

beautiful – yes, always that – but today it would be a dangerous beauty, it would be war-paint: a mask for Ogun. And he
would have no shame.

As if insomnia was epidemic, or due to some prefiguration
that something significant was coming, Evill too had been
unable to sleep. Eventually, defeated, he got up and stumped
downstairs. Music pumping through his Beats he slumped on
the couch in his bleak lounge and stared blankly at the
gently-hissing gas fire. Above it on the mantelpiece a dull
silver container sat among curling cards. The container was
about a foot tall, sealed at the top, and stood on a dark-wood
plinth. On the plinth, inlaid in gilt, was an inscription,
Annette Evans – Mum, above some dates. She had had
thirty-three years on this planet. The cards were cards of
condolence, with conventional words inside them that had
meant nothing to him then and meant nothing to him now.

He sparked up.

One bad day he had unstoppered the urn and looked
inside. There had been knobs of bone in there among her
ashes; brute reminders that cremation wasn't some sort of
alchemical process, it was just burning something – someone
– up.

Evill alternated drags on his cigarette with pulls on his
inhaler. One day, when he could afford it, he would get those
ashes made into a diamond, and he would have the diamond
set into his front right tooth.

When he could afford it. Which wasn't just a matter of
money. When he could let go of his anger at her for what she
had done to him; for what – which was almost the same
thing – she had done to herself, and let her be something
beautiful.

His gaze drifted round the room. Everything was dulled
by a layer of dust. The pot-plant next to the sofa was dead, its
spindly leaves clutching, its parched soil an ashtray. Dead
from neglect. Was he dead? He breathed, still. But you could
breathe and be dead: you could be on a ventilator. And
anyway he could barely breathe, his lungs as constricted as
his life. He sucked on his inhaler again, felt the chemical mist
force his stunted alveoli open as Duke Blade spat lyrics into

his head:

> *Pussyole gangstas you must murk dem*
> *Boom ting bitches you should work dem*
> *Crying tongues ya haffi hurt dem*
> *Cheating hos you must desert dem*
> *Haters and traitors dem na understand*
> *Them soon feel the sting a the backa my hand*
> *Cos a man is a man is a man is a man...*

Time passed. He zoned in and out. Beyond the blinds the sky lightened. The phrase 'ten life sentences' came into his mind from somewhere. A prison sentence. Life, over and over, never free. Jailed even in death. Chained bones. What time was it?

He struggled up from the couch and went through to the kitchen. A couple of lines were left over on the counter from the night before. He snorted them. Synthetic energy coursed through him. Now he only felt dead in his soul, and his life didn't require him to have a soul. In fact it was better not to.

Cos a man is a man is a man is a man.

He climbed the stairs to go and get himself ready to face another day. On the landing he realised the door to his mother's room was closed. This wasn't due to any ghostly activity, it was just the way the house sometimes channelled the wind when you opened the front door, but for some reason this morning it bothered him. He set it open again, though he didn't so much as glance in. He didn't need to see the velvet painting on the wall of a black Jesus, mournful, effeminate and futile. Or the unused packets of gauzes, sterile bandages, latex gloves and disposable incontinence pants, the boxes of antibiotics past their use-by date, the blue plastic container for sharps that would still be contaminated by his mother's long-since rusted blood.

To start with social services had provided a carer, but Evill had been so rude and aggressive towards her that after a week of his abuse she had refused to come back, and they had refused to send a replacement. Convulsed with self-loathing and disgust, he had had to care for Annette himself. Was that what he had intended? If so, why? As punishment for her? For himself? For them both? He hadn't done it well: every day had felt like a dirty defeat; and having to deal with his mother's rapidly-deteriorating physicality had only made him hate her more.

He had never talked to anyone about about those last six months. Not Solid, or Cuts, or even Pit-Bull, with whom he shared the most. They didn't know he had moved back in with her; didn't know anything beyond that he wasn't around much. They had assumed he was kicking it with some boom ting and he hadn't contradicted them. Up till then he had always given them the impression that Annette was dead. And now she was. And every day he sold what killed her.

Awoy, woe is me, shame and scandal in the family.

While he was upstairs the landline began to ring. He never answered it: it was Annette's, and no-one he wanted to speak to would call him on it. None of his bloods knew the number, and who else was there? The council. The hospital.

The old-fashioned ansaphone clicked on. 'Hello, Everill,' a Jamaican-accented woman's voice said. 'It's your auntie Esther calling to see how you're doing.' She sounded uneasy. 'It's strange to hear – to still hear your mother's voice as the message. I would have thought you would have changed it by now.' He could hear her breathing. 'It's been ages since we saw you. Everyone asks after you. Nana, the kids. How are you doing at college? You know your mother would have wanted you to do well at your studies.'

Evill snorted softly and his expression hardened.

'Well, I know the anniversary is coming up so I just thought I would call even though you never call us. We're all praying for you. Well, goodbye, then.'

The ansaphone shut off with a clunk. Evill levered up the floorboard in his bedroom, reached into one of the bags between the joists and peeled off five twenty-pound notes. His hand went for the hunting knife, then passed on to the Glock and closed round it. Today he wanted the weight of a gun in his hand. It was power and slow-motion suicide in one.

Cos a man is a man is a man is a man.

He posed in front of the wardrobe mirror practising different types of quick draws from the back of his track-pants: the classic Clint Eastwood Western-style straight draw; the James Bond draw, turning fast with a hand up; the gangsta draw, crook-armed against recoil, almost discreet, the gun held flat on its side and aimed in a downward slant: all the time staring into his own eyes in an autoerotic Mexican stand-off. Once he had the moves down slick enough to satisfy his sense of being a hard man he wedged the Glock into the waistband of his track-pants at the back, flicked the top over it, pulled up his hood, went downstairs and left the house.

On his way out he pressed 'erase' on the ansaphone.

It was colder today, but brighter. Winter was coming to an end, and as Evill rolled down the street he could sense the vegetable energy latent in the bare branches of the trees, aching to burst forth in shoots and buds; and the skewed angle of the sun signalled to him subliminally that the change of seasons was on its way. A city boy born and bred, these things were obscure to him, but still he felt them.

The cold made the gold in his teeth ache, reminding him he was alive. A police-car cruised past him at a crawl, the pigs inside hoping, he knew without a glance in their direction, that he would crack and run, which would give them the excuse to pursue him, violently subdue him, forcibly search him and arrest him. Though the gun felt both suddenly heavy and grotesquely, juttingly obvious wedged down the back of his track-pants he didn't break his swagger, and a few seconds later the driver of the cop-car, disappointed at his non-responsiveness, made a fast u-turn and accelerated away. Movie style gun-battles with the feds ran through his head, played out on streets that, while looking like they did, were also somehow American.

Today he was the first to reach the Rock.

He felt a surge of annoyance. He never carried the product himself, never even touched it, except what he took for his own personal supply: he had the others run that risk. That was what rank meant. But it also meant that if any customers pitched before the rest of the Crew showed up he would be left stood there like a twat with nothing to sell. He could leave and come back but there was nowhere to go. Well, there was the parade of shitty shops, but he hadn't needed anything when he passed them earlier, and the idea of trailing back through the underpass and up the other side to buy some unneeded something purely to waste time irritated him out of all proportion to the problem.

A white man in grey office-type trousers and a parka came hurrying out of East Tunnel. Evill, keeping his hood up, turned away from the man so his face, even his race, would not be seen. That was partly why he wore gloves: to cover all skin. A moment later the man was gone.

Once there had been benches to sit on in the central area: an effort had been made to turn the underpass into a civic space, to encourage contemplation of the sculpture the council had purchased, perhaps even commissioned out of some improvement fund back in the day. The benches had long since been removed, however, in an effort to discourage loitering, and all that remained of that piece of social planning were several sets of metal slots in the tarmac to which the legs of the benches had once been tethered. Into each slot was set an iron hoop. They were the sort of things chains got attached to, latently sinister.

Evill hawked and spat. Despite the gloves his fingertips were burning with the cold. He realised he couldn't stand this much more. In summer it was better. It almost felt good then, lying back on the warm Rock in the sun, kicking it while the slaves went to their offices and warehouses and call-centres. Evill could tell from their looks they at least half-envied him and his Crew their lawless idleness.

But now the Rock was cold and damp with dew. The whizz he had snorted earlier had worn off and he felt flat. A fresh wave of annoyance swept over him as Stats came skulking out of one of the tunnels.

'Aright, E,' Stats said huskily, hands thrust as usual deep into the pockets of his thin, dirty hoodie, a lop-sided, gap-toothed smile on his ashy-brown, narrow face.

'You oughtta get that sorted,' Evill said.

'What?'

'The tooth business. Makes you look like a regular junkie.'

Stats shrugged nervily. 'One day,' he said. 'You got a ciggie?'

'What am I, a vending-machine?'

Stats shrugged again, jigging from one foot to the other.

The movement made Evill see Annette. All junkies are the same, he thought. One pathetic stitched-together mugged-up animal with a needle-hole for a mouth. Still he found himself making conversation, to keep Stats on the line till the food arrived. 'Oily getting his beauty sleep, then?'

Stats coughed a laugh, looked down at the ground then up again. 'Where your boys, then?' he asked.

'On their way.'

'Soon come, is it?'

'Yeah.'

Even in the cold, still outside air Evill could smell Stats, a creeping sweetness that made his stomach turn over. He could tell Stats to fuck off and go and wash, play that game: refuse to sell until he went and had a bath. It was tempting but too much effort. Stats would just stand there hoping he didn't mean it until Evill was forced to drive him away with a kick or a slap.

'Sup, souljah?'

Evill turned to see Pit-Bull rolling up. 'You're late, bruv,' he said, 'and we got a customer.'

'Is it?' Pit-Bull said indifferently. 'Whey di others-dem?'

'They're later,' Evill said flatly. The cold air was making his chest tighten. He took a suck on his inhaler. 'You got the business, then?'

'Enough,' said Pit-Bull.

'Go stow it then.'

'Aiight.'

'Just give me – What you got?' he asked Stats. Stats held up a dirty, drooping twenty-pound note. 'Two,' Evill said, taking the note, and Pit-Bull palmed two wraps to Stats.

With a bob of the head Stats pocketed the drugs, turned and hurried off. Pit-Bull ambled off down North Tunnel to hide the rest of the stash. Evill looked about him. For better or worse there were no other customers.

Finally Cuts and Solid pitched.

'Where you been, then?' Evill asked annoyedly.

'Magistrate's court,' Cuts said.

'For what, though?'

'He told you yesterday,' Solid said.

'Affray,' Evill said, remembering. 'So what dem give you?'

'A fine and bound over for six months to keep the peace.'

'I hope you told 'em good luck with that.'

'As well you didn't have no blade though,' Solid said. 'Time mandatory with a blade, now.'

'True-dat,' Pit-Bull said.

'How much is the fine?' Evill said.

'Two-fifty an' a month to pay.'

'Best hope we get some customers, then.'

'It can go with the CCJs though,' Cuts said with a shrug.

'Still, though,' Solid said, 'jail-time ain't a laugh, though.'

'Brer scared of doing a lickle stretch, then?'

'I ain't *scared*, blood,' Solid said irritably. ''Llow dat. It ain't good, that's all I'm saying. The only kinda pussy in jail is punk pussy, an' I ain't check for that.'

'You got your fist, though,' Pit-Bull said. 'I can get by on a couple month wrist-action easy.'

'Cos you're sick, bruv,' said Cuts.

'Just practical, bruv. When I ain't got time to chase the gash, you know?'

'Gash is work,' Cuts agreed. Solid nodded.

'You getting the skirt, bruv?' Pit-Bull asked Evill.

'Getting all the gash I need,' Evill said. 'But right now it's all about the dollars, though.'

The others fell silent as he turned away from them and clambered up onto the Rock. A little grudgingly they followed him, taking their usual positions on its lower parts.

For a while no-one passed. Then a mother appeared, a fat white woman shepherding a little girl on a pink tricycle. The moment she noticed the Crew she tried to hurry the little girl along. Oblivious to her mother's urgings the girl trailed her feet on the ground, making progress more difficult, and the woman's face flushed as she took hold of the handlebars and dragged the tricycle forward.

From under the shadows of their hoods Evill and the others watched the woman's reddening face and hated her for judging them. As the presence of a tiny amount of blood in the water is enough to trigger a shark to attack, so just the expression on her averted face was enough to trigger them. Fortunately for her, however, at that moment a shifty-looking, studenty white boy appeared, blatantly looking to buy, and they turned to business.

The boy bought, and left. Then came more waiting around. Their mood sank. The sun above was bright but gave little warmth, and the angle of it left most of the central space in shadow anyway. Their butts cold and damp, they perched on the Rock in grim silence.

Then the African battyboy appeared.

Finally, something.

It was an ecstatic relief.

He was wearing his usual school uniform, but today he had not only a red headscarf knotted round his skull but also actual, obvious make-up on. White crosses were on his cheeks and forehead; green eyeshadow glittered on his eyelids, and his full lips glistened crimson. The sight of this unexpected carnival queerness charged the four youths of the Crew with one massive, liberating surge of adrenalin. Whatever they did next, he had asked for it: it was on him.

As one they dropped down from the Rock. The African boy kept on, heading in a straight line towards the tunnel opposite, not looking at them but oh, so aware of them, not coming towards them, pretending, in fact, that he was trying to keep away from them, but confronting them nonetheless with his painted face, with the swish in his hips.

'Da fuck?' said Solid as he and the others began to circle the youth, not stopping him at first but with each orbit drawing closer, moving clockwise and counter-clockwise, at all times keeping their eyes locked on him.

'I didn't used to reckon they had battyboys in Africa,' Evill said, and his heart thudded in his chest as he stated that thought.

'Then we did see this one,' Cuts said, and it was as if he was Evill and Evill was him.

Now they were close enough around him that the African youth was forced to halt. His face was impassive. Evill wondered what masochism made someone do what this boy was doing. Perhaps his queerness made him need punishment. 'Maybe it ain't no man whatsoever,' he said, staring into the youth's face. 'Maybe it's a bitch for real.'

'Let's see, then,' said Pit-Bull, and he made a grab for the African boy's crotch. With a sharp movement, the first definite action he had ever taken in the Crew's presence, the youth batted Pit-Bull's roughly-groping hand away. His expression still did not change.

'Bitch feisty, man!' Solid laughed.

'Bitch got balls, then?' Pit-Bull asked the unmoving carnival mask-face.

Evill and Solid took hold of the youth's shoulders, wrenching them back as Cuts drew a large kitchen knife from the back of his track-pants, a single dully-glinting piece of razor-sharp steel. 'Bitch don't need balls, though!' he said excitedly, holding the knife up in front of the young African's painted face, his own flushing in anticipation.

'Oh, man,' Solid said teasingly, and his tongue flicked over his lips. 'You wouldn't, though.'

It was a dare, not a deterrent. Pit-Bull went down on one knee before the blank-faced boy and reached for the waist of his trousers to rip them down at the front. 'Bitch don't need no balls,' he repeated breathlessly.

Up to that point it had all gone as it should have gone, as they had known it would go: them the predators, him – it – the prey, smaller, weaker, paralysed, helpless. Stupid. The only point of uncertainty had been how far they would go. Even now it was open. Would this be the time they went all the way?

And then the youth's knee came up fast as a piston and caught Pit-Bull under the chin, driving his teeth into his protruding tongue above and below, and iron blood flooded Pit-Bull's mouth as he stumbled backwards onto his arse with a strangled yell of pain and surprise.

Without hesitation Cuts raised the knife, intending to bring it down in a stabbing arc aimed directly at the African youth's chest. But the youth, wrenching his shoulders free from Evill and Solid's grip, moved not backwards in a desperate attempt to avoid the blow but forwards, stepping into Cuts, economically and effectively blocking the plunge of the blade by bracing his forearm against Cuts' wrist. Snake-fast he turned Cuts' momentum against him, twisted Cuts round, caught his hand and folded his wrist over. There was a gristly sound like a chicken-leg being snapped, and with a shout Cuts dropped the knife and the youth forced him down onto the ground, wrenching Cuts' wrecked wrist up behind him as he did so.

Once Cuts was down the youth kicked him just a single time in the side of his head. He was only wearing trainers but the kick was well-aimed and left Cuts half-stunned. Then the African bwoy turned to the still-sitting, bloody-mouthed Pit-Bull and kicked him in the side of his neck, the toe of his trainer crushing a nerve-bundle there and knocking Pit-Bull sideways, leaving him spasming on the ground, choking and gasping like a goldfish on the carpet.

As the African bwoy turned away from Pit-Bull Solid tried to rush him. Again the youth stepped into his opponent, this time ramming two stiff fingers up the heavier boy's nose. There was a crackle of gristle as he forced Solid's head back, pushing on into him until the pain of having his nose broken forced Solid to rear up and back. He tipped over backwards, banging his head sharply on an angular knob of the Rock as he fell.

The youth now snapped to Evill. His glitter-framed eyes were fire and ice, and his fey movements had the economy of a hunter's. His eyes never leaving Evill's, he stooped and picked up Cuts' knife, and that simple action was made with the deftness of one who has used such a weapon many times before. Evill moved back, the youth's advance compelling him towards the act he knew had been coming, an act now made easy for him because we all know it is acceptable to kill in self-defence. He pulled the Glock from the back of his track-pants. The African bwoy was on him, raising Cuts' knife. There was no doubt that it was in his mind to kill, and there was no doubt that he would feel no way about it afterwards: that he was not, and never had been, what Evill and the others had taken him to be. Evill pushed the Glock up under the youth's jaw and, without hesitation, pulled the trigger.

Chapter Seven

Stanlake had no time to react as the cold polycarbide muzzle of the Glock pushed up bruisingly hard against the gland in his neck just below his jawbone; no time to think that in the end it had all gone wrong. He heard the click of the trigger being pulled, felt the muzzle twitch against his abruptly-electrified, prickling skin.

Then nothing.

The gun had misfired.

Stanlake gripped the jackal's gloved wrist and forced the weapon aside, pushing him up against the inclined plane of the sculpture as he did so, leaning his full weight on the jackal's now-outstretched arm, forcing it back against the elbow-joint until with a grunt the youth had to drop the Glock. It hit the ground with a clatter. Stanlake was on top of him now, he was the priest, the witch-doctor, and the sculpture was his altar. Was this the sacrifice the gods were asking for? The thug's body stiffened against his. Stanlake raised the knife and stared into the thug's face and saw fear there and inside he laughed: this one who was not afraid to kill was afraid to die.

And he himself, he who was not afraid to kill either, what did he want?

Something about this youth, something in the cast of his features, reminded him a little of Big Gun.

'Makinde says it is good to kill,' Big Gun had said to him once.

But Makinde was wrong.

Keeping the knife raised, Stanlake slid backwards off Evill. His eyes on Evill's, he bobbed down and picked up the discarded Glock. The rest of the jackals lay crippled and moaning on the ground. He palmed the knife and slid it into the waistband of his trousers at the back, flicking his school jacket over it so as to hide it from sight. Then, without taking his gaze from Evill, and surely watched by the others, he stripped down the defective Glock. Big Gun's trick in the bag, not in the bag now. Out of the bag. The cat out of the bag for these fuckers, to show these fuckers what he could do. Big Gun had taught him. It only took practice.

The fault was just below the trigger mechanism: he could feel that the stop-lever had slipped down slightly within the housing because the pin had worked loose on one side. This gun had been owned by someone who didn't know how to take care of it. Not like a soldier would. Like a bride. Like your cock. With dextrous fingers Stanlake rotated the pin until it clicked into its proper place.

These movements that have saved your life many, many times you do not forget, and they sleep in you but barely.

The damaged jackals looked up at him as he slotted the Glock's slide back into place, pulled it back experimentally, released it, and rammed the magazine up into the hand-grip. There was a smooth click, a penetrating sound in the attentive stillness. Stanlake slid the magazine's floor-plate back on and snapped the slide back, lifting a round into the breech. It rose smoothly into place. He held the gun up in front of his war-painted face.

'Did you see?' he said.

They didn't respond. But they had seen. He hoped the lesson would be enough.

As Stanlake backed away from them into the darkness of the tunnel that led back to his block the youth on the sculpture, the youth in black he had taken the gun from, sat up slowly, rising like the dead, and watched him with strange eyes until the dip in the tunnel cut him off from sight. Stanlake turned and, wedging the gun into a jacket pocket, hurried back to his block.

As he waited for the lift the adrenalin began to pass from him, and by the time he had reached his floor shudders were running the length of his body. All he could think was: thank God no-one came while all that was going on. The lift made no stops during its ascent, and that was a mercy. He glanced at his watch. It was 12.15. He just had time to leave the gun and the knife and get to school for his exams.

After hiding the weapons under his mattress Stanlake

turned to study his face in the mirror. He had planned, to the extent he had planned anything beyond confronting the jackals, to remove the make-up and go on to school after-wards. But something had changed today and he needed to mark it, and he needed to show himself and the world that he was moving beyond it. He removed his headscarf. Then with cottonwool and cleanser he wiped the white crosses from his cheeks and forehead, carefully leaving the eye make-up and lipstick intact. Though he was long past being sent into shock by combat everything felt like it was happening in slow motion. Past and present intercut in his mind in jump-cuts, in flashes.

Gunfire exploding all around him in the night.

The knife he had shoved into somebody's stomach: it had been easy.

He checked his watch again: he would have to hurry to be in time for the first exam. He got up to go. Though he hadn't worn his coat earlier, out of fear it would constrict his movements, he pulled it on now. It was a too-large grey duffle coat that was offensively shapeless but warm. He slung his lunc into a carrier-bag and exited the flat, flipping up the hood of the duffle coat as he left his block.

At the entrance to the underpass he hesitated, but only for a moment. They know I have the knife and the gun, he thought. They do not know I am not carrying these things with me. And they know what I can do, and they do not know what else I can do.

Still, he was relieved to find the central area deserted. He crossed it quickly and hurried down the tunnel opposite. Which exam came first? Geography. He tried to claw his thoughts round to glaciers and cloud-formations but the fight kept forcing its way back into his mind, and beneath it reverberations of other fights, other situations. He had once brought a knife down on a prone prisoner's throat with enough force to feel the tip grind against the bone of the man's spine behind the larynx, and as he did so he had looked into the man's eyes and watched him die. He had taken a gun from a man who surrendered to him and shot the man in the face just to see what would happen, to see if all faces came apart the same. Things he tried never to think about; things today had forced him to recall. The way in which killing became easy. He had seen films where someone doing a wicked act had been so disgusted with him- or herself that person couldn't do it again, but he knew it wasn't true.

But that had been war, and war is a different animal with different stripes.

But these youths called themselves soldiers.

Very well, then.

It is done.

Geography.

Clouds.

Below 1800 metres: cumulus. Altrostatus, 1800-6100 metres. Nimbus, above 5500 metres. He looked up at the sky. It was clear today, blue and blank, rendering his knowledge abstract and schoolbookish. He walked faster. Blood pounded in his ears. He wanted to do well. To make his mother proud as she could not be proud of what else he had done today.

He was still some way off when the bell began to ring. He started to run. By the time he reached the gates his fellow students had already gone in. He crossed the deserted schoolyard and hurried over to the sports hall, pushed his way through the double doors and slipped in at the back.

The others were already in their seats.

He made his way to his place. The rest of the students had already turned over their papers and were busily ticking boxes. An invigilating teacher gave him a long, blank stare, glanced up at the clock on the wall, then made a mark on a sheet of paper. One or two of Stanlake's neighbours shot him desultory looks as he shoved off his duffle coat and took his seat. Seeing his make-up one of them looked again and smirked. It was Yvonne. The rest were too focused on what they were doing to pay him any attention. Yvonne made a 'psst' sound and an urgent half-gesture to the boy sitting next to her, but was curbed in her attempt to get his attention by a sharp cough and a warning look from the invigilator. At that moment Stanlake didn't care what Yvonne thought, or what any of them thought. They weren't his friends or his family or his peer-group or his tribe: they were just strangers. He felt more himself than he had for a long time as he turned his paper over.

After completing the multiple choice section the exam let you choose two longer questions from a number of more specialist modules. Stanlake chose weather and glaciers. For weather he had to draw and label a transection of the troposphere illustrating 'at least five' cloud types, then draw and label a diagram showing the meeting of a hot and a cold front and the resultant precipitation. For the glaciation module he also opted for a transection, showing the snout at the front and the terminal morain to the rear of the glacier's passage: he understood things that had a visual element, although to him glaciers were as remote as science-fiction. Even snow he had only seen this year.

Those had been strange days: the snow swirling down blindingly; the city grinding to a halt; the cold white carnival spirit the snow induced in people, a sort of exultant panic underpinned, or so he had thought, by repressed ferocity. The abrupt, almost instantaneous collapse of both infrastructure – buses and tubes and trains – and psychological boundaries – the flinging of snowballs at strangers; building snowmen in the middles of roads – had disturbed him deeply: no difference, it turned out, between here and home. Human beings always and forever on the edge of craziness.

And yet the snow had been beautiful too, something out of a fairytale. *The Snow Goose*. Narnia. He had never thought he would see it. And a few days later it was gone, leaving inexplicably ripped-up roads and dirty tide-marks on the pavements.

Due to poor scheduling and staff shortages those students sitting both Geography and English had only a twenty-minute break between exams, just the time it took the invigilators to put out the next set of papers on the desks and replace lost or removed pens, pencils and erasers.

Stanlake waited with the other crossover students in the lobby of the sports hall, leaning the back of his shaved head against the rough yellow brickwork and staring into space. There was a coolness about him that held the others back from commenting on his appearance.

For a limited amount of time, anyway.

Yvonne's sometime boyfriend Trevone was the first one to nerve himself up to say something. After checking to make sure that he had everybody's attention, he swaggered gangsterishly over to Stanlake and looked him up and down.

'So why you got that on, then?'

Trevone had the bearing of a bully – he was tall and broad for his age, and his brow was permanently furrowed – but he didn't have a bully's spirit, so when Stanlake met his stare levelly, and with no trace of intimidation, he was wrongfooted, and didn't deliver whatever follow-up diss he had in mind. Instead he stood there, waiting for an answer.

'It makes me feel good,' Stanlake said.

'Why, though?' asked another boy who hung around with Trevone, but whose name Stanlake didn't know. He was light-skinned, with cane-rows.

'Why not?'

'Don't you worry people think you're queer or summink, though?'

Stanlake shrugged. One of the invigilators appeared at the doors and signalled. 'It is time for us to go in,' he said.

As they re-entered the exam-room Stanlake felt a touch on his arm and looked round. It was Shelley, the white girl who sat at his table in class. 'I think you look really beautiful,' she said.

'Thank you,' he said, suddenly shy.

Shelley giggled and flushed. 'You're Stanley, right?'

'Stanlake.'

'Good luck with the exam, Stanlake.'

'And you,' he said. Reluctantly, he thought, she let go of his arm and took her seat.

Stanlake made his way to his seat and waited for permission to turn over the paper. He hadn't given the slightest thought as to how the others at the school would respond to his appearance. He had just known that he wasn't afraid of them, and that he didn't want to censor himself any more. He certainly hadn't imagined it might connect him with them, that it might intrigue them.

'You may begin.'

As one they turned over their papers. Stanlake flicked through the pages until he reached the section on the book his class had been studying, *Doctor Jeckyll and Mister Hyde*. Other classes had been doing either *Great Expectations* or *Jane Eyre*: the school was ambitious for its students, and pushed them towards what were called 'the classics'. Stanlake liked that his book was set in the city in which he was living: it made him feel somehow more connected to it. He began with the multiple-choice questions, the quick part of the exam, then turned to the essay-questions, which were thematic. He chose one that asked you to discuss ideas of good and evil in the story.

Doctor Jeckyll thinks he can remove what is bad from inside him and be a totally good person, Stanlake began. *But the bad has to be somewhere because it is part of who he really is. He thinks the bad is not who he really is, so to his head it becomes another person called Mister Hyde. He learns that sometimes strength comes out of the bad things in him. But he cannot accept this, so he kills himself with drugs. This part is not realistic because people always want to live.* He wrote as neatly and quickly as he could.

'Pens down, please.'

With a collective sigh of relief or defeat the students put down their pens and pencils and sat back, flexing their aching wrists as the invigilators went round gathering up the papers. A minute later they were streaming out into the weak spring sunshine, turning on their mobile phones, shouting to release tension, chatting loudly, making plans for the half-term holiday. Even Stanlake felt lighter, though he walked alone amongst the others with the hood of his duffle coat up.

'Stanlake?' He turned to see Shelley catching up to him. Yvonne stood nearby, chewing gum ostentatiously, watching. Shelley flicked her hair back. 'So you coming to Euan's party Saturday, then?'

'I have not been invited.'

'You can like come as my date if you want.'

'Maybe.'

'I'll text you the directions.'

'I do not have a mobile.'

'Oh.' Shelley frowned, unable to think of a way round such an unexpected obstacle. 'Well, I guess I'll see you around then. Have a nice half-term, yeah.'

He looked after her as she went and joined Yvonne. Trevone sauntered up to join the two girls, and the three of them fell into a conversation Stanlake couldn't hear. Evidently he was mentioned because at one point Trevone shot him a glance. It was neither hostile nor friendly. Stanlake turned away from them and headed off.

With his hood up most people in the street didn't notice his made-up face, and in his oversize duffle coat he didn't even look particularly male except that he was wearing trousers. Older people avoided looking at youths anyway, he had noticed; and as there was still half an hour to go before the school day was officially over there were few other youngsters on the streets to be in his business.

Nobody bothered him.

The underpass was still deserted.

The display unit on the wall of the Housing Office clicked over. 752. Poppy's ticket was 763, so there were eleven people to be got through before her turn came, and today, of the three service counters, only two were staffed. She shifted uneasily on the uncomfortable plastic seating. To get here she had had to leave work an hour early. This was because, it being a Friday, the Housing Office closed at 3.30 instead of 4.30.

Mr Patel, the company's Cleansing and Housekeeping Co-ordinator, had initially been reluctant to accommodate her request for time off. 'Especially without so much as a day's notice for consideration,' he had grumbled. Poppy explained to him that it was just last night that she and her son had been threatened with knives by the gang of drug-dealing youths who loitered outside their block. On hearing that, Mr Patel, who had had to work in his father's corner shop in Dagenham as a boy, managed to drag up some compassion, and was only a little grudging in giving her permission to leave early.

Of course the unworked hour would be deducted from her pay.

In defiance of the despair that crowded the room Poppy forced herself to sit upright. Others slumped in their seats, looking down at their hands or at the ground, already broken. A baby grizzled in a pushchair, its mother rolling it back and forth inattentively with her foot, gesturing towards offering comfort while texting on her mobile. Everyone in this room was poor; most of them were not white. Most of them were women. Several of the women were in burqas. This was foreign to Poppy. Back home the Muslim women, most of whom lived not in the villages but in the town where Stanlake and his friends went to school, had covered their heads, but never their faces. One of them, Amina, had helped Poppy train as a midwife, and they had become friends, occasionally visiting each others' homes. Religion had been a source of, or an excuse for conflict, but those women had never been her enemy.

'It's because they are the same thing, that is why,' Pacific had said to her once of her ecumenicality. 'The religions of the sand people.'

'Please do not blaspheme, enh,' Poppy had replied mildly. 'God does not like it, and one day you will need Him.'

'I have the God I need,' Pacific said. 'The Gods.'

In the U.K. these women hid all of their faces except their eyes. Did they shut everyone else out, Poppy wondered, or themselves in? Certainly it was a barrier.

She studied the texting mother and her grizzling baby. The baby was pale brown with soft, ringletty black hair, and dressed in a blue romper-suit. The mother was white and young, with straight, dark-brown hair she had scraped back into a scrunchie. Her pink puffa-jacket was open, exposing a too-small top that showed she wasn't wearing a bra and rode up over the seed-pod of her flabby, post-natal belly. Silvery stretch-marks striated the pale skin, an almost pretty effect. Round her folded-over navel a design had been tattooed, possibly a sun, though it was too squashed in on itself for Poppy to be sure. A piece of jewellery glinted in there. The girl wore tight, low-cut jeans and Ugg-type boots. Poppy watched as she put her phone away and with nervy fingers rolled a cigarette, spilling tobacco as she did so.

At least the baby looked healthy and cared for: only a little undersized, and cleanly dressed. He would be handsome when he grew up, Poppy thought. The mother might have been pretty had her face not been so sharp with suspicion, its lines not so hardened by poverty. Until she came to the U.K. Poppy had not thought there were poor white people in the world.

The baby quieted. The mother didn't give it a glance. Poppy looked around her. Notices with information about this or that lined the walls of the drab, overheated room, and the high, dirty windows were fogged with condensation. The glass in the windows had wire mesh in it, and she was reminded of the asylum centre, and how it was ending up there, despite having survived every terrible thing you could imagine, that drove people to suicide. This was the same sort of place.

The next number clicked up. One of the women in burqas, a large, older woman, heaved herself up from where she was sitting and lumbered over to the counter.

'You cannot come in,' a voice, male, stern, Nigerian, said to someone else.

Along with the other people waiting, Poppy looked round and saw a security guard preventing another woman in a burqa from pushing a double-width pushchair in through the swing-doors. There were two little girls in the pushchair, dressed in matching pink. The woman said nothing, just tried to force her way in.

'You cannot come in, the office is closed,' the guard said. He was tall, in a grey uniform that was snug on his muscular frame, and he blocked the doors so they couldn't open wide enough for the pushchair to get through. 'This people – ' He jabbed a finger in the direction of the fully-occupied row of chairs where Poppy was sitting. 'They were on time. They will be seen. You will not be seen. You must come back again next week.'

'Tomorrow?' the woman said.

'Tomorrow is the weekend. You must come back on Monday.'

Seeing his implacability the woman backed off, turned the pushchair awkwardly in the corridor and went away. Another number was called. Poppy glanced at her watch. It had gone 3.30. A pulse of unease went through her. *Would* she be seen? Housing Officers could refuse to see any more people whenever they wanted, it seemed. Poppy had seen it happen in other council offices. What if they sent her away?

Back to the boys with their knives.

That thought returned her to what she had forced out of her mind while sitting there in bureaucratic limbo: what had happened after she left for work? Had the jackals hurt her son? Had he done something that would make their troubles worse? Better he put on make-up than war-paint she had thought last night, but was that true? She found herself squeezing her hands together so tightly it hurt. Perhaps nothing had happened. Perhaps they hadn't been there when he left for school and she was worrying needlessly. But the jackals had their knives, and had hatred in their hearts for her and for her son, and that wasn't nothing. Had he even gone to school? Yes, surely: he had exams to sit and he wouldn't miss those. Or not by choice.

And afterwards?

Her hands were cold in the too-warm room.

He had no mobile she could reach him on. She had no contact number where he could call her, or where a hospital could call her, or the police. She fought a growing desire to leave the Housing Office and rush home.

She thought of saying a prayer, at least silently, inside her head, but it was too late for prayer: what had happened had happened already. All she had now, false or not, was hope. And she did have hope, though she hardly knew how, for as horror lay behind her, so she was sure it also lay ahead. But that was God's business. Hers was to endure. She forced her hands to lie in her lap. Still they were restless, reaching down to smooth her dress, searching for her son's undetectable stitches.

Whatever had happened, she would go to church tonight.

Someone else tried to come in but was rebuffed by the security guard before they could even get the door open. A fat Asian man with white stubble on his unshaven chin coughed, then coughed again, not covering his mouth, and Poppy thought of tuberculosis, which had killed her aunt. She wanted to say something but felt no connection with the man, or with any of them, that would permit her to speak. Anyway he was fat, so it probably wasn't T.B. Kemi had been thin, so thin.

At last the display unit flicked over to show her number. Fearful of somehow missing her chance, Poppy bustled forward to take her seat at the counter. Facing her on the other side of the protective glass was a plump woman in a white satin tie-neck blouse. She wore large spectacles and had a small, pursed pink mouth and very blue eyes. Next to her monitor stood a narrow vase with three violets forced into it. The building was old, and the room had evidently at some point been converted from some other purpose. It meant the woman had a large window behind her and was backlit like an interrogator.

Poppy pushed her rent-book, utility bills and Indefinite Leave To Remain papers into the slot that dipped under the glass. The woman took them and looked over them wordlessly, flicking backwards and forwards, then tapped something on her keyboard. Her fingers were stubby and she had short, candy-pink nails. She stared at whatever came up on her computer screen.

'Right,' she said eventually. 'How may I help you today?'

'I am having trouble,' Poppy said. 'I need to be moved right away.'

Tap-tap went the fingers. 'Have you reported this trouble to anyone?'

'No.'

Tap-tap. 'Right.'

'But everyone knows it is bad.'

'Everyone?'

'The other people in the building.'

'Have you spoken to your estate manager?'

'No.'

'What is the nature of the trouble?' The woman moved her mouse around and clicked it, checking, Poppy supposed, onscreen boxes. Categories.

'It is young men loitering,' Poppy said. 'They are selling drugs.'

'And have you actually seen them selling drugs?'

'No.'

'I see.'

'But they do. Everyone knows.'

'Right.' Click, click.

'And they threaten. They threaten my son each day as he returns from school.'

'What form do these threats take?'

'So far it is words. But – '

'And is the school aware of this?'

'I don't know. I don't think so. But they know he is doing well at his studies.'

'And how old is your son?'

'He is seventeen, and he is very studious and gentle,' Poppy said, and at that moment her description of her son was simply and honestly true.

'And has he been in trouble with the authorities?'

'No, never.'

'Right.'

Poppy felt indignation flushing through her. 'It is true,' she said, bridling. Who was this indifferent woman behind her glass screen to ask such things? What did she know about anything? Catching her tone, the woman looked at Poppy, her eyes magnified by the lenses in her glasses. Poppy forced her anger down. After all, this woman did not know her, and every day she must hear many stories equally full of need and want, and many lies. 'My son is good,' Poppy stumbled on, knowing the woman had heard that before too. But persevere, she thought. 'He – '

'Basically the problem is on a borough-wide basis we've got residents dissatisfied with young people hanging about,' the woman interrupted. 'So that's not restricted to a particular area, so wherever you're placed you would have that problem. Unless you're saying that they're picking on you and your family in particular as opposed to more generally.'

'Yesterday one of them threatened me with a knife.'

Tap, tap. Click, click. 'And did you report this to the police?'

'No.'

'Was there any reason why not?'

'No-one saw, and I was afraid to make worse trouble.'

'So, no witnesses?'

'No.'

'The difficulty is, until you speak to the police and get a report reference number I can't start to progress your reallocation claim. The most I can do for you today is to start a bundle listing your allegations – '

'They are not allegations,' Poppy said. 'They are true.'

'We currently have an increasing number of priority-need housing claims,' the woman went on. 'Due to government policy there's a fairly chronic housing shortage within the borough. So those claims that are better supported by documentation do tend to get to the front of the queue in regards to re-housing within the borough.'

'But the things that have happened have happened,' Poppy protested. The woman looked at her blankly. 'I can't go back and make proof about them.' The woman said nothing. Her fingers hovered over the keys. 'What about other boroughs?' Poppy asked.

'We can only assist with relocation within the borough.'

'It is what is going to happen next I am worried about,' Poppy said. 'I do not think they will stop at threats. That is why I need to be moved right away.'

'I have to tell you that even starting right now we're looking at nine months,' the woman said. 'Minimum. More likely a year.'

'Is there nothing that can expedite things?' Poppy asked, a note of desperation she couldn't suppress sliding up inside her voice. She was rewarded with another blank stare. 'Speed things along?' she added.

'A concretely-documented incident of racist, faith-based or gender-specific or homophobic or transphobic persecution, or being in danger from an abusive male partner or relatives.'

'They do not like that we are immigrants.'

'Are they white?'

'No – well, one is, I think. They are all races.'

Poppy and the woman sat there in silence, not quite looking at each other. The woman's moist rosebud mouth was slightly open. Perhaps she was thinking, or maybe it was just her brain idling at the end of a long week of other people's problems, problems to which she had no solutions.

'My son is small,' Poppy said. 'He is not of big build and he is not very – ' She groped for an appropriate word before reluctantly making do with 'manly'. It made no impact on the woman. 'They are bullies. I worry that things will carry on like this and we will have to do something to defend ourselves.'

It was a weak gambit but it broke through. 'I'd have to immediately advise against that,' the woman said quickly. 'The best thing you can do is follow proper procedure and inform the appropriate authorities when incidents occur. The police, the estate manager, the tenants' association, us. Keep a record including time and date of incidents. Anything else just makes it complicated in terms of our statutory obligations, and can actually work against your claim.'

'Is there nothing you can do?' Poppy asked, and now she couldn't hide her frustration. At least back home you could bribe someone. Not that she had any money for dash, but it gave you the hope that something could be achieved. Here there was just the machine, impervious, inflexible, barely human.

'As I said, we can start a bundle.'

Poppy gathered her strength, forcing stoicism, humility. 'Let us do that, then,' she said. She could do this. She had faced worse. She would twist and force her way through this system until she got what she needed from it.

If there was time.

'Right,' said the woman. 'Address?'

Poppy left the Housing Office twenty minutes later with nothing she could use and a sense of futility. The system only seemed to work if you started to complain before you had a problem. And of course the woman was right: there were youths like that everywhere.

Back home they would have become soldiers. On the side of the government or on the side of the rebels, it would have made little difference. Civilians were prey, and looting was policy.

The wait for the bus seemed endless and, though she was at the front of the queue, when it eventually came it was so crammed with passengers she could barely squeeze on. For a moment she thought of waiting for the next one, but no doubt that would be equally crowded, and might even pass by without stopping at all. Ignoring the hostile looks of her fellow passengers she wedged herself on board. She could only get hold of one of the support-poles by twisting herself at an uncomfortable angle. Everything about this day felt like an ordeal.

The underpass, when she reached it, was deserted. Increasingly uneasy, she hurried on.

'We gotta off the cunt, fam,' Pit-Bull said, blazing aggressively. The tip of the joint glowed and a cannabis-seed popped and fell to the floor, briefly showing red on the pale yellow laminate, then turning black. As the hot smoke passed over his tongue Pit-Bull cursed blurrily. The mucus-covered muscle was still lacerated from where Stanlake's knee had driven Pit-Bull's teeth into it during the fight, and a bruise like a livid, exploded star spread out across his pale neck from where Stanlake had precision-kicked him.

'Open him up,' Cuts agreed, reaching for the joint. His right wrist was held in rigid alignment by a plastic brace and the movement was awkward. A wad of gauze was taped over one of his ears from where Stanlake's kick had ruptured his eardrum. He winced as he brought the joint to his lips, the lower one of which was split and scabbing.

Solid nodded. 'Murk the fucker,' he said. His voice was thick and he was breathing through his mouth. His nose was braced on either side with plastic strips and taped across. There were plugs of gauze in each of his nostrils, and his eyes were bruised and puffy. He had needed stitches in the back of his head from where his close-cropped skull had struck a jutting edge of the Rock. He turned to Evill. 'But so what you sayin' 'bout alla dis, fam?'

Evill took the joint from Cuts and blazed as they waited on his answer.

The four of them were resting up in Solid's flat, on the twelfth floor of Cardinal Three. It was the block diametrically opposite the one Stanlake and Poppy lived in on the other side of the estate. In size and layout it was the mirror-image of theirs, except that Solid had kept the lounge as the lounge. Which was where he and the other members of the Blows Crew were sitting around now, beefing.

It was a bleak room, warm but unloved, with no domestic touches. A large grey leather sofa, an outsize plasma-screen on the wall, an X-Box and handsets, a Wii, a Bose iPod dock and speakers were the fruits of Solid's lifestyle.

Trappings, Evill thought as he blazed. Traps.

Dirty clothes, foil takeaway trays and pizza boxes, pop and beer-cans lay about, along with a few dvds, action movies and torture porn. A computer sat on a cheap blond-wood desk in one corner and a sleeping-bag lay rumpled on the floor. It belonged to Cuts, who often crashed there, having nowhere else to go but an aunt's who loathed him. The air was blue with smoke and the ashtray was overflow-ing, and the room with its sealed windows smelt stale and slightly rancid.

Evill exhaled. The fact that he alone had been physically undamaged in the fight with the African bwoy had somehow cemented his superior status within the Crew; had made him seem untouchable. More significant than that, though, was their witnessing his unhesitating pulling of the trigger. All of them now knew that mentally he had crossed that line. Yeah, the gun had misfired, but shit like that happened and it didn't signify: the intention was what counted, was what earned respect. And now they knew: he had the mindset of a killer. He let the smoke curl up from his mouth and drew it back into his nostrils.

Still he said nothing, and in his silence the others, his soldiers, believed he was wise, or at least that he knew something they didn't. And perhaps they were right. But beneath the façade his mind was churning, as it had been since the fight.

Once they had admitted, grudgingly and resentfully, that their injuries were too serious to be dealt with by the self-medications of skunk and alcohol and plotting revenge, he had helped Pit-Bull, Solid and Cuts limp off to Casualty. Solid's nose had had to be reset, and he had needed a local for that, as had Cuts for his dislocated wrist. One of Pit-Bull's teeth had been cracked and would need remedial dentistry to save it. He'd been lucky not to need stitches in his tongue, a thought that made them all wince. Solid and Cuts had both needed stitches in their gashed scalps.

When asked how they came by their injuries the Crew had blamed them on a game of American football in the park that had got out of hand, a story which convinced no-one. While they were being examined the triage nurse's aide had sloped off and spoken to a woman on reception who gave them a look and made a phone-call, presumably to the police to see if any incident had been reported.

Evill hadn't been worried: he knew the boy wouldn't have belled the feds – why would he, when he had won? – and no police had appeared during the three hours the Crew had been stuck there, most of it, after the brisk but cursory initial examination by the triage nurse, waiting to get their injuries actually sorted.

Too minor to be a priority.

As Pit-Bull, Solid and Cuts stoked themselves up Evill thought of the African youth's wide, kingfisher-lidded eyes, eyes that were a tunnel into something both terrifying and compelling. Or were a mirror. And if that was so, then the depth and the terror were inside himself.

'He's got the gat, though,' he said.

'And like you see how he like fixed it up, though?' Pit-Bull said, and there was admiration in his voice. 'Like out of a computer-game or summink.'

'Like he had training, bruv,' Solid agreed.

'Where a queer get training, though?' said Pit-Bull.

'Africa,' said Cuts. 'All kindsa fucked-up shit goes down in dem places dere, innit.'

'Shut up about Africa, fam,' Solid said, a sudden spasm of identification with the continent of his unknown parents flushing through him. 'What you know about it?'

'Wars,' Evill said. 'They got bare wars down there, don't it? And they start 'em young.'

'But so what we gonna do, fam?' Pit-Bull asked. 'Cos we can't just chat an' do jack. And we can't let the Blows Crew be disrespected so.'

'Innit, though,' said Solid.

'He got the Glock off of Evill, though,' Cuts said.

'And he got the blade off of you,' Evill said acidly. 'He got that first.'

'He fixed it so it works,' Pit-Bull said, coaxing the joint he'd just rolled into life by running the flame of his Zippo along its underside. 'And he did it like it weren't nothing, you know? Like he'd done shit like that x times or whatever.'

'That fucker Oily,' Evill said. 'Selling us whack shit. He's gonna get a kicking.'

'Fuck Oily, bruv,' Cuts said. 'What about the queer?'

'What about business, bruv?' Solid said. 'We been off the corner now for like six hours not selling. That's a worry, blood.'

'We can't sell looking like we just been give a beating though,' said Pit-Bull.

'Yeah, but there's one of us ain't marked whatsoever, though,' said Cuts, reaching across with a grunt.

Evill shifted uncomfortably as he let Cuts lift the joint from between his fingers. The last thing he wanted was to be lumbered with selling on his own, which would mean carrying both the gear and the money, and would therefore put him at maximum risk of getting busted by the feds or, without support from his soldiers, getting ramped or stabbed up by another crew. 'This is fuckeries,' he grumbled.

'You know?' Pit-Bull agreed. 'But there ain't no other option I'm seeing right now, bruv.'

'Sometimes you got to lead from the front, fam,' said Solid.

Evill shot him a look. 'What you sayin', blood?'

Solid shrugged. 'What it is, blood.'

'Management pon di shop-floor.' Cuts looked down to hide a smirk.

Evill made a growling noise in his throat. 'Bare fuckeries,' he said.

'Blame the queer,' said Pit-Bull.

'Yeah, 'bout that,' Solid said.

'I'll deal with the queer,' Evill said, though he had no clear idea what he would do: just, it would come down to him. What if the gun had fired, he thought. Who would I be now?

'Business gotta come first, though,' said Pit-Bull.

Evill nodded tightly and gestured to the others to turn out their pockets. Soon on the coffee-table in front of him were around thirty wraps of crack, two hundred ecstasy tablets and forty meph, a dozen or so wraps of H, and £50 in notes and coins to go with the £100 he had brought out with him that morning. Grudgingly he tipped the pills and wraps into a carrier-bag Pit-Bull offered him. Cuts passed him a knife, handle-first. Evill took it. If he was done by the feds for possession the knife wouldn't signify next to the amount of drugs he was carrying; and if he was bothered by rivals it could come in useful. It was eight inches long and its rubber handle had indentations to ensure a firm grip. He slid it carefully into an inside pocket of his tracksuit-top.

'Aiight, then.' He took one last drag on Pit-Bull's joint, passed it back to him and got to his feet.

Leaving his stewing, battered crew to loaf about in the warmth and comfort of Solid's flat, Evill made his resentful way back to the underpass. As he trudged along, shoulders hunched against a cutting wind, he cursed his life, and cursed the others for being such a bunch of pussies. Beaten down by a lickle queer-boy in make-up! That was pitiful. Yeah, they'd been taken by surprise, but a real soldier is ready for anything the road throws at him, always. A real soldier has a Zen mind with all channels open, just his heart closed.

What had the youth seen in him that made him not bring the blade down, Evill wondered. That was the question that had kept his mind in turmoil ever since the fight: what had made him not do what had been the obvious thing to do? It hadn't been fear, or not any obvious kind of fear, but he couldn't think of any other reason, for neither pity nor compassion had been in the African bwoy's eyes.

The underpass smelt of piss and decay. A solitary street-light lit the deserted central area a dull orange. As he swung up onto the Rock a fine, steely rain began to fall, haloing the light's fluorescent tube. He hunched against it and stared ahead balefully. He should have gone KFC on the way, at least got a cappo or some popcorn chicken to hold him. What was wrong with him tonight? Why couldn't he get any focus?

I could've been a killer. If the gun had of worked I would've become that. A path chosen, no going back.

Or was it chosen? Wasn't he just a slave to this? There were people in the world who had the sweet life: people who had fresh-cut flowers in crystal vases on polished tables; people who could take a deep breath and enjoy the scent of those flowers because their lungs weren't fucked because they weren't born a crack baby. Who had clean lives. What was this invisible fucking wall that kept his world so absolutely separate from theirs? Youts only stabbed up other youts, never the rich. His bladder felt tight.

He dropped down from the Rock, ambled off into the shadows of East Tunnel and pissed against the dung-coloured ceramic tiles. They were part of an abstract mural, or maybe whoever was doing the tiling just ran out of tiles all the same colour. It came to the same thing, which was nothing much.

When he got back to his spot he found Rula waiting for him.

Immediately he felt irritated. She was a regular customer but she rarely had money. Blonde and scrawny, with a wide mouth and high cheekbones on a taut face, she could have been any age between twenty and forty-five, though she dressed teenage-young, in knock-off Ugg boots, skinny low-rise jeans and today a diarrhoea-brown fun-fur jacket. From a distance she could have been a model but closer up she was thin in a bad way, and she radiated a whore's desperation, that puncture in the spirit through which neediness poured out.

Evill hated her.

'Hey,' she said, tossing her hair. She had a heavy accent, Polish or Russian or something, she'd said a couple of times but he'd never paid attention: what difference did it make?

'Rula,' he said, not looking at her, climbing back onto the Rock so he was above her: in heels she was taller than him.

'How you doing, Evill?' she said, hugging herself, moving from one foot to the other as if following some abstract, dislocated rhythm.

'Not so good, Rula,' he said.

'Oh, yeah?'

He hadn't meant to give even that much of himself away, but he was cold and frustrated, and right now any attention, even from someone like her, was better than nothing. Still, he pulled back: never let a punter think you're their friend or next it'll be freebies for favours. 'Business ain't been so hot,' he added meaningly.

'It's because it's so cold,' Rula said. Despite this, above her self-encircling arms her jacket was pushed open at the front to display a scoop-necked top that framed the flat, bony area where her breasts met her chest. Her ribs were visible through pale, blue-veined skin. 'You got a light?' she asked, producing a cigarette. It was a proper cigarette, not a roll-up. Maybe she had money today. She did sometimes, from whoring, Evill assumed.

'I quit,' he lied.

'I should quit too,' she said, putting the cigarette away and looking around distractedly, pushing a hand through her tangled hair.

'What you want, Rula?' He was bored with her now, even disgusted. Why couldn't she just buy if she was going to buy and fuck off and leave him alone?

'Just my little good time,' she said. The junkie's pointless mystification.

'What you got, then?'

'Ah.' Rula tilted back her head and smiled. Her attempt at an alluring look didn't come off, however, undermined as it was by the cold and the rain, by the softened greyness of her teeth and the all-too-visible recession of her gums. She had sucked off all the Crew at one time or another, sometimes even one right after the other. He had let her blow him once. Just once, though. He shuddered at the memory and wished someone would come. Not even a punter, just someone who would end this. He thought of suicide.

'Aright,' he said abruptly.

'Where?'

'The tunnel.' He indicated one of the tunnels that didn't lead either to the African boy's block or to the school. Rula shrugged and went on ahead of him. Flashing looks around him, Evill slipped down off the Rock and followed her into the dark.

'You want blowjob?' she asked.

'I want a fuck.'

'You got rubbers?'

'No.'

'I got rubbers. You will wear one?'

'No,' he said. 'Fuck that shit.' Then he wavered. A sket

like Rula was going to have everything going, herpes, syph, gonorrhoea, Chlamydia, maybe even AIDS. 'Yeah,' he corrected himself. 'But you got to put it on with your mouth, though.'

He had carried a gat earlier and almost been busted by the feds, had a knife and hard drugs on him now, and yet fucking Rula without a rubber seemed like a self-destructive act too far. Raw with a whore, he thought. I don't think so. He had been to the clap clinic enough times. The thought of the plastic scraper in his piss-slit made him clench.

The tunnel was dank and rank. Evill pushed his track-pants down to mid-thigh. The air was cold on his crotch and he struggled to get hard. She sucked him for a while before trying with the condom. He stared into the darkness ahead. The cheap smell of her perfume was laced with the rotten-ness of old leaves under floodwater. As her mouth moved warmly on him there flashed into his mind the image of the scarlet, glittering lips of the African youth. What would he smell like? Taste like?

Evill's erection grew rapidly in Rula's mouth.

He felt the chilly brush of her fake-fur coat against his bare skin as, still on her knees, she moved to rip open the foil packet with her teeth. Deftly she rolled the latex sheath down the length of his cock, which at once started to waver. She used her fingers, not her mouth.

'You want it from behind?' she asked, getting to her feet and turning away from him.

'Whatever,' he said thickly.

'I don't mean up the ass,' she added, unzipping and shoving her jeans and underwear down to mid-thigh, her urgent movements a parody of lust. She bent over, bracing herself with outstretched arms against the tunnel wall.

He guided his half-hard dick into her crack and awk-wardly worked it in. It wasn't firm enough and slopped straight back out. He wanked briefly to force some rigidity into it and shoved it back in, pushing his hips up against her flat backside to keep it inside her.

'Is it in?' Rula asked breathlessly.

'Course it's in, you stupid bitch,' he snarled. It was like being in a bad porn movie. He began to pump aggressively,

making sure to withdraw the minimum with each stroke out
of fear his dick would drop out of her again. Disgust and self-
loathing intensified in him. He fucked her until he couldn't
stand it anymore, then pulled out. His dick was barely firm.
Turning away from her, he peeled off the condom and threw
it down.

'You come, then?' Rula asked.

'Yeah, yeah,' he said. His lungs were tight and he needed
a hit of his inhaler. But not in front of her. She was wriggling
her skinny-fit jeans back up.

'I get my treat now?' she asked.

'You're just a sket, Rula.'

'I want my treat, Evill. You promised.' In the dark he
heard the crisp sound of a zip being tugged up.

'I never,' he said. 'I just thought you was horny and
needed a jook.' But winding her up gave him no pleasure. He
reached into his pocket and threw a couple of wraps down in
front of her. 'Two,' he said. 'Cos I'm a gentleman.'

She dropped to her hands and knees and started grub-
bing about, searching by touch in the dark for what she
needed among the litter and debris. He left her to it and went
back to his spot. Now rain-wetted, the Rock was even less
comfortable to sit on than before.

Rula found her treats and left without a backward glance.

Time crawled by. The rain stopped, started again,
stopped. Other customers came and went, paying ones after
Rula, and their eagerness to be out of the cold and out of
their heads made the transactions brief and businesslike.
The impersonality was a relief. If any other fool had come
begging he'd have put a foot in their arse. After a couple of
hours most of the crack was gone. A student planning a party
took thirty of the Es, half the meph and some of the heroin,
and, though he was weary and his stomach was cramped
Evill began to feel less angry at the world.

Mid-evening the mother of the African youth passed by,
a large white wrap on her head, church-style. Coming back
from some African community thing, he supposed. He
remembered her and the youth arriving, carrying their stuff
in binliners. He watched her from under his hood as she
crossed the space, but said and did nothing. With her large

backside, her full but fully-covered bust, her handsomeness and lack of make-up, she was everything a mother was supposed to be.

He had always found it hard to tell hate from longing.

He still didn't know what he would do about the African bwoy.

Chapter Eight

Poppy got back from the Housing Office to find Stanlake sitting in the kitchen sipping a mug of tea. He had on a white skinny-rib tank-top; a length of blue and green floral wax-print material was wrapped round his hips sarong-style, and he was wearing green eyeshadow and wet-look red lipstick. He was calm and seemed uninjured. Without a word he rose and switched on the kettle, taking a second mug from the drying rack and dropping a teabag into it. The kettle boiled while Poppy was unbuttoning and hanging up her coat in the hall. She took the steaming mug her son offered her with questioning eyes.

'It is dealt with,' he said.

'How can it be dealt with?' she said. He shrugged. 'Please, Stanlake, what happened today?'

'Were they there when you came back?'

'No, but they are not always there. What did you do?'

'I showed them some of what they had not seen.'

'They are gone for now,' Poppy said. 'But they will come back.'

'Yes. But they won't bother you.'

'Why not?'

'They will not dare.'

'You do not know what these boys will dare,' Poppy said. 'You don't know what they're like.'

Stanlake looked at her levelly and took a sip of his tea. Poppy noticed he left an imprint of lipstick on the rim of the mug. She shivered.

The sound of the television in the flat below came up through the floor, the voice of a newsreader, judging by its urgent, stylised tone. Though the words were muffled the voice would be telling of famine, terror, economic unrest, disorder on the streets.

War.

Stanlake, staggering out of the forest with a tiara on his head.

Pacific kneeling in the dust in the village square, the tears on his face following the lines of the scars on his cheeks.

The blade the boy who loved knives had held up close to her face, the sourness of his breath, the depthless eyes.

You have to work to be human, she thought. It doesn't just happen.

Was this, then, God's plan? Had He made Stanlake into what he was so he would have the ruthlessness to do what was needed here at the end of their flight? She had been so afraid of him when he returned out of the forest that day. But he had taken her by the hand and his hand had been warm in hers, and he had told her they must run because war was coming.

'Leave that!' he had ordered when she started to gather up a few things for a journey to who knew where. She ignored him and quickly threw together a bundle of necessities. All the while he was looking back towards the line of dusty trees beyond the compound wall. From nearby there came the sound of gunfire and hoarse shouting.

'Hurry!' he said. 'Or we are dead!'

She knotted the bundle with awkward, nerveless fingers, and they fled the village.

There had been no moment of reunion, much less reconciliation, not then; and later, during the long days they spent walking the road, neither of them could find the words. During that time he became a stranger to her again, a spirit in her son's skin, trudging beside her in the wavering heat.

Stanlake discarded first one piece of his uniform and then another as they toiled along, stripping away in stages the outward signs of the soldier, the rebel, the killer, laying bare the slender-armed youth who had never gone to war. With each piece of clothing he put aside he looked more and more like who he had been before the rebels came. Yet the sameness was an illusion, a lie. He could not go back, as she could not. No-one could: only forward.

He volunteered nothing about the more than two years he had been away, and amidst such utter uncertainty she

didn't ask, unable to drag up from within herself the sympathy that asking would require; and too she was afraid of what
he might disclose.

The ache in her right ankle began on that journey. It had
never fully left her.

And now these boys, these jackals, have brought back all
those things that I and my son ran away from, that we
thought we had escaped. And even if the youths stopped
bothering them, as she feared they would not, would
Stanlake be able to discard the mentality of the soldier a
second time? In the everydayness of their lives in the U.K.
she had almost forgotten her fear of him, but now it was
beating at her again: her son, her boy, was a killer.

Yet there he sat, sipping tea, renouncing with the make-
up on his face the desire to do the harm that men do,
wanting only to live his life. And he had returned to what he
had been only after they had physically assaulted her, wasn't
that true? Hadn't he acted as any good son would? A good
son would not stand aside and do nothing.

And now it was done.

But the world was full of threats, full of people who
wanted to make trouble, who would not let you be. There
were so many triggers for what was still inside him, and not
buried far down: like his father, the soldier lay in a shallow
grave. And not dead, but sleeping. She had read that on an
old gravestone in a churchyard off the Walworth Road where
she went sometimes to sit and think: 'not dead, but sleeping',
and it had stayed with her. She thought of the uncountable
dead in their graves, waiting on Judgment Day. Dead and yet
waiting. The thought was oppressive. She had seen the dead,
touched them, smelt them. And not just the war-dead: she
had once delivered a baby at full term that was pale and
strangled by its own umbilical cord, its lips and nostrils blue.
She had been unable to think of the goodness of God that
day. The baby, a little girl, had been as warm as if she was
alive, but that was only the mother's warmth, and soon the
baby was cold.

Not dead, but sleeping. Perhaps that was part of why her
own sleep was so light and wretched: a fear of sinking too
close to the level of the dead she had left behind. The dead

that waited.

My husband.

'I'm going to church,' she said. Perhaps the pastor *could* help, though she struggled to imagine anything he might say that would be of any use to her. So long as he didn't just tell her to pray. What she needed was advice beyond what she could think up for herself as she sat in front of her son in his woman's make-up. She swallowed the last lukewarm dregs of her tea and went through to the bathroom to wash her hands and face.

Stanlake listened to the pipes judder as his mother spun the taps. Was she right? Would the jackals make more trouble for them? Was it not dealt with after all? But of course she didn't know about the gun, or that it was now in his possession, which meant that always in the jackals' minds from now on would be the fear he had it with him, or if not the gun, then at least the knife. And they knew he knew how to use such things. That would deter them, surely, for they were bullies who did not seek an equal fight, still less a fight with someone more skilled in the techniques of war than themselves. And they wouldn't want trouble on their doorstep, driving off trade, drawing the police. But too they were thugs, and like all thugs they were prone to violence through boredom and unspent energy; and Stanlake knew that such young men often acted against their own interests, only weighing the costs later.

He sighed. He didn't want to have these thoughts anymore, the thoughts of a warrior in the combat zone. To be dragged back like this was almost a form of attack by evil spirits. Jackal spirits, seeking to assail and then possess him. Would only a sacrifice end it? Could it be – this thought had never come to him before, but it did so now, and vividly – that he himself would have to be the sacrifice? That all of this had been only a reprieve?

After Poppy left for church he would light the candles and ask his Masks for guidance, perhaps even offer them a little of his blood.

He felt exhausted.

As if from some parallel world the thought came to him

that he was now on holiday. The other pupils at his school were no doubt relieved to have a week of not having to think about their studies, but for him his schoolbooks were a bulwark against the endless massing of the past. Better to think about Doctor Jeckyll and his potions and how they could possibly work scientifically than to find his mind returning over and over to the cabin by the roadblock, to strange days and stranger memories.

Big Gun standing in front of him wearing the red beaded dress he had taken from the body of the girl.

Big Gun lifting a charm of bones and who knew what else over Stanlake's inclined head and saying, 'For this will turn bullets, my brother.'

And Stanlake had smiled and said, 'But still I will not test your favour with the gods by lying down in front of one of the trucks.'

The conventional reply made Big Gun smile too, and they hugged. Makinde had been out reconnoitring and he came in fast then. Seeing the packets around their necks he bared his teeth in a feral parody of good humour and said, 'Good, good, my Beasts. Now you are invincible!' He was holding something in his hand. 'And there is this.' He placed on the table, among the grimy playing cards and heaped cheap jewellery, a bulky object the size of a fist. It was wrapped in olive-green material soaked black, and where the black had touched the commander's hand it showed wet and red. Stanlake, Big Gun and Blondie looked at the thing with appalled fascination. It was smaller than a human head, at least that. Makinde peeled back the damp cloth, revealing with a conjuror's relish what lay beneath.

'Is that a cow's heart?' asked Big Gun, once the glistening, purple-red muscle had been laid bare.

'It is too small,' said Stanlake.

'The heart of a goat?' suggested Blondie. Makinde shook his head. 'Maybe a pig?'

'No,' said Makinde. When they offered no more ideas he grinned and said, 'Eat.'

Stanlake, Big Gun and Blondie exchanged glances. None of them was prepared to be the first. Makinde produced a bayonet, flipped it deftly round his hand, then brought it down with such force that the blade was rammed an inch into the soft, splintering wood of the table. He left it there, upright as a warrior's spear, waiting to be claimed.

'Eat,' he said again. He turned to Big Gun. 'You.'

Big Gun swallowed. There was no way out. Something died in his eyes as he pushed out his chest and stepped forward. With an effort he wiggled the bayonet-blade free from the table. It took both his small hands to do it. Then, gingerly holding the heart steady with one hand, with the other he attempted to cut a sliver from it. The blunted blade slid about unhelpfully on the slick membrane covering the bulging surface, but eventually he managed to cut through it and slice into the muscle beneath. He made first one cut, then, near to it, a second, and levered out a slice of raw flesh. Fastidiously, Big Gun didn't touch it with his fingers. Instead he lifted it on the tip of the bayonet and, staring levelly into Makinde's eyes, raised it to his open mouth and placed it on his tongue. Big Gun's teeth closed on the metal. He withdrew the blade smoothly, then, with a shudder and grimace, he swallowed.

'You see!' cried Makinde, delighted. 'You see how it gives you courage! You – ' He turned to Stanlake. 'Little Gun.'

Woodenly Stanlake stepped forward and did as Big Gun had done. By that time he had no thoughts. The heart was firm and slippery as he pressed down on it with his finger-tips. Following Big Gun's cut made the task easier. As Big Gun had done, Stanlake raised the slice of flesh to his mouth on the blade of the bayonet. The texture was slimy, and all he tasted was iron and something rancid. He swallowed. It was done. He stepped back, saying and showing nothing.

Only Blondie remained: Diamondz was on duty outside. Blondie had killed and raped but doing this thing made his hand tremble. In his clumsy nervousness he cut off a bigger chunk than he had meant to, dragging with it a large vein that was webbed with part of the mucus membrane. He tried to imitate Big Gun and Stanlake and put the entire piece of flesh in his mouth and attempted to swallow, but it stuck in his throat and he began to gag and retch. He turned away from the others and bent over in a corner of the cabin, trying to hawk it up. After a long, ugly minute of hacking and dry-heaving Makinde went over to Blondie and struck him hard between the shoulderblades with the heel of his hand, hoping most likely to impel the youth to swallow the lump of raw flesh. His blow had the opposite effect, however: Blondie dropped onto all-fours and threw up the slimy, veiny chunk of muscle, along with everything else he had eaten that day.

Makinde flung a rag at him. 'Clean it up,' he said, a look of disgust on his face.

But Blondie didn't clean up his vomit. Instead he stood and wiped the back of his hand across his mouth. His eyes met his commander's. Without a word he took up the knife and cut another slice from the heart. His face was hard as wood, and a tear ran down one of his cheeks as he lifted the limp sliver into his open mouth, placed it on his tongue, closed his mouth and swallowed.

'Good,' said Makinde. 'Very good.' The feral grin returned to his face but now a twitch pulled at the corner of it, and for the first time Stanlake saw in Makinde a tiny shard of fear, fear that Stanlake suddenly understood could only have come from the Commander's realisation that he had trained his Beasts too well. And seeing that fear, Stanlake also knew this: he will want us to die; he will want to be rid of us.

He swallowed the last of his tea. As he rinsed out his mug in the sink he tried to force his mind to think of other things: the holiday, for instance, and how to fill it.

There was always reading, and he had borrowed from the school's library Wilkie Collins' *Woman in White* and Charlotte Brontë's *Wuthering Heights*. But he didn't want to spend the whole seven days indoors; nor did he want to live only in his head, even if in the happier realm of his imagination.

His mind filled then with thoughts of make-up and women's underwear – or, more precisely, underwear that he, while still being a boy, could wear that had the qualities he associated with what women were allowed to wear and men were not: skimpy cuts, lacey or silky materials, provocative stylings.

Stanlake had always assumed such things didn't exist for boys because who, except for him, would want them? Then, a few weeks ago, in a bin at a bus-stop, he had happened to notice lying on top of the other rubbish a men's underwear catalogue. He had wanted very much to take it, but because other boys and girls from his school were there too he hadn't dared. It had been hard to control himself, so powerfully had he been drawn to the images on the double-page spread the catalogue had happened to fall open at. Slick, shiny pouches, sheer semi-transparent thongs and exceedingly low-cut black vinyl and leather swim-briefs were displayed on sculpted, hairless male bodies. Pouting men sprawled across the page in supine poses, male, muscled, but receptive as women, Photoshopped faces free of any shadow of shaving, free of anxiety, of personality, of blemishes, of history; free of everything but a diffuse, passive sensuality. Stanlake's cock had rammed itself stiffly against the zip of his trousers at the sight of them, and his heart had rammed itself against the cage of his ribs.

No-one else noticed.

He had to get hold of those things, or things like them, or things he could at least slice and stitch into something that was a homage to them.

If he got away from the local area he would feel less awkward in his search for such undergarments. The thought of going to the Primark down the road or the nearby T K Maxx filled him with dread: there were too many African girls on the tills, too many black boys stacking the shelves. The bravado he had felt earlier in the day was slipping away from him, and while he could convince himself that he didn't care what the rest of the world thought of him, he was afraid of being judged by those who were nearest to being his own.

A larger obstacle to his quest for self-transformation was that he didn't have any money; nor could he think of a ready way of getting some. He could try and shoplift again, but he knew that the bigger shops, unlike the local chemist's, had proper security-systems: tags that set off alarms; cameras that covered all the angles; plainclothes operatives spying in the aisles and uniformed security guards watching the doors. Yvonne had got herself barred from the Lewisham Primark for trying to boost a fun-fur jacket, and had been lucky not to get taken to court. Shelley had run out at the same time with a necklace and had got away with it, but she hadn't dared go back there until she'd dyed her hair a different colour. The necklace was made of plastic and metal and had been priced at £2.50.

The girls had made it sound like a crazy escapade when they bragged about it at school the next day but it wasn't, it was theft. He couldn't imagine facing his mother, who not only worked Monday to Friday in the City but also had a second cleaning job at a pub on the estate on weekend mornings, and saying to her, 'I needed these things, and you do not earn the money to provide them for me, so I stole them. And I got caught.' Not to mention the embarrassing nature of the things, and the nature of his need for them.

He thought again of Big Gun in the red beaded dress. Big Gun had started wearing it about a week after the girl died, putting it on one night when they had all been drunker and more stoned than usual, laughing and staggering around the cabin in it, still wearing his army trousers underneath, and he kept wearing it until the end. No-one had commented, and indeed all their identities became looser and stranger as the weeks ground by. Diamondz wore earrings, a tiara and necklaces, and sometimes white satin wedding-gloves that went up to his elbows. Needing a realer transformation, Blondie discarded his filthy wig and dyed his hair repeatedly with looted hair-dye, turning it whiter and whiter until his scalp was permanently inflamed and peeling. Always up and down both wrists he wore stolen watches, none of them set to the right time. 'All of them are right somewhere,' he'd say. Stanlake wore lipstick and eye-shadow, garishly applied, and sometimes nail-varnish. They no longer knew who they were, and they had never known where they were: there was just the red mud of the road, the sodden, steaming forest, the relentless rain and the endless waiting.

Then came a day after many empty days when three trucks arrived at the roadblock in a convoy and in a hurry. As Stanlake and his comrades came stumbling out of the cabin with their weapons at the ready the commander in the frontmost truck barked at them to get the barrier down. 'And leave it down,' he ordered. 'Others are coming.'

'What is going on, sah?' Stanlake asked as he slung his rifle across his back and clambered up onto the barricade to start pulling it apart. Diamondz, Blondie and Big Gun followed him.

'Never mind what is going on. Just get those tyres out of the road. You, you and you,' the officer picked out three soldiers not much older than Stanlake who sat slumped in the back of the truck. 'Help them.'

Wearily the soldiers put aside their weapons and climbed down from the muddy, rust-holed vehicle to join in with the moving of the tyres, either throwing them down where they were or sending them rolling into the flooded gullies that flanked the road. The rain, which had fallen off for the last half-hour or so, began to patter down again, and they moved faster.

Within ten minutes a gap had been cleared just wide enough for the trucks to fit through. Stanlake, Diamondz, Blondie and Big Gun were brusquely waved aside and the order to move out was given. The three soldiers who had helped them were pulled back up onto the truck by their comrades; and with engines revving, first it then the other two nosed their way through the gap, the drivers crunching the gears as the wheels spun and each vehicle lurched and slithered about in the mud. Once they were past the barrier they picked up speed. In a little while they reached a bend in the road, then they were gone from sight. A minute or two later the sound of their engines had wholly faded away.

A now-sodden Stanlake, Big Gun, Diamondz and Blondie hurried over to the shelter of the cabin's awning. Blondie was the one officially on watch, but none of them went back inside: they needed to talk. With some difficulty Stanlake lit a damp joint, toked on it and passed it round.

'What do you think is going on?' asked Big Gun.

'It looks like a withdrawal,' Diamondz said.

'Or a retreat,' Stanlake said. 'And if that is so – '

'Then the enemy is coming this way,' said Blondie.

As one they scanned the road the way the trucks had come. It looked the same. They listened to the rain on the tin roof, the rasping and creaking of insects and the croaking of toads. The sky above was grey and heavy, and everything was so green it was almost a violence. Some way off lightning lanced down once, then twice. Thunder rumbled.

'It is coming our way,' Big Gun said, though it was unclear whether he meant war or the storm.

'Should we stay?' said Blondie.

'We have been ordered to stay,' said Stanlake.

'It is our duty,' said Big Gun.

'If we are losing and the enemy is coming it will all be fucked up,' said Blondie. 'We could go. Who would know?'

'If we follow the trucks they will know we have deserted,' said Diamondz. 'We would be punished. But if we go another way we might head straight into the hands of the government forces. Do you want to be caught and tortured? They will cut off your cock and stuff it in your mouth, and only then will they kill you. I have seen it.'

'But if we stay here the same thing will happen,' Stanlake said. 'Unless we get shot and die first. I do not want to die either way.'

They peered out dispiritedly through what was now a curtain of rain. The boredom of standing endless guard over that mostly-deserted road had combined with drunkenness and being stoned to dull in them what had been to start with a fanatical loyalty to their commander and to the cause. How all-consuming it had been! Stirring their hearts, burnishing their spirits, burning up their minds, overwhelming and drowning out their personalities. But once momentum was replaced with stasis, once endless ideological haranguing was replaced with silence and being ignored, their own thoughts soon came seeping back, and whatever vision it was that Makinde had inspired in them began to fade. What was the cause for which they had all been so ready, so eager to die? They had long ago stopped discussing it, and now none of them could remember. Something to do with freedom, they dimly recalled. But who of them was freer today than he had been before the war? Now all they wanted was simply to live. To forget what they had done and carry on as if there had been no war. It was in those last uncertain hours that they shared, for the first time, a little of what their lives had been.

Diamondz was an orphan. He never knew his father, and his mother had died of T.B. when he was eight. He had been a bright boy, but with no relatives prepared to pay for his schooling he hadn't been able to study. Owning no land, and having no desire to labour at farming, he had come to the city at the age of thirteen to make something of himself, but had soon enough found that without contacts or sponsors the only way forward for him was outside the law. He became a block boy, involved with drug-dealers, though he himself did not deal, or so he said. 'I was too young and small.' Instead he kept watch and ran errands, for which he was given tips. Somehow he saved enough money by the age of fifteen to put a downpayment on a motorbike, a red Sanya, his pride and joy. He kept the chrome mirror-clean, the paintwork buffed and free of blemishes, and the leather fed so it was smooth and supple as living skin.

One weekend he went to visit his deceased grandmother's sister, his great-aunt, a widow who he heard was living in extreme poverty way out in the bush. Out of Christian charity he planned to help her with money, he said, but Stanlake and the others assumed he had also wanted to flaunt the success he had made of himself without her family's help.

He never got there. On the way the bike broke down, and as he was struggling along the road with it, wondering what to do as he could not fix it himself and there would be no garage for many miles, rebel soldiers had appeared out of the forest and taken him.

The commander of the rebel unit that had abducted him took a fancy to Diamondz' motorbike and had it repaired. He tore around on it for a week, showing off. Then he hit a landmine and was killed. As he had been heartless and arrogant, and careless with the lives of the men under him, none of them mourned his passing. With a shrug they chose his replacement and carried on, leaving his scattered body-parts for the dogs to pick over, along with the debris of the motorbike.

That was, Diamondz reckoned, three years ago. A year or so after, they happened to pass through the village where his great-aunt had lived. It was deserted, and nothing but stumps and ashes remained.

Big Gun was from the country too, but unlike Diamondz, until the rebels came he had never been more than a mile from the place where he was born. His mother had been the mistress of a preacher in town, but when she fell pregnant with Big Gun the preacher's wife, enraged, drove her out, and she went back to the countryside to live with her parents. She was fifteen at the time, and her parents had been disappointed in her. Having failed to extract any financial support or compensation from the preacher to help raise him, they had shown Big Gun little love when he arrived. Yet he had found life with them pleasant enough, and had enjoyed caring for the goats and pigs and chickens and doing small tasks about the place.

One day when he was ten government soldiers arrived. They accused the villagers of shielding rebels, though Big Gun could not remember ever having seen any rebels, and talk of the government and its difficulties with the secessionists had seemed a faraway thing. The soldiers took the goats and pigs and chickens and left behind them threats of reprisals and fear.

That night gunfire was heard in the distance. It went on into the next day, sounding further away. A week later the government soldiers fell back, burning as they went so the rebels would have nowhere to rest their heads. Nor would the villagers whose homes the soldiers destroyed, but the army considered the people of the village little better than the rebels, and told them they should be grateful to be alive. Then they left.

Afraid and uncertain, the villagers didn't know what to do for the best. Some harvested what of their crops had not been burnt or despoiled; others gave in to despair and became apathetic. And then the rebels came out of the forest, red-eyed, ragged and crazy as devils. Big Gun did not tell the others what he had told Stanlake about what happened next, just that he too had been taken away.

Blondie was a town boy. His parents were comfortably off, and he had received a good education. Life had been sweet, studying for his Senior School Certificate, partying with schoolfriends, smoking weed and dating girls. Keeping up with his studies had been his biggest challenge, and chasing this or that girl his biggest problem. Then the rebels came.

'We used to be nice people, you know?' he said sadly. 'Now all that seems like fairytales. As I say these things, it's like I'm making it up.'

The others nodded. Still none of them revealed their real names: even in the face of death something had to be held back.

Another hour went by. Two more trucks passed. As the barrier was still down the Beasts merely stood stiffly to attention under the awning, their rifles hefted to their shoulders. The vehicles barely slowed as they barrelled through the gap in the tyre-wall.

In the back of the second truck, which was uncovered, were many wounded soldiers. They had received some medical attention but the rain had drenched them and they lay like sacks, blank-eyed, with limbs thrust out at odd angles like hacked branches. The red of their seeping blood stood out starkly against the white of the bandages. At least they hadn't been abandoned in the field by their commanders: that was something, the Beasts agreed later. But it wasn't much. Wheels churning muddy water up into their arches, the trucks laboured on. Then they were gone.

Stanlake, Diamondz, Big Gun and Blondie stood easy, not knowing what to do next. Nothing else happened and no more trucks came. After a while Diamondz went inside to boil water on the stove and make them all tea. There was no condensed milk or sugar left, and the tea tasted bitter. They stood outside under the awning, sipping from tin mugs, waiting. Minutes bled into hours, morning became afternoon. Still no more trucks came and their unease grew.

In the late afternoon the rain slackened. It was a relief, a lessening of pressure both physical and mental, and though it made no real difference to their situation they relaxed a little and stopped straining to hear above the clatter on the roof, the creaking of the toads and insects, and the furtive pattering of drips and raindrops on the forest's billion sodden leaves, the sounds of nearing war.

The rain stopped, and in the boiling humidity the ground began to steam. It seemed somehow to mark to Stanlake and the others some larger shift in things, and their talk turned once more to what they should do.

'If we go, go where?' said Blondie.

'To our homes?' Big Gun's suggestion had a hopeful

inflection to it.

'No,' said Diamondz. 'Our homes are gone. And even if we could go back to them,' he added, 'do you know the way from here?'

Big Gun shook his head.

'Wherever we go,' said Stanlake, 'the question is, should we go together, or separately?'

'I do not want to go alone,' said Big Gun.

'No,' agreed Blondie.

'Or me,' said Stanlake.

They fell silent then, thoughts of the homes they had had, the homes they could never return to, weighing like lead in their hearts.

It was as dusk was falling that they heard another vehicle on the road. Blondie and Big Gun were inside, preparing maize porridge; Stanlake and Diamondz were outside, standing guard. Mist hung across the road in ghost-curtains. Stanlake punched the underside of the awning. As the roar of the approaching engine grew louder he and Diamondz slipped their rifles from their shoulders. The cabin door opened and Blondie and Big Gun came out, weapons at the ready.

The vehicle that came barrelling out of the mist a moment later, its headlights tunnelling through the deepening twilight, was a jeep. It was travelling at high speed, bouncing and skidding along the rutted, flooded road, and seemed barely under the driver's control. As it sped towards the gap in the roadblock Stanlake saw it was Makinde's jeep, though in the deepening gloom he couldn't see who was at the wheel. Was it Makinde? Was he going to pass them by and leave them behind and vanish into the night forever?

At the last moment, as if out of a change of heart, the driver wrenched the wheel round and the jeep slewed off the road. It came straight at them, still going fast. Stanlake, Diamondz, Blondie and Big Gun stood there facing it down, muscles tensed, rifle-butts tight into their shoulders, ready to shoot or, if it failed to stop, to throw themselves aside. The jeep finally slithered to a halt when it was just ten feet from them. Dazzled though they were by its beams they kept their rifles trained on the driver's side of the windscreen. The headlights snapped off, and for a moment they could see nothing but ghost-lights flaring and floating on their retinas.

The driver's-side door swung open and a man got out. It was Makinde. Leaving the door hanging open and the engine running he strode up to them.

'Good, good, you are still here,' he said as the Beasts thumbed on their safety-catches, shouldered their rifles and snapped to attention. 'Unload the jeep.'

'Yes, oga,' they replied in unison, slinging their weapons over their backs and following him round to the rear of the vehicle.

'What is going on, oga?' Stanlake asked.

Makinde pulled back the canvas flap to reveal five or six rifles and four boxes of ammunition, a lidless plywood box with several old-looking grenades inside packed in straw, and a machine-gun and several spare magazines for it. 'This roadblock is the new frontline,' he said. 'Once I am through you must close it up again and let no-one else through.'

'Are the government forces near?' Big Gun asked as Stanlake passed him one of the ammo-boxes.

'I do not think they will reach here tonight,' Makinde said. But he glanced back along the road as if, despite his words, enemies might appear at any second. 'Quickly with this, enh?'

Within a minute the weapons and ammunition had been brought into the cabin, the rifles and machine-gun laid out on the cots to keep them dry and free of dirt. Your weapon is your lover, Makinde had said many times out in the forest, and now here they were, Makinde's Beasts, lovers of death with iron brides in their beds.

Makinde paced back and forth, his eyes darting, the muscles in his face twitching. Sweat blotted his uniform, and he smelt of stale beer and cheeba. 'You must defend this road,' he said. 'It is a vital route. The enemy must not win control of it or we are done for. We are counting on you. You must not let them get through.'

'But there are only four of us, oga,' Diamondz said hesitantly. 'It is not enough against a whole army.'

'Ah, but you are my Beasts!' Makinde said, and his bloodshot eyes glinted. 'You have great courage! And look!'

He gestured towards the cots. 'You have many weapons! You have grenades. You have ammo. And more than that, you have the hearts of warriors!'

'But still we are only four,' Stanlake said. 'However many weapons we have, we have only so many hands to hold them.'

Makinde turned on him. They were no longer the toys of his rhetoric, and he knew it. Strangled-looking veins squirmed across the gelid whites of his eyes and the irises were rimmed a dirty yellow. The pupils had a dull sheen, as if blooming with cataracts of the spirit. His fingers drummed on the pistol-holster at his hip, one-two-three, one-two-three, then he reached up fast for Stanlake's face. Stanlake flinched but didn't move to resist him. With two quick movements Makinde smeared the turquoise eye-shadow on Stanlake's eyelids outwards with his thumb. Still Stanlake didn't move, just kept his eyes on his commander's.

Makinde took a breath, and now his manner turned would-be sincere and grave. He put his hand on Stanlake's shoulder, gripped it and shook it. 'You must do what you can,' he said. 'Do as I trained you. Do your best. That is all any of us can do.'

He turned to the others. 'Just a little way on we have set up camp. I will go there now and send back reinforcements. I will come back myself. I will return with many men, and we will be there with you, fighting alongside you. Do not fear, Little Gun,' he said to Stanlake. 'You will not die alone.' He smiled a lightless smile. 'Now I will go. Close the barrier behind me. Anyone who comes from now on is an enemy. Kill them without hesitation.'

'Yes, oga,' they replied in unison.

'I will be back soon.'

'Yes, oga.'

They followed him outside and watched as he got back into the jeep, reversed a short way and turned. Gears crunched. The wheels spun in the mud, briefly gained purchase, jerked the jeep a foot forward, then spun again. Makinde stuck his head out of the window.

'What are you faggots looking at, enh? Standing there like whores no-one wants. Get over here and push!'

Big Gun hung back, but Diamondz, Stanlake and Blondie came forward, and though they got sprayed with mud in the process, the three of them managed to shove the jeep back up onto the road. Once it was on the level it lurched away from them. It kept going, bumping along slowly, and they watched as it passed through the gap in the roadblock. A minute later the night had swallowed it up.

Wearily they rebuilt the tyre barrier. Once that was done they returned to the cabin. It was unbearably hot inside, so they doused the oil-lamp and dragged chairs and boxes outside and sat beneath the awning in the dark, gazing out into the enemy-concealing shadows, rifles propped against their thighs or leaning to hand against the wall behind them.

'I do not think he will come back,' Blondie said after a while.

Diamondz nodded. 'I think there is no camp and they have kept going. No-one will be sent to help us.'

'Then should we stay?' Stanlake asked. He and Big Gun naturally deferred to the two older boys.

'I don't know,' Blondie said. He turned to Diamondz. 'What do you think, man?'

Diamondz hawked and spat. 'I think that fucker would betray us,' he said. 'Those weapons are shit. I think he only left them so we would believe we could do a good job fighting, so we would think he must be sending people back or he wouldn't leave them. But he won't.'

'I agree,' said Blondie.

'Perhaps the government forces will not come this way,' said Big Gun.

'Who knows what way anyone is going,' said Stanlake. 'But I think they have left us behind to be swept up like rubbish.'

'Sh!' said Big Gun.

They all fell silent and listened. The forest seemed alive with furtive movements that were both purposive and threatening. Sweat trickled down Stanlake's sides in itchy tracks and his mouth was dry.

'I need a smoke,' Blondie said hoarsely.

'No,' said Stanlake. 'We need our wits. And if they are somewhere round here but guessing where we are they could smell it from a long way.'

'Not in the rain.'

'Still.'

'What did you hear?' Diamondz asked Big Gun.

'Maybe nothing,' Big Gun said nervily. The others exhaled.

'If Makinde was the last,' Stanlake said, 'we wouldn't hear gunfire.'

'Or trucks,' Blondie said, 'because trucks follow, they don't lead.'

'Just a stealthy approach on foot-o,' Diamondz said.

They stared out into the impenetrable blackness of the forest. The night sky above their heads was tented in with cloud, and now the lamp was out there were no light-sources anywhere. No moon, not even stars.

'We should fall back into the forest,' Diamondz said. 'Take what we can and hide there and watch the cabin. If they come they will expect us to be inside. If they see we are gone and we keep quiet, then they will think we went with the others and just go away.'

The others nodded agreement, though they felt no desire to abandon shelter until it was absolutely necessary. It was unlikely the night would pass without another violent downpour, and they wanted to keep themselves and their weapons and whatever supplies they took with them dry for as long as possible.

But how long was that?

'Let us get our things together at once,' Blondie said. 'That way, whenever we do leave, we can leave in an instant.'

'Little Gun, keep watch,' Diamondz said. Stanlake nodded and the others disappeared inside to pack. His rifle heavy in his hands, he surveyed the wet wall of the forest. With every passing second the feeling that the enemy was drawing near intensified in him, and his skin prickled.

'Hey.'

He looked round. It was Big Gun, calling softly from the doorway. He reached out and handed Stanlake a knotted tangle of necklaces, chains and pendants, and a spare clip of bullets for his Kalash. Stanlake slipped the clip into his breast pocket, shoved the jewellery into one of his trouser pockets, and went back to watching. Muted clattering and banging about came from within, and each clumsy attempt to marry speed with care added to his rapidly rising levels of anxiety: couldn't they be quieter?

Now it was Diamondz' turn to shove his head round the door. He was wearing the tiara. 'Do you know how to fire a machine-gun, Little Gun?' he asked. Stanlake shook his head. Diamondz vanished back inside.

At the exact moment the cabin door banged shut there was a sharp cracking sound and something passed close by Stanlake's right ear. He snapped his head round in time to see it hit the breeze block wall behind him with a thud and puff of concrete-dust.

Stanlake dropped flat to the ground. 'They are here!' he shouted as gunfire exploded from the forest, raking the cabin wall at waist-height above his head. Taking only the roughest of aims he returned fire into a darkness now flecked with flashes of killing light, at the same time squirming backwards as fast as he could towards the cabin doorway, all the while keeping pressed as flat to the ground as possible.

Chapter Nine

Within moments two of the Beasts were at the windows above Stanlake's head, jabbing the matting screens aside with the muzzles of their rifles and discharging them explosively into the enemy-shielding darkness of the forest. Someone inside the cabin evidently knew how to use the machine-gun, because seconds later a third person raked the wall of trees beyond the small clearing with bullets; at about groin height, Stanlake judged, from the way the vegetation was chopped about by the back-and-forth sweep of destruction. Whoever was firing the machine-gun kept his finger on the trigger till the magazine was empty: the noise tore through the night, then stopped abruptly with a click.

There was no immediate return of fire from the tree-line, or shouting of orders; nor was there any other sound, the insects of the forest having been shocked into temporary silence.

Stanlake skittered backwards on his knees and elbows, flat and fast as a lizard. Keeping his gun-sights trained on the forest wall he thrust the cabin door open with a heel and squirmed backwards through the doorway. Once inside he swung the door closed and jumped up into a squatting position. Blondie and Big Gun, who was the one using the machine-gun, were at the far window; Diamondz was at the one next to the door. Like Stanlake they were squatting on their haunches, and their chests were heaving. The breeze block was solid, and no bullets had penetrated it, though a few had come in through the windows and hit the wall behind.

Keeping as low as he could, Blondie peered out over the sill.

'What are they doing?' Diamondz asked hoarsely as, next to him, Big Gun rammed a fresh magazine into the side of the machine-gun.

'I cannot see,' Blondie said.

'It does not matter,' Big Gun said. Recklessly he stood up and, framed in the window, sprayed more bullets into the forest wall, not stopping until the second magazine was empty too. 'Give me another,' he said, dropping back into a squat. Stanlake reached over to the cot where the magazines were piled and passed him one. Big Gun wrenched out the empty magazine, threw it aside and clicked the new one into place. Then he stood and fired again, just a brief burst this time. 'So they know we have plenty-plenty ammo left,' he said, squatting back down.

Still there was no returning fire. 'What do you think they are doing?' asked Blondie. 'No way we killed them all-o.'

Suddenly it was obvious to Stanlake: 'They will be circling round to attack us from a different angle,' he said. 'We must go at once. Out of the back windows.'

The others agreed instantly. The cabin had two windows on the side that faced away from the road. At a nod from Diamondz, Stanlake and Blondie moved to the right-hand window, reached up and ripped away a length of netting that had been nailed over it to keep out mosquitoes and other insects. Leaving Big Gun standing sentry Diamondz wormed his way over and joined them. Half-rising he stuck his head out of the window, looking first in one direction, then the other. No shots came and evidently he saw no-one, because without another word, with his rifle in his hand he clambered over the sill.

A moment later he reached back in to help Stanlake climb through after him. Stanlake took his hand and let Diamondz pull him up and out. Blondie quickly followed. Big Gun let off a final burst of machine-gun fire out of the front right window then hurried to join them. He struggled to get up onto the sill, as not only was the machine-gun cumbersome, he was also still wearing the red sequinned dress. He was awkwardly dragging it up into a tangle round his hips when Stanlake and Blondie reached in, took hold of him by the elbows, and lifted him bodily through the window. When they set him down on the ground outside he was holding the machine-gun at the ready. Stanlake saw he had jammed a spare magazine down the front of the dress where breasts would be.

In silence and without a backward glance they made their way into the forest, going in single file and choosing a slantways path that would lead them away both from where they guessed the government soldiers were circling round to, and the rebels' road. The rain began to fall, pattering lightly on the leaves at first, but quickly turning drenchingly heavy.

'Perhaps they will go in the cabin for shelter and stay there and not follow us,' Big Gun said, shaking diamond droplets from his hair and wiping his wet face with his hands.

'The commanders will stay in the dry,' said Diamondz. 'The rest will be sent on after us. Let us pick up the pace.'

They did so, jogging along. Diamondz led the way, followed by Blondie, then Big Gun, with Stanlake at the rear. The ground was slippery and tangled with roots and under-growth, and they were following no trail. Big Gun stumbled: the machine-gun was a heavy weight for his small frame, and he jammed its muzzle in the dirt as he tried to save himself from falling flat on his face. Stanlake caught his arm and helped him up, then took a moment to help him sling the weapon across his back so he could run better. Impulsively Big Gun took his hand, and for a little while they ran like that, hand in hand, behind Diamondz and Blondie through the wet, black forest.

Without moon or stars or reference-points of any sort, since the ground was level and in its vegetable density featureless and uniform, it was impossible for them to keep going in a straight line. The fear began to grow on them that they would accidentally circle straight back into the rifle-sights of the enemy. They slowed down, and began to pay more attention to moving as silently as possible.

It was strange to be away from the cabin that had been their home for – how long? Six months, at least – and find themselves toiling through the largely unfamiliar forest around it. Here the spirits dwelt, and the beasts of the forest; and here too the enemy lay hidden. The only light was the firefly luminescence that came from the watches on Diamondz' arm, and in the absence of context it was hard to tell if those darting dots were near or far away.

After about an hour's slow going they came to a halt by a crowded grove of banana trees. Pushing through the wet, furled leaves they found themselves in what felt like a hidden place among the stems, a shelter in its enclosedness, though it offered little protection from the rain above. Diamondz brought out a bottle of whiskey, took a swallow, and offered it round. It reached Stanlake last, and by then there wasn't much left. He swigged, then spared a slop for the spirits of the place before returning the bottle to Diamondz. Diamondz noticed but didn't comment: they needed all the help they could get. After a brief rest, they went on.

For a time the going was slow and difficult, as they were still having to force their way through extremely dense undergrowth, then they struck a trail. For better or worse they took it, relieved that at least for a while progress would be easier. Stanlake was still at the rear of the line. The feeling they were being observed began to grow on him again. He reached ahead and touched Big Gun's elbow. Big Gun looked round.

'I think we are being watched,' Stanlake said quietly.

'Yes,' Big Gun agreed.

At that moment gunfire broke out on their left. With a gasp Big Gun went down. As bullets tore into the foliage around them Stanlake threw himself onto the ground next to him. Though he could no longer see them in the dark, he thought Blondie and Diamondz had run on ahead. There was no sound of them returning fire.

'Are you alright?' he hissed to Big Gun. Big Gun didn't answer. Stanlake reached out for him in the dark and accidentally struck his face, one finger jabbing Big Gun hard in the eye. Stanlake withdrew his hand sharply, but Big Gun didn't respond. Stanlake reached out again and in the blind dark explored Big Gun's unmoving lips, nose, eyebrow, cheek. His fingertips slid into a crevasse below Big Gun's right cheekbone that should not have been there. It was warm and wet, soft yet needled with shards and splinters. Raindrops struck Big Gun's open eyes and still he didn't move. Stanlake bent over him and kissed him on the forehead. Then, keeping low, he left Big Gun and went on, following the way he thought Blondie and Diamondz had gone.

There was a further flurry of gunshots, coming from the same direction as the first. Stanlake hoped it was just random fire intended to intimidate; and that, crouched low as he was, he couldn't be seen. He moved as fast as he could.

To begin with, getting away was Stanlake's only thought. But after a while he began to look back, to see if by the flash of gunpowder he could work out where the enemy was firing from. If they are a small patrol we have a chance, he thought. They do not know how many of us there are, or how well we are armed.

More shots cracked out, and he began to see that they were all coming from a slight rise, not far off, where the trees were less dense. He reckoned there couldn't be more than four or five men up there, close together, firing. A little way ahead the sound of returning gunfire broke out: evidently Blondie and Diamondz had had the same idea as him and had also located the enemy's vantage-point. Bent almost double, Stanlake hurried along what had become a narrow defile in the hope of joining them.

A half-minute later he was throwing himself down next to his comrades and aligning his rifle with theirs. They didn't ask where Big Gun was. He watched for the next flash of enemy fire, and when it came he fired back.

The firefight went on intermittently for perhaps an hour. First Blondie, then Stanlake, then Diamondz ran out of bullets.

'I could go back for the machine-gun,' said Stanlake.

'Could you find the way?' asked Blondie.

'Forget about all that,' Diamondz said when Stanlake hesitated. 'We must go right now.'

Unlike Diamondz, Blondie and Stanlake it seemed the enemy wasn't short of ammunition: the firing continued as they tried to slip away along the defile. Two or three rounds hit tree-trunks just above their heads and, though he was crouched on his haunches, one hit Diamondz in the side of his chest, flinging him sideways to the ground. There he lay shuddering and heaving as his punctured lungs collapsed and his split, spasming heart pumped out into his body-cavity. Stanlake gripped his hand in the dark. Less than a minute later Diamondz was dead. Stanlake took the tiara from his head and jammed it onto his own shaved skull. Then he ran, following Blondie he thought, though soon he was just blundering forward through the slapping wetness of leaves and the eye-jabbings of twigs. Something scampered through the branches above his head, a monkey, probably, disturbed by the nocturnal firefight, or a spirit, friendly or unfriendly, who knew.

He threw his now-useless rifle aside and ran faster. Caution would not save him; speed might. Eventually he ran head-first into a tree-trunk in the dark and fell back, stunned. Breathless and concussed he lay on the sodden ground, shivering despite the smothering heat. He could feel a trickle of blood run down from where the inner rim of the tiara had been rammed into the flesh of his forehead.

He stared up at the black undersides of the leaves. There was no point in trying to go any further: he was now so disorientated that every step was as likely to take him towards his enemies as away from them. Better to rest up here and wait for daybreak and the possibility of working out where he was, and therefore which way he should go. Some distance off he heard yelling, over and over. No words, just bursts, expulsions of agony. Then it stopped.

He propped himself up on his elbows then hauled himself backwards so he could rest his back against the trunk of the tree he had run into, heedless of ants, centipedes, spiders and scorpions. He thought of Anansi and his tricks and wiles. He thought of his grandfather, who had died when he was only five, who he had barely known but he remembered had told him stories. If he could sleep he might be guided by a dream: his grandfather might aid him. But now Pacific had joined the older man in the village of the dead, who knew what anger his grandfather might hold in his heart; who knew what tale of blood his son had whispered in his ear. Stanlake closed his eyes but no sleep came, just a zoning out that did little to refresh him.

The insects fell quiet shortly before dawn. Birds began to chatter. Stanlake's surroundings started to emerge from the gloom, though at first all he saw was the dense and pathless forest walling him in on every side. Brushing a fly from his cheek he rubbed his face. He was hungry now, and thirsty. With an effort he struggled to his feet. He reached up and bent down one then another of the large, furled leaves of a nearby banana tree, in the grooves of which rainwater had gathered, and managed to drink enough to hydrate himself. His resilience and wits returning, he looked about him more intently.

Studying the ground he saw only his own footprints: no-one else, friend or enemy, had come there recently. In one direction the land rose slightly, and he decided he would go that way, in the hope of getting a wider view of the territory around him, of which at present he could see nothing. Carefully he pushed his way through the tangled under-growth, doing the least damage he could, trying to leave no trail. Wet leaves and muscularly-twining suckers trailed over his face and arms and chest. Backlit by the rising sun everything glowed a vivid light green, and the dark earth steamed.

A little way along he struck a track that ran parallel to the rise he was heading for, which seemed to be less a hill than a ridge. Many booted feet had passed along the track since the last rain, so within the last twelve hours. He hesitated, then changed his plan and began to follow them, moving warily.

After perhaps an hour, during which time he heard and saw no-one, and the sun had boiled the water from the forest, he came to a clearing where the track he was following converged with several others.

There, under the tall trees in that non-place, lay Blondie. He had been hacked to pieces with a machete or axe. Flies crawled greedily over his butchered flesh. The peroxide hair on his damaged head was now piebald red. Crows had already taken his eyes. His hands had been hacked off, his brace of watches taken, the pale and latticed imprints of their straps still visible on the now blood-laced skin of his fore-arms. One foot was gone. Stanlake looked down on him. Who lived, who died: it meant nothing. Except that he, being still alive, had to carry on until his life was done.

So he walked, heading always as far as he could east-wards, for his memory of when he was first taken by the rebels was that they had been going west. East was hope. East was home, though he put all thoughts of what he would find there, if he ever did find it, out of his mind.

Those had been hallucinatory days, walking with the spirits and the ancestors, starving and soaked repeatedly by sudden deluges. Thunder rumbled, lightning lanced and he toiled on. It was then that he had first spoken with the dead Masks, and, as the drugs he had been using daily for the last two years passed from his system, they answered him.

As he walked, the rainy season ended.

From time to time he heard gunfire, mortar explosions, vehicle-engines, shouting and yelling, and he skirted round it, keeping his distance and crouching low. He passed through many villages, most of them burned, all of them deserted, now only for ghosts to dwell in. In some of the huts were the dead, abandoned unburied, and in some compounds sleek-looking dogs foraged. He spoke to no-one so heard no news. Had the rebels lost? He doubted the war would have such a clean and decisive ending, and in any case he could no longer imagine a world that was not at war. He kept the tiara on his head, wearing it like a talisman, and perhaps it was, for after a fortnight, during which time he had avoided all human contact, he came to an area he thought he recognised. Pressing on, the possibility became a certainty, and soon he was taking familiar paths.

It was then that the fear came on him. Up until that point home had been a symbol of hope, abstract. Now it was real. What would he find? Perhaps only horror. Undoubtedly he had left horror behind him the day the rebels took him. But there was nowhere else for him to go, and so he kept on, though more slowly now as his uneasiness grew. Noon came and went and still he saw no-one. No-one walking, cycling, driving cattle. No-one working in the fields.

Then he heard the sound he had been dreading: trucks on the road, coming up behind him. Government forces or rebels, it made no difference: he must not be found by them. He left the road and barely had time to conceal himself in a nearby patch of scrub before a convoy of five trucks came into view, carrying rebel troops and going fast. Keeping crouched low Stanlake peered out at them, searching chiefly for Makinde, but also for any other officers or soldiers he recognised. To his relief there was no sign of his former commander, and none of the other faces were familiar to him. Were they heading towards conflict, or away from it? None of the soldiers seemed wounded: that suggested towards.

At a fork in the road the trucks swept round to the south, away from Stanlake's village. The moment they were out of sight he returned to the road and, reaching the same fork, took the other way, which now ran straight ahead. Home was less than two miles away. The sky was wide and grey above him. Emotions roiled in his chest. There were things ahead he could not face that he would nonetheless have to face; things that required a different courage from killing, from taking orders no matter what, from risking your life for your comrades.

The tiara was still on his head. He scarcely noticed it now.

The village would be deserted. They would all have fled. No.

They would be waiting for him, for revenge. They would take hold of him and hack him up. No.

They would all be dead, their innards devoured by dogs.

The army would be there.

The rebels would be there.

Oh, my brothers help me, he prayed. And as if a hand had touched him gently on the shoulder, the thought came to him that somehow things would be alright. It seemed to be expressed in Big Gun's voice, or perhaps Matthew's voice through Big Gun's lips: he thought he felt them brushing his ear but he didn't look round. Spirits do not care to be seen.

He was on the outskirts of the village now. There was no sign of life, but it hadn't been burned. The mud-brick walls of the huts and the compounds, and the thatch on the roofs were all intact. Looking closer he saw small signs of deterioration and decay: things had not been renewed, or not as recently as was customary. But it hadn't been destroyed. Only the wooden statue Patrick had carved and placed by the road at the entrance to the village, a guardian spirit in the half-comical shape of a guinea-fowl, had been hacked down.

In one of the compounds a small fire burned brightly, making little smoke, and a pot of water bubbled above it on a trivet. No-one seemed to be tending the fire or the pot, though he sensed life in a hut nearby. If he went into the hut he would see a face he knew, who had once known him. The thought was unbearable. He went on.

If I need news I will go back and ask, he thought. It was odd: he couldn't recall whose home it was.

The other compounds were empty. No people, no animals. He didn't smell corpses.

Within five minutes he had reached his own yard. It was so little changed it was like a dream.

In the distance came the sound of gunfire. Was it coming his way? It was hard to tell. Perhaps he should have kept his gun after all. True he had run out of bullets, but at least he could threaten with it. But then perhaps he had been watched walking the road, and the unseen watchers only hadn't shot him because all they saw was just some ordinary boy without a gun.

Perhaps his father was watching over him. He wished he could believe it was so.

At the threshold of his compound he hesitated. More gunfire came, definitely closer: only minutes away now. Whatever he found or failed to find here he would have to move on without delay. A bowed figure dressed in blue and white emerged from the doorway of his parents' hut and straightened up.

Yes, it was his mother.

He raised his hand in a weak salutation. She saw him and she flinched. He never forgot it. A machine-gun chattered briefly. She turned her head in the direction of the sound. From the same direction came shouting. There was no time. He came forward jerkily, stopping a few feet from where she stood. 'We must go at once,' he said. 'The soldiers are coming.'

'I will pack a few things,' she said, and turned and went back into the hut.

'There is no time.' Glancing over at the line of trees beyond the compound wall he approached the building that had once been his home and leaned in through the doorway.

His mother was bent over something busily. 'Leave all that-o!' he said urgently. 'They will be here any second!'

Poppy ignored him, deftly gathering up the corners of a square of fabric around some hastily thrown-together items of clothing, food and other bits and pieces. A framed photograph. Stanlake hung back, his heart thudding in his chest so hard it was choking him. He would never enter this house again. Its completeness tore at his soul. Finding a ruin would have been so much easier: if his home had been destroyed as his innocence had been destroyed it would have been final and therefore simple. He would have been a Beast forever. But no: here it was, the same as when he left it. Where did his father lie? He wanted to ask his mother, but that was sentimentality, and there was no time.

'We have to go, Mummy,' he said, and the word sounded strange to him, foreign. He reached out for her and the movement was the same movement he had made to grab hold of Florence in the back of Makinde's jeep. Every move he made, every action, was poisoned.

He could hear the trucks now – they could only be moments away – but at last Poppy was ready. He took the bundle from her as she exited the house and hand in hand they hurried across the compound. From another compound, the one where the fire had been burning, they heard a woman scream.

They ran.

'I'm going to church now,' Poppy said, bringing Stanlake back to the present.

'Okay.'

'Are you sure you won't come?' She was dressed all in white, and her hair was covered by a high white wrap.

'I have nothing to wear,' he said, half-smiling, half-disdainful, perhaps trying to goad her into challenging his make-up, his unnaturalness in the eyes of her Lord. She made a face, put on her coat, and left.

The instant she was gone exhaustion swept over him. With an effort he pushed himself up from the kitchen table, staggered through to his bedroom and collapsed face-down on the mattress. Rolling onto his back he closed his eyes.

Almost at once he felt as if he was floating on blackness, tilting and rising, being born up gently and set and carried on shoulders as a coffin is carried by those who love the dead one inside. Here, though, the order was inverted: here it was the dead who bore up the living, his Masks lifting him. The heads of the two spirits who led the way flanked his head, their ears brushing his ears, and they were singing of yams and milk and blood.

By the time Poppy found a place at the back of the packed meeting hall the sermon was already underway. Reverend Obasanjo was shiny with sweat. The microphone he held delicately in his gold-ringed hand was spattered with spittle, and the speakers screwed into the low ceiling above his head crackled from the liquid electrolytes that had infiltrated its inner workings. Though heated only by the radiance of bodies the rammed room was almost unpleasantly hot, and the faces of the worshippers were sheened and glowing. Behind the Reverend the organist, a lean, bearded man with an Afro who wore traditional blue-and-green robes and opaque sunglasses, pointed up his words with stings on the keyboard, and the congregation responded to his exhortations with full-throated Amens and Hallelujahs and Praise Jesuses.

'My brothers and sisters,' the Reverend was saying, 'people in this country, people in this country are *blind*.' He pointed with his index finger at his own staring eyes.

'Amen!' someone called out.

'Blind to the spirit of the *Lord*.'

'Praise Him!'

'They dwell in darkness and ignorance and confusion!'

'Preach it!'

'Pity them!'

'Yes, Lord!'

'Pity them, for they are bound for the Pit! They are bound for eternal damnation!'

'Hallelujah!'

'In this country of no belief there is a belief – '

'Have faith!'

'– a misguided belief that *things just happen*. They just

happen for no reason whatsoever!'

'God moves in mysterious ways!' a woman cried out.

'Yes, my sister.' The Reverend took a moment to mop his face with a hand-towel proffered him by one of the ladies of the church who most intimidated Poppy, Mrs Ige. The towel was silky white and as brightly clean as a towel at a top hotel, as transcendently clean as Christ's winding-cloth. 'His miracles to perform, yes, that is so. But today, my brothers and sisters, today I am talking about' – and here he paused dramatically – '*Witches.*'

He pushed his voice down on the word so it came rumbling from the speakers, and at that the congregation ceased their responses and fell silent. The organist added no flourish, in fact withdrew his hands from the keyboard and folded them in his lap. This was serious business: there was to be no cathartic air of performance to release the faithful from the weight of it.

'Witches and demons,' Reverend Obasanjo continued. 'We know, all of us here know, that in God's plan there cannot be chance. He knows all and sees all. He planned all. He created all. So there cannot be chance. Come, sit and listen.'

With audible creakings and flutterings of fans the congregation sank onto the close-packed rows of folding chairs. Those at the back, like Poppy, had no chairs and continued to stand.

'These people who believe in chance, in randomness, they live in a state of confusion. They think a lottery ticket will solve all their problems. But nothing will solve their problems except faith.'

This statement was met with general nodding and a few muted Amens.

'Still,' the Reverend went on, 'we have free will. God took Adam and said to him, "Do not eat of the fruit of this tree", and Adam – though yes, he was tempted by Eve as many men have been tempted by a woman, who was herself tempted by the Serpent – Adam chose to eat that fruit. So we have been given free will: to choose to do good, or, in our weakness, to choose to do evil. But it is not that that I am speaking of today.'

By now there was so little air left in the room that everything had a sort of glinting intensity. Poppy listened, they all listened as they did every service, intently, waiting for this: for the moment the Reverend would affirm their faith as the one true faith, their perceptions as the true perceptions. He would lift them above those around them who toiled in darkness and ignorance, and give them for that brief period of grace a superior vantage-point; and then he would humble them again in the face of the greatness and terror of the Lord and His works, and send them out chastened and purified into the night. But tonight's talk was different.

'Things do not just happen,' the Reverend said emphatically. 'Behind every action there is a reason. Behind every deed there is a will. *Every* deed, good or bad. And there are people, people who have turned from the path of righteousness, people who have turned their face against God, people who practise *wickedness*, brothers and sisters. And when I talk about wickedness I don't just mean everyday wickedness. I don't mean a little bit of greed, a little moment of lust or envy. The Lord will forgive us these small-small transgressions if we come to Him in sufficient humility and with our hearts open and bare. He knows we are not perfect, and He forgives us our trespasses. No, what I am talking about today is that class of persons who seek intercourse with the forces of the damned. I am talking about witches, brothers and sisters. Witches!'

The Reverend's eyes moved challengingly round the room, and though they did not on this occasion meet Poppy's, still she felt revealed to him, for she, like all of them, had grown up with tales of witches, rumours of witches, fear of witches. They flew at night. They hung upside-down from trees like bats. They poisoned wells, and animals, and children. They were all over the place, and numerous. They killed their own children to gain power from the spirits. They invited spirits in and were wilfully possessed. Even children could knowingly invite demons in and become witches and do great harm. Faith in Jesus Christ saved you from that. He protected you from that, if you only gave yourself to Him. Things don't just happen, the Reverend had said, and in that intoxicatingly airless room Poppy had agreed, and she too had muttered, 'Amen.' But later she thought, Yes, they do.

'Why is your daughter answering you back? Why is your son lounging around the house not working and taking drugs and speaking insolently? Why does he not care if he is sent to jail without women where homosexuality occurs?' A susurrus of disapproval passed through the congregation at the mention of sexual deviance. 'Why is your daughter acting like a slut? Why is she going down to the clinic for venereal diseases or having abortions?'

Poppy's skin prickled. Suddenly she felt sure that the Reverend was addressing specific people in the room, people who had come to him with problems, though he did not identify them individually or by name.

'These are not our traditions. These are not our values. Where have they come from? Television, yes. The internet, yes. Secularism, yes. But there are deeper things, my brothers and sisters, things that were there before TV and satellite and Facebook and mobile phones. You don't need an iPhone for the Devil to whisper in your ear. Reality shows won't tell you how to identify that witch who is pretending to be your friend but behind your back is doing you harm.'

'How can we know?' a strangled-sounding man's voice broke out.

'Tell us, father!' a woman called.

'Pray!' the Reverend exhorted. 'Pray for guidance!'

As if by prearrangement the organist added a rousing flourish on his keyboard, and the tempo of the sermon shifted.

'Father, you know!' someone cried out. 'You know how!'

'God has gifted me,' the Reverend said, raising his voice above what was now a swirling swell of organ music and mopping his face again. 'Yes, my brothers and sisters, He has given me that knowledge.'

'Praise Him!'

'Come to me and I will help you!'

At once a worried-looking woman rose from her seat. She approached Mrs Ige, who stood at the Reverend's right hand, stately in a headwrap like a white flame threaded with silver and gold. Mrs Ige took the woman's hand in her own bejewelled one and, with a concerned expression on her face, listened to the urgently-whispered words. Was it her son who courted jail, Poppy wondered, or her daughter who was being promiscuous? Joining in with the others she began to clap her hands to the building syncopation of the music. Mrs Ige and Mrs Bankole were the intercessionaries. No, the gate-keepers. She couldn't imagine sharing her problems with them in order to get to speak to the Reverend. And they would want money, she presumed. Dash. No, not dash: a donation to church funds. But either way she could ill afford it. She looked for Lucy but couldn't see her in the crowded room. Surely she was there, though: Lucy never missed a service.

She let the music lift her and carry her thoughts and fears and worries away. It got harder every time.

Fuck this shit, Evill thought to himself. It was gone two a.m. and the rain had begun again. He could shelter from it in one of the tunnels, of course, but the thought of lurking about in the stinking dark like one of the zombies revolted him. He had shifted most of the gear anyway, and the idea of waiting on the need or whim of some junkie loser who might not even show up sent the rage that was always within him surging to the surface. If anyone had come then he would have murked them just to release it.

The African bwoy.

He could of stabbed me but he didn't.

I gotta sort it.

How?

Fuck this.

He recovered the bag of unsold pills and wraps from its hiding-place, shoved it in a pocket and left the underpass. Where to go, though? Solid's, where the Crew would be chilling, or home? But that was like asking, what do you want, too much or not enough? He wondered what the youth's drum was like. The layout of the flat would be exactly the same as Solid's, but beyond that? Warm, probably. Colourful, he imagined. What floor did the bwoy live on? There was no easy way of finding out. Even if Evill had known his name no-one put their names in the slots by the entry-buzzer; no-one wanted to give their business away to random strangers.

The Cardinals were twenty-two storeys high.

If he watched the lobby long enough, eventually the bwoy would have to come out.

Then what?

Evill felt, in some way he couldn't explain, that the bwoy could be a way out of something. A way into something.

Perhaps.

He imagined cutting himself. When he was fifteen he had started cutting his arms. That was after he realised he preferred boys to girls. Then he discovered violence against others and stopped cutting himself. The scars were now just tiny pale lines that didn't absorb the sunlight properly. Perhaps too much light had leaked out of him that way for the brownness to ever be replenished: the skin could never forget the loss, however bright the sun got. But he was safe: only a loving eye would ever notice those ghostly lateral lines, and in his life there was no such eye.

Evill didn't think of himself as gay, or even bisexual, because he only fucked girls. The need that was at the core of him was totally detached from the mask he wore for the world, and so his life was both pure and grotesquely twisted, and he knew it. Whenever anyone mentioned love something icy trickled down inside him.

Solid, Pit-Bull and Cuts might as well be faggots too, he often thought, for all the pleasure they got from fucking women, for all the desire they had to spend time with women.

He would go home.

He sparked up a joint and started to walk faster, hood up, hunching his shoulders against the rain. The sensi dulled his mind but sharpened its edges: the usual paranoid buzz. No-one was about. As he made his way down a quiet residential street he heard the sound up ahead of a dustbin being tipped over. A fox darted out of a garden and across the road. On the far side it stopped and looked back at him, its damp fur spiky and sparkling.

You and me both, he thought. We got our noses in the garbage, looking for the good shit. A word flashed into his mind then: scavenger. Anger followed it. He looked round for something to throw at the fox but nothing was to hand. When he looked back, it had gone.

The walk home seemed endless.

Stanlake was asleep but twitching like a cat. His eyeballs moved rapidly beneath their lids and his face was greasy with sweat. He was back in the forest, in the lightless night, and rifle-fire was cracking out on every side. There were trees all around him – he could hear the bullets thudding into their guessed-at trunks – but it was cold, cold as the U.K., and he had the sense of being in an underground tunnel: there was an earthy smell, a smell like corpses. Perhaps what seemed to be tree-branches were in reality roots? He had a sense he was making a descent. Was this death? Beneath his feet was concrete, not earth, the concrete of the underpass. Gunfire exploded around him.

Awake and not awake, seeing and not seeing, he rolled off his mattress combat-fast. In a single sinuous movement he drew the Glock from its hiding-place and slid his finger round the trigger. For a moment he crouched there, looking around him, assessing threat but not seeing reality. From the cool weight of the gun in his hand solidity spread out into the room but in his head rifles were still firing, he was still in the forest. Barely aware he was naked he slipped out into the hall, his movements economical as good engineering, though inside the machine his gut was churning, and his heart thudded and his head buzzed, clogged with bees and honey and venom. Once he and Matthew and Robert had climbed a tree to get at a beesnest and they had all got stung. He was in the hall in the tunnel in the forest in the realm of the ancestors in the passageways of the dead. Veins radiated out from his temples into the vibrating black, veins and no arteries because veins carried the blood out, arteries returned it, and no blood was returning to him. Only the blood of others could replenish him. Hadn't he always known that?

He was at the front door of the flat.

He didn't know where he was.

The rifle-shots were nails driven into his screaming head.

He was in the forest. He was turning the key in the front

door. Wet banana-leaves brushed his bare shoulders. His eyes were wild and his throat was dry. Now he was in the lobby-area outside the flat, naked, the Glock ready in his hand, the floor-tiles icy beneath the soles of his cringing feet. A fire-door gave onto the stairwell. He pulled it open. It opened onto death and horror and slantwise grave-mouths.

He was about to step into the stairwell when he felt a presence behind and a little way above him. One of his Mask brothers, he knew without turning, and that broke the moment. The echoing shots shrank, resolved themselves into the sound of a girl's high heels ringing on concrete as she trudged up the steps, and now he could hear, as he had not been able to before, that she was talking on her mobile phone.

'I told you, Shanice,' she was saying, 'I ain't goin' blues witcha. Not with them man-dem in there. Yeah, she did, and they cut her, yeah. She needed *stitches*. Plus with this lift out of order *yet again* my feet can't take it. Fuck off, gal!' she laughed. 'If it was a penthouse the lift'd work. It's just *high*.'

Stanlake put up his gun and stepped back, letting the fire-door swing shut in front of him. Oblivious, the girl clomped past, heading on to one of the floors above. Shudders began to run the length of Stanlake's body, a combination of the chilliness of the air on his bare skin, the aching coldness of the tiles beneath his feet, and the draining from his system of nightmare-ignited adrenalin. He returned to the flat. It was a relief to close and lock the door behind him, to assert that there was a difference between inside and outside, and that he knew what it was.

'Stanlake?' Poppy, sounding sleepy, calling from her bedroom. 'Are you alright? What is it?'

'Go back to sleep,' he called back softly. 'It is nothing.'

I could have shot her, he thought. The girl in the stairwell, or my mother. I wouldn't even have known what I was doing.

Rubbing his tired eyes he went through to the kitchen, ran the tap and filled and drank a glass of water. Hanging from the handle on the back of the kitchen door was a bulging bag of vegetable-peelings. He ejected the clip from the grip of the Glock and pushed it down into the soft, yielding mass until it couldn't be seen. Then he wiped over the body of the pistol with a tea-towel and pushed it in too. Once he was sure it was out of sight he went back to bed.

Chapter Ten

The next morning was a Saturday and the day of Poppy's other job, which was cleaning a pub on the estate not far from their block. From the outside the pub looked like a concrete bunker, but inside it was carpeted and boasted dark wooden furniture with carved legs and tapestried cushions, and a gas fire that was made to look like real logs burning. To Stanlake these things gave it a fairytale quality, though this was because he had only ever been in there when it was closed and he had come to meet his mother to go on with her to the market. When there were customers it was evidently a brutal place: often outside there would be purple-red spatters on the pavement, evidence of the fights that had taken place the night before, along with pancakes of drying vomit and shattered glass. It was called the Trafalgar, which Stanlake knew was a famous battle. A painting of a sailing-ship hung on hooks from a pole outside. Almost all the people who drank there were white.

Poppy didn't have to be at the pub till eight, which meant neither she nor Stanlake had to get up until seven. The extra sleep was welcome, and to be getting up in daylight, however grey and dim, made both of them feel more a part of the world around them.

Their routine was otherwise unchanged. Stanlake rose a little before his mother and prepared a mug of tea for her while she washed and dressed. As always they spoke little.

'When I came back from church last night there was just one of them there,' Poppy said eventually.

'Did anything happen?'

'No.'

'Good.'

Her son wore no make-up this morning. Poppy didn't know if this was a good thing or not. A little later she left for work. She took the bag of vegetable peelings with her to throw down the rubbish-chute. For some reason it was unexpectedly heavy.

After Poppy had left Stanlake mooched around the flat feeling idle and somehow dissatisfied. Perhaps he, like Evill, was sensing the imminent arrival of spring, the shifting season's release of gestated energy, and it was that that was making him restless. As he had yet to experience the rebirth of the year in the U.K. the small signals were unfamiliar to him. He had a bath, towelled himself down, moisturised, then lolled on his bed and flicked through magazines. There was nothing in them he hadn't seen or read already. Jumping up, he went over to the window, drew back the material he had pinned up as a curtain, and saw it was bright and sunny outside. There were no clouds in the sky, and even up here on the fifteenth floor no wind was buffeting the windows. Could it actually be – *warm* out there? He had never had a warm day in England yet.

Even though he'd come up with no plan for raising money, and all he had on him was the three pounds left over from school yesterday, it seemed crazy to spend the day stuck in the flat, where nothing could happen, on his own. He decided to go out.

Choosing what to wear delayed him. Having make-up on relaxed him but it also made him conspicuous, and that might not serve his plans today, whatever they turned out to be. He compromised on light day-face: discreet enhancement that wouldn't draw attention. He pulled on a skinny-rib vest, low-rise jeans and a thick oatmeal jumper, (lifting the neck-hole carefully over his made-up face), knee-high socks, bright red knock-off trainers, and his duffle coat. To keep his head warm he tied a dark blue headscarf round his shaved skull, knotting it tightly at the back.

Looking in the mirror he was pleased: his skill with the brushes and pencils, the powders and paints, was growing.

He left the flat at a little after ten. The lift was working.

He had no destination in mind. East Street Market, maybe: there were always things to see there. But he felt a desire to wander at will through unfamiliar streets. Quite unexpectedly he found himself missing Patrick, Matthew and

Robert: in the natural order of things his Mask brothers should have been here with him, keeping him company as he explored this vast new city. And though they were beside him always, and were his brothers still, their relationship to this, to him, was different now they were no longer alive.

He couldn't imagine Big Gun, Diamondz and Blondie here. They were with him too, but they were spirits of the forest, not the city. Here they would run wild like the jackals.

The events of the day before returned to Stanlake's mind. It was likely too early for the jackals to be out selling yet, but they would be there later when he came back. They knew now that he could, and would, fight, but still they might go for him, fear of the gun he might be carrying pushed out by abruptly-surging aggression.

More likely they would bide their time, thinking to torture him with anticipation. And that would be their mistake. For Stanlake had lived so long with fear, it was so much a part of him, that he could experience it without being paralyzed by it; in a way without feeling it at all. This was not worse than what he had gone through already. This did not worry him more. It was just another thing. If they were planning to torment him in that way they had already failed.

If they tried to do anything, he would react. That was all. Though he hoped they would not.

The door of the building swung shut behind him with a clunk. Despite the inviting dazzle of sunshine and lack of wind the air outside was as cuttingly cold as usual. Was this country ever not cold? Images of heat and holidays were always of faraway places.

Stanlake put up his hood and dug in his pockets for his gloves. He was fond of his gloves. They had cost three pounds off a market stall, and were woollen, and each finger was made of a series of different-coloured bands. They were 'for girls', the trader had said, but of course Stanlake hadn't cared. Men in this country seemed afraid of colour. Stanlake didn't understand it, but then he had never understood why men and women were supposed to wear different things, or had different colours and articles of clothing forbidden them.

Here bright colours were reserved for children. The playground he had to go through to get to the underpass, for instance, fenced in though it was by prison-like bars, was painted in primary reds, yellows and blues. Despite this attempt at cheeriness, and though it offered two swings, a slide, a seesaw, a small merry-go-round, a two-level jungle-gym climbing-frame, and benches for parents to sit on while keeping an eye on their children, it was usually deserted.

Today, however, there was someone there. A single figure in a black tracksuit, hood up, perched on top of the jungle-gym. Being a frame of metal tubes it couldn't be comfortable to sit on, and the figure jumped down from it with evident relief when he saw Stanlake approaching. Gold motifs printed on the material of his tracksuit glinted in the sun-shine, and Stanlake realised it was the leader of the jackals. He looked around him hastily but the others weren't lurking about anywhere he could see, and there were no places they could be hiding. If this was an ambush, it wasn't an obvious one.

As the jackal drew near, his movements oddly tentative, Stanlake saw him as if for the first time, as if some screen between them had been removed. He too was short, maybe five centimetres taller than Stanlake, and his wrists and narrow neck suggested a skinny frame beneath his baggy clothing. Though a vicious life had hardened their outlines, there was an unexpected delicacy to his features. His skin was mid-brown and smooth, his eyebrows fine and minimal. His mouth was wide, his lips full, and his teeth were large and one of them was block-framed in gold, but it was his eyes Stanlake had not seen before, and these were both naked and opaque.

Hands thrust into his pockets, the jackal came to a stop just over an arm's length from Stanlake and stood there looking at him, saying nothing. Then he pushed his hood back, a gesture of revelation. His skull like Stanlake's looked to be shaved, and was wrapped in a dark blue do-rag against the cold. Stanlake removed his hands from his pockets, so as to be ready for anything.

The jackal pulled out a pack of cigarettes, tapped one out and put it to his lips. He produced a lighter and after a couple of nervy clicks got a flame from it, and sparked up. He took a drag, then wordlessly inverted the cigarette and offered it to Stanlake. Stanlake shook his head. The jackal shrugged and took another drag.

Stanlake glanced about him again. No-one was around. There were no witnesses to this encounter, foe or friend. Although the towerblocks loomed above them with their thousand windows, this, whatever it was, was private.

'So.' The jackal ducked his head, looking suddenly shy and boyish. 'So what you go by then, fam?'

'Go by?'

'Name. What's your name?'

'I am Stanlake. You?'

'I'm Evill. Uh, Everil.'

'And the others?'

Evill looked around vaguely. 'They ain't up yet. This is well earlydoors for them.'

'And you?'

Evill coughed, hunched, and, as Stanlake watched, took first a hit on his inhaler, then a further drag on the cigarette. 'I know, fam,' he said, off Stanlake's look, 'it's fucked up.'

Stanlake shrugged. 'The drugs,' he said.

'Yeah?'

'Do you make a lot of money?'

'You wanna get in on it, then?'

'I do not want to get in on it.'

'You wanna buy?'

'No.'

'Good.'

Evill looked away and Stanlake had the feeling that this was not the conversation they were meant to be having; that somehow he had pushed it down a wrong path. What had this Evill come here for? What did he want? Was his name the truth of him? But then he had corrected himself: Everil. He did not seem to be intending harm, but yesterday he had jammed the muzzle of the Glock under Stanlake's jaw and pulled the trigger without hesitation. Was that panic or the instinct to kill? Still, would not Stanlake or any of his comrades have done the same, back in the forest? And did these boys in the U.K. not call each other 'soldier' and believe that they too lived in a forest, as they said, an urban jungle? For the first time the thought came to Stanlake that they might have it in them to become, as the Beasts had become, comrades.

For all the terror and dread and simple boredom of those times, Stanlake missed his comrades.

But no, I do not want to go back to all that.

He watched as Evill produced a roll of banknotes from his pocket. The roll was fat, with rubber bands round it. Evill peeled off six twenties. 'Here,' he said, holding the money out to Stanlake. When Stanlake didn't move to take it he added, 'Buy yourself something pretty, yeah.'

Something simultaneously tightened and expanded within Stanlake's chest. Should I do this? Yes. No. I don't know. Do I want this involvement? But perhaps this is his atonement. Almost without will he found himself reaching out and taking the proffered notes, keeping his eyes on Evill's as he did so, wary of Evill trying to take hold of him but noting peripherally the delicacy of Evill's hands. He knew he should say something, he should not just take this money, but what words would not be a mistake?

Evill's face was twitching with suppressed emotion, its expression almost hostile now, his eyes channels into a black unknown. Abruptly he turned on his heel and walked away, flicking his hood up as he went. Stanlake watched him until he disappeared, not in the direction of the underpass as Stanlake had expected, but round a corner and down the ramp that led into the rat-run. His swagger was confident, but there was a hunch to his shoulders that was vulnerable. He didn't look back.

What was this?

What could this be?

It was like a dream. But the money was real in his hand.

Evill had been waiting in the playground since half-past seven that morning, after a night during which he had been unable to sleep. Instead, as so often, he had sat in his drab front room blazing and zoning in and out, preoccupied with the thought that he had told the Crew he would sort it with the African bwoy and knowing that he hadn't done so; that he didn't even know what he wanted to do. And they would expect him to have the shit resolved because he was the don, and he had to be what they believed him to be. He thought of slave-masters, and of his own position near the rectum of the digestive tract they were all a part of, that the African bwoy was not a part of.

Dawn came bright and cold. He showered and left the house. In the small gardens of the street he lived in tiny blades of plants were starting to show. He passed a single tree that was heavy with pink blossom. All the others were still bare. Wasn't blossom meant to be for bees? He thought so. But bees only came in summer. But there the tree was, as if it had decided to be beautiful for its own sake. Cramps jerked at his stomach: he hadn't eaten for over twelve hours. He made a detour to an all-night garage and bought a Snickers to hold him. Everything in there seemed garish and ugly under the fluorescent lighting.

He wouldn't wait for the bwoy in the underpass: he wanted to meet him in the light, not down a hole in the ground. He went further into the estate, came to the play-ground, and decided that would do, as the bwoy would have to come through there too.

For no particular reason he remembered at age eight a social worker asking him about his mum. The social worker had had a plump, kind face, but even then he had known she was a part of something impersonal and merciless; that her little smile and soft, auntie-ish voice were the sheath cover-ing a knife.

'A ruined child.'

A phrase he remembered from somewhere, and he thought it had been applied to him. It sounded too poetic for a social worker, though: too revealingly judgemental. Social workers never admitted they made judgements even though they did it all the time: that was their job. His mother wouldn't have said it either, because it implied defilement, a lack of inevitability. A responsibility that might have been hers.

Maybe it was me, he thought. Maybe I said it about myself. For a while he had written raps, and they had maybe even been quite good. Then that dream died with the rest. Was there a moment when? He didn't recall one.

He sat on one of the swings, his hips slightly too wide for

the low seat, his feet flat on the rubberised tarmac, too tall and heavy to actually swing on it. Not a child any more. There was no going back. His body ached from the hours he'd spent slumped on the sofa. He struggled up from the swing, went over to the climbing-frame and did some pull-ups on it. That helped a bit, the weight of his lower body stretching out his spine. Then, for want of anything else to do, he clambered up onto it.

Now he felt more like a child. How soon all that went, he thought: how quickly your whole physical self was reduced to walking, sitting, shitting and fucking. Zipping his pants pockets as he remembered doing at school, he hooked his feet under one of the bars and arched backwards until he was hanging upside-down from the top of the frame. His fags and lighter tumbled out of his tracksuit top. He extended his arms above his head towards the ground. The tracksuit top slipped down, exposing his flat belly to the chilly air.

As he hung there the African bwoy's mother came hurrying across the playground. She was wearing a drab housecoat and on her head was a powder-blue wrap. She noticed him peripherally, an odd dark shape hanging from the climbing-frame, looked properly and started. She kept going. Then she was gone.

Tensing his stomach-muscles, Evill swung himself back up. He got down from the climbing-frame and reclaimed his cigarettes and lighter.

Time passed with numbing slowness. The sun crawled up and without seeming to move the shadows shortened. He went down into the underpass for a piss and came back. People passed by, heading in and out. A postman wheeling a mail trolley went down into the rat-run. Evill might as well have been a shadow himself for all the notice anyone took of him. No children came to play.

Then the bwoy came, and they had their halting, misfiring conversation, a conversation that had to avoid being about the gun and his pulling of the trigger, anything but that, but became instead and against his will about drugs and dealing: that other pit. And he offered a cigarette from his lips to the bwoy's lips, a kiss at one remove that was refused, though the bwoy did at least share with him his name:

Stanlake. An old-sounding name, at a slant to the usual. In its seeming more-than-Englishness it concealed rather than revealed, but for the first time Evill saw Stanlake as he was instead of projecting bullshit onto him, and he found in Stanlake's feline agate eyes not the expected – he had thought inevitable – twin locked-off rifle-sights of an enemy, but some new thing that made his heart leap. And he wondered then about Stanlake's body, hidden and muffled by his duffle coat today, but surely lean and athletic given the litheness of his movements during the fight before, a fight from which Evill now felt as remote as if he had been not the instigator but only a witness: as if he was Everil watching Evill, though he knew that such a simple separation was a lie.

He imagined the joy and terror of touching Stanlake's body and wanted to say something to express that heated, tensile longing. Not having the words, as how could he, such words never having been spoken before in the history of the world, instead he gave Stanlake money, saying as he did so the one thing that surely laid his intention bare, as much to himself as to Stanlake, because even by then he had had no plan. And such a revelation had been too much for him, and he had had at once to turn and go, and he had headed over to Solid's with nothing resolved, only made more complicated by what he had done.

Gotta rally the troops, though. Gotta get paid.

And pay.

He had to keep his finger on the buzzer for over a minute before Solid answered, sounding sleepy.

As the lift rose Evill wondered what the bwoy would buy, and how he could get to see it.

The unaired flat stank of stale cigarette-smoke, and Pit-Bull and Cuts were sparking up as Evill followed Solid into the lounge. Their bruises had developed yellow and green-potato tones, he noticed, and looked worse than when they were fresh the day before. The darkness of his skin meant Solid's were less visible, tho he still had the – now-wrinkled – strip of pink bandage across the bridge of his nose. If they kept their hoods up it would be okay though, Evill reckoned: they wouldn't look like total pussies.

'So you deal with it, then?' Solid asked as Evill took the

joint from between Cuts' thick ivory fingers and toked.

'My call is, lef' it,' Evill said.

'What you mean, blood, lef' it?' asked Solid.

''Llow it, that's what I mean, fam.'

Cuts looked at him. 'What, just do nothing?'

'A wha gwaan, fam?' asked Pit-Bull, his brow wrinkling, pink touching his earlobes.

'There ain't no percentage in it,' Evill said.

'I say we jump him,' said Cuts.

'Yeah?' Evill turned and locked his eyes on Cuts'. 'Zat right, then? You say that?'

Cuts shrugged and looked down, mumbling something inaudible.

'What you say, though?' Evill pushed. When Cuts didn't reply he spat, 'Chief.'

'We could though, bruv,' Pit-Bull said, his tone almost apologetic.

'Or we could be out there selling,' Evill said. 'We gotta be about the business, souljah, not about lickle wars on the side.'

'You afraid of some lickle battyboy now, blood?' said Solid.

'The lickle itty-bitty battyboy what broke your nose and fucked Cuts' wrist and gash up your head, you mean, bruv?' Evill said. 'That battyboy? No, I ain't afraid of him.'

'Plus true-say there's the gun,' Pit-Bull said, switching sides. 'He's got it, and we ain't. And he fixed it so it works. And he'd use it, no doubt.'

Solid and Cuts subsided. They weren't convinced long-term, Evill knew, but for now they'd toe the line. 'Come,' he said, taking a final drag before stubbing the roach out in the ashtray. 'We haffi business.'

When Poppy left the flat she wasn't thinking about the jackals: they were never up that early. Her mind was on the Reverend and the advice he might give her. Yet what could he do for her really? He couldn't change the past, and what were her problems today? So her son wore make-up, so what? She knew a little of why he wore it; she knew what he was repudiating, and she wasn't going to tell anyone at church about that, not even the Reverend. Perhaps it was just a phase.

Something caught her eye as she crossed the playground. To her surprise she realised it was one of the jackals, hanging upside-down from the jungle-gym.

She thought of witches, shivered, and hurried on.

It was strange to have money out of nowhere. Stanlake decided he would go up to the West End, to the most famous shopping street in London, Oxford Street. He had never been to Oxford Street before, and just the name excited him. He put £10 on his Oyster card at the newsagent's, caught a bus to Elephant & Castle, and took a tube to Oxford Circus. It was by then midmorning, and he emerged to pavements already thronging with shoppers.

This was the other London, where people had money, and today, for the first time since he reached the U.K., he was a part of it.

Oxford Circus seemed to be in the middle of Oxford Street. Randomly Stanlake headed west, turning back only when he reached a large arch of white stone – Marble Arch, he realised later – with beside it a huge metal sculpture of a horse's head, upended so it was standing on its nose. Beyond that, across a dual carriageway and behind railings, was an expanse of drab parkland and still-leafless trees. In plots between the safety barriers that edged the dual carriageway daffodils were starting to open, silently trumpeting spring.

But it was the department-store windows that captured Stanlake's attention. Their displays featured many of the designers whose work he had fallen in love with in magazines back home, and all of them had some theme or other that bound the clothes together. In one window every piece of clothing was either yellow like the daffodils or green like their leaves, and the theme was spring. Another had an undersea theme, and all the fabrics shimmered and were blue and green. Just seeing all this close-up made Stanlake feel reconnected with those hopeful times when anything had seemed possible.

And would not even his Beasts, Big Gun in Florence's beaded dress, Blondie and Diamondz with their watches, dye-jobs and jewellery, like this street?

One of the stores was like some great presidential palace, with a broad, pillared portico and sets of brass revolving doors through which shoppers passed in and out. It was called Selfridges. He stood before it for a while, awed, getting jostled, unable to enter. But I am a shopper too, he thought. I can go in. No-one will stop me. And if they do, I can show I have money.

He went in.

Inside the store the still, warm, antiseptic air was interlaced with dizzying trails of scent from the dozen or so perfume and make-up counters, islands scattered across the ground floor in a gleaming chrome-and-white archipelago. Ties, scarves, costume jewellery, wallets, handbags and other accessories were displayed around the walls. In the centre crossed chrome escalators rose and fell smoothly, endlessly. The cosmetics counters were staffed by women in make-up heavier than Stanlake would ever dare to wear, yet without looking like prostitutes. Strangely, they were dressed in white smocks, as if the services they offered were somehow medical. All around him bottles and boxes glinted and shone and sparkled.

Stanlake pushed back the hood of his duffle coat as he drifted round the counters, hoping his own foundation wasn't melting in the sudden warmth, looking at things only obliquely, not wanting to catch anyone's eye in case he was asked what he was interested in, and why. At the same time he wished he'd taken his own look further. Why had he been so conservative? He looked at a range of Mac waterproof make-up and felt excited, though all of it was forbiddingly expensive.

No-one challenged him, and his confidence grew. He pulled out and sniffed the crystal stoppers of various tester bottles. Floral, citric, musky and woody scents filled his swelling nostrils, all of them tempting him with their different moods and accents, but even a small bottle of *eau de toilette* was £35.

He soon noticed that the make-up at the counters mostly favoured paler skin-tones, though there were some ranges that suited his complexion too. Wealthy-looking women with soft, puffy skin sat on chrome bar-stools with delicately-closed eyes as the women in surgical smocks applied make-up to their faces. If he loitered about would one of the women offer to make up his face, he wondered. In this other world the idea seemed not impossible.

His eye was caught by a panel of highly-patterned, richly-coloured silk squares strikingly displayed against dark wood. He imagined the silk against his shaved skull and closed his eyes in sensual abandon. He wanted very much to buy Poppy something, but if he did then he would have to come up with some sort of lie: she would know such a gift wasn't something cheap off a market stall.

And Evill gave me the money for me, he thought.

The store was like a vast market laid out over six floors, each floor divided into different stalls for the many famous fashion labels that were being sold there. Each stall had its own shopkeepers, who wore the clothes of that label. As happened naturally in a market there was some grouping together of stalls according to the sort of things they sold, like underwear, and there was a café from which the aroma of roasting coffee-beans wafted, making his mouth water. I'm here, he thought, as he stepped onto the escalator and began to ascend. Patrick, Robert, Matthew, I'm here as I said I would be.

On the third floor he found displays of women's lingerie. His heart started to beat faster; and he felt a generalised sensory arousal that was only partly sexual as he gazed at the elegant display-mannequins with their artificially-elongated limbs, the flawless smoothness of their cool, shiny surfaces enhanced by skimpy lace and slivers of silk, rayon and mesh. His nipples prickled and his cock stirred.

His excitement was short-lived, however: soon he was noticing price-tags and realising that all the money he had on him wasn't enough for a single Agent Provocateur basque or teddy. Agent Provocateur was the best. There were other brands that were cheaper, but they were less appealing as well. Plainer and more ordinary, they suffered by contrast with the top brand. Deflated, Stanlake decided that in any case it made sense to explore other shops before making any purchases. He took the escalator back down to the ground floor and left Selfridges.

Bathetically, the next department store that caught his eye was an enormous Primark. Deciding it would be better to get a lot of different things for his money rather than just one single pricey thing he might not, when it came to it, enjoy wearing that much, he went in. The store was thronging with girls shopping for an outfit for the weekend, and a fair number of boys and men. Stanlake passed a rack set up next to the tills that was weighed down with jewellery. Mostly it was made of wood, plastic or resin, and some of it was in attractive ambers and earth tones. Maybe he'd get some bangles, he thought: chunky bracelets looked good on his delicate wrists. He made his way through to the lingerie section, which was easily four times the size of the one in his local branch, and had a far more extensive selection of styles.

Here he was going to bump into no-one he knew. Here he felt free.

In the end he spent more than three quarters of an hour making his choices. He quickly realised he should avoid basques, bodies or chemises that had fitted cups because his chest was flat and he had no desire to pad. He wanted the clothes to enhance his physique as it was, not to deny it. This wasn't really about trying to be a woman: it was about giving himself the freedom to be a sensual human being who was allowed to think of nothing but pleasure.

He was drawn to stretchy fabrics that were intended to hug every curve of the body. In particular he liked lacy or spider's-web designs, though he did pick out one free-flowing chemise in black silk. It had spaghetti straps, a simple cut, and he reckoned it would come down to just below his butt. The slippery iridescence of the material excited him. He found some stretch lacy short-shorts that excited him too, a pair in black and a pair in white; a see-through black mesh stretch mini-dress, a mesh-and-spider-web body, and a sheer mesh bustier that came with stockings and suspenders. While queuing to pay for his choices he took some wooden bangles from the display rack, along with an amber plastic necklace. Altogether his purchases came to £87.50. That, plus the Oyster top-up, meant he had spent £97.50 of the £120 Evill had given him.

The line was long and the tills were busy. The girl who eventually served him looked Somali, and wore a brightly-coloured hijab and wet-look pink lipstick outlined in black. She barely gave him a glance as she scanned the barcodes on his purchases and shoved them into a small carrier-bag. He left the store feeling elated.

Part of him wanted to hurry straight home, but at the same time he also felt an urge to carry on wandering, to keep the wonder of the day going for as long as possible. Also, unless she had gone to church, by now his mother would be back in the flat, and though he didn't mind experimenting with make-up while she was around he could only imagine trying on women's underwear when she wasn't there, or after she had gone to bed.

And too he thought of Evill and the jackals, waiting as they surely would be waiting down in the underpass. The others will not know he has spoken to me, he considered. And even if they do know we have spoken, they will not guess what was said. If he is with them when I next see him then what he said when we were alone will not apply. So I will not hurry towards that.

Back at Oxford Circus he looked down what he noted was Regent Street and his eye was caught by the flagship Apple Store, blazoning a world of technology, none of which he could afford; and then, further down and across the way, by a strange, old-fashioned-looking building with upper storey gable-ends that overhung the pavement. Its whitewashed walls were framed by black beams, and like a house in a fairytale it had diamond-paned windows and little wooden balconies. A sign like the Trafalgar's hung from a pole outside. Stanlake went down to have a closer look. On the sign was a coat of arms and the name of the shop: Liberty. He wondered how it had come by such a wonderful name, and it seemed part of the magic of the day that he should go in and explore.

Inside Liberty was the same still, perfumed air there had been in Selfridges. Richly patterned rugs hung from internal balconies, and swathes of gorgeously coloured fabrics were draped over antique furniture or pinned up in tented opulence. Everything in the store seemed somehow to be from the past, some better past, and that both intrigued and troubled him. There was nothing from Africa here, and while he had not expected there would be – had not thought about it at all – that total absence made him feel abstracted from himself in a way he had not been in Primark. In Primark there was no past: just what was happening now, today, this weekend, and you expected no more. But this store was proud to tell you that its precious things came from all over the world, from other cultures, from places you would be excited to hear about and long to, but maybe not dare to, visit, and where was Africa in all of that?

All the clothes in Primark were made in China, but they didn't come from there.

Disquieted, he left the store. Emerging from a different door to the one he had gone in through, he found himself in a backstreet. Unsure which way Regent Street was from there he wandered along the side of the building. Though he had no sense of where places were in relation to each other, as if hoping for a clue he looked up to check the name of the first street he came to. It was, unexpectedly, a name he recognised: Carnaby Street. He knew nothing about it except that it had once been a centre of fashion, some time in the remote past. The association felt propitious, and he turned down it to see what there was to see.

The street had been pedestrianised, and was a mixture of small boutiques, shops selling shoes and trainers, cafés and pubs. The people who worked in the boutiques looked more unusual than the people who worked in Primark or Selfridges or Liberty; somehow more extreme. In the doorway of one a dark-skinned black man in tight-fitting leather jeans and a stripy tank-top leaned smoking. His dyed-blond Mohican made Stanlake think of Blondie.

We could have been here, he thought, having lives. We didn't have to be stuck in that fucked-up place. You didn't need to be crazy to dye your hair or be a boy and wear diamonds: you could just do it wherever you were. We didn't need to be killing.

He blinked away sudden tears.

I must keep my eyes wide open.

There was too much to take in. He could sense there were

undercurrents – associations of colours and shapes and fabrics and patterns – underpinning everything he was seeing. Some of those undercurrents were aesthetic; some seemed symbolic, although the meaning was obscure to him; some were even political. It would take him time to sort all of it out in his head. He knew, knew strongly, that he would come back here: this street offered him something he wanted to take. Was this the first time since arriving in the U.K. he had thought about the future? It felt like it.

He wandered on. The streets grew narrower. He passed through a small market selling fish, Calvin Klein underwear, and metal bowls of fruit and vegetables, just like in East Street. Some of the shops alongside the market announced that they sold porn dvds, and some of the porn dvds they displayed in their windows were gay. Handsome white men with muscular physiques posed next to each other in briefs or swimwear and smiled out at the viewer or tried to look manly and serious. Stanlake wondered what it would be like to see them doing what they did, and his crotch stirred, though he had then no sense that they had anything to do with his life and how he might live it.

He came to a street of cafés, restaurants, bars and shops that even had a theatre in it, though at that hour it was locked up. In the bars, he noticed obliquely, there seemed to be only men, and several of the shops seemed devoted exclusively to men's underwear. He stopped outside a shop that sold underwear for both men and women. Much of it seemed to be made of black or red vinyl, or studded leather, but what caught Stanlake's eye was that one of the male mannequins in the window was wearing nothing but a pouch made of stretchy lace. This collision of the masculine and feminine so embodied what he wanted for himself that he entered the shop without hesitation: this was the completion of his day.

Again it seemed that the spirits were smiling: the lace thong was in a sale, and he managed to get three pairs for eighteen pounds, though he had to root through a bargain bin to find three small sizes: unwanted XL and XXL items predominated. The plump white girl behind the counter gave him a friendly smile as she took the thongs and his boldly-offered money. Her hair was dyed black and pulled back in a ponytail, and she wore black lipstick and had a ring through her lower lip. She was dressed in a black leather scoop-necked top that thrust her breasts together and forward, and she wore a short leather skirt, fishnets and high-heeled ankle-boots. In her friendliness and confidence she was a glimpse of yet another world to Stanlake: you could be like this as if it was an everyday thing, as if it was nothing, just fun.

Including yesterday's unspent lunch-money, after paying he had £5.70 left. It seemed prudent not to spend all of it, but he could spend a little more before going home and still have something left over.

Despite the cold, because it was sunny people in heavy coats and sunglasses were sitting outside the cafés, sipping steaming hot drinks. He could join them, he thought, and have a cappuccino and some sort of sweet cake. Except he would sit inside, where it was warm. Wasn't that what supermodels did, between shows? Sit in the windows of cafés, drinking black coffee? But he didn't really like coffee, he had never had a cappuccino, and he didn't know what the cakes were. He wasn't used to sweet things, anyway. And a supermodel would rather have a cigarette, wouldn't she?

It seemed both easy and impossible to go into one of these places, order something, find a seat and sit and watch the world go by. He had eaten nothing since breakfast, and suddenly he felt both hungry and tired. Looking around there was no sign of anything familiar, like Nando's.

There was a Nando's at Elephant & Castle.

He realised he didn't even have enough for that, and what wasn't enough for Nando's surely wouldn't be enough for here, where the rich went.

Save your little money and go home, he told himself.

Keeping on going, he came to a larger road with bookshops. Looking along it he saw a sign for an underground station, Leicester Square. From there he took the Northern Line to Waterloo, changed to the Bakerloo line, and went one stop to Elephant & Castle, all the while keeping tight hold of his Primark bag, afraid he would somehow leave it on the train, as if desire inevitably makes you careless.

The sky had greyed over by the time he was back above ground, accentuating his sense of having left a different world. The bus, when it came, was crowded, and he had to squeeze past youths and pensioners and mums with kids and unfolded pushchairs to get to the stairs to the upper deck.

Up there there were plenty of empty seats. He took one at the front.

He thought about Evill. Yesterday he tried to kill me. If the gun had not misfired I would be dead. Today he gave me money to make myself look pretty. Back on the roadblock I kissed Big Gun and he kissed me back. I was fourteen and he was thirteen, but we knew what love was. And Big Gun was one of those who came to my village, who made me do what I did, but I forgave him, or anyway by then it did not matter. Can I forgive this Evill for threatening and ill-treating my mother, the indecency of that? But love is not about decency, or I do not think so. Big Gun had killed, in hot blood and cold blood, and tortured, and raped, and I too did many of these things. We did not forgive each other: that was not what we were asking for.

But why was he thinking about love? Was it because Evill was the first person who had shown an interest in him here in the U.K.? No, not the first person: the first boy. Stanlake could face that now. Evill was the first boy to search for something in his eyes and find it there, or at least find a puzzle he might want to solve. And if Evill wasn't nice, nor had Big Gun been nice.

For the first time that day Stanlake considered Evill not as an unexpected conduit for his own private self-expression, but as an object of desire. His hands were strong and square and his wrists delicate, an intriguing collision of elements. His movements were smooth. And if his eyes were wounds his lips looked sensitive and like they might respond to kisses; and if his face was hard his skin was smooth, perhaps receptive to caresses.

Since Stanlake came to this country he had not been touched.

But still Evill was a jackal, a jackal among jackals.

But then had not he, Stanlake, been a Beast among Beasts?

Somewhere his sacrifice waited.

With a start he realised the bus had reached his stop. He jumped up and hurried down the stairs, pressing the bell as he went to discourage the driver from closing the doors before he got off.

He was on the streets again.

Ahead was the underpass.

Chapter Eleven

here was a damp bite to the air, and dusk was leaching light from the sky. Here and there street-lamps stuttered into random life. Stanlake folded up the carrier-bag carefully, his purchases still inside it, and pushed it deep into his coat pocket. Whatever happened next, what he had bought today wouldn't get dropped or easily taken from him.

Still, as he went down into the underpass his mind was divided. Part of him was eager to get home and put on a show in front of his mirror for himself alone: to become a fantasy object desired abstractly by imagined multitudes – this, of course, assuming his mother was out. Another part of him wanted to see Evill again as he had seen him that morning and somehow put on a show for him, impossible though that seemed. A third part of him anticipated Evill's necessary betrayal of that earlier encounter, and was ready for trouble.

For combat.

Why do I have to do this, over and over?

To give out energy on so many psychic wavelengths was in and of itself exhausting.

He emerged into the weakly-lit centre of the underpass. As he had expected the jackals were there with their hoods up, perched on the sculpture like vultures. Evill, still in black and gold, but now with skeleton-gloved hands, was in the highest position. The heavier-set black youth sat on a ledge a little way below him, his dangling legs making him look boyish despite his bulk, a bright pink sticking-plaster across the bridge of his nose like a tribal paint-mark. The white youth sat next to him with head bowed, absorbed in his mobile phone, thumbs moving restlessly on the keypad. The Chinese one stood leaning against the sculpture, flicking a depleted lighter, trying to light a cigarette. Some sort of surgical wrist-support protruded from his sleeve, and his thumb-movement was awkward.

First Evill noticed Stanlake, then the others. Stanlake came to a stop, tilted his head back and looked at them. Coolly he waited. This had to be seen through.

Evill's eyes were shadowed by his hood, and the set of his mouth was unrevealing. Neither he nor the others said anything, nor did they move from where they were. The Chinese youth gave up trying to light his cigarette and put it and the lighter away. The white youth pocketed his mobile. Still no-one spoke. Then Evill gave Stanlake a small gesture of acknowledgement with his left hand. Stanlake responded with the ghost of a nod.

The others sensed the near-subliminal connection that had been established between the African youth and their don, and they waited wordless and impassive for the next development. But Evill said nothing, and the moment stretched out, and in the end it was the white boy who spoke, just as Stanlake, having judged his point was made, was about to continue on his way:

'So where you learn that with the gun, blood?'

'In war.'

'What war, though?'

'In my country there was a war. *Is* a war,' Stanlake corrected himself. Things carry on even if you are no longer there. It is a lesson the dead can teach you.

'And you was in it, then?' asked the black youth with the plaster on his nose.

'I was a soldier.'

'It's like a war here too, though,' the white youth said.

'Is it?'

'Yeah.'

'What are you fighting for?'

The youth hesitated, and it was Evill who answered: 'Survival.'

'For myself and my mother I want only peace,' Stanlake said, and his statement brought their interaction to some convergence of intent.

'We – ' Evill began.

'Business,' interrupted the burly black youth, who

Stanlake would learn later was called Solid, breaking the moment and indicating with a tilt of his head that someone was emerging from one of the tunnels. They all looked round. It was the too-thin mixed-race youth Stanlake remembered from the day before: him and his white friend hurrying away with their drug purchases, blind to everything except feeding their addiction. Today he was in dirty, diaper-arsed skinny-leg jeans, broken-down trainers and a yellow hoodie made of some thin, cheap material. His hands were thrust deep into its front pocket, pulling the fabric out of shape and stretching the hood down round his taut, narrow face.

There is something in his eyes, Stanlake thought, something metallic. But Solid was smirking as the youth drew near. 'Heyyy, blood,' he said. 'Back so soon? You must love us.'

Cuts laughed at that. 'Got your Junkies' Club Card, then?'

'Yeah,' the youth said, and Stanlake could see the jackals not seeing the tightness in him, too caught up in their own bullshitting.

'Frequent flyer,' Pit-Bull said.

'High flyer,' said Cuts.

A constriction that was born of adrenalin, tensing muscles and something else –

'We don't do no air-miles though,' Pit-Bull said.

'Or no mile high club,' Solid added, sliding down off the Rock.

'But we got a bone to pick with you though,' Evill said as the youth reached the foot of the sculpture, eyes lowered like a supplicant.

– eyes hidden –

'The gat,' Pit-Bull said.

'It was shit,' Evill said.

'Here,' the youth said thickly, only now looking up at Evill. And he drew out from the front pocket of his hoodie a kitchen-knife and without hesitation rammed the short blade into Evill's inner thigh. 'That's for Oily, you cunts!'

Before the others could react Stanlake was on the youth, grabbing his head in both hands and twisting his neck, forcing him to let go of the knife-handle with a yelp and shoving him away from Evill.

Stats stumbled onto all-fours like a beast. Then he was up and running. Stanlake and Pit-Bull took hold of Evill's elbows as with a grunt of shock he slithered down from the sculpture, helping him to the ground. He was unexpectedly heavy. Caught by surprise and unsure as to what most needed doing, Solid and Cuts stood there, momentarily frozen.

Stats turned in the entrance to West Tunnel and looked back at this sudden urban pietà. 'You killed Oily, you cunts!' he bellowed. His eyes were glittering with tears, his posture distorted. 'I fuckin' hate you!' He turned and vanished into the dark as, their paralysis broken, like dogs off the leash Cuts and Solid pelted after him.

'Solid! Cuts!' Pit-Bull yelled. 'Where you going, you cunts? Fuck that junkie! What about Evill?' Gesturing helplessly he turned to where Stanlake was lying Evill flat on his back. Blood was pumping from around the blade that was still embedded in his thigh, soaking the leg of his track-pants at a frightening rate. 'What you doing, man?'

'Flat is better,' Stanlake said. He pulled off his headscarf and started to unknot it. Evill was wheezing.

'Pull out the knife, though,' Pit-Bull said.

'No.'

'But look at it, though.'

'If I pull the knife out the blood will spray faster and he will die.'

'You done this before, then?'

'Yes.'

Stanlake flicked his headscarf into a roll to make a tourniquet. The air was cold on his exposed scalp. Pit-Bull watched as he knotted the tourniquet round Evill's thigh above the wound. Evill grunted breathlessly, fumbling in his pocket for his inhaler as Stanlake pulled the tourniquet tight and tied it. Stanlake looked up at Pit-Bull. 'You must call an ambulance,' he said.

'But they'll send the feds too, though,' Pit-Bull said, his eyes going to the blood that was pooling on the ground under Evill. 'That's the drill.'

'Call them anyway. I will stay with him.'

'Fuck it,' Pit-Bull said, as if resolved in his mind to do so, but still he hesitated, gesturing weakly with his mobile, 'They'll know it was this number, though.'

'Use my phone, bruv,' Evill said thickly.

'Yeah, we can use your phone, bruv,' Pit-Bull agreed, kneeling down and going into Evill's pants-pocket.

'Then fuck off out of it.' Evill took Stanlake's hand and gripped it so hard it hurt, and closed his eyes.

'What is it, 911?' asked Pit-Bull, fumbling the phone's lock off.

'999, you cunt,' Evill gritted, keeping his eyes shut. 'This ain't – this ain't America's Most Wanted.'

'I got it,' Pit-Bull said. 'Yeah – I need a ambulance. There's been like a stabbing. In the leg, in the whatsit, thigh. Yeah, it's serious, there's like blood all over the place. I dunno, I was just passing by. I dunno, this is his phone, I don't have a phone. I was – yeah, no, there's a geezer here with him what knows first aid. Yeah, a lot of blood. I dunno.'

Evill opened his eyes and stared up at Stanlake. 'Am I gonna die, blood?' he asked, and he looked very young and very afraid. 'Is this it?'

'I do not think so,' Stanlake said. 'Not if the ambulance comes soon.' He looked round at Pit-Bull, who had turned away and was now stumbling through directions to the underpass. 'But I will stay with you. If you die, you will not die alone.' His words were well-meant, but Evill only looked more afraid.

'Done, bruv,' said Pit-Bull, pushing the phone into Evill's hand alongside his inhaler. He gave Stanlake a look. 'You stay with him, yeah?'

'Yes.'

'Then I better blurt.'

After a long, hesitant moment he turned and loped off the way Solid and Cuts had gone, picking up speed as he went.

And Stanlake stayed with Evill, as he had not been able to stay with Big Gun, or Diamondz, or Blondie, and in a while he heard sirens on the dual carriageway above, and a minute later two paramedics came running, and they were dressed in green with milky latex gloves, and one of them complimented Stanlake on the professionalism of his tourniquet as he cut through Evill's track-pants with surgical scissors and examined the wound. They put Evill on a stretcher with the knife still stuck in him, and he wouldn't let go of Stanlake's hand, and so Stanlake went with him as the paramedics carried him to the ambulance. At the ambulance doors Evill opened his eyes and looked up at Stanlake and said, 'Don't leave me, man,' and his chest was heaving and his breath was shallow and rapid. One of the paramedics glanced at Stanlake and asked, 'Friend?' and Stanlake with only the smallest hesitation answered, 'Yes,' and at the man's nod, and still with Evill's hand in his, he clambered up into the ambulance. The paramedic gestured to the policeman standing waiting nearby that he should follow, yanked the doors closed, and, siren blaring, the ambulance pulled out and sped away.

After she had finished at the pub, work for which she was paid cash in hand, Poppy caught the bus to Peckham to get her braids redone. This was her one indulgence. She had never had 'good' hair, but more closely-coiled hair like hers was better for braiding, she believed, and it was healthy and strong. She could braid it herself, of course, if she wanted just simple rows, but she loved the fancy patterns and decorative shapes the hairdresser could give her. This attention to her hair was essentially a private pleasure as most of the time – at work, while sleeping, at church, travelling to and fro on the bus – she kept her head covered. Perhaps it represented to her the possibility that there could be something good ahead, because otherwise why bother?

As much as the result she enjoyed the environment: being among other black women, even if they were British, Caribbean and from all over Africa, made her feel at home in a way she didn't anywhere else, not even at church. She didn't have any friends there in particular. Mostly she just sat quietly and listened to the talk, and let the warm, sharp smells of the chemicals used to treat and straighten the women's hair, the shampoos and dyes and lacquers and lotions, float her away from the heartless present. The hairdresser's, which was called Shiny Style, and which Lucy had recommended to her, was down a sidestreet just off Peckham Rye. Through the window she could watch the Nigerian and Ghanaian traders selling fish and vegetables and palm-oil from their temporary Saturday stalls. The shop was crowded but Poppy didn't mind: there was no hurry, and she had nowhere to be. This was her time.

When she was growing up she had always thought that she would have a daughter, or many daughters, as well as a son; had taken it for granted, really, as if it was simply the natural order of things. Now she wondered who that young woman had been who imagined that life turned out as you expected. Because had that ever been true? For anyone? Had anyone in the history of the world ever got through their life without some big interruption turning it upside-down? Even without the war she would never have had a daughter. How huge a tragedy that would have seemed! How small a tragedy it really was.

She thought of Stanlake. Was he trying to be both son and daughter to her? But she knew he wasn't doing what he was doing for her. Sunlight slanted in through the plate glass, warming her where she sat. Being with these women and girls reminded her, no, more than that, proved to her, that life went on. One of the hairdressers, a young girl in a turquoise teeshirt and jeans with butterfly designs sewn on the back pockets, was obviously pregnant: her bump brushed the client whose newly-straightened hair she was crimping as she moved gracefully around her.

Someone had put some daffodils in a vase on the window sill, and they were opening in the sunlight. Poppy thought of her flat, and how she had got into the habit of always keeping the curtains drawn and the blinds closed against the cold and the grey, in an attempt to keep what was within cosy and warm. Today, for the first time since arriving in the U.K., she thought of throwing the curtains wide to let in the light; that the outside might bring in something good. R&B played softly on the radio, a singer with a gospelly voice telling her man that she deserved adoration.

Poppy listened idly as the woman sitting next to her, a Ghanaian like Lucy, told the friend she was with a convoluted story about a relative who was being ill-treated by her husband, a heavy drinker. The wife was always offering excuses for his conduct until eventually, put off by her complaining martyrishness, the heavy drinker left her for another, younger woman. 'And this other woman turned out to be the very friend to whom she had been in the habit of confiding her marital woes!' the Ghanaian woman concluded, and she and her companion tutted and shook their heads.

'Some women you cannot trust,' the friend said.

'Or some men,' the storyteller agreed.

Poppy thought, I had fifteen good years. That is not nothing. My husband never beat me, never took another woman. We loved each other and we made a life together and we had a son. However it ended, what was good was good.

She looked at the daffodils yielding to the sun, to the new season, and for the first time thought that perhaps, though she had no-one in mind, she would not spend the rest of her life alone.

Dusk had sunk into neon night by the time Poppy reached the underpass. Her braids were wound so tight against her scalp it hurt, but the pain made her feel sharp-edged and purified, and the attention she had received over the course of two still, meditative hours in the chair had lifted her spirits. It was the exact opposite of the elevation she received from church: a nurturing of the body. Yet somehow it also fed the soul. Such oppositions that weren't oppositions troubled her, though she never tried to express why, not even to herself.

As she emerged into the centre of the underpass she was pleased to see there was no-one hanging about. Perhaps Stanlake *had* somehow dealt with the bullies in a way that ended things. Then she noticed something on the ground in front of the sculpture. With nervous steps she went over to examine it more closely: a rough purple-red oval over a foot across that she knew from direct experience was a potentially lethal outflow of blood. There were spatters on the surface of the sculpture too.

A noise behind her made Poppy turn. A Somali woman in a mauve burqa was standing there with a little girl in a push-chair. Her mouth was slightly open, and there was a blank expression on her face. Bulging carrier-bags hung from the pushchair's handles.

'Did you see?' asked Poppy.

The woman shook her head. 'I hear sirens,' she said. 'Ambulance come. And police-car.'

'You didn't see who was hurt?'

The woman shook her head. 'I saw the ambulance go.'

'But not who was inside?'

'No.'

'When they went, did they sound the sirens?'

The woman thought for a moment. 'Yes,' she said.

'Thank you.'

They would not sound the sirens if the person was dead, Poppy thought as she hurried back to her block. That was something. And it might be that whatever had happened had nothing to do with her son anyway.

But the flat she let herself into was empty.

It took the ambulance ten minutes to reach King's College A&E. The contact between Stanlake and Evill was broken when the paramedics rushed Evill away through swing-doors for immediate treatment deeper inside the hospital. Stanlake was left to wait, the ghost of Evill's hand in his, his status as 'friend' no guarantee the medical staff would bother to tell him how Evill was doing, or even whether Evill had survived a loss of blood that tight bandaging had only slowed, not stopped.

A bored-looking policeman came over to Stanlake, sat him down and took a statement from him. Stanlake told the policeman that he had been coming through the tunnel when a figure in a hoodie – in the dark, he said, he could make out nothing of the figure's appearance – had bumped into him. Stanlake had gone on to find Evill – 'Everil' – lying on the ground and bleeding from a knife-wound, and had used Everil's mobile to call an ambulance.

'Turf war,' the policeman said, making desultory notes in a pad and suppressing a belch. 'Mate of yours, is he?'

'I know him only slightly,' Stanlake said.

The policeman took Stanlake's name and address, and wandered off.

The reception area of the casualty department was busy but depressing. Nurses and orderlies bustled back and forth, doing their best to avoid catching the eye of anyone waiting. They often stopped and spoke in low voices with the woman on the admissions desk, occasionally breaking into laughter as people do in the workplace however serious the work is, as he himself had sometimes laughed as he tortured, indifferent to the suffering he was ordered to cause, at times even resentful of it: resentful of the effort it required to suppress his natural empathy. How long had it been since he laughed?

Many of the people waiting to be dealt with had small but ugly injuries. Some were sitting rigidly upright, their faces stiff with pain. Others were drunk and feeling nothing, or nothing coherent, anyway, and these slumped in their seats. It had been like that in the war, and Stanlake felt tense and nervy. He wanted strongly to leave, but he needed to know whether Evill was alright. The rest of the patients, those who weren't visibly injured but had some internal problem, a blown heart, maybe, or an alcohol-stiffened liver, looked fundamentally unhealthy to him, and a sense of poverty hung over many of them. The air smelt medical and antiseptic, but this was the reverse of the perfume hall at Selfridges, with its flawlessly sterile women in white.

Looking up at the clock on the wall Stanlake was aware his mother would be home by now, and worrying about him. Just when he had decided he would have to go and maybe come back later, a male nurse emerged through the swing-doors. Stanlake recognised him as one who had gone through with Evill on his arrival. The nurse was pink-faced, with messy, dyed-blond hair spiked up, and was carrying a clipboard.

'Excusemeismyfriendalright?' Stanlake asked, running the words together to make it harder for the nurse, who was obviously trying to hurry through without being pestered, to ignore him.

'Your friend?'

'He was stabbed in the leg.'

'Oh, yes.' The nurse looked at him more attentively now, and Stanlake felt suddenly selfconscious, as if his insides were on display to this person who, it struck him now, was slightly effeminate in his manner, who might therefore know things. 'Everil, right?'

'Yes.'

'The knife-blade nicked an artery. We had to give him quite a large transfusion, just under a litre, but Mister Cannery managed to repair it under local. He'll be okay.'

'Can I see him?'

'He'll be tired, but – ' The nurse wavered. 'Alright, I'll take you through. Just wait there a minute.'

'Thank you.'

The nurse went over to the front desk and handed the receptionist the clipboard. They had a small conversation, then he came back and led Stanlake through the swing doors and down a succession of corridors to a small ward of ten beds, seven of which were occupied.

Everil lay on a bed by the window, eyes closed, looking drained. The window had neither blinds nor curtains; outside was the night. The room was overheated. Saline ran from a bag on a hook into the crook of Everil's right arm, and a plastic clip on his right forefinger was attached to a heart-rate monitor. He wore a short surgical smock that left his legs bare from just below the crotch. They were slightly spread in a way that was both suggestive of the sexual and like a newborn's. His right thigh was neatly bandaged, and a pale blue blanket covered his feet. Stanlake was struck by the delicacy of his features in repose.

'Everil?' the nurse said, touching his shoulder. 'You have a visitor.'

Everil opened his eyes sleepily and looked up at Stanlake, who was standing at the foot of his bed. 'Come round, blood,' he said creakily, indicating with a small movement a chair on the side of the bed that wasn't occupied by the monitoring equipment and IV bag-stand. The nurse left them. Everil offered Stanlake his hand. Stanlake took it, and they sat there for a while, hand-in-hand. In hospital, it seemed, you could express feelings that elsewhere were forbidden: none of the other patients paid them any attention. Everil stared ahead. Stanlake studied his profile, feeling the quiet pulse of Everil's blood against his fingertips as if it was his own. Muffled sounds of television shows bled from the head-

phones worn by some of the other patients, each of whom
had a miniature TV screen attached to his bed on an arma-
ture. This was disconcerting luxury to Stanlake, who had
heard on the news that the National Health Service had no
money.

'I'm tired, man,' Everil said, and now he looked at
Stanlake, and some shield or membrane had been drawn
back from his eyes, and his gaze was open and direct. 'They
say I got to stay in overnight at least.'

'Yes,' Stanlake said.

'If you ain't doing nothing better you could come visit.'

'I could.'

'Well, will ya?'

Stanlake bobbed his head. 'Yes.'

'Good,' Everil said, and he lay back and closed his eyes.
After a while the pressure of his fingers on Stanlake's
gentled. Stanlake withdrew his hand from Everil's and got up
to go.

It took two buses to get back to the estate, a tedious journey
with a boring wait in the middle, but Stanlake was barely
aware of it. It was strange to see the bloodstain in the
underpass: dulled to maroon by the deadening streetlight it
no longer looked like blood at all.

He who tried to give death would have died, he thought. I
have given death, and yet without questioning it I saved him.
He felt the ancestors strong within him then: not his direct
linear family but the Masks and the Beasts, those young
spirits who were tied to him by gifts of blood: a different kind
of family. He entered the block.

The lift rose, an ascension.

By the time he got the front door open Poppy was in the
hall, her chest heaving, her eyes wild.

He felt guilt then. He should have come home sooner: he
shouldn't have waited at the hospital, not for some boy he
barely knew, some boy who until yesterday had been an
enemy. He, Stanlake, was selfish, misdirected, disloyal. Yet
still for a moment he thought his mother might set all that
and all the rest aside, might come forward and embrace him,
and he could see the urge to do so was strong in her. But she

pushed it down, defied it, and stayed where she was. 'I was worried,' she said.

'I'm sorry,' he said.

'But you're alright.'

'Yes.'

And that was all. He turned from her and closed and locked the door. Not looking at her, he took off his coat and hung it up. His fingers brushed the folded bag of underwear. He would take it out later: it didn't seem to be part of this moment.

'I was worried,' Poppy repeated. 'The blood, and then you weren't here.'

'I went out.'

'What happened, Stanlake? Was it anything to do with you?'

'No. But I was there.'

'So tell me.'

He went through to the kitchen. It was easier to speak not looking at her, and perhaps easier for her too, because she stayed in the hall. 'When I went out they were where they usually are,' he said, raising his voice above the water from the tap as he ran it into the kettle. 'A boy came who I had seen buy drugs from them before. He was very angry about something. He stabbed Everil in the leg.'

'Everil?'

'The boy who leads them, who wears black and gold.'

'He told you his name?'

'Yes.'

'What happened then?'

'The others ran away. I called an ambulance. I went with him in the ambulance to the hospital. That is where I've been.'

'Why you and not one of his – would you call them friends?'

'The police were coming, and they are afraid of the police.'

'Because of their crimes?'

'Yes.'

'Stanlake?' He looked round. Now she was in the doorway. The kettle began to gurgle softly as it reached the boil.

'Is all this because – do you think these – these jackals can be new comrades?'

He looked away from her and got teabags from a jar. 'It is better they are comrades than enemies.'

'And you are lonely.'

His hand lingered on the lid of the jar. 'Yes.'

And he wanted her to hold him then, but he knew she wouldn't, couldn't. The kettle clicked off. Somewhere someone's TV was blaring, a Saturday night chat-show accompanied by hysterical laughter. He made two mugs of tea, handed one to Poppy, then went to his room. He thought of Everil in the hospital bed, thighs slightly spread, bandaged, with a tube in his arm, revealed as human as in a different way he had been revealed that morning, when he had bounced up to Stanlake without his crew and given him money and asked for nothing in return.

His mind went to the things he had bought, but just then he had no interest in them: they were only things, and people were more important.

He would visit Everil tomorrow. It would be good to have a reason to leave the house, even if it was to do something Poppy would disapprove of. Not the performing of an act of charity, which was to her a virtue, but becoming involved. He went back to the kitchen, washed up his mug, went to the bathroom, removed his foundation, washed his face, moisturised, and brushed his teeth. Poppy was in her room, sitting at her small dressing-table reading her bible. She didn't glance up as he passed back and forth before her open doorway.

He hunched the duvet to his shoulder and closed his eyes, hoping he wouldn't dream. But he did.

His dreams were filled with blood that night and he woke repeatedly. Somehow he felt the moment of his sacrifice was drawing near. He thought of his father, and he thought of Evill – Everil. And Florence in the red beaded dress, and Big Gun, later, in the same beaded dress. Big Gun had been trying to escape from something, that was why. Stanlake's mind flashed to what he had bought earlier: yes, those things could help.

Pulling on his track pants he padded down the hall, dug

into the pocket of his duffle coat, tugged out the bag and returned to his room.

Neither he nor Poppy ever closed their doors on each other, and Stanlake didn't do so now, though he did push his partway shut, angling it so he couldn't be seen from the hall if he was in front of the mirror. He tipped his purchases out onto the bed, delightful, intriguing, slippery, provocative packets of pleasure. Whoever wore such things would be wholly a creature of the sensual world, a person who lived in the pure present and sought only to give and receive physical enjoyment. He tugged at the plastic packaging in which the things were sealed. It stretched fleshily, then tore. He drew out the contents. Such small scraps of material, yet somehow they promised so much! He shucked off his track-pants and stood there naked, already half-erect.

The things were harder to wear successfully than he had expected, and he realised he had fallen into the mistake of imagining that they would do the work of transformation by themselves. Now he saw that they were only the basic elements of transformation: that he himself had to be the catalyst. He remembered the many magazine articles he had read by women about the work it took to perform feminine desirability.

Unexpectedly the lingerie emphasized the masculinity of his frame, a frame that up till then he had considered femininely slender: the lacey, scoop-necked bodies emphasized the width of shoulders that had seemed narrow before, and revealed the breadth as well as the flatness of his chest. This was an alchemy the reverse of what he had expected – one that reinscribed the fundamental maleness of his body. Yet still it released him from some pressure, as he had hoped it would, and his pleasure in his evolving appearance showed him clearly something he had always known: that he did not want to be a woman.

The lace shorts, worn over one of the lace thongs, were his most successful purchase, as these not only looked good, enhancing his butt perkily, but were fairly comfortable. The black silk baby-doll nightie was sensually pleasing but hung down from his chest in a way that concealed his shape, and so lacked a sexual charge. The mesh bodies were pleasingly

form-fitting, though as the material was black they contrast-
ed less with the darkness of his skin than did the white lace
of the shorts, and that was somehow disappointing. The
suspenders and stockings were awkward to put on and adjust
and keep in place, though they were perhaps the most
visually provocative of all his purchases when he checked his
reflection in the mirror: the most connotative of the sexual.

Dressing this way made him think about sex. It was
perhaps the first time he had ever thought about sex in terms
of what he himself might actually want to do. Before the war
he had just been a boy listening to other boys talk about girls,
and in the war everything to do with sex had become so
twisted it was better not to think about it at all. The kiss with
Big Gun had been romance, not desire. Like the other boys
he had masturbated, of course, but his mind had been blank
as he did so.

Now he thought of Everil.

He would like me in these things, I think, he considered,
staring at his reflection as he stood there in a bulging lace
thong and a lacy suspender-belt. He lifted himself up onto
the balls of his feet, lengthening his legs. His dick stiffened,
stretching out the material of the thong. He gripped it
through the lace and, staring into his own eyes, which were
wide and without make-up but as darkly receptive as if they
had been outlined in Kohl, he began to move his fist.

Everil lay back on the hospital bed, exhausted from the shock
of the attack, the anaesthetic and the transfusion, but
restless and unable to sleep. It was as if the adrenalin from
all that had, instead of passing away like piss, somehow
stained his flesh and left his nerves vibrating. He propped
himself up on his elbows and looked around him. All the
other patients seemed to be asleep. At least their uncon-
sciousness made him feel like he was on his own. He had
never shared a bedroom with anyone, except one night near
the end, when his mother was close to being in a coma, and
he had pushed his way onto her bed and fallen asleep lying
cuddled up to her.

He had never told anyone that.

He thought of Oily, dead. He couldn't feel anything about

what had happened either to Oily or to himself, except perhaps an intensification of the sense that he was nothing but a machine-part, a component. Oily had been another part of the same machine, and they had had no more choice in their actions, no more control over their destiny, than the parts of the Glock had had when he put it to Stanlake's jaw and pulled the trigger and it fired or didn't fire. Dead as lead, he thought. Bullets were made of lead, and he seemed to remember that pipes used to be made of lead, and people who drank the water that ran through them got sick.

Now they were plastic.

He checked his phone: 4 a.m. and no messages. The charge-light glowed a fading red: the battery was down to under ten percent. In the morning it would be dead. Too many apps, he thought. Bullshit apps he never even asked for. He texted Pit-Bull where he was, and that he and the others had to carry on selling, reminding him they'd all be in the shit if they fucked it off and stopped bringing in the dollars even for a day. The phone refused to send the text. He tried again. It dropped from eight percent to zero and shut down. He kissed his teeth and returned it to the bedside table. His bandaged thigh throbbed dully, and one of his elbows was bruised and jarred from where it had struck the Rock.

The thrust of the blade had been like a punch: he had only felt it on the outside of his body, hadn't realised at first that he'd been stabbed; and when the blood started to run down his leg he had had the light-headed thought that he had pissed himself, ridiculous though that seemed as the result of only a punch. And then, with no possibility of resisting, he had collapsed forwards, and Pit-Bull and the African boy had caught him and brought him down slow.

The African bwoy. Stanlake.

Just the thought of him made Everil's dick stir.

I'd like to –

But what *would* he like to do? He had never had sex, never been intimate with another male. Fucking women was a non-experience, didn't count. When it came to it, *if* it came to it with Stanlake, what would he want to do? He believed – hoped – that his body would tell him, but if it didn't then he would have to make some sort of decision about who he was, and what that meant.

In the meantime his thoughts were vague. But still his dick grew painfully stiff. At least the loose-fitting surgical gown concealed it. Not that there was anyone to see, though he supposed a nurse must wander round every so often to check on the patients. He needed the relief of a wank but didn't want to do anything that would make his blood pump faster, afraid it would rupture the stitched blood-vessel in his thigh. Also it seemed disgusting to wank in a room with other people in it, and there were no tissues, and he knew the sharp smell of spunk would spread throughout the overheated room and then everyone would know what he had been doing. Why did he give a fuck, though? Everyone wanked, didn't they? It was as if other people – other men – in becoming aware of the act would also somehow become aware of the desires that motivated it. Queer, battyman desires that added to the weight that had his whole life pressed down on him, but at the same time shot a light clear and sharp as a blade through that burdensome, tumerous mass.

He thought of Drilla, to whom he reported, from whom he got supplies, who larged it in his gold Rolex and his matte-black Bimma but was not free either; who was in the end just another stretch of the intestinal tract that took in meat and money and pumped out shit; and he and his soldiers were no more than hookworms taking little bites on the way down, excreting trinkets. Everil didn't care about things, he realised; had never cared about things. The brands and fashion labels, the Wiis, phones, flash trainers and other bullshit status items he obsessed on with the crew were just a way of filling a void inside him, the true nature of which he had never even tried to understand. But now he was beginning to.

Lying next to his mother that night she had mumbled and stirred without opening her eyes, and had blindly and repeatedly tried to push him away. He hadn't let her, had held onto her hot, thin, sweaty body, and eventually she had quieted. Did that make him a good son, pushing comfort onto her because beneath her resistance she surely needed it? Or was it just selfishness on his part, pimping her struggling, oblivious body for his own emotional needs? Two nights later she died in her sleep.

He had been downstairs, buzzing on dope and coke and playing online poker, which marketed itself as something cool and sexy but was in reality just a pathetic way for shut-ins to flush money down the toilet. He had lost £800 that night. Anything would have been a better use of it. He remembered a line about casinos: the house always wins. Stomping resentfully up to bed he had glanced in on his mother, and though he hadn't heard her breathing there had been so much churning inside his head he hadn't taken that absence in; had thought she was just asleep. When he went to her room late the next morning, red-eyed and resentful at another looming day of care-giving, she was already cold and stiff. He had a shower before calling the ambulance. The delay had made the police suspicious but they let it slide: she was just a junkie.

I could of died today. Yesterday I could of killed. I didn't do neither. Could that somehow be a beginning? I ain't had a smoke, he thought. That's what's wrong with me. And there ain't nothing I can do about it.

He closed his eyes and tried to force himself to go to sleep.

Chapter Twelve

Every Sunday morning was like this for Poppy: she stripped the beds, bagged up the sheets and duvet-covers, and took them and the rest of the week's washing in two large, nylon-threaded carrier-bags to Sudz, a launderette that was one of a row of commercial units round the back of the block. All the others had long since closed down except for a Paddy Power betting-shop, which at that hour was shut. In front of it, on the cracked paving-slabs, discarded betting slips shifted languidly in the stirring air, and cigarette butts lay about.

'For the poor you shall have with you always,' Jesus told His disciples.

Although the launderette was supposed to open at eight Poppy had a ten-minute wait before the woman showed up to unlock the door. A cigarette hung smouldering from one corner of her mouth, her hair was ratty and her eyes were bleary.

'I've no change,' she said by way of a welcome.

'I have the correct change,' Poppy said. 'And soap-powder.'

The woman grunted and turned away.

Back in the flat Stanlake planned his look for the day. Under his regular clothes – track-pants and vest – he would wear the lace thong and the lace short-shorts. That would be enough to begin with. For his make-up he would go a little bolder than he had yesterday: a touch of gold on the lips and eyelids; a touch of mascara to accentuate the feline shape of his eyes; an enhancement of the arch of his eyebrows with the soft black eyebrow-pencil.

Today he was aiming for neither the carnival voluptu-ousness he had been experimenting with in private nor the combative drag mask he had worn when he confronted the

jackals. Today, for the first time in his life, he was consciously using make-up to make himself appealing to someone else.

To a man.

Yes.

To acknowledge that was strange and unnerving and
exciting all at once, and curiously and unexpectedly it was
natural too.

Because nature is what arrives when you're not thinking:
you look round, and there it is.

The hospital's visiting times were 2-8 p.m. By 9.20 a.m.
he had made all his choices, which left him with four and a
half hours to fill, allowing forty minutes to get to there. He
was too distracted to read either a course-book or for
pleasure, and he had no new magazines to browse.

Sitting staring at his reflection it struck him that he
would have to hand-wash the new underthings he had
bought: he would be too embarrassed to give them to his
mother, and even if he found the nerve, the industrial-sized
washing-machines in the launderette would ruin them, as
they did anything delicate.

He thought of Big Gun, and how, if not for the war, he
would never have worn a dress.

If not for the war I would never wear what I am wearing
either, he thought. But that is different.

He squeezed the wooden bangles he had bought from
Primark over his hands, shook his wrists, checked himself in
the mirror, and felt pleased. It was by then nearly ten: the
dryers would be finishing. He went down to help his mother
fold and bag up the laundry. This too was their routine.
There was no-one else in the launderette, though several
machines were churning through their cycles, wads of
sloshing washing visible through scratched glass portholes.

Poppy was reading a dog-eared copy of *Heat* someone
had left lying about. 'These girls,' she said. 'Fourteen and
wanting breast implants!' She opened the door of one of the
dryers and felt the tumbling laundry. 'They should value
being children and not having to worry about that kind of
thing, not thinking about plastic surgery and botox and
anorexic dieting to get a man.'

'They say anorexic girls are afraid to become women,'

Stanlake said mildly.

'Either way it isn't good,' Poppy said. 'These are dry now.'

'Will you be going to church today?' Stanlake asked as he and Poppy pulled things from the dryer, folding and stacking them in the laundry-bags. The sheets they folded between them, their movements, choreographed by habit, requiring no direction.

'Later on,' Poppy said.

'Will you be gone all evening?'

'Yes. If you don't want to be on your own you should come.'

'I don't think so.'

It was a conversation they had had many times, and usually Poppy gave up at this point. Today, however, she took a breath and went on:

'All those things you believed in,' she said, and there was a tremor in her voice that made him look at her. 'All those things that were part of our lives back then, what use are they now, here? Termite-eaten masks in a hut? Dusty old drums in a shrine? Chicken- and goat-blood on a rock? I didn't think such things were right, but where we were they were at least part of something. Of history, or at least habit. But how does any of that help you here? The shrines are gone, the groves are cut down, everything is burned and gone. You can't cut a bullock's throat, they will call the police or the RSPCA. You need something you can use.'

'Those things are not gone,' Stanlake said. 'They are inside me, and I can use them. This' – he tapped his forehead – 'is my shrine.'

And he wanted to ask her how her religion helped, what use sin was, what help Christ being nailed to a cross two thousand years ago could really, truly be. But he knew she would give him the obvious answers: salvation, community, hope – and that was true, though underneath such words he was certain lay a void, or worse: a darkness. But to express all that was too hard and so he said nothing, just looked down and folded a bath-towel. One corner of the towel had caught on something in the machine and was coming unravelled: he would have to remember to snip off the loose threads to slow its deterioration.

They returned to the flat, put away the laundry and made their beds together. There was something reassuring about stretching a warm, clean sheet over even a tired and saggy mattress. How many people had slept on those mattresses before they were passed on to him and Poppy, Stanlake wondered. There were sweat-stains on them and perhaps, somehow, dream-stains too. Poppy folded a blanket and placed it on her bed so she could iron the dress she was going to wear to church. For some reason that morning the lack of such a mundane thing as an ironing-board emphasized the material poverty of their lives to Stanlake: seeing his mother having to kneel, perhaps.

1.30 finally came around, and, telling Poppy he was going out and would see her later, but not telling her where he was going, though she surely guessed, Stanlake pulled on his duffle coat and left the flat.

Someone had pissed in the lift.

The Crew weren't in the underpass.

Two buses and forty minutes later he was at the hospital. The ward felt different by day: most of the patients were awake, and several had visitors. Flowers added splashes of colour to the room. Everil sat propped up in bed. He was gazing out of the window with earphones in, and so was unaware of Stanlake's approach until Stanlake touched his shoulder. He looked round and his hard, pretty face broke into a boyish smile.

'You come, then,' he said, tugging out the earphones. R&B sounded tinnily.

'I did.'

Everil reached forward with a grunt and turned off the radio. 'Why come you ain't show earlier, though?'

'Visiting hours are from two.'

'Oh. Okay. Well, come sit, yeah.'

Stanlake sat. 'You look better,' he said, and it was true: the strained, grey-tinged look had left Everil's face.

'I been filling up on blood like a vampire is why,' he said. 'Like, a litre and a half, plus.'

'That is a lot.'

'Yeah. The nurse said.'

'Yes.'

They ran out of words then, and suddenly found it hard to look at each other. Everil turned his hand palm-upwards, offering it without demand, and Stanlake took it, closing his fingers around Everil's, and the connection felt good. For a while they didn't talk.

'Zat your mum, then?' Everil asked eventually. 'In the headwrap an' that?'

'Yes.'

'Thought so.'

'Why?'

'Cos she looks like you. Well, kind of. No offence, but you're prettier, though.'

Stanlake smiled, flushing with embarassment.

'I'm dying for a smoke, fam,' Everil grumbled. 'How you spose to get well if they ain't let you do what you do? And the food's shit.' Then, abruptly: 'You got a father at all?'

'He is dead.'

'What of?' Stanlake hesitated and Everil noticed and quickly added, 'You don't have to tell me, though. I mean like, not if you don't wanna.'

Lowering his voice and keeping his eyes on Everil's, Stanlake said, 'I killed him.'

And Everil's hand didn't flinch in his, as Stanlake had hoped it would not, had believed it would not: this hand that had held the Glock, that had pulled the trigger without hesitation not knowing the gun would misfire. And Everil didn't look away either, and he and Stanlake saw into each other, and in that interpenetration both of them understood that yes, this was a beginning, and Everil said, 'In the war, yeah?'

'In the war,' Stanlake nodded. Tears started in his eyes, and as he blinked them away he glanced around self-consciously, but the other visitors were occupied with their loved ones; were not aware that something had occurred at the bed beside them that to those involved was as momentous as the world shifting on its axis.

'If they give her time off in lieu,' a woman was saying to a middle-aged man with tubes clipped under his nose, 'she thought Australia might be nice. Or there's Spain.'

'With a cutlass,' Stanlake said, and his voice was now so

low it was all husk and no resonance. 'I saw my father's brains wet on the ground.' He looked away then, out at the blank sky. 'That is something, enh?' he said. 'That is something.'

And my father was kneeling and they were chanting and I was crying so hard my body was convulsing and I raised the cutlass above my head high as the sky, and I looked into my father's eyes and at that moment I believed in nothing, no gods, no ancestors. Everything was causal then, everything was basic, mechanical. I told myself I saw acceptance in those eyes, or at least the understanding that in this way I might save his wife, my mother; that I might save myself, his son. And that I could not save him.

I could not save him.

And I brought down the blade as hard as I could and I called that mercy, for him and for me, because I never could have struck a second blow, not to kill, I did not have that in me, though I hacked the body in a frenzy as things, energies, spirits left me like lightning leaves a storm-cloud.

And she watched me: my mother watched me do this thing with eyes flayed. And as I did it one of the grinning Beasts who had lifted her skirt not with his hand but with a machete-blade, let the material fall back into place, and she was at least spared that as later I was to learn Big Gun's mother was not, as his sisters were not.

But I was not spared.

I don't remember who was doing what. Their faces were nothing to me at the time, Big Gun, Diamondz, Blondie, others I came to know later: it was as if whichever way I looked the sun was behind their heads, their faces black holes burnt into a nightmare radiant nothingness, absences framed by a dazzling corona, Makinde's most of all, haloed with death-energies like spikes, a blazing crown for a saint in negative. And he was always behind my mother, laughing, and she heard him but never saw his terrible face, and she sobbed so hard snot ran down her face and her whole body was shaking, shaking. And they chanted, 'Souljah! Souljah! Souljah!' to mark my conversion, my perversion, and fired into the air, driving the maddened spirits of the departed from the village, and I looked down at the red and white and brown confusion of my father's open head, and at least he died fast, and they took me away into the forest and there they brought the Beast out from inside me who could do these things without tears.

And later Stanlake did not think, which boy held the gun to my head, which one held the machete at my mother's genitals, because by then he was them, and it would have answered nothing, would have relieved nothing for him to know. Who could he blame? All of them? None of them? God? Himself? The war? Fear? Fear had had power over all of them, that was for sure. It stalked them; it hung over them like smoke. Even Makinde was filled with fear – of the enemy, of those above him, and at the end of those below him too: his creations, as he believed them to be, Stanlake supposed, though that was the vanity of a man who was no more than a channel for darkness, a conduit for fear as if fear was a thing in itself that had its own needs and purposes.

Stanlake had seen the tunnels, the cells and corridors of his father's brain momentarily pulsing then sagging among splintered bone and hair on a darkening spray of speargrass. He hadn't seen his father's face, not then – he had fallen face-down – though later it came to him in dreams. Sometimes it was the face of other people, and he wondered what that meant.

And now Everil's fingers did tighten round his, but reassuringly. 'C'mere, fam,' he said, sitting up awkwardly in the bed and pulling Stanlake to him. And Stanlake leant forward and let Everil hug him, and he slipped his arms round Everil's hot, hard back, and they held each other like that for a long while. To be held was a new thing for both of them, and when they finally drew back there was a moment of fear.

'You alright?' Everil asked, and he was asking on many levels.

Stanlake had to clear his throat. 'Yes,' he said. 'I am okay.' He smiled weakly.

Then, perhaps inevitably, not knowing how to go forward, and afraid of making some wrong move, they pulled back a little. 'You didn't get no bother off the Crew,' Everil asked, 'when you passed by?'

'There was no-one there.'

Everil kissed his teeth. 'Idle fuckers,' he said. 'One day I'm down and they're fucking it off. And my phone's outta charge so I can't even bell them to pressurise.'

'Pressurise?'

'For them to be out there shifting the gear. Getting paper.' Off Stanlake's look he added, 'Getting paid.'

'To pay you?'

'So's I can pass it up the line and get more shit to sell.'

'It sounds like a business.'

'Ain't nothing but. And I'm like middle management. Fucked about by the bosses and the workers.'

'And that boy? The one who – '

Everil sighed. 'We was at school together,' he said. 'The same school you're at now, right? Back in the day. Stats, we called him. Cos he was good at maths. He could do it in his head, like without a calculator. Back then that meant he was a genius. Funny, ain't it? Cos I can do all that now. Keep figures in my head. Cos you can't be writing shit down: you gotta keep it all up top. You work the muscle and build it up.'

'He shouted about his friend,' Stanlake said, both he and Everil reflexively coding their conversation against being overheard.

'Oily,' Everil said. 'Yeah. Thing is though, if that's what you're doing with your life, I mean what they was doing, then it's your mentality that you always push it, you know? You take it the most to the edge you can, cos that's where you get the most intensest rush. Like whatsit flying too close to the sun, like a moth. And sometimes, like, inevitably, you fuck up, you know? And sometimes that ain't a lesson you can learn from. And I feel bad for him, I do, but then I ain't free either, you know? I don't keep bringing in the paper, then it's me what's gonna get fucked up. Me principally, but the crew as well. And that's on them, but it's on me too. So we gotta do what we're doing. And if it weren't us, it'd be someone else. Cos ain't no-one pure in this life, is it?'

Stanlake thought of Makinde, and Florence, and of himself. He had thought it would be different here, but it was the same.

No, not quite the same.

Everil misunderstood his silence, it seemed, because he said, 'Don't judge me, man.'

'I do not,' Stanlake said.

'My mum was a crackhead,' Everil said quietly. 'When I come out of her my lungs was fucked. It's why come I got to use that.' He nodded to where his inhaler sat on the bedside table. 'It's why come I'm small. So tell me: what were the odds drugs weren't gonna figure big in my life?'

'Was?'

'When she was alive,' Everil said, and his eyes retreated. Stanlake took his hand. Then, making himself not think about it, he bent forward and kissed Everil gently on the mouth. Everil inhaled sharply but his lips responded. It wasn't a passionate kiss, though it began a stirring in both of them: it was, rather, an affirmation of what was human in them; a simple act that gave sensual pleasure and relieved pain and dread, though in its unexpectedness it startled as well.

Stanlake sat back down. Everil now had a little gold on his lips. Smiling, Stanlake reached across and brushed it away with his thumb.

'So did you?' Everil asked.

'Did I what?'

'Treat yourself to something pretty?'

Stanlake flushed. 'Yes,' he said, dipping his head shyly.

'You got any of it on now?'

'Yes. Underneath.'

'Don't worry, fam,' Everil said. 'I ain't gonna ask to see it. Unless – ' His eyes went to the curtain above the bed. It was designed so it could be pulled round on a rail to give a patient privacy. He and Stanlake looked at each other, then, daring rising in them, they glanced round the ward. No-one was paying them any attention and there were no medical staff to be seen. Stanlake took hold of the curtain and drew it briskly round the bed. Everil was grinning as, his heart pounding, Stanlake quickly took off his duffle coat and pulled his hoodie up over his head to reveal the close-fitting red vest beneath. He pulled up the vest to show his flat, trembling stomach.

'I would like to get a piercing in my belly-button,' he said breathlessly. Then, taking a breath, he pushed the track-pants down to mid-thigh, turning sideways-on to Everil to show off the lace-covered globes of his butt and the bulge of his crotch simultaneously. The white fabric stretched provocatively over his smooth, dark skin.

Everil smiled. 'C'mere, blood,' he said. Stanlake turned front-on and awkwardly shuffled forward. With the confidence that comes from realising that what is natural to you is as naturally reciprocated, Everil reached out and took the bulge of Stanlake's crotch in his hand like a ripe fruit. Stanlake gasped, and his cock began to expand painfully inside the confining mesh. With some difficulty Everil bent forward and kissed the swelling, stiffening bulge, and Stanlake's chest heaved.

From beyond the curtain they heard the clatter of an approaching hospital cart. With a grunt Everil slumped back. Stanlake hastily pulled up his track-pants and tugged his vest and hoodie down, and he and Everil suppressed excited laughter as he whisked the curtain back, exposing them to the ward once more. The trolley passed the door and went on. The woman who had been talking about Spain and Australia gave Stanlake and Everil a dark look: who were these unnatural youths who were laughing in hospital?

Demurely, Stanlake sat back down by the bed, angling his hips to conceal his erection from her and the other people in the room.

'Can I beg you a favour, blood?' Everil asked, reaching out and taking his hand again.

'What do you need?'

'A couple things. But I don't wanna drag you into my business, though.'

'Perhaps it is my business now.'

'Kinda maybe. But I don't want you in it, fam. Just if you can do this one ting for me one time and then it's done.'

'Okay.'

'Go Solid's and tell the Crew they got to be out there selling. They'll bitch you out but tell 'em its orders from up top. From me, from Drilla. His drum's in Cardinal Three. I'll give you the number. Cuts'll be there, he practically lives there, and probably Pit-Bull, the white brer.'

'Why would they do what I say?'

'Take my phone. That way they'll know it's coming from me. And Pit-Bull saw what you done when I got murked.'

Stanlake nodded.

'Get 'em to charge it. Then come back here again later, yeah, and on the way you pick up whatever dollars they make, plus the phone. When's visiting time till?'

'Eight.'

'Come back just before then, yeah? Zat okay?'

'Yes.'

Everil's brow furrowed. 'True-say I don't wanna put this on you, blood. I want you to be part of something else for me, you know what I'm saying? Like, not what my life is now: something better. But you got my back to the ultimate so I'm arxing. Say yes or say no, either way I won't put nothing on you again, I swear.'

Stanlake squeezed Everil's hand. 'I will do this for you,' he said.

An hour later Stanlake was looking up at Cardinal Three, a slab of black haloed by the pale sun behind it.

Could these be new comrades, his mother had asked. He hadn't answered.

Yes. No. Maybe.

The entry-door was propped open with a brick. That was good: he wouldn't have to buzz Solid to get into the building. He would be a surprise.

To not be alone. It was possible, yes.

And as the Beasts had accepted him, so he could make these jackals, this crew, accept him, whatever they thought of his appearance and what it might signify.

Yet there would be a delicate moment when they first saw him. Ought he go back to his own flat first, at least bring the knife with him? No: they are uncertain; they will want to discuss things. That boy Pit-Bull will have said what I did. And I think they are just enough afraid of me still.

Solid's flat was on the twelfth floor.

The lift was working.

A minute later Stanlake was standing outside Solid's featureless front door. On the aluminium flap of the letterbox was written in marker pen, 'Fuck Off Junk Mail Cuntz'. Bass from within was making it rattle, and through it he could smell sensi. There was no bell. He banged the letterbox sharply twice, and waited. There was movement inside, then a slight shift of light as someone pressed an eye against the spyhole. Locks were turned and bolts shot back. The door opened a little way and Solid looked out, a bovine expression on his face, his bloodshot eyes blankly hostile.

'The African battybwoy,' he said. The pink strip of tape across his nose was wrinkled. 'What you doing, coming my drum?'

'Evill sent me.'

Solid raised his eyebrows. 'Yeah?'

'That is how I have your address.'

Solid thought this over. 'Come, then,' he said, and he opened the door and held it so Stanlake could enter, though this meant Stanlake would have to pass under his arm.

'I will follow you,' Stanlake said.

Solid shrugged. 'Push the bolts across when you shut it, yeah,' he said, turning and going into the lounge.

Stanlake did so, then followed him. The lounge stank of dope, takeaway tins, stale beer, and sleepers' breath. Cuts and Pit-Bull slumped on a grey leather sofa. A large HD TV hung on the wall. An X-box and gamers' pads sat on the floor below it. R&B thumped from speakers attached to an iPod in its dock. A computer sat on a desk. In the middle of the coffee-table a pub ashtray overflowed with stubbed-out cigarettes and roaches.

Solid muted the music. 'We got a guest,' he said.

At the sight of Stanlake Cuts and Pit-Bull tensed, but they kept their expressions indifferent.

'He makes out Evill sent him,' Solid added.

At that Pit-Bull sat forward. 'He's okay, then? Cos we didn't know – '

'They gave him surgery,' Stanlake said. 'He is okay.'

'How we know that's true, though?' asked Solid.

'He told me your address.'

'Maybe.'

'And this.' Stanlake produced Everil's phone and held it out. 'He asked that you charge it.'

Pit-Bull took the phone from Stanlake. The bruise on his neck where Stanlake had kicked him was yellowing now. 'Looks like his,' he said.

'Charge it and you will see,' Stanlake said. 'And he told me to say you must keep selling.'

'How he know we ain't?' Cuts asked sharply.

'I told him.'

'How you know that, though?'

'I went through the underpass and you were not there.'

'Since when is our business your business?' Solid said.

Stanlake shrugged.

Cuts kissed his teeth. 'And you told him that, yeah? That we wasn't there?'

'He asked me.'

'But he's alright, though?' Pit-Bull asked, and Stanlake sensed a concern in him that wasn't felt by the other two. 'You ain't lie, though?'

'They repaired the artery in his leg under local anaesthetic and gave him a transfusion of blood,' Stanlake said. 'He is in King's College hospital, perhaps for one more night, I don't know. I went with him in the ambulance. I was there today.'

'Twat getting murked in the first place,' Cuts said. Then, to Stanlake: 'You can tell him we're gonna gut that fucker Stats.'

'Open him up,' Pit-Bull nodded.

'He said to never mind that, you must go and sell,' Stanlake said. 'He said I am to come there at seven-fifteen and collect the money and take it to him.'

'Oh, yeah?' Solid straightened up from where he had been putting Everil's mobile in a cradle to charge. 'He said that, yeah? And who made you the don's lieutenant all of a sudden?'

'He did.'

Solid grunted and fell silent. Stanlake watched as Pit-Bull built a joint, his pale pink tongue moving tremulously along the two thin pieces of conjoined paper before he broke off to split a cigarette, tipped out the tobacco, then toasted, crumbled and sprinkled the resin. The white boy put the result to his lips, sparked up, drew deep, then, still holding his breath in, offered it to Stanlake roach-first. Stanlake took it and toked delicately. As the smoke poured from his nostrils he passed it to Solid. Solid noted the dusting of gold Stanlake's lips had left on the paper, shrugged, put it to his own lips and blazed. Exhaling, he passed the joint on to Cuts, who blazed too.

It felt like years since Stanlake last smoked cheeba, and he no longer found it pleasant. Mixed in with the mellow tone was a more jagged one, an awareness that was both heightened and, he knew, distorted. It was time for him to go.

'You must sell now,' he repeated, and he stood there, and he was short and slight and effeminate, but he had been younger and given orders and been obeyed. He had shot grown men for disobeying him, and he couldn't leave until the crew acknowledged his order.

'You got nerve, blood,' Cuts said.

Stanlake said nothing, standing his ground as the moment stretched and strained.

'You know what, 'llow it, fam,' Pit-Bull said, struggling to his feet. 'Brer's right, we gotta get selling.' After a pointless pause Cuts followed suit. Solid remained sitting. Stanlake turned to him.

'I will come to the underpass at 7.15,' he said.

'Aright, aright,' Solid grumbled, giving in and getting up too. 'Cheese an' bread.' Seeing Stanlake's wrinkled brow he said, 'Cheese an' bread means we're doing it, yeah.'

'Good.'

Stanlake turned and left the flat.

He had hoped Poppy wouldn't be home when he got back but she was. Knowing his clothes stank of dope-smoke, and not wanting her to smell it, he didn't take his coat off in the hall as he usually did, but instead went straight through to his bedroom. There he hung it over the back of a chair and changed into a pair of low-cut white jeans and a skinny-rib vest, also white. He left his other clothes spread on the bed to air.

'Where have you been?' Poppy called as Stanlake went through to the kitchen. She was in her room, reading her bible.

'Visiting a friend.'

'A girl?'

'A boy. Do you want tea?'

'No.'

Stanlake fixed himself a mug and sat at the kitchen table in a fading slice of sunlight. He thought of kissing Everil again and his heart began to race. He had kissed Big Gun, but he and Big Gun had been boys: he and Everil were men, young men it was true but still men, and it was different. Realer, if reality admits of gradations, and more serious, despite how serious things had been back then out on the roadblock, because here there was the possibility of a future.

He thought of the Masks. Was it a betrayal of them to want a life? Surely they would not think so. Surely they were not a hole into which all his future happiness must be poured just because he, by chance, had survived. No. They were my friends. They still are my friends. And my mother is wrong: they have not been left behind to gather dust. I share with them all I can.

Dusk fell softly, sinking through twilight into night.

Poppy left for worship at six. The minute she was gone Stanlake went to his bedroom, pushed down his track-pants, the lace panties and thong, and masturbated thinking of Everil on top of him, pushing his tongue into his mouth. As he moved his fist reggae music began to pulse through the ceiling from the flat above, as if the building was resonating and amplifying his desire. Soon hot seed flooded his navel.

He went down to the underpass just after seven and found Pit-Bull, Solid and Cuts waiting for him, resentful and hunched against the cold. No punters were about. Stanlake brushed knuckles with Pit-Bull and Solid as he had seen other youths do. Cuts stood aloof, refusing his fist. Stanlake followed Pit-Bull down one of the tunnels. Pit-Bull produced a roll of dog-eared banknotes and handed it to him.

'Is this everything?'

'Yes, blood,' Pit-Bull said, and though in the dark Stanlake couldn't see his face, from the tone of his voice he believed Pit-Bull was telling him the truth. 'Oh, and here.' Pit-Bull drew Everil's mobile from his pocket and passed it to

Stanlake. 'Charged.'

'Thank you,' Stanlake said, pocketing the money and the phone.

'We'll be out here till the shit gets old or we're outta stock,' Pit-Bull said. 'Then we bounce, aright?'

Stanlake nodded in the dark, adding as he turned to go, 'That is cool, fam.' He could feel Pit-Bull smile at hearing those words in his accent.

By the time Stanlake reached the hospital it was ten to eight and an orderly tried to bar his way, only grudgingly letting him through after Stanlake explained that he was just dropping off some personal items for a patient. When he reached the ward he found Everil twitchy and wired.

'Where the fuck you been, man?'

'I have been doing what you asked me to do.'

Everil took a breath. 'Sorry, blood. I've been going up the walls in here with no fags and no dope and not knowing a wha gwaan, you get me? Feeling just totally fucking – powerless.'

'Your phone,' Stanlake said, and passed it to him. Their fingertips brushed, and the contact earthed something in both of them, and they became more human. The other patients were asleep or plugged into their entertainment centres.

'Everything go okay?' Everil asked as he thumbed in his password. There was a muted musical flourish. 'The Crew do what you say?'

'Yes.'

There was the beep of a text waiting. Then another. 'Shit.'

'What?'

'Drilla.'

'Drilla?'

'The boss-man. Shit. I gotta get outta here directly,' Everil said, struggling up. 'I gotta go see him.' His breath was short and he reached for his inhaler on the side-table.

Stanlake took his elbow and helped him swing round into a sitting position on the edge of the bed. 'Did the doctor say you could – ?'

'Fuck the doctor. I gotta run this. You got the dollars,

yeah?'

'Yes.'

'How much?'

'Eight hundred and twenty pounds.' Stanlake had counted it discreetly on the largely passengerless bus on the way over.

'Just enough with the rest.' Everil took a hit on his inhaler, bent over and began to root his street-clothes out of the bedside locker.

'I could deliver it for you.'

'I already put you in harm's way once today, fam,' Everil said. 'So no. A man's gotta own his business, pay for his own self. Plus I got to swing by mine to get the rest of the dollars, so you couldn't just go dere anyways. But – ' He looked at Stanlake and hesitated. 'Would you come with me, though? Not go in, just – '

'Yes.'

Everil was wearing black trunks and a white vest under his surgical smock, and low socks. He found his hoodie and trainers but no track-pants. 'Ah, man, this is fuckeries,' he moaned. 'Dem get tief?'

'They were cut off you by the medics.'

'Fuck. I'm fucked.'

'Wait.'

Stanlake went off and found an orderly and explained that his friend was leaving the hospital but had no trousers: were there any spare pairs he could borrow and return, or have? The orderly, a plump and sweetly helpful Nigerian woman, disappeared into a storeroom and came out with an average-sized pair of grey track-pants, which she gave to Stanlake with a smile. He hurried back to Everil's ward. The charge nurse was just leaving.

'She said I oughtta be alright so long as I ain't put no pressure on the stitches,' Everil said. 'Like jogging or kick-boxing or shit. Thanks, blood' – he took the track-pants from Stanlake. 'So I promised her I wouldn't do none a dat.' He bent forward and slid his feet down the legs of the track-pants, then wiggled them up awkwardly over his thighs and butt. Then he pushed his feet into his trainers. 'Tie my Nikes, fam?'

Stanlake knelt and did so. 'Can you walk?'

'I better.'

Stanlake took Everil's hand and helped him stand. His first few steps were tentative, but once he realised the stitches weren't going to burst instantly his movements became easier and more natural.

Outside the hospital minicabs waited in line. Stanlake and Everil went to the frontmost one. Stanlake opened the door and helped Everil in. Everil slid over and Stanlake got in after him, pulling the door closed as Everil gave his address to the driver, a lanky Somali with khat-reddened teeth. Everil spread his thighs and with a tight grunt hooked the leg with the stab-wound in it over Stanlake's leg and Stanlake rested his hand on Everil's knee. The driver glanced in his mirror but said nothing. Congolese music played softly on the stereo.

Twenty minutes later they were pulling up outside a terraced house in a quiet street lined with budding beech and blossoming cherry trees. Stanlake was surprised that Everil lived in such a place: he had assumed he would have a flat like Solid's, in a block. Something uglier. He stayed in the car while Everil hobbled quickly up to the front door and let himself in. Five minutes later he re-emerged in a different tracksuit, an all-white Adidas one with inset black pvc logos, and with a fresh black do-rag on his head and different trainers on his feet. His movements seemed more confident now, though he still had trouble getting into the cab. He gave the driver a new address, which turned out to be a modern house on a small new-build estate off the Old Kent Road, down Lewisham way. The house was featureless but the cars outside it – a matte-black Saab and a customised silver Range-Rover with tinted windows – were stand-out expensive.

'Stay here, fam,' Everil said to Stanlake.

'Hey, man, you got the money for this?' the taxi-driver asked as Everil swung the passenger door open and lifted his legs out one at a time.

'I got the money, blood,' Everil flashed his roll. 'You'll get yours, aright. So chill, yeah.'

The driver nodded. Stanlake watched Everil roll up to the

house, disguising his limp as much as possible. Before he reached the unlit porch the front door opened a crack. Inside was dark, and no-one was visible from where Stanlake was watching. The door opened further. Everil went in. The door closed.

Stanlake sat back and exhaled. The driver turned off the engine, leaving the ignition key in so the music still played. After a while Stanlake became aware of the man's eyes studying him in the rear-view mirror.

'What?'

'I think you have seen war,' the driver said.

'Yes?'

'I have seen war, so I know.'

Stanlake saw something of himself reflected in the darkness of the Somali man's eyes, in the constant flickering of his pupils. He did not want to have this conversation with this man, not here. Yet he was not an enemy, and it is always good to have allies, so – 'I too,' he said.

'Would you go back,' the driver asked, 'if you could?

'No,' Stanlake said. 'Here is better.' When the driver didn't reply Stanlake asked, 'Where is home for you?'

'I grew up in Mogadishu.'

Stanlake nodded. 'I hear it's very bad there,' he said.

'People here don't know how things can go,' the driver said sadly. 'They take it for granted what's here today will be the same tomorrow. They don't know it can all just – go.'

We didn't either, Stanlake thought: we were no wiser. He looked round at the house. As if his look was a cue the front door opened and Everil came out. The driver turned the key in the ignition. The music cut out momentarily and the engine juddered into life as Everil got back in.

'Sorted,' he said. He smelt strongly of cigarettes and dope-smoke.

'Where now?' asked the driver.

Everil didn't reply at once. A sudden contortion passed over his face.

'What is wrong?' Stanlake asked. 'Is it the wound?'

Everil turned to him and his eyes were glinting pits. 'I don't wanna go home, blood,' he said breathlessly. 'I know it sounds like bollocks, but I proper can't go back there tonight.'

He pulled out his aspirator and took a hit. He wanted Stanlake with him, needed him with him, but not in that dead place where love had only ever been a damaged, twisted thing. It could be made to live, maybe; could be redeemed. But not easily, not with one grand gesture, and he didn't have the strength to try tonight. His first thought was a hotel, though he had never stayed in a hotel in his life, but before he could voice it Stanlake said, 'We will go to mine.' And before Everil could protest, if he had been going to protest, Stanlake had given his address to the driver and they were on their way.

Twenty minutes later Stanlake was helping Everil out of the taxi on the edge of the estate. Everil leaned in the window and paid off the driver, giving him an extra ten. The driver slipped the money into the breast pocket of his denim jacket and nodded to Stanlake before winding up his window and heading off into the night.

'Won't your mum be home?' Everil asked, suddenly aware that this dreamlike, longed-for moment was as real as the Glock, as the knife-blade. 'I mean cos I ain't up for – '

'Not for two more hours, I think,' Stanlake said. 'She is at church.'

'Maybe this ain't a good idea, blood.'

'Maybe,' Stanlake said. Everil couldn't read the look in his eyes. 'If you want,' he went on, 'you could call another cab on your mobile and go somewhere else.'

'Nah,' Everil said. 'Nah, you're alright.' He took a breath. 'Let's do this, then.'

They went down into the underpass. It was deserted. 'Idle fuckers,' Everil said. 'Can't they stick at nothing for two fucking seconds if I ain't cracking the whip on 'em?'

In truth he was relieved they weren't there; that he didn't have to explain – or refuse to explain – what he was doing with Stanlake, where he was going with him. His dick stirred in his track-pants though he had no clear sense that anything sexual was going to happen tonight. Yet he was still the don, and so he pulled out his mobile to bollock them. Pit-Bull's phone went to answer, as did Solid's. He didn't even bother trying Cuts. 'So why come I mission over the Rock and find

you ain't selling, though?' was the message he left on Pit-
Bull's phone.

They went on to Stanlake's block. Stanlake held the door
for Everil to go ahead. It swung shut behind them with a
solid clunk.

The lobby was empty. The lift was working. They rose up
fifteen floors in silence.

'Mummy?' Stanlake called as he opened the door. Everil
tensed but there was no reply. He peered over Stanlake's
shoulder into the dimly-lit interior. What am I doing here, he
wondered. But then Stanlake took his hand and drew him
over the threshold and he knew. What if his mother *had* been
here and seen us coming in this way? Well, so what if she
had? It wasn't like he was afraid of her. What, then? Shame?
Everil rarely felt shame. To him it was mostly a shallow
word; the shame of being seen with a butters sket or in a pair
of gay trainers; or it was bragged of in garish talk of manhood and disrespect, a glinting surface masquerading as
heart. But here, now, it had weight. Yes, he would have felt
shame. For his treatment of her before, now he was confronted by her humanity; for what he wanted from her son,
which she would not have failed to see as it poured from his
eyes searchlight-bright. This was what family was, he
realised, and it was something he had never known. He had
known only its shadow, and its absence had given him
freedom to walk in desolate places, and he had thought that
good.

Not now.

I got a house but not a home, he thought. To take
Stanlake there would have been to reveal everything he
lacked; to lay bare that he didn't know if he was even capable
of love. Not the love between mates, brers, bloods that was
wound up inextricably with cheerful cruelty, but the love that
demands and exposes.

Stanlake's flat was the mirror of Solid's, and in every way
its opposite: dark and close, cluttered, colourful and homely.
Glancing in the kitchen Everil saw washed-up plates stacked
neatly in the drying rack, pans scoured shiny waiting on the
stove, and a sink that wasn't full of rancid, oily takeaway tins
budding mould. Onions hung in a basket; on a shelf yams

and sweet potatoes waited quietly, and in the air was a saturation of spices. Stanlake drew him on past what in Solid's flat was the lounge, but here was a bedroom. An African-print dress was draped over the back of a chair, a duvet with a small floral pattern was drawn taut over a mattress. A bible sat on the dressing-table, the gold cross that inlaid its burgundy cover glinting.

As Stanlake led Everil to his bedroom he too asked himself what he was doing bringing Everil here, what he would do or say when Poppy returned. He didn't know, but he found that he didn't care either, because this was something he needed to do: this man was some sort of answer.

I will light candles for the spirits, he thought. He took the lighter from its place on the shelf, clicked it into life and lit the six candles that flanked the mirror, three on each side. Patrick, Robert, Matthew, he thought. Big Gun, Diamondz, Blondie, watch over me. Watch over us.

The candle-flames glowed gently, and in their soft warmth Everil found himself watched by flawless faces, exotic birds of fashion cut carefully from magazines and stuck up around the walls with tape and Blu-tack. Offcuts of material had been made into a bedspread and throws that were draped over the chair and table and pinned up at the window: African wax-prints, Asian paisleys, Arab geometries. The world in a room, the variety defying the poverty that underlay it: the sparse furniture, no sound-system, TV or computer. Not even a bed, just a mattress. Yet richer than Solid's drum, and richer, Everil knew, than his own home.

Suddenly he was so tired he could hardly stand. Stanlake, whose hand he was still holding, was instantly aware of the shift in his balance. 'Come sit,' he said.

Everil nodded and let Stanlake help him sink down onto the mattress. His thigh ached deep within the flesh. He had hated being stuck in the hospital but from his exhaustion now he realised he should have stayed there. But then Drilla had texted and he had had to go because Drilla wouldn't deal with any of the others, and Drilla didn't hear excuses.

I used to want to be him, Everil thought. Get rid of me and just be him. But when he had been in Drilla's drum tonight he had seen not something to aspire to but a horror show of inhumanity. The same-old-same-old, the no-horizon girls, the guns, the futile gold, the empty posturing and brag.

He lay back and closed his eyes. He didn't want to think about Drilla, or the Crew, or any of it. He felt a great and overwhelming relief as Stanlake unlaced his trainers and worked them off his feet. He was almost – not asleep, but in some other place – but came to enough to sit up and let Stanlake raise his arms and slide off first his tracksuit-top and then his vest. Then Stanlake slid his track-pants down, working them gently over his ankles. Everil was now in only his trunks. Small rustling sounds told him Stanlake was undressing too.

'Turn on your side,' Stanlake said softly. Everil rolled over and Stanlake slid into place behind him, and he could feel the warmth of Stanlake's chest against his back. Stanlake put his arms around him, and silent tears squeezed from the corners of Everil's eyes as Stanlake held him as he had never been held. Stanlake kissed the back of Everil's neck and a shudder passed through him and something was released and left his body. He could feel Stanlake's rising stiffness against his butt, and it felt right. He drew one of Stanlake's hands to his lips and kissed it. The scents of cocoa-butter and cinnamon touched his nostrils. He gripped Stanlake's hand and held it tight to his breast, a fist like a heart.

They hadn't meant to sleep. The candles had burnt down and gone out, and the room was in darkness when Poppy returned from church. The sound of her key in the lock didn't wake them, nor her gentle closing of the door behind her once she had come in. She was in a pensive mood, and that made her move through the world trying to create as little disturbance as possible. Reverend Obasanjo had preached on the duties of mothers that evening, and it seemed to Poppy that he was saying mothers were to be held accountable for all the failings of men, and his words had left her spirit burdened. They had been harsh and, she felt, unfair: yet hadn't she failed with her son?

But what options did I have, she asked herself as she hung up her coat. Without choice, what does it mean to fail? And Stanlake was headstrong: he had been determined to follow his own path even before –

She wandered through to his bedroom, assuming he was still out as it was too early for him to have gone to sleep, wondering who this friend was that he had taken to visiting. She smelt candle-wax and something else: radiant body-heat, though she didn't consciously recognise that second scent until she saw the shadowy shapes on the mattress. Two young men in just their underwear: her son and the leader of the jackals, and her son's arms were around the jackal holding him close, the jackal she had seen hanging upside-down from the climbing-frame that morning as witches were said to hang upside-down from trees like bats, and there were no trees round here, so – All those stories she had her whole life dismissed as foolishness seemed not so foolish now; seemed no longer hysterical ignorance but plain and possible fact.

She turned and stumbled off down the hall, needing to get away from – she couldn't name it yet – the *situation*, needing to breathe. She wrenched the front door open and stepped out into the blank, bare lobby area. A gust of wind sliced through the louvred windows that made up one wall of the lobby and slammed the door shut behind her with a gunshot bang.

Stanlake started awake. He sat up. Everil stirred. 'What, fam?' he asked sleepily.

'Nothing. Stay here.'

Stanlake pulled on his track-pants and left the room. He saw Poppy's coat hanging on the back of the front door. She came and left and I heard it slam, he thought. She left because she saw me in bed with him.

I do not care.

He stepped out into the lobby. Poppy stood there, turned away from him. Her shoulders were hunched, her arms were tight around her, and in oblique profile he could see she was blinking rapidly.

'How could you do this to me?' she said, palming tears from her eyes. 'And with that – that – devil?'

'He is not a devil and it is not to do with you.'

'It is a crime against God! The Bible says – '

'Daddy didn't believe in the Bible and nor do I.'

'Don't you dare speak his name!' Poppy said, and now her eyes were on him like wet stones, whetting stones and as hard. 'You think he would have accepted your – lifestyle? You think he would have accepted this *filth*? You're a killer! A murderer before God!'

Stanlake's face froze immobile as carved coal, only his eyes alive, raw as wounds, the needles of her words sliding into the tissue of his soul, going as deep as it gets. Energies criss-crossed the air between them. Behind Stanlake's face was a mask, behind the mask was his father's skull, split upon. Behind that a son sat with his father looking out across a valley as the sun set, and behind that, where a heart should be, a cutlass sat before a mirror.

Tremors running up his body, Stanlake turned from her and went back into the flat.

'What is it, blood?' Everil asked as Stanlake for the first time closed his bedroom door. He was now fully awake and propped up on his elbows.

'Nothing,' Stanlake said thickly. He had to lift and then lean on the door, which was warped, to make it shut all the way. His chest was heaving. Shucking off his track-pants he burrowed under the duvet, winding it round himself, rolling Everil off it then pulling him under it alongside him. 'Hold me please,' he said in a small voice, and he shuddered with relief as Everil wrapped his hot, strong arms around him. Was his mother his sacrifice? Was this the price of it all? He would not believe it.

'Your mum?' Everil asked, after Stanlake had stilled a little.

'Yes.'

'She won't come in, though?'

'She won't come in,' Stanlake said. 'Let's go to sleep.'

The front door creaked open then creaked shut, and the key turned. Then another door shut: Poppy too had closed her bedroom door, against her son.

Despite what had happened, in the reassurance of their intimacy Stanlake and Everil drifted off to sleep again, and there in that room they protected each other, and were protected, perhaps, by other powers. And Everil slept despite the lack of cannabis in his bloodstream, the lack of alcohol, and if he had dreams, good or bad, he didn't remember them. Several times Stanlake cried out in his sleep, but each time Everil hugged him close and he quieted again without waking.

Everil woke in the small hours with a mouth dry as cotton and bursting for a piss. A glance at his mobile told him it was 4 a.m. Surely Stanlake's mum would be asleep by now? He sighed. He wasn't used to being disapproved of by anyone who might matter to him.

Carefully he slid his arm out from under Stanlake. Stanlake mumbled something and rolled onto his front without waking. Everil swung his legs round and sat quietly on the edge of the mattress waiting for the circulation to return to his arm, feeling the prickle of the restored blood-flow. Then, with an effort – he could feel the stitches in his inner thigh tug creepily as he did so – he struggled to his feet. He crossed to the bedroom door and, lifting it carefully on its hinges, opened it. There was a sharp squeak and he swore under his breath.

The hall was empty.

The mum's door was closed.

The bathroom was beyond it, next to the front door. Wearing only his trunks, Everil padded down the hall. He fumbled in the dark for the bathroom light-cord, which brushed the back of his hand like a cobweb before he caught and pulled on it. The bulb gave out a feeble light. All the fittings were worn, he noticed. I live better than this, he thought, and that meant he had to face the fact that he had, after all, had some luck in his life, some privilege. A purple and orange velure bath-mat hung damply over the edge of the bath. On the windowshelf sat a row of toiletries, mostly cheap cleansers and moisturisers, scent, and a spray to keep braids shiny. It was a relief to empty his bladder.

He washed his hands and, not wanting to go into the kitchen, which was opposite Poppy's room, bent over and drank from the tap. He wavered over whether to flush the toilet or not, decided not to, and put the lid down. He rinsed his hands again because of touching the seat and, finding no towel, dried them on the bath-mat, then left the bathroom.

The mum's bedroom door, which he was certain had been closed before, was open. From the blackness within came her voice, low and dangerous: 'Hey! Jackal!'

That voice stopped him as forcibly as if a cold iron bar had been placed on his chest. He peered into the room's dark interior but could see only a vague shape.

'How did you bewitch my son, jackal?'

At that, to his own surprise, he almost smiled. 'Nah, nah, you got it wrong, though,' he said. 'It ain't dat way at all.'

'What way is it?'

'It's *him* what's bewitched *me*.'

When no reply came Everil added, 'I won't never hurt him, though. Believe dat.'

And Poppy watched him from the dark as he hesitated before turning away from her and going back to her son's bedroom, and she had seen even in the low light the new openness in his eyes, though she refused to acknowledge it then, even to herself, for what it was; refused to see it as anything other than a threat. Am I to lose everything, she wanted to cry out, both my values and what I value? She was as alone at that moment as she had been in those empty days in the village after she had buried Pacific, when there had been nothing to do except endure as dully and pointlessly as a stone. Her son had taken her husband from her. Then he had been taken from her, and then he had returned. Was what was happening now God's punishment for failing in her duty to bring her son to Him? Or in her duty to forgive him?

But I couldn't, she thought. I tried, but I couldn't.

It was him what bewitched me.

Tomorrow she would speak to the Reverend. She would push past those women who barred the way with their assurance that as below so it would be above; that those who ran the show here would run Heaven too. She would push past them and question the Reverend until he gave her answers she could use.

From the dresser drawer she took the framed photograph, the one thing remaining to her from their old life. No, she corrected herself: from their life. There is no new one, it is all the same thing. In the dark she couldn't see the image, but she didn't need to. Her fingertips brushed the crack in the glass that ran across her husband's face. She gripped the frame in both hands as if it was an aid to prayer. And she prayed then, without words, almost without thought, out of nothing but the need that was all that was left to her. A sudden wind rattled the window-frame. Something would change. Something had to change.

Chapter Thirteen

The alarm sounded what seemed like only moments after Poppy had eventually drifted off to sleep, jolting her from what had been no more than an impoverished doze into another day of toil. It was just after five a.m. and still dark outside. She washed and dressed. No mug of tea was waiting for her in the kitchen, no toast browned on the grill. Stanlake's door was still closed. She ate her breakfast in grim silence, tasting nothing, listening out for the slightest sound from her son's room, but there was only the click of her own jaw moving, her throat swallowing. She washed up and packed her lunch. Her hands moved as they had after Pacific died: hands carrying on when the heart could not.

The rebels came and took her husband and her son and went away. The army passed through and went away too, seemingly taking the fighting with it. Once the dead were buried and the bruises of the girls who had been raped were healed – the visible bruises, at least – and their torn dresses stitched back together, there settled on the village the illusion that nothing had happened. The dead had just gone away, that was all. The boys who had been taken had just gone on some trip, perhaps organised by the school, or the church. Pacific was away on business.

Some really did go away: those who had family in areas away from the fighting that weren't too hard to get to left at once. Others hung on, but the community was shattered: every family had lost at least one member, and people avoided meeting each others' eyes, not wanting to see their own pain reflected back at them. There was much praying but it brought small comfort. The crops rose and ripened in the fields – it was a good year for growing – but there weren't enough people left to harvest them, and their abundance felt like a mockery.

When she and her son first came to the estate Poppy had been confused by the ugly concrete sculpture that was placed at the centre of the underpass. Large and pointless it had seemed to her then; inhuman, almost offensive in its lack of meaning. Why this, she had wondered. Later she had noticed its name, *Genius Loci,* and soon she had realised that it was true: this harsh grey lump, barely the product of human hands, did embody the spirit of the place, and was, almost against its intention, art.

The spirit of the village died after the rebels came and went. Before that Poppy had thought of herself as someone who always had a plan. And it was true: back then she had been all plans, for her family, for her son, for herself. But when it came to it she just sat. Cleaned mechanically, cooked mechanically, swept the yard as if there was still a household around her to notice her keeping up standards, and sat. At first she listened constantly to the radio, trying to work out how the war was going from what the rantingly-propagandist government broadcasters were omitting to say, but after a fortnight she gave up because what did it matter? Bad things happened everywhere. Sense was no help. Planning was no help. Pray and cross your fingers.

In a window of stability a nurse came from town to do HIV tests on the girls who had been raped. Miriam, a Muslim. 'Insha'Allah,' she said, taking the tea Poppy offered her. 'As God wills.'

She pulled on her coat and went down to the bus-stop. No jackals on the way. That was something, but it felt like nothing today. She was so tired and distracted that everything seemed to be happening in slow motion. Lucy was already there, bundled up in a coat, a woolly hat pulled down over her ears, her round, unmade-up face glowing. Poppy had been dreading seeing her; dreading her bright, worse than useless pieties, but Lucy, seeing the expression on her friend's face, at once caught Poppy by the hands and said, 'Sister, you're upset. What's wrong?'

Seeing Poppy was reluctant to answer in front of strangers, Lucy led her a little way away from the other people waiting in the shelter. Keeping Poppy's hands in hers she said, 'Please tell me.'

'My son is gay,' Poppy said. 'He likes to wear make-up and he is gay.'

'Are you certain?' Lucy asked. 'Some of these fashions the young people wear nowadays are quite confusing.'

'It isn't fashion,' Poppy said.

'No,' Lucy said. 'Okay.'

The bus arrived then, and they had no option but to break off their conversation and get on or be late for work. They managed to find seats together away from the few other passengers and continued their talk.

'Don't blame yourself,' Lucy said. 'It is this rotten country with its confused values.'

'It is everything,' Poppy said. 'Yes, it is here. But it is me too, and it is what happened before. Being a man has become an ugly thing to him. But he is also under someone's influence.'

'A new man in the home can – ' Lucy began.

'No, no, it's nothing like that.' The bus swung round a corner. Poppy reached out and gripped a metal upright to stop from sliding off her seat. 'This is some boy from the streets.'

'Ah,' Lucy said, 'these boys and girls lose their way in the streets. They become up for anything. Is he taking drugs?'

'No,' Poppy said. 'Or – I don't think so.' What do I know about him really, she thought. Did I make him like this? The Reverend might say yes. But if so, how? Did life make him like this? Or God? He was always too friendly with the girls, I think, and nothing but friendly. But he was only a boy and it didn't seem to matter: there were boys who were his friends too, Matthew and Robert and Patrick.

All dead now.

'Lucy, tell me, what should I do?'

She expected Lucy to offer the usual bromide, but Lucy said, 'See the Reverend. Today. Your son is being influenced on many levels, and the Reverend can help you. I will cover for you at work.'

Her manner was eager, her eyes bright. To her this is a bit of an adventure, Poppy thought. But she is helping, and she is right. 'When should I go?' she asked.

'The Reverend doesn't get up early,' Lucy said. 'He is up

till all hours studying the Bible and working on his sermons. He comes to the church to open it up at about ten, and works in his office all day at church matters.'

'And Mrs Ige and Mrs Bankole?'

'They normally come around lunchtime, after sorting out their families and their businesses.' Off Poppy's tight nod Lucy added, 'Yes, I know. They're too proud of their role in the church.'

'I'm sure they are good people,' Poppy said, conventionally.

'Still, they are nose-in-the-air types.'

This was the first time Lucy had said anything to Poppy that was critical of any aspect of the running of the church, and it made Poppy like her more. 'You said 'many levels',' she said.

'Don't you think so?' Lucy asked.

'I don't know.'

Poppy looked out at the passing streets. *Could* there be witches here? It seemed far-fetched, but after all there was wickedness everywhere, and selfishness, and malice. If witchcraft was ill-wishing made concrete, then why not? And hadn't the Reverend preached on just that subject yesterday, and on the dangers of blindness to it? Certainly there were things this mechanical world of clockwork cause and effect did not explain.

The breeze off the river was stiff at their backs as they got off the bus, hurrying them on to their day's work.

Stanlake woke with a yawn and stretched, feeling lazy. Everil's arms were still around him, warm and new and reassuring. He glanced over at his alarm-clock: seven a.m. A spasm of guilt shot through him. He hadn't made his mother's tea; hadn't even woken in time to think of it. He was a bad son, rebellious, neglectful and with no excuses.

But then he remembered Poppy's words to him on the landing the night before and his heart hardened against her, against the endless abnegation of his own needs. I am not a bad son, he thought. And over this I had no choice: my road to becoming a man.

In the U.K. the young lack the rituals and traditions to

mark such transitions in their lives: here they have to make them up. Cigarettes, drugs and other such rubbish. Without tradition they get lost. This I have seen all around. But the fact is if I had never come here, still because of my nature I would have had to come up with new acts and markers just like they do, brand-new things made up out of my imagination. This is something maybe they have taught me. Because I am a young man in *this* country, I am here like they are, and I am having to do what they do: invent my new life as I go along.

He felt the the soft warmth of Everil's breath on the back of his neck.

Yes, this they have taught me.

The shift crawled along. Work had never seemed more endless to Poppy. Janina and Paramjit were in a talkative mood but she took in nothing they said, and she was sure their chatter made them perform their tasks more slowly than usual. Lucy had spoken to them on her behalf, and they had agreed to cover for her. All she had to do was wait for Mister Patel to make his customary appearance, then she could slip away. As he might appear any time between eight a.m. and mid-day, however, she remained on tenterhooks. Working faster would have assuaged some of her guilt, and she tried to hurry things along, but not so much as to annoy the others.

Maybe I should've properly asked for the time off, she thought. But if he had refused her, then what?

She had arranged with Lucy that if her absence was noticed Lucy would say she had fallen sick. 'If I say women's problems he won't ask further,' Lucy said. And Poppy had nodded because wasn't this, after all, a woman's problem?

Mister Patel came round just before ten. He asked Poppy how her housing problem was going, which added to her guilt, and she hoped she wouldn't get him or the others into any trouble.

She gave it ten minutes, then went and got her coat and slipped out.

The bus seemed to take forever to come, and the South London streets were even more congested than usual.

Roadworks were everywhere, though no actual work was being done in many of the coned-off areas: they were just purposeless obstructions, small gestures of the Devil's to delay her. Poppy shifted restlessly on her seat. She felt as if she was trapped in a race with the awful Mrs Ige and Mrs Bankole, and that things were contriving to slow her up and – who knew? – speed them on ahead of her.

And she didn't even want to get there.

In her bag was the framed photograph of herself and her husband and son. Why had she brought it with her? As evidence they had once been a normal, respectable family, perhaps. She held it against her belly like a talisman.

It was a little after eleven by the time she reached the Anointed Joy and Prosperity Mission but she found the building still locked up. Defeat swept over her then, and she felt utterly alone. The sky was clear blue overhead and the air was cold and tasted metallic. I will wait, she thought. He will come. There was a café a little way along, but when she went and looked in the window she saw it was very white English, with a menu of fried eggs, sausages and bacon, a television turned to some sporting event, and only men for customers.

I should go back to work, she thought as she looked back at the church's unyielding breeze block façade. It would be more sensible than hanging about here when the Reverend might not show up for hours for whatever reason.

At that moment, glinting in the bright sun, a silver Saab drew up in front of the church, flawless, incongruous, almost surreal in that run-down sidestreet strewn with market debris and uncollected rubbish, a material miracle with blue-tinted windows and an almost silent engine. A door opened and Reverend Obasanjo emerged from behind the wheel. He was wearing a pearl-grey suit of such immaculateness it made him and the car seem all of a piece, and the perfection of its cut added to the broadness of his shoulders and the narrowness of his hips. His eyes were hidden behind dark glasses. Later, when she looked down at those dark glasses lying on his desk, she saw the letters 'Gucci' imprinted on one of the arms, and she knew from her son that that was a costly brand. Not that she had ever doubted it would be.

'Reverend!' she called, hurrying across the street towards

him as he headed up the steps. He turned and for a moment his expression was hostile. Then he broke into a welcoming smile.

'Sister,' he said. And he reached out and took her hand in his, and his grip was strong, and she felt he was lifting her up.

'Can you help me, please,' she said breathlessly.

'Of course.' He unlocked the padlock on the door and slithered the chain away, and with a gesture ushered her in ahead of him.

The church was somehow different by day: laid bare as a building that had once been council offices bereft of spiritual intent. Not that Poppy found that deterring: for her the people were the church. Though she could see the beauty of old churches and appreciate the faith that went into their construction – some, she knew, had taken more than a lifetime to build: what faith in continuity! – it was to her a simple truth that the spirit, the heart of a church was its congregation.

Reverend Obasanjo steered her towards his office, snapping on lights in the windowless corridors as he went. There was a faint smell of dry rot Poppy had never noticed before. Other rooms in the building were hired out to various community organisations: pinned to the walls and Blu-tacked to the doors were flyers and posters, some hand-drawn, for mother-and-toddler groups, Yoruba drumming classes, debt-counselling workshops and a Caribbean senior citizens' lunch-club.

She had never been in the Reverend's office before. It was plainly furnished and dominated by a large desk. On the desk sat an outsize leather-bound bible from which an ornate gold bookmark protruded like the handle of a dagger. In front of the desk was an upright wooden chair and behind it was a fancy wing-backed one covered in oxblood leather. Behind that was a wide window with blinds half-turned against a view of bins and a concrete wall topped with razor-wire. To one side was a small workstation on which sat a computer, keyboard and fax-photocopier-printer, and next to that was a filing-cabinet. A box of cartridge paper sat on the grey-carpeted floor. A door gave onto a kitchenette with a steel sink and above it, cupboards. One of these was partially open, and on a shelf a bottle of whisky was visible: Glenmoranji. On the wall opposite was a gold-framed print of the Last Supper, a version of a classical painting in which Jesus and all His disciples had gentle African features.

Reverend Obasanjo indicated that Poppy should take the chair in front of the desk, a large ruby winking in his cuff-link as he did so. 'Now, sister,' he said as he sat opposite her. 'Tell me.'

Suddenly Poppy was tongue-tied. Almost absent-mindedly the Reverend drew a mobile phone from an inside jacket pocket and placed it on the desk next to the bible. It displayed the time in large numerals: 11:17. Chapter and verse. 'But you're busy,' Poppy said, and started to get up.

'Not at all,' the Reverend said. 'Sit. Please.'

Reluctantly Poppy sat back down. Unable to meet the Reverend's eyes, instead she looked at his hands. They were large, diamond-ringed and perfectly manicured. The skin was dark and smooth and even, yet there were scars on the knuckles and on the backs of the fingers: shiny testaments to old wounds. That seemed hopeful. This man had known troubles: he had had to fight. Perhaps he could wrestle this devil.

'I am worried about my son,' she began. Then she stopped. Why should she burden this man with her dirt? The cologne he was wearing was citric with a chocolatey under-tone. The window glowed behind him like a halo.

'Go on,' he said.

'He is being influenced.'

'In what way?'

'It is bad, Reverend. Very bad.' Why was she struggling so to get to the point? The Reverend heard troubles and wicked things every day, and offered guidance on them: that was his job.

'Is it gangs?'

'No. Well, yes, that is part of it, but – '

'Sister – '

'I know. I'm sorry, it is difficult.'

'We are all sinners, sister,' the Reverend said. 'We are all fallen. We all need to beg God for forgiveness.'

Poppy glanced at the Last Supper on the wall. Jesus' face was pretty; almost, despite the beard, girlish, his large, limpid eyes surely touched with eyeliner as well as filled with absolution. 'My son is gay,' she said.

'Does he have brothers?'

'He is my only son.'

'Is he too much among your daughters?'

'I have no daughters. And my husband, he died.'

'And how old is your son?'

'Seventeen. He will be eighteen in two months.'

'And how far has this thing gone?'

'At first he just seemed interested in things it's mostly girls who like, like fashion magazines. Then he started – just at home, not outdoors – wearing make-up. Lipstick and eyeshadow and all that. And then lately he's been wearing these things outside.'

'Why don't you stop him?'

'I'm afraid.'

'But you must be strong, little sister. I know we are in a place that makes it hard, that tells you these things are okay when you know and I know they are not. The Good Lord loves us all – '

'Amen,' Poppy said.

'But you know and I know what He likes, and what He doesn't like.'

'It has gone further,' Poppy said. 'Last night when I came home from church I found him in bed with another boy.'

There, it was done. And at once it seemed both cataclysmic and utterly trivial. Almost she wondered why she had come here, why she had worked herself up as if this one thing that wasn't even a surprise was so much worse than everything else.

'Who is this other boy?' the Reverend asked.

'A tough boy from around the estate. He deals drugs and carries a knife. He is older.'

'And he is using your son like a woman.'

The Reverend's words stung Poppy. The youth's arms had been around Stanlake protecting him, not using him. And hadn't Stanlake fought him and defeated him? She didn't think it was to do with dominance. 'Not that,' she said.

'But I think this boy has influenced him.'

'With drugs?'

'With witchcraft.'

'But your son was already wearing make-up before this boy was on the scene.'

'That was different.'

'In what way?'

'It wasn't to do with sex, or other boys, it was – Please, Reverend, is there anything that can be done?'

The Reverend sat back and pressed his fingertips together. The cuffs of his shirt were pierced and pinned by the ruby links. Poppy too was pierced and pinned. He seemed to be weighing her up, though his expression was hard to read.

'An investigation of this sort takes a lot of time and work,' he said. 'It is costly.'

'Yes,' Poppy said, her voice catching. Of course it would end this way. 'I have nothing,' she said.

'It is not an easy thing, to divine witchcraft and to drive it out.'

'No.'

'I do not remember seeing your son here.'

'No.' Her voice broke on the word.

And why should he help me with my heathen son who I cannot even get to come to church? There is the weakness of being human, which is God's business to forgive; and then there is weakness of character, which is just a shortcoming.

The Reverend glanced at his mobile. Her chance was slipping away. She had no money. This was all hopeless. In any case she should not have said to Stanlake what she said last night, even if it was true. With a sense of having already failed, she reached into her bag and brought out the framed family photograph. Turning it so it was the right way round for the Reverend she placed it on the desk in front of him. He reached out indifferently and touched the metal of the frame.

'This is my husband and my son,' Poppy said.

Reverend Obasanjo's hand twitched as if he had been stung, making the picture jump and clatter. He gave her a strange, searching look she did not understand.

'The glass is cracked,' she said pointlessly.

'Yes,' he said, and it was as if speaking was all of a sudden a great effort for him, and a tenseness filled the room. His eyes remained on hers, but she had nothing else to say. She got to her feet and reached out for the picture. She would return to work and finish her shift: at least that.

'There are things that can be done with your son,' the Reverend said. Poppy hovered, waiting. 'I believe I can help you, sister.'

'I can afford little,' Poppy said. 'But perhaps I could help out round the church more?'

'As you know, in the usual way it would be a lot of money,' the Reverend said, and his voice was smoother now. 'The Lord asks that we prove our faith by what we are prepared to give up for Him.'

'I understand,' Poppy said.

'But I am a compassionate man. And I understand it can be difficult in these times of economic hardships.' The Reverend looked at the photograph again. 'So you are all alone in the world,' he said.

'I have Jesus.'

'Of course.' He smiled at her again, a kindly smile, and his eyes were warm and gentle. 'That is what our church is for: love and community in Jesus Christ.'

'Amen,' Poppy said. Then, feeling she was being some-how presumptuous in keeping her eyes on his, she looked down at the large, leather-bound bible, the gilt edges of its pages so fine they made a single block of gold; the Gucci sunglasses; the crystalline, steel-framed mobile phone.

'I will do this for you,' the Reverend said. 'I will come to your home this afternoon and speak to your son.'

'But the jackal – '

'From what you are saying to me, the jackal, having taken his pleasure – ' Poppy flinched. ' – will have gone back to selling his drugs. He will not be there. But even if he is, I am the Lord's worker and he will not stand in the way of the Lord's work.'

Poppy risked another glance at the Reverend Obasanjo's face: yes, there was no fear in him.

'I personally will determine if some spirit has entered your son, or some curse or spell has been put on him, which may be the case, or may not. Whether he is being attacked in that way and needs specific actions to be taken, or if he is just choosing sin over virtue, I will stay and pray with him for guidance.'

'Thank you, Reverend, thank you,' Poppy said breathlessly, heeling away sudden tears with the palm of her hand. Could this be the help, the solution she so desperately needed? Could this be the beginning of a return to order, to sanity, to things as they were before? If so, why was she so afraid? 'He is on his half-term holiday,' she said. 'He has no money to go out, and should be at home all day.'

'Good. And sister,' the Reverend said, 'it is better I see him alone. A young man may say things to another man that he would not say if his mother was present.'

Poppy nodded. 'If you think that is best,' she said.

'That is how it must be.'

'Okay.'

Always this world of men's secrets, she thought.

'Now give me your keys and tell me your address, and allow me two hours.'

'Two hours?'

'That will be enough for a beginning.'

'Thank you, Reverend,' Poppy said, digging in her bag. 'I was at my wits' end. Thank you very much.'

'No, thank *you*, my sister,' the Reverend said, and he was smiling again as she placed her keys in his hand, 'for finding the courage to come and confide in me today.'

Back out on the street Poppy took a deep breath to clear her head. The slight oiliness anchoring the Reverend's cologne had coated her nasal passages, making them itchy. Why did she feel so uneasy? She knew she was doing the right thing, yet almost she felt she should go home and warn Stanlake that the Reverend was coming, even though she knew that if she did so he would simply leave. Still, not to warn him felt like a betrayal.

Betrayal or not, I am doing my duty, she told herself firmly. I have been weak and let things slide and look where we have got to. Now, for my son's sake, I must be strong. I will return to work, finish my shift, and then and only then go home.

And what if Stanlake's – friend – *was* still there when the Reverend arrived? What would happen? Perhaps something dreadful; dreadful, that was, beyond having her priest witness her son and his friend's deviation so nakedly. Oh, but surely even such a boy as that wouldn't assault a priest? Still, if a bad spirit was in him, then who knew what a jackal might be capable of. And Poppy knew all too well that vile things happened every day, spirits or no spirits.

What am I going to come home to?

Every day seemed worse than the one before.

Poppy caught up with Lucy and Janina in one of the washrooms on the seventeenth floor. Lucy was surprised to see her back so soon. 'How did it go?' she asked eagerly.

'Good, I think,' Poppy said, taking a handful of paper towels and getting on with drying the sinks the other two had just rinsed clean. 'He says he is going to help me personally.'

Lucy was impressed. 'Eh-eh, how did you pull that off?'

'A priest is supposed to help, isn't he?' said Janina, to whom Lucy had evidently tattled while Poppy was away.

'But there are degrees of help,' Lucy said as Janina disappeared into one of the stalls. There came the sound of her tipping the dirty water from her mop-bucket into the toilet-bowl.

'When will he come?'

'He is going to speak to my son today,' Poppy said.

They were in the men's washroom. The door opened and a young white man in a suit started to come in, saw them there, blushed and withdrew.

'Let's get finished,' Poppy said.

Eventually Stanlake couldn't sleep any more. He wriggled round to face Everil, who opened his eyes and smiled. Stanlake smiled back and they kissed. The kiss was warm and soft, but behind it was muscularity and strength. Everil tasted of tobacco and something sweet. They slid their arms around each other. Stanlake pushed his tongue into Everil's mouth and felt Everil's chest rise against his in excitement. Through the stretchy lace of his pouch his rigid erection jostled against Everil's and they both gasped at this sudden, revealing contact and Stanlake pulled his hips back: what if this repels? But Everil moved his hands down to Stanlake's waist and held him in place, angled his own hips forward and began to grind his crotch against Stanlake's, hard-on sliding over hard-on inside the underwear they were both still wearing. Their stiffening nipples brushed, electric.

Everil laughed breathlessly, then reached back awkwardly for his inhaler, keeping his hips welded to Stanlake's as he did so. Gazing into Stanlake's eyes he took a hit, and the undertone of menthol was what Stanlake had been unable to identify in his kiss. The bright morning sun made the fabric at the window glow orange and blue, and the air in the room was warm. His heart thudding in his chest, Stanlake kissed his way down Everil's body, pressing his lips first between Everil's flat pectorals, then working his way down the lean, trembling length of his stomach, finally reaching the rigidity of his dick and kissing the arching shaft of it through the black lycra of his trunks. There was a darker circle at its head, blacker than black. Everil moaned and closed his eyes as Stanlake tugged down his trunks. His erection sprang up and slapped against his belly, leaving a gleaming bead of precum just below his navel, then stood proud and thrusting as a ship's prow. Stanlake carefully worked the trunks down over the bandage round Everil's thigh, then slid them off altogether. He reached up and took hold of the rigid shaft of Everil's cock.

Everil, he saw, was circumcised: like himself a man in this at least. If he hadn't been then this act would have had another level of taboo: the redundant female flap still there, contradicting the man. But no –

Stanlake bent down and kissed Everil's hot, smooth cockhead, probed the slit in it with the tip of his tongue. The taste was both sweet and salty. Everil gasped throatily, and said, 'Fuck.' Stanlake opened his mouth and took in Everil's erection. Its veins pulsed against the insides of his cheeks and it was hard and hot. It was life. It made life and gave life, cousin to Elegba, the black domed stone in the sacred grove, but unlike Elegba it asked for no sacrifice. And if it did require an offering then what was freely given was offering enough, though in truth this was less an offering than an exchange, since to give pleasure in such a way was itself a pleasure.

And so this was a new thing to Everil, Stanlake's open-heartedness transforming utterly an act which, after all, was not a new act; and finally and for once Everil felt like a human being. Later he would think of Rula and the grotesque parody of intimacy he had performed with her and with other girls, and realise that he had come to Stanlake a virgin, but for now he thought only of this remarkable person he was with, this human being who wanted nothing at that moment but to bring him joy.

Everil turned slowly onto his side, the stitches in his thigh pulling a little but not enough to deter him. He pushed his cock deeper into Stanlake's mouth, which Stanlake didn't resist, and pulled Stanlake round until he could nuzzle, kiss and nip the African youth's erection through the bulging lace of his thong. *My gift to him.* Everil tugged it down and Stanlake's dick sprang up, somehow unexpectedly large and heavy, demanding attention, all the more male for the contrast it made with the delicacy of the material that had constrained it. *This is a man. I am with a man.*

Like Stanlake, Everil had never sucked a cock. He had used those words for casual abuse ten thousand times, never imagining the doing of it could be so intense a pleasure. He cupped the smooth, muscular globes of Stanlake's butt in his hands and buried his face in Stanlake's crotch, swallowing him in a greedy slurp, gagging excitedly as the head of Stanlake's dick slid down into his throat and filled some emptiness in him. His lips tingled, electrified, as they reached the smooth, shaved skin at the base of Stanlake's shaft.

In their youth and eagerness they moved fast, sucking greedily and building rapidly on rising waves of heat and sweaty breathlessness to thrusting climaxes that pumped seed so deeply down each others' throats it went untasted. And then for a long strange moment they lay there, a single, sensual creature slick with sweat, dicks that were reluctant to soften still in each others' mouths, complete. Finally, needing to breathe, they moved their hips back and rolled onto their backs, disgorging slick erections, leaving lips shiny, faces

flushed and pumped with blood. Their hands searched for
and found each other as, chests heaving, they gasped for
breath in the amber air. And Everil laughed with pure joy,
and Stanlake laughed too in that simple present moment.

After a while Stanlake got up and padded naked through to
the kitchen. Everil heard the tap run and he came back with
a pint glass of water, which they shared greedily. Then they
cosied up again, pulling the duvet over themselves for
shelter. Everil felt a strange surging of energies inside him.
The two nights in the hospital, and now this night without
dope, speed, coke or anything else – even at Drilla's he had
taken nothing – had emptied his body of poisons, and he
both craved a cigarette, a joint, a line, and wanted never to
touch any of that shit again. The usual jangling nerves and
sense of being dead inside that plagued him every morning
were absent: being with Stanlake was powerful healing.
Tears welled up. He tried to blink them away but they
quickly overflowed their ducts and ran down the sides of his
head in silver lines. Not wanting Stanlake to know he was
crying he tried to quietly sniff them away, tasting salt in the
roof of his mouth. The sniffing was not enough, however, and
things long held down rose up in his gorge as irrepressible,
gasping sobs.
    Stanlake hugged Everil to him, holding his hot, quaking
and suddenly fragile body close, and Everil buried his face in
Stanlake's chest and Stanlake felt Everil's tears wet on his
skin. Tears started in Stanlake's eyes too. It had been a long
time since he had cried for another's pain; since he had
dared to be open to that. You cannot be open and kill, or not
as he had killed; or beat, or torture. And at that moment he
became aware in a way he never yet had been how badly he
had been damaged, and he felt the paradox: that that was
why Everil was here with him. That that was why he could
understand Everil, and be understood by him; and that
within that understanding was the possibility of repair.
    Sometimes a thing can be missing and you don't even
know. Could there somehow be restoration in the arms of
this boy? This morning he could believe it.
    Everil quieted. After a while he lifted his head from

Stanlake's chest, sniffed, coughed and wiped his face with his hands. Pecking Stanlake on the cheek, he got up and vanished off to the bathroom. Stanlake heard the squeak of the toilet-roll holder and Everil blowing his nose, then the splash of taps as he washed his face.

When he came back he was buoyant. He slid on top of Stanlake and kissed him on the mouth. Both of them were erect again in a moment. This time they brought each other off with their hands, mouths glued together, rapidly deoxygenating breath shared in a speedy loop as their fists pumped them to a fast peak. And once they had achieved this second sweaty release Everil moved down Stanlake's smooth, shiny body in kisses and, with the tip of his tongue, tasted Stanlake's seed where it had spattered across his belly, then came up and kissed him again on the mouth.

They lay quietly, chests heaving, bruised dicks aching from sudden proper use. This was being alive. This was a beginning. Now Everil did want a cigarette, but somehow it seemed wrong here, in this room that had been purified by their shared acts of intimacy, and so he let the urge pass from him as best he could. He drank more water. For once he didn't have a headache. His bandaged thigh throbbed, but only in a small way, like a simple creature with just enough consciousness to be aware of itself.

Later they allowed themselves words, and the words did not, as they had both feared, divide them. Arm-in-arm and with hands clasped, more often looking up at the ceiling than meeting each others' eyes, they shared with each other things they had never shared with anyone. Everil surprised himself by talking about his mother, and his months of nursing her, without shields, without bravado.

'She died just about when the hospital was gonna take her off of me for real,' he said. 'She'd gone down to where she was needing full-on care like twenty-four seven.' The stains on the ceiling looked like old maps of lost or unexplored lands. 'Like technical shit I ain' know how to do. Drugs they wasn't gonna lef' me with. She died and I ain't touched nothing in that room since, like it's a shrine, you know? It ain't like I need it clear anyway. I mean, for what? Guests? Before that it was a mission, though: me caring for her,

changing her, washing her, alla dat grim shit. It's a funny
thing though, blood: you can hate someone and still do that
for 'em. Change 'em and wash 'em, all dem tings you did
never want to do for no-one, not even a baby what's yours for
certain, never mind this person spose to be your parent, your
mother caring for you. And I did hate her.' He sighed. 'Not all
the time, still. Cos she did what she could, I suppose: she put
a bit of love in me somewhere even without meaning to. Cos
or else I wouldn't have that to put back out, would I? I
thought I didn't, but it turns out I do. A little.' He smiled.
Then the smile faded. 'When you say 'Mum' you imagine
kind of a ideal, don'tcha? Like someone who actually wants
to be that person and do what mums do. Like, choose dat.
But she was just some selfish little gal what got up the duff
and didn't even notice till she was too far gone to get rid of
it.'

Stanlake kissed Everil on the cheek. 'I'm glad she let it go
too far,' he said.

Everil blinked, then blinked again. 'You know what,
fam?'

'What?'

'No-one's ever said that to me before.'

'What?'

'That they'd rather I was here than I weren't. That I
existed. No-one's ever said that.' He cleared his throat. 'Sorry
I'm causing bare ructions with your mum, though.'

'That is between her and me.'

'Still, though. And sorry about all the other shit too. I
mean, what we – what *I* – did before. I'm thinking now it
was envy what made me so harsh. Over you having a proper
mum an' dat.' Everil turned and looked at Stanlake. 'I'll make
it up to you, though,' he said. 'I don't know how, blood, but I
will.'

'Tell me about your friends,' Stanlake said. 'Your crew.'

'We all kinda dropped out together,' Everil said. 'Like
when we was thirteen, fourteen. Fucking school off felt like
freedom back then. Cos what they was tryna teach us never
felt like it was gonna take us into – I dunno, *life*, you know?
It's funny, though: sometimes my brain feels like it's starving
but I ain't know how to feed it. I mean like, say books.

There's like nine trillion of 'em, so whey a brother a go start?'

'Perhaps with anything you ever heard where you thought, I wonder what that's about,' Stanlake said.

'Maybe, man. Yeah, maybe suttin' like dat. The idea of going in one of them bookshops, though, I dunno.' Strange what makes us afraid: things that seem so easy to others they ain't even a thought can be impossible for us. On road I'm a expert. A specialist. But going in a bookshop: they'd know I ain't spose to be there. They'd – what? Kick me out? Nah, they'd never. But – 'You gotta fit somehow,' he said. 'It's like with Pit-Bull, you know? He's white an' alla dat, but he don't fit where he is any more than the rest of us. He's white but inside he's us. And he thinks we're like – I dunno, the future or suttin'.' Everil smiled a small smile. 'And maybe dat's true. And Solid come up in care, and he's African still, but he don't know nothing about it 'cept what he sees on TV, which ain't nothing but famines and fuck-ups. So he's like hollow too. And Cuts' old man walked out and left him with his mum, and she's like the white half, so he don't know much about being Chinese 'cept being called chink and slant-eyes. It's like we're all ripped up and fucked up.' He turned his head and looked at Stanlake with large eyes. 'I useda think liking mans was parta being fucked up,' he said. 'But it ain't.'

'No. It is not.'

And then Stanlake spoke a little of his childhood; of setting off for school before dawn, of walking barefoot with his friends through the cool dew on the grass beside the road before the sun rose and boiled it off; of sitting outside his parents' home with his father looking out across the village as the sun set, or sipping sodas with Robert, Matthew and Patrick in the shade of the banana trees and making plans for the future. He talked too of the rites and rituals of becoming a man: just a little, betraying no secrets, breaking no vows whether the shrine still existed out in the forest or had been destroyed and lived on only in his head. And he allowed himself to feel the joy of those times with no foreshadowing of what was to come; and Everil knew or guessed enough to not ask him about it, not then, anyway.

Eventually their rumbling stomachs and aching limbs told them it was time to get up. Sniffing one of his shaved armpits and pulling a face, Stanlake went and ran a bath. He and Everil shared it, an experience that was enjoyable but awkward, and made more so by Everil having to keep his bandage out of the water. As host Stanlake took the taps end. And if there wasn't enough room for either of them to lie back fully, the heat of the water and the scent of the bath-foam was relaxing, and they knelt facing each other and moved soapy flannels over each others' chests and thighs and faces and heads, gently at first then, as their tactile confidence grew, more vigorously. The caressing contact gave them half-erections, but the need to do anything about these fresh arousals had not yet recharged itself. They took it in turns to stand and, with sudden propriety, wash their own genitals and backsides.

As he sloshed water over his face and head Everil found himself thinking vaguely about Drilla and the Crew and shifting merchandise. That whole situation felt like something from someone else's life a thousand years ago, and on this lazy, sensual morning he found it impossible to engage with the reality of it or care about the consequences.

Still, it led him to other thoughts. There had to be something he could do with the whole rest of his life other than sling rocks off of the Rock. If Stanlake could come through the shit he'd come through, shit Everil was well aware he hadn't heard half of; if Stanlake could get through that and get here and be dumped in a shitty flat on a shitty estate and be hassled by thugs and still pick up a book then why couldn't he, Everil, do the same? Or, if not a book, *something*. There were other lives out there, brilliant lives: why couldn't one of them be his? He thought of the thousands of hours he had spent on PlayStation and X-Box, and for what? Distraction. From what? Life. Why? Because it was shit. All that gaming: just one drug among many, and none of them any use for anything. He wondered if he could ever be simply clean. Who was the real him, unnarcotised, unpoisoned, not writhing in self-hatred? He hoped it was this, now.

'I gotta take a leak,' he said, levering himself up out of the bath with a grunt.

Stanlake admired Everil's tapering back and high,

sculpted buttocks as he stood at the toilet-bowl legs apart and pissed. Someone who had been a stranger, who was now known. His skin was brown and shiny as a seal's, and the suds from the bath-foam traced the groove of his spine, the arch of his butt and the swell of his calves as they slid slowly down his body and winked out. The bandage on his thigh was still mostly dry: just a few damp discs on the elasticated cream fabric.

'So whatcha wanna do next, man?' Everil asked, glancing round over his shoulder, a cheeky expression on his face as he shook his dick.

'Do?'

'Day like this, mans oughtta go do something, blood. Not settle.'

As he said that there was the sound of a key in the lock of the front door. Getting quickly out of the bath, Stanlake stepped over to the bathroom door, closed it and slid the little bolt across. Everil flushed the toilet. Stanlake began to dry himself hurriedly with a towel, handing Everil another one from the airing-cupboard as he did so. The bathwater gurgled and belched noisily as it sank away, and Everil suppressed a nervous giggle as he towelled himself down. He and Stanlake felt more naughty and awkward than guilty or ashamed: teenaged in a way neither of them had ever had the chance to be until today, simply brazen in their delight in each other, and fearless with youth. Because what, really, was there to fear? Poppy already knew what there was to know, and she had gone and now she had come back: the only worry was a matter of etiquette. Still, though –

'I'll go first and see,' Stanlake said. 'Follow when I call, okay?' Everil nodded. Stanlake kissed him quickly on the lips, slid back the lock, opened the door and, his towel wrapped tight around his hips, stepped into the hall. 'Mummy?' he called.

Away from the humidity of the bathroom the air felt cold on his bare skin. No answer came. He shivered. Why had she come back early from work?

He heard the rattle of the blind being winched up in the kitchen, and a guillotine-blade of sunlight slid across the floor and partway up the wall opposite.

'Mummy?' There was a trace of some unfamiliar scent in the air, subliminally disquieting. Now he was in the kitchen doorway.

The figure in the kitchen turned to face him, a tall, broad-shouldered man in a well-cut suit, silhouetted by sunlight so that for a moment he had no face. Within the black blank Stanlake saw a cold, broad smile.

'Little Gun,' the man said. 'It has been too long.'

Chapter Fourteen

'**O**ga,' Stanlake said tonelessly. His chest shrank and his fingers felt electric-wet and began to prickle. How could this man, this shark of a man, be here? The jackals, he thought. Their knives and guns made me back into a soldier, released from me some stink of violence a creature such as Makinde could pick up on. That morning I went out there to fight. I went out there with redness in my head and no mercy. And now my oga has smelt me out and come for me.

Back there, in the forest, I didn't deserve to get away.

I am a Beast.

He has reclaimed me.

I am his Beast.

To think I could escape was vanity.

'I have found you out, Little Gun,' Makinde said, the smile still on his face as he looked round the narrow kitchen with its peeling walls and cracked ceiling, its worn units and air of transience. The black stain on the Blu-tacked map was worsening, obscuring home.

I am poor, Stanlake thought. I am a nobody. But I am not alone. Not any more. 'You deserted us, oga,' he said. 'You left us to be killed.'

Makinde's smile tightened then, became a painted pattern of curved-bone teeth, and Stanlake remembered what he had seen on the commander's face those last weeks of the war: fear. Fear not of the enemy but of his creations, his Beasts. And Stanlake remembered this too: that Makinde was right to be afraid.

'We all died,' Stanlake said. Inside he was cold as stone, and at that moment as inhuman. 'Blondie, Diamondz, Big Gun. All dead.' As he spoke he was transported back to those days as totally as if what came after was just some TV show he'd happened to see in the asylum centre, and no more pertinent to his life or important: a tiny distraction from the brute reality.

Except for Everil, who now hovered in the hall just out of Makinde's sight-line, a towel round his waist too.

'But not you,' Makinde said. 'You lived.'

'You are wrong, oga,' Stanlake said. 'I died too.'

'Then we all died, Little Gun,' Makinde said. 'The war killed us. It killed our country. But some of us were reborn here, enh?'

'Yes.'

'A wha gwaan, man?' Everil said, coming forward then as if this was all natural, forcing casualness into his voice, a pugnacious expression on his face. Looking up unblinking at Makinde, who was eight inches taller than either him or Stanlake, older, broader, heavier, Everil slung a bare, skinny arm around Stanlake's shoulders as casually as a mate might do, defiant, unashamed. 'Who's this, then? Why come he's in your drum?'

'I am Reverend Obasanjo,' Makinde said, before Stanlake could answer. Turning to Stanlake he went on, 'Your mother came to see me at church. She asked me to come here and pray with you. She said you have fallen into deviation.'

'Fuck dat, man,' Everil said, his arm tightening around Stanlake's shoulders.

Makinde shot Everil a sly glance. 'She informed me you had fallen under a malign influence. She said you were being controlled by an evil person nearby, a witch, or you had a spirit in you.'

'I am not bewitched, oga,' Stanlake said. 'And I am not possessed. I am human.' His voice was even, but inside his head his mind was racing. How did this happen? What lies are these? What is this?

'At first I was not interested in this woman who came to see me so upset today,' Makinde said. 'She has no money, she is nobody, she is nothing. I do not care about her small-small worries. But then she showed me a photograph. Your photograph, Little Gun.' Makinde's smile broadened. 'I did not remember her, but I recognised you. And so I came from my church to do God's good work. Here in your home.'

'What is this bullshit, bruv?' Everil said. 'Why you

listening to this foolish church chat fuckeries for? Why not tell this chief to bounce?' He had no fear in him, and Stanlake loved that fearlessness. But still –

'This man is not what he says,' Stanlake said. 'And he is very dangerous.' To Makinde he said, 'I want you to go.'

'I cannot go.'

'Why?'

'You know why.'

'I don't know why, oga. And why did you come in the first place?'

'To rescue you from your perversion, Little Gun. Because your mother begged me.'

'That is a lie,' Stanlake said. 'And I told you: there is no Little Gun. He is dead and left behind.'

Makinde shrugged. 'Your friend: is he a Beast?'

'Say what, blood?' Everil said sharply.

'He doesn't mean what you think,' Stanlake said, his eyes on Makinde's. 'He means are you like me. Like I was. Still, he is a liar.'

'Ah, Little Gun,' Makinde said, shaking his head. From the breast pocket of his jacket he drew out a cigar. From another pocket he produced a silver cigar-cutter. It glinted, and the rings on his fingers glinted as he looked down to cut off the end of the cigar. It was the first time he had taken his eyes from Stanlake's. He put the cigar in his mouth, patted for and found a box of matches, struck one and puffed it into life.

On the draining-board the kitchen knife winked in the sunlight. He is bigger than me and stronger than me, Stanlake thought. But if I get a good stab in I will have the advantage. And I can stab many times quickly and that will shut him up and finish him off. He knows this. He broke eye-contact not because he is super-confident, which is what he wants me to think, but because he is afraid. That is good. He does not hold all the cards. And he did not expect Everil to be here, or if he did, he didn't expect a faggot who knows violence and isn't so easily cowed.

'When I came here – ' Makinde began.

'And how did you come here, oga?' Stanlake interrupted.

'You can call me Reverend Obasanjo.'

'That is not your name.'

'Ah, but did you ever know my name, Little Gun? My real name? Did I ever know yours until today?'

'No.'

'Then call me Reverend.'

'No.'

'Then call me father.'

Stanlake's face hardened. 'No, oga, I will not call you father. How did you get here, to this country?'

'How did you?' Makinde countered.

'Enh, so you don't know everything about me after all, oga.'

'I had a dream,' said Makinde. 'I saw Jesus. His golden light rained down on me. He told me it was His divine will that I serve the Lord, so I served the Lord. He told me, come here. So I came here to this country to do His good work.'

'Please do not talk such rubbish,' Stanlake said.

'Faith is never rubbish, Little Gun. Faith brought me here, to this place, to this room, now.' Makinde's expression turned grave. 'I have many contacts, Little Gun. Business contacts, contacts in governments all over the world. I didn't spend all my time waiting about in the forest like you did. I am smart-o, and I used my brains. I fought. I was a warrior, oh yes. But behind the scenes at all times I businessed. I traded. I imported and exported. I provided services and investment opportunities of every sort. The war was not everywhere and even where there was war people wanted to make money, because money is power. Opportunities were all over the place for those who could see them. In the end it did not matter which side won. Because I learned this-o: it is money that wins. So I became – international.'

He puffed on his cigar. The tip glowed, and Stanlake remembered a village they had overrun late on in the war, remembered Makinde putting that glowing tip to the eye of a young man they had taken prisoner. 'Keep it open or I will cut your cock off,' Makinde had said, and in a grotesque exertion of willpower the young man had done so, keeping his head still while the rest of his body arched and convulsed. The seared eye had gone blue-white like a boiled egg and the youth had screamed shrilly as a girl, as if he had been castrated anyway, and had urinated on himself. From then on the smell of cigar-smoke made Stanlake want to vomit.

I was one of those holding that boy down. It was me and Blondie. At the time I admired his strength: to not close his eye as the heat came nearer and nearer and finally touched the shrinking iris. And we were helping him to not move by holding him, helping him to stay alive. Survival and will-power were all that was left, because by then there was no pretence it was for a great cause, for the liberation of the people. The boy had done nothing against us. We wanted no information from him. What had happened to him after-wards? Stanlake couldn't remember.

'What do you want, oga?'

'To help you, Little Gun.'

'That is bullshit.'

'To save you.'

'You are so far from God it's a joke, oga,' Stanlake said. He could kill easily now. Do it and feel no way about it: resolve consequences later. 'You couldn't even pray to the shit in the toilet.' Everil would help him get rid of the body: maybe just drop it down the stairwell. Who could say what floor or what flat it came from? It would be just another dead African. Armani suit or not, no-one would care.

Thinking such thoughts, once again he felt a dread of the spirit. Just standing there speaking his lies and deceit and manipulation he is robbing me of myself. He is turning me back into a Beast, a thing that is all teeth, something without love.

'I'm not here to save you from Hell, Stanlake Olusegun,' Makinde said. 'That is between you and your faggot.'

Everil's chest heaved as he bridled at that word, the ultimate trigger-word out on the streets, and Stanlake knew he was forcing himself to not respond to it, to hold himself ready but let Stanlake make the decisions.

Everil too had seen the knife on the draining-board, had heard it calling to his hand. This fucker's big, he thought. He's taller than us, heavier than us and built strong and fast. But there's two of us and we could take him, standard. His skin prickled: the heat from the bath had drained away and the air in the hall was chilly. A slight draft bled in under the front door, making his bare ankles ache. The adrenalin in his system ebbed, unable to sustain itself at full pitch, and the wound in his thigh was throbbing: standing in one position was putting pressure on it. He shifted slightly, making sure the bandage was hidden by the towel. Na let the fucker know you got a weak spot.

'I am here to save you from being sent back,' Makinde said to Stanlake. 'If the authorities find out what you did they will send you back. They will say you are not a victim, not a refugee. They will say you are a war criminal who committed war-crimes and they will tear up your papers.'

'You made me do those things,' Stanlake said with an effort, a constriction forming in his throat. 'I was just a boy.'

'It makes no difference, Little Gun. Your hands were small but you did bad deeds with them.'

'Not willingly.'

'At first, maybe. But later on, enh? Once you got the heat in you – '

'No,' Stanlake said in a strangled tone. Almost he darted forward to grab up the knife from the draining-board, but Everil's arm tightened round his shoulders, telling him: don't let this man control the situation.

'Why we listening to this pure fabrication, fam?'

Makinde rolled the cigar to the corner of his wide mouth. His teeth had the evenness of expensive dental work. 'Were you there?'

'Course not, but – '

'You are stupid, faggot. You think your little friend is nice-o but he is not nice.'

'I think if he's a war criminal then you're one too,' Everil said. 'I think if you grass him up then you're grassing yourself up and you'd get deported out the country too. I think you should go fuck yourself.'

'Ah, you faggots. So full of emotions, like little girls.'

'Fuck you!'

'Look at me,' Makinde said, gesturing as expansively as the galley-kitchen would allow. 'Look at this suit. Armani. These cuff-links with diamonds and rubies. Look at this gold on my fingers. This watch with diamonds and platinum, Tag Huer. These shoes, hand-made. I am a somebody. I have friends in high places, so high you have never been in them. I provide things for them, things they need that are hard to come by. They will not want me to fall because I am their friend, and their friends are kept clean, do you understand? I am a man, Little Gun, and you are a boy. I live in the world. You still live in the village. I have contacts. I have money. You have nothing and no-one. You have rags and you are a faggot. I snap my fingers and you go! And your mother goes. And you and I both know there is nothing to go back to, enh? Not for failed rebels who committed crimes against humanity.'

'But you came here, to my house,' Stanlake said, trying to push uncertainty from his voice. 'For what?'

'Because I need my Beast once again.'

'What do you mean?'

'In my role as priest I help people. Many people. And they are all very grateful. But sometimes they are not grateful. And at those times I need someone to speak to those people.'

'Speak to?'

'Shut them up.'

Stanlake said nothing.

'I need someone they can smell death on, Little Gun.'

Makinde turned away from him and stubbed the part-smoked cigar out on a saucer. 'You will come to the church after hours tomorrow,' he said, his broad back to Stanlake and Everil now, defying them to rush him. 'No, better, come with your mother to the service. Then you will stay afterwards. We will tell her it is for prayers to drive the evil spirit of homosexuality out of you and send her home. You will require many such sessions. Don't worry, Little Gun,' he added, turning back with a grin. 'I will pay you for your work. Life will get better, Little Gun. Life with money is always better. And maybe I can find work for your faggot friend too.'

'No.'

Makinde shrugged. 'But you know the heat is in him, Little Gun. Dirt draws dirt to itself like flies to shit.'

'Get out,' Stanlake said. Makinde looked at his watch. Sunlight blinged on the diamonds that rimmed its face like frost. Keeping Everil with him, Stanlake moved back from the kitchen doorway. 'Go,' he gestured, but the gesture was without force.

'I will see you tomorrow, Stanlake Olusegun,' Makinde said, pushing the now-extinguished cigar back into his breast pocket. Stanlake and Everil braced up as he passed by them into the hall, but he didn't try anything. At the front door he paused. 'Your mother will be back soon, Little Gun. It would break her heart to hear all the little bad things you did apart from the one big bad thing. And why should I have to tell her if you keep your mouth shut? Oh – ' He took Poppy's keys from his pocket. 'I will not need these.' He tossed them to Stanlake. 'Your door is never closed to me.'

Stanlake caught the keys. The door swung closed. Makinde was gone.

Stanlake and Everil stood in the hallway looking at each other, barely daring to breathe. After what seemed like a long while they heard the lift door open then close, then the lift sink away. Stanlake took a shuddering breath. He and Everil hugged, but their skins were now cold and clammy, depleted of reassurance.

'Come let's get dressed, man,' Everil said. Hand in hand they returned to the bedroom and, awkwardly and in silence, pulled on their clothes. Stanlake put on his boy underwear, and did not attempt make-up.

'So your mum'll be back soon, then,' Everil said.

'I suppose so.'

'So time to bounce, then.'

'Yes.'

Of course. Of course he would go. Why would he want to stay and deal with this?

Seeing the expression on Stanlake's face Everil's brow furrowed. 'I ain't mean it that way though, is it,' he said. 'I ain't going nowhere – '

'But – '

'I mean, not without you, fam.' And his use of that word at that moment was a claim and a commitment.

'Thank you.'

'I ain't need thanking, fam,' Everil said. 'It's what it is. You an' me versus whatever.' He looked around him. 'We need to chip, still.'

'Yes. We will go now,' Stanlake said. But he stood there uncertainly, not putting on his coat.

'Your mum's keys?'

'Yes.' Then, taking a breath and forcing decisiveness: 'I will leave the door unlocked. What do we have to steal? And no-one worse can come in than who she has let in already.'

Everil shrugged agreement and flicked up the hood of his tracksuit: he was ready to set off.

Stanlake pulled on his duffle coat. He had no thoughts of where they might go. Well, weren't there many places in this big-big city? It shouldn't be difficult to find somewhere. He went to his bedroom and shoved the underthings he had bought with Everil's money into a small carrier-bag and pushed it into a pocket of the coat. He crammed all his make-up into the glittery make-up bag and shoved that into the other pocket. Because I may not be back, he thought. Keeping his own, he hung Poppy's set of keys on the back of the front door and swept up the loose change on the shelf. 'Let's go,' he said, yanking the door open.

She was standing there, as if waiting to be let in. For all he knew she had been there the whole time. But no: Makinde would have returned her keys to her when he left, not thrown them at him. She looked at her son with wounded eyes. Perhaps she felt guilty for the hurt she had done him; or perhaps she believed he was part of her trial, her cross, and that she was his victim and not the other way around.

'Come,' he said thickly over his shoulder to Everil. Poppy stepped back to let them pass and, avoiding her eyes, Stanlake and Everil left the flat. Like a sad, silent ghost she watched them as they waited for the lift. They didn't return her look, seeing her only as one sees a ghost, at the periphery of one's vision.

Once they were gone Poppy went in. Her hands were cold and clammy. Whatever she had expected it wasn't this. Closing the door she found her keys hanging on the hook on the back of it, proof that the Reverend had been there. She moved nervily around the flat, as if in search of – what?

The jackal had still been there. The Reverend hadn't even managed to kick him out, and now he had taken her son away. I think the Reverend has just made things worse, she thought. But perhaps he couldn't sort it out all at once. Perhaps this was just a beginning. It must be hard to drive out spirits: it must consume energy on many levels.

If there are spirits.

She thought of the accusations people made in churches back home, their always-hysterical, sometimes blatantly vindictive tone, and felt uneasy. It was so easy to accuse someone you didn't like of putting a spell on you; to refuse to accept that your misfortunes were God's will or simply blind chance; to believe that your wayward child had a bad spirit inside him and then place your trust in a spiritual surgeon like Reverend Obasanjo to diagnose the sickness and prescribe the cure. But even experts weren't always right, were they? What then? And what was the cure? Browbeating? Physical chastisement? Pacific used to say often that Christians hated the body, that it was a sickness in them.

What was this thing, homosexuality? Here in the U.K. it was an identity, though Poppy did not understand what that meant. Since she was young she had known there were people who did things that were against nature, but so long as they also married, raised families, cared for their parents and did their duty around the place, people didn't mind too much. Just so long as it wasn't talked about. And that had seemed – and still seemed – a sensible arrangement to her.

These days, however, it was talked about a lot, and it was pastors who were doing the talking. These modern pastors went on the internet, looked at hours and hours of homosexual pornography, and reported back on it to their congregations, going on about the things these men did together in bed in great detail, and blaming the modern world and its moral pollution for causing it.

But my son was what he was anyway, she thought, never mind the internet: he never saw it, never saw this pornography they go on and on about. He did not become this because we came to the U.K. He did not become this because of the war. If I am honest, it was always in him. Or, to put it another way: he was always this. Perhaps that is what 'identity' means. How, then, can the Reverend browbeat it out of him?

He cannot.
I have made a mistake.
I have driven my son away.
Poppy paced, not knowing what to do.

The sun was still high when Stanlake and Everil left the block, and that surprised them both, that only a part of the day had passed. The air was cold but there was no wind. They walked without talking along the Cardinal's short shadow. As they descended into the underpass their hands brushed but didn't link.

The central area was still deserted, adding to the sense that their old lives were falling away, though behind that was the knowledge that nothing was resolved, and ahead was – what? Everil looked up at the spot on the Rock where he had been sitting when Stats stabbed him.

'Do you want us to go to Solid's?' Stanlake asked.

'Maybe later.'

The blood on the ground had faded to a dull purple. Everil was struck by how large an area it covered. I almost died here, he thought. He kissed his teeth. 'Let's blurt, yeah.'

They left the underpass. Stanlake always felt relief at leaving the estate, but for Everil the post-codes cut into him like cheesewire: to transgress their boundaries could lead to a shank in the gut, a beating, even a cap in the ass. His ability to imagine the future shrank back like a dick in ice-water: isn't it just always this? They were moving, but with no purpose.

'Let us go up to the West End,' Stanlake said as they came to a bus-stop.

Everil shrugged. 'Aiight.'

They waited. Everil felt naked without his crew. Any second some next challenger could step to him with brag and worse. And though Stanlake was there standing by him, to embroil him in such foolishness would be a wrong thing, and Everil had his honour. His autonomic systems dipped and surged. He tapped out a cigarette and lit it. The nicotine stabilised him a little.

He was halfway through his smoke when the bus came.

They sat upstairs at the front, like tourists, Everil on the outside, the man, protective. 'So tell me,' he said.

'I knew him as Makinde,' Stanlake said, staring out at the passing streets, staring into the past. The only other person on the upper deck was a studenty white boy who sat near the back, music bleeding from his earphones, looking down, playing a game on his phone. 'But I think that was not his real name. He was our commander in the war. I was fourteen. He was my kidnapper. But I am not a victim.'

'But you are, though.'

Stanlake looked at him.

'You ain't weak, blood, I ain't saying that. Course I ain't. But you was victimised still. Like what you done, dem bad tings, you'da done them if you did never meet him?'

'No.'

'Well, then.'

'But it shows you the bad things that are in you. That are already in you, not put in you by someone else.'

'But dem tings is in everyone, bruv. Like, did anyone not do them?'

'No. Well – perhaps Matthew. He ran into the forest and was killed.'

'Yeah, but see, if you die and they don't, then they win, innit? Maybe your spar run cos he could like see that bit further than the rest of you. Like see in advance what he was gonna have to do to get through. Not cos he couldn't do it, though: because he *could*, you get me? I mean, who ain't do harm under deep pressure?'

Stanlake shrugged. Everil hooked his arm over the back of the seat, framing Stanlake's shoulders in an almost-hug. 'But what now?' Stanlake asked. He had no thoughts in his head.

'First off, we eat something. Mans can't strategise on a empty belly.'

The bus made its slow way up to Waterloo Station, round the Imax cinema and over the river. They got off on the Strand, and Everil bought them burgers and fries from a McDonald's. They didn't sit in but wandered, passing theatres as they ate. The shows in the theatres seemed to be mostly old films turned into musicals, or plays based on pop songs Stanlake didn't know. The streets were rush-hour crowded with tourists.

'I know where,' Everil said, tossing his Styrofoam burger-box onto a heap of bin bags left like Christmas gifts around a lamp-post. He led Stanlake through to Leicester Square, where more tourists milled and entertainers touted for trade, offering flyers for plays, comedy nights, or having your portrait drawn. 'Bwoy sweet like you gotta have a sweet tooth, yeah?' Everil said.

Stanlake smiled, not denying it.

'Cool.'

Next to a multiplex cinema was what seemed to be an ice-cream restaurant. It had two doors. One led to a take-away counter, and people were queuing there. Everil opened the other door, which led to the restaurant proper. He gestured to Stanlake to go in ahead of him. Embarrassed but charmed, Stanlake did so.

It was good to be out of the cold: even after the burger and fries he still felt ice in his bones. A smiling Asian girl in a pastel-striped paper cap handed him and Everil large card menus. The restaurant wasn't busy and she led them to a semicircular booth that could have seated six. Everil let Stanlake sit first then bumped him round on the smooth red leather, enjoying the gentle, cheeky contact.

Looking around Stanlake noticed that many of the customers were young Middle Eastern couples, the boys clean-cut, clean-shaven, with sharply-gelled hair; the girls demurely pretty in colourful headscarves, with beautifully made-up eyes. A pair nearby were sharing a milkshake, two plastic straws in the same tall glass.

'Cos they're Muslims,' Everil said. 'This place stays open till like three a.m. on a weekend. They come here cos they can't do no alcohol. If we get three flavours each we can split 'em. Or you can pick a sundae or whatever, no probs.'

They chose mostly the sweeter flavours – Belgian chocolate, butter pecan, rocky road, strawberry cheesecake, chocolate chip cookie-dough and caramel cone – along with Cokes to drink. The Cokes – slurry from a machine – were disappointing, but the ice-cream was not, though Stanlake soon found his teeth were aching. Still, the combination of the meat and the sweet gave him and Everil energy and heart, and being in the warm, and being pleasantly-treated by the waitress, made them feel hopeful that the world might somehow bend in their direction.

Beyond the plate glass tourists shuffled in a parallel dimension where apart from shopping opportunities only old and picturesque things existed. To them the natives were merely props in a play, and Stanlake and Everil were invisible, except perhaps as the shadow of a threat. They sat thigh-to-thigh, and under the table Everil let his hand curve down between Stanlake's thighs and casually cup his crotch. To be this natural was a new thing to him, and though there were other, urgent things to discuss he found himself asking, 'So, you ever like done it with a gal?'

Stanlake shook his head. 'No.' He smiled a little. 'I think girls are pretty, but that is as far as it goes. You?'

Everil's brow furrowed. 'Enough times,' he said. 'More'n enough, as it goes. But it never meant nothing to me, though.'

'And boys?'

'Never. It sounds dumb but I kinda never exactly knew, you know? Not till I saw you. And even then, not till the day you was wearing the – ' He gestured at Stanlake's face and Stanlake understood though he was currently wearing no make-up. 'Like, it was like a bridge into me, you get me? Into my heart. Girls was just some next ting, like wearing such-an'-such trainers cos other peeps is wearing 'em even if you don't like 'em or they don't fit right. And you and like dating? I mean, with boys.'

'I kissed a boy,' Stanlake said. 'But that was as far as it went.'

'What happened?'

'He died. In the forest, in the dark. He was shot by the government soldiers. I closed his eyes and I ran away.'

'Cheese an' bread, fam.'

'Big Gun was his name, although he was smaller than me. I never knew what his real name was. Or perhaps that was his real name by the end.'

'Like Oily,' Everil said. 'The boy what died of the O.D., why come I got murked up. Olly was his name. Oliver. Posh boy, till he got on the pipe. Then I guess Oily come what he really was. Something like that, anyway.'

'Was there a day,' Stanlake asked, 'when you became – Evill?'

Everil pulled a face. 'Nah, blood. That happened like one drop at a time. There weren't no big Darth Vader ting what turned me. First off it was like a joke-name. Pit-Bull give it me. It was like his name, OTT. Later on I made it so it weren't funny.'

'To me you are Everil.'

'That's cool. And you ain't no Little Gun neither, aiight? Cos I know what your one big thing was, but that ain't you. That was put on you, an' you ain't that. You're – I ain't got the words, still.' Everil looked down, embarrassed. 'I gotta apologise, fam.'

'What for?'

'For the business with the gun. What I wanna say is – ' He broke off, and his voice dropped to a whisper. 'I'm glad the gun was fucked up. More'n anything ever.'

Stanlake smiled. 'Me too.'

'It's why come I ain't wanting no beef with Stats for the knife business,' Everil said. 'Cos if Oily ain't palmed me off with no wack piece then where I'd be now? Or you. Bad places, man. Cold places you ain't come back from, dead or alive. That's the main thing, but also cos Oily snuffing it, that's on me, you know? His life was on him, I know that: his choice, and if it weren't me it'd've been some next man businessing him. But it *was* me, though, and I do feel that. Yes.' Everil heeled a glint from his left eye and smiled. 'Gettin' soft, blood,' he said throatily.

'You should make a sacrifice for him,' Stanlake said. 'For his spirit.'

'Like what, kill something?'

'Or give something of value.'

Everil shrugged, not knowing how to respond. 'We got more urgent problems, still,' he said.

'Yes.'

'You gonna do what that phoney preacher said? Go there an' dat? Play along?'

'I don't know,' Stanlake said. 'But I can't ignore it and do nothing: the risk is too great, to me and my mother.'

'She's the one dropped you in it, though.'

'She's my mother.'

Though he had never felt his emotions so simply and directly, Everil accepted the primary nature of the response. 'I reckon he was bullshitting, though.'

'In what way?'

'Alla dat deportation shit. Like say he grasses you up to the feds, whoever: how they'd prove what he said about you? They couldn't, right? Except from what he said. But if he said shit then you could drop him straight back in it cos what he's done's worser than what you done, cos he was like the whatsit – instigator. You was a kid.'

'But then we both get kicked out of the U.K., him and me, and my mother,' Stanlake said. 'We go back as pariahs, to face poverty, prison, perhaps death. And don't we deserve death for what we did? The war criminal and his eager helper?'

'But you wasn't eager.'

'He will say I was. No-one remains alive to contradict him. And if they find survivors, what mercy would they show me? Who knows what they would say or do in their pain and anger.'

'He ain't want that either, though: being deported an' alla dat.'

'But he has money and influence. I have nothing. He could weasel his way through the system and dispose of me.'

'You believed that crock 'bout 'knowing people'?'

'Maybe. I don't know.'

'It was bullshit, fam. Chief was ramping.'

'But you do not *know* that.'

'I could smell it, still.'

'Those with money or power can buy their way out of any situation,' Stanlake said. With a nervous jerk of his hand he knocked one of the empty drinking-glasses to the floor. It fell with a clunk on the linoleum but didn't break. He picked it up and set it back on the table.

And Everil, surprising himself as much as, if not more than Stanlake, turned to Stanlake and kissed him on the lips. The kiss was neither long nor short: just enough. 'It'll be alright, fam,' he said. 'I got your back.'

Stanlake flushed. Everil sat back and tugged briefly at his rapidly-stiffening dick through the fabric of his track-pants. A girl in a sky-blue headscarf a few tables away watched with an amused smile. The boy she was with had his back to them. After a moment he touched the girl's hand to bring her attention back to him. She's gonna say something, Everil thought, waiting for the boy to turn round and gawp at the two youts who had lipsed each other in public. He found that he didn't care, not here, anyway.

The boy didn't look round.

Everil checked his phone. Still no messages. He had never thought of himself as charismatic, as a leader, but here was the proof: without his presence the Crew instantly fell apart, like troops with no commanding officer.

Troops.

He was at the beginning of a thought.

'We best go back, fam,' he said, a decisive note now in his voice.

'To where?'

'Solid's drum.'

'Then I will adjust my appearance,' Stanlake said.

Chapter Fifteen

S tanlake went to the restaurant toilet and applied fresh make-up. Everil paid for the ice-cream and Cokes, Stanlake contributed a few coins for the tip, and they left. The sun had gone down and the street-lights were winking into life. Shop windows glowed yellow and alluring but the two young men didn't give them a glance. Their breaths misted, and that seemed something to notice after an hour in the warmth. Stanlake dug in his pockets for his multi-coloured gloves, Everil pulled on his skeleton ones. Stanlake's eyelids shimmered green and his lashes were Kohled. A dust of silver-green sparkled on his cheekbones and scarlet lips. Under the hood of his duffle coat he had retied the red headscarf. He now moved more confidently in the world.

Something about heading back to the bus-stop made them think of home. Not the homes of the past, which Stanlake had lost, which Everil had never had, but the home that might lie ahead, for which they were trying to lay down foundations. Hopeful thoughts, if underpinned with grief and anxiety.

The bus was crowded: the rush-hour had begun, and the only seats they could get were across the aisle from each other upstairs near the back. Breath and body-heat fogged the windows, and there was a damp, oniony smell. At Waterloo the woman who had been sitting next to Everil on the window side – heavyset, with three bulging shopping-bags – struggled past him to get off, and Everil moved over and Stanlake slipped across to join him as the next wedge of passengers crammed on. They couldn't talk without being overheard so they sat in silence, half-companionable in their physical proximity, and their thoughts came rushing in.

Are these jackals new comrades, Poppy had asked him, and Stanlake hadn't answered, though the question, the possibility, had been in his mind too. He remembered Big Gun, Diamondz and Blondie high on coke and gunpowder dancing to music on the radio, and he had danced and smoked and snorted too. Blondie had shot bullets into the roof and they had laughed as if the retorts were punchlines to good jokes, only regretting the holes when the rains came.

And he remembered dancing with Patrick, Matthew and Robert to Fantastic Mash-up Sounds, the mobile sound-system that came to the village on the last Saturday of every month, the day after payday, and played a mix of American R&B and local artists. The four of them had got tipsy on Star lager, and had stumbled away from the dance and gone and sat in the dark away from their parents so as to avoid a scolding. Along one side of the square where the weekly market was held were benches where courting couples would come and sit and talk and hold hands, though there were none there then. Patrick had produced cigarettes, and they had lit up a couple and passed them between each other, coughing in their inexperience. And Pacific had found them by the smell and the glowing cigarette-tips, and to their mild alarm had sat down heavily among them, making them hutch up on the bench to accommodate him, and he had swigged from a bottle of Guiness, and he was as drunk as they were.

'Smoking is bad for you,' he said, taking the lit cigarette from between his son's fingers. 'It gives you cancer.' He took a drag and didn't return the cigarette. 'It can kill you.' He exhaled. The young men kept quiet, nervous but also excited at being treated for this brief time as equals by an adult. How long was it since their initiation? Six months maybe. Long enough to have forgotten the pain, anyway, and feel only pride in their progress towards manhood; and now this, another, albeit smaller step towards being men among men.

Discreetly the boys continued to share the other cigarette while Pacific finished the one he had taken from Stanlake. 'It is a good dance,' Pacific said, and he raised his bottle as if for a toast. After a moment's hesitation Stanlake and Matthew lifted their bottles and clinked them against his. As one they swallowed the last of the contents. Behind them the sound of insects was dense as the night. Before them the music floated on the air. Overhead the stars were thick. 'Your mother will be wondering where I am,' Pacific said. He pushed himself up with a grunt and ambled back to the dance, saying without looking back, 'I will see you boys later.'

To be able to think of his father in this way, simply living, without at once being taken back to the blistering heat and dazzle, the half-blinding sting of tears, the chromatically-distorted look on his father's face the moment before he brought the cutlass-blade down on his head, the cruel, harsh laughter as his father's skull yawned, disgorged: that was a new thing to Stanlake, something given him, it seemed, by the youth sitting by his side.

I am loved, he thought. And in me there is love. I do not need to be trapped forever in that moment, as if in my life, as if in my father's life, there were no other moments, when there were years.

Everil too was thinking of fathers, wondering as he almost never did about his own father, who he had never known, who he had mostly never cared to know about even had his mother cared to tell him, which she hadn't; wondering about roots and forebears and finding himself in a maze that had, perhaps, no centre, and brought him no reassurance. How could a fuck little better than a rape between two people who felt nothing for each other make a centre? A family?

Family, he thought. Could he and Stanlake somehow become that? Could he – through mechanisms equally obscure – become part of Stanlake's family? Because however filled with death it seemed, he knew there was love there. And for him to see that, to be able to see it, reminded Everil that he too must have been loved, though he couldn't remember when.

He would scatter his mother's ashes, he decided. He didn't know where yet, but when he did, when the right place came into his mind, he would do it.

Once the bigger business was done.

He thought of the Crew: family of a sort. Enough of one, he had believed, until now.

The traffic gridlocked. It would probably have been quicker to get off, walk down to Elephant & Castle and pick up another bus on the far side of the double roundabout, but they were stuck between stops. Once, Everil remembered from back when he was very young, there were buses where the back of them was open, and you could get on and off when you wanted, and there were conductors who would tell you off but couldn't stop you. He remembered his mum hurrying him off ahead of her one time and almost getting hit by a cyclist pumping along the inside lane.

In the seat in front of Everil and Stanlake a heavy-set Eastern European man was bellowing into his mobile in some foreign language. Rude fucker, Everil thought. Wouldn't be yelling his business if he thought we could understand it. Further up two girls, one black, one white, were eating KFC and throwing the bones down. Everil thought of rats. He thought he might like Stanlake to fuck him and shifted in his seat, wondering what it would feel like. Several times he had slid lubed fingers up inside himself and enjoyed it. One time he had got three in there and his dick had bucked. He thought too, how good it would be to be inside Stanlake. Better than pussy: more right.

Both of them had queasy stomachs from the juddering of the bus by the time they finally stepped down onto the pavement. It was a relief to gulp cold, unbreathed air. With that suddenness that still surprised him about Britain, Stanlake noticed that the entire sky had clouded over while they were on the bus. A tiny snowflake landed on his cheek, so dry that at first he thought it was cigarette-ash, then it melted.

By the time they reached Solid's block the wind was up and the snow was blowing about, light and powdery, getting in their eyes and mouths and nostrils. The security-door had been repaired so they couldn't just wander in as Stanlake had before. Everil buzzed, and when Solid answered with a crackly, 'A who dat?' said, 'It's me.' The door hummed and clunked open and they went in and got the lift to Solid's floor. Everil rattled perfunctorily at the letterbox. Cuts answered. He and Everil spudded, then he fell back to let the don and his spar enter. It was strange to Stanlake to be there again.

The air in the lounge was close with the smell of dope

and damp laundry. Solid and Pit-Bull were playing a video-game. Up on the plasma-screen, in the dust-yellow ruin of a desert town, American soldiers shot Arab insurgents while angular black helicopters clattered overhead. A figure in a burqa rushed forward screeching 'Jihaaad!' and exploded. Solid and Pit-Bull swore: the game was over.

'Fucking suicide-bombers, man,' Pit-Bull grumbled.

Solid tossed his pad, flinching involuntarily as he did so and touching his tightly-bandaged right wrist. He took a swig from a can of lager and turned to Everil. 'Thought you was the pizza-boy, bruv,' he said.

'Why come you ain't out there selling?' Everil said.

'Fresh outta supplies, bruv.'

'Yeah?'

'A true, fam,' Pit-Bull said.

'Let's see it, then.'

Grudgingly Solid pulled out a roll of dirty banknotes. He passed the roll to Everil and they all watched as he flicked the notes over deftly as a teller.

'This all of it, though?'

'Yeah.'

'Ya rampin'.'

'Nah, bruv,' Solid said. 'It's all there.'

'And you sold the lot?'

'What I said.'

'Then I reckon you been selling about quarter price, then.'

Solid gave no answer. Everil looked at the others in turn. Cuts' expression was bovinely unrevealing but Pit-Bull soon blushed and looked down. 'It's been chilly, bruv,' he said apologetically.

'So I gotta stand over yous lot like 24-7 or you just instantly fuck it off, then?' Everil said. 'Like there ain't no consequences for alla us if we ain't shift the shit? Like you're working at KFC or something and you just walk off the job and hey-fuckin'-ho no problem, no blowback? Two fucking nights,' he said, working himself up. '*Two fucking nights* I was off road and you couldn't even keep it together for that?'

'The feds was about some cos of the stabbing, though, fam,' Pit-Bull said. 'I mean, if mans-dem was busted that woulda been worse fuckeries, right? Cos we'da lost the stock *and* the paper. So, I dunno,' he shrugged, then added, 'We shoulda come hospital, though.'

'Why you lying so, Pit-Bull, man?' Everil asked angrily. 'Alla yous. Lyin' one lie 'pon another. You think I'm a cunt?' Pit-Bull mumbled something. 'Why you all so lazy?'

'Fuck dat, man.'

Everil turned to Cuts. 'Say what?'

'You sent your bitch round, tell us what to do – '

'He ain't my bitch, fam.'

'Like I give a fuck what he is – '

'Best watch your mouth though, fam, or you'll be giving a fuck with your teeth down your throat.'

'We done the selling, though,' Cuts said hotly. 'We shifted the shit, give your blood the dollars, then what?'

'Then you keep on working,' Everil said. 'Like we done every day since time.'

'Maybe we wanted a bank holiday.'

'What, you think me getting shanked was a holiday?' Everil said. 'You ain't answer my calls, send me to voicemail like I'm a cunt, make me come over here like I ain't got nothing better to do – '

They know he doesn't want this anymore, Stanlake thought. He has said nothing to reveal it, in fact he has said the opposite, but they can tell he no longer wants to lead them, and they despise themselves for wanting to be led, for having their lack of vision, their submission exposed. They feel humiliation and betrayal.

I understand them very well.

Solid got to his feet. 'So what about our cut from that roll you just took, though?' Everil's jaw tensed as Solid squared off with him.

'Solid, bruv,' Pit-Bull said. 'What you doin'?'

'Gettin' paid, bruv.'

Everil made four with Solid, and his lack of fear, his cold self-control reminded them all he was the don. Without looking Stanlake's way Everil tossed him the roll. 'Fifty each,' he said as Stanlake caught it. Stanlake nodded, tugged off the rubber bands, and counted out the notes. Pit-Bull and Cuts watched him as he did so, this pretty, diminutive boy in a duffle coat with a made-up face and delicate fingers that would suit nail-varnish. He counted off five tens and handed them to Pit-Bull. Then he counted off a twenty, a ten and four grubby fives for Cuts. Cuts gave him a long look, weighed up the shifting power-relations in the room, shook his head and took the money. He made a point of recounting it, a small challenge that Stanlake and Everil let pass.

Deprived of back-up Solid stood down. He turned to Stanlake and waited as Stanlake counted out his pay and handed it to him.

A long, uncertain moment followed, then Solid cleared his throat and said, 'You want a beer, blood?' Stanlake shrugged a nod. 'Bruv?' Everil nodded.

Solid went off to the kitchen and returned with two tins of Stella. He lobbed one to Stanlake, one to Everil. They popped them and went and sat on the couch alongside Cuts and Pit-Bull, who shifted along to give them room. Solid took the armchair.

'You wanna play?' Pit-Bull asked Stanlake, picking up one of the X-box pads and gesturing at the angular, hyperreal image of a square-jawed, unshaven U.S. marine frozen on the TV screen.

'I do not think so,' Stanlake said.

'You just don't reckon you could win, though,' Cuts said, reaching for the other pad.

Stanlake shrugged, sipped his lager. 'What would it tell me? To win?'

'Like if you could – ' Cuts began, then stopped, remembering perhaps Stanlake reassembling the gun, or the look on his face as Stanlake took the knife from him combat-style, or the time he spoke of war. He glanced down at his bandaged wrist and shrugged.

'What's it like though, fam?' Pit-Bull asked. 'To kill someone?'

Everil kissed his teeth. 'You don't just arx that, blood,' he said.

'Why do you want to know?' Stanlake said, though in truth he understood perfectly well, and his question was only a test of Pit-Bull's self-knowledge.

'Cos it's a ting, innit,' Pit-Bull said awkwardly. 'A ting

what'll change you. What'll make you, I dunno...' He flushed and shrugged as Cuts had done.

Stanlake looked round at the others. Outside the window snow was moving fast. The metal frames rattled, and the wind moaned round the building like something wanting in. 'You think it will make you a man,' he said. 'It does not.'

Cuts made as if he was going to come out with something smart, but a look from Everil cut him off. Instead he said, 'Why not, though?'

Stanlake looked at him. His green and silver eyeshadow glinted, and silver dust sparkled on his lips, and he said, 'Because girls kill too.'

'It makes you something, still,' Cuts said, and his agate eyes glittered as Pit-Bull's sapphire ones had done.

'It makes you less.'

'It proves you got heart, though.'

'No, that is not what it proves,' Stanlake said, and he met Solid's eyes unblinkingly and held them until the joint Solid was holding burnt his fingers, and with a sharp grunt and a flick of the wrist he flung it across the room and swore. It landed still lit by Pit-Bull's foot. Pit-Bull picked it up, blazed on it, and placed it smouldering on the lip of the ashtray.

'You want to become men,' Stanlake said, and it was not a question but a statement. The others said nothing but stirred awkwardly in their seats, even Everil. The windows rattled again, more violently this time, and chill currents of air drifted across the closeness of the room.

'What you mean, blood?' Cuts said, after a long, stoned moment.

'Drugs cannot do it,' Stanlake said. 'Thieving cannot. Or fucking, or dealing, or violence.'

'What, then?' said Everil.

'Connection.'

'Connection?'

'With the spirits of the men who came before you. Fathers and grandfathers and great-grandfathers. To become part of the tribe of men.'

'We ain't know our fathers, though,' Everil said. 'Well, 'cept for you, yeah, bruv?' he said to Pit-Bull. 'And Cuts, kinda.'

'He's a cunt, though,' Pit-Bull said. 'Card-carrying BNP cunt. Yous lot is my brothers. My family.' And he reached out a fist, and first Everil, then Solid, then Cuts met it. Brown, brown, yellow, white.

'And you want to become men?' This time Stanlake was requiring an answer.

'How?' asked Pit-Bull.

'Tell me you want it, and I will tell you how.'

'Yeah, we want to become men,' Pit-Bull said, his face reddening. He looked round at the others. Grudgingly they nodded.

'But – ' Solid began.

'Do not resist,' Stanlake said, cutting him off. 'Do not resist me. Do not resist yourself, my African brother.'

Solid subsided, brow furrowing, keeping his eyes off Stanlake's, to hide, perhaps, the longing they would reveal: the restless, only-now-acknowledged pain of alienage. 'You are all my Africans,' Stanlake said. 'Do this thing with me and you will be my brothers, my comrades. You will be warriors. You will be men.'

They are boys, he thought. As my Masks were, as my Beasts were. And now they are my jackals, through whom the dead will find an open door. Yes, I can do this. Yet what could he do? What rituals would be right in this place? How could he reshape these shapeless, these misshapen lives? There was no blood-fed shrine, there were no circumcisers' knives, no dusty sacred hut of masks and drums, no generations of elders standing to receive them full of joy at the making of these new men. But I am my father's son. As he knew there so I will know here. He will guide my thoughts, my words, my hands. And he will show me the path to my atonement, my sacrifice.

Over Solid's fireplace was a mirror, and he caught a glimpse of his own face in it, and it was strange to him, and he knew that somehow being with Everil, being intimate with him, that that too, whatever his mother and the church might believe, had made him a man.

'What about selling, though?' Solid asked.

'Fuck selling,' Everil said. 'Selling can wait. So – ' To Stanlake: 'What we need to do this, then, and when we gonna do it?'

'I will make a list,' Stanlake said. 'We will do it tonight.'

The bus-doors dragged open and Poppy stepped out into the swirling snow. Dry and light, it stung her eyes, and she kept her head down as she hurried forward, and the word 'sanctuary' was in her mind. As she turned the corner the wind plucked at her headwrap as if it was a candle-flame, and she had to put up a hand to hold it in place. She thought of the lamb Abraham had offered – had been allowed to offer – in place of his son. Had been allowed to offer, yes, but only after he had taken it to the limit; only after he had proved that he would offer his own son.

No, not 'offer'. Kill.

The streets were emptying fast as people hurried homewards. Poppy had always criticised her husband for making sacrifices – so primitive: yes, back then she had seen it as primitive, cutting animals' throats – yet wasn't it in the Bible, over and over? But why did God want all that blood spilt? Why was God, so good, so perfect, also so cruel? And if He did none of the things He was supposed to, saved and spared no-one in this world, then what did faith add up to?

From behind a row of wheelie-bins outside a Lidl a fox with a raggedy tail, its back frosted with snow as if it was a creature of gingerbread that had escaped from a bakery, darted across the street in front of her and vanished down a snecket. Poppy thought of the men of the village going hunting, their eyes bright with anticipation as they gathered in the cool grey of the morning, bows and spears on their shoulders, their gaze turned towards the forest. When she was young she had asked her mother why girls weren't allowed to hunt; complained that it wasn't fair. Her mother had broken off from pounding cassava and told her it was tradition, and then told her to study her bible passages for Sunday school. At the time Poppy had felt her mother was ducking the issue, and had resented her lack of engagement with the principle of simple fairness and equality. Later on she saw that becoming a Christian was a way of getting past too much tradition; that in life you need to embrace something new in order to get past something old, or all you will know is loss.

The majority of the congregation in any church she had ever attended were always women and girls. Did women really care more than men about being close to God?

Up ahead she saw Lucy on the church steps and called out to her, but the wind blew her voice back into her mouth along with some snow. Poppy broke into a run to try and catch up with Lucy before she got inside, but the unmelted snow lying on top of the greasy pavement had made a slippery skin and one of her legs shot out from under her, tugging a muscle in her groin painfully, and she had to catch at a lamp-post to stop herself falling. Lucy vanished into the building. Poppy pulled herself upright with an effort and limped after her.

Reverend Obasanjo's car wasn't parked outside and she couldn't help feeling relieved, even though part of her intention in coming early to service this evening had been to try to speak to him in private before things began. Uncertain what exactly she wanted to say, she had also hoped to have a chance to speak to Lucy before she tackled the Reverend.

Poppy stamped her feet on the mat and brushed the snow from her headwrap before it had a chance to melt and make stains. Then she went through to the meeting-room, from which she could hear the sounds of setting up.

'Ah, Poppy,' Mrs Ige said, before Poppy had even had a chance to unbutton her coat. 'Good. Come and help us with the chairs.' A few other women were already doing things. The keyboard player in his kente-cloth shirt was flicking out cables; a teenage girl wiped down one of a row of trestle tables.

'I was hoping to speak to the Reverend,' Poppy said.

'He is running a little behind,' Mrs Ige said, smiling the smile of one who has inside knowledge. 'There are the chairs.' She waved a plump hand at two rows of folding chairs propped against the wall. Her nails were red and, though small, sharp. 'Quickly, enh?'

'Is Lucy about?' Poppy asked.

For a moment Mrs Ige looked blank, evidently not able to put a face to the name. Then with a dismissive wave of the hand she said, 'She's around somewhere.'

Poppy took off her coat, hung it up, and went over to the chairs while Mrs Ige stood in the middle of the room, one bejewelled hand on her sturdy bust, looking around for another chance to give orders. As below, so above, Poppy thought, unfolding a chair. The hinges were stiff and it was a struggle. A burst of static came from one of the speakers as the keyboard-player plugged something in, then unplugged it. For a short time this place had seemed like home to Poppy. Like sanctuary.

Not anymore.

In a magazine someone left on the bus one time she had read about a curious mental condition, and for no reason perhaps but the oddity of it the name had stuck in her head: Capgrass Syndrome. Sufferers believed that everyone around them had been replaced by exact duplicates, perfect in every way. But the sufferer knew, impossibly, that they *were* duplicates, and the more exactly other people behaved as they should, the greater was the deluded person's conviction that this proved they were fake. Looking round the room, that was how she felt now.

Lucy emerged through a side-door with an armful of folded white sheets to prettify the trestle tables. She set them down on the table the girl had just cleaned and came over to help Poppy with the chairs.

'Praise Jesus we get a good turn-out despite the snow,' she said.

'Yes,' Poppy said.

'Are you tired?' Lucy asked. She was all smiles this evening, and Poppy suddenly wondered if she was bipolar. That had been another article in the magazine. If she was, then what did her happiness mean? Or her sadness? In her head Poppy scolded herself for having such uncharitable thoughts about a fellow congregant. Or were they uncharitable? Weren't they really just about the facts?

My son is a homosexual.

Wasn't that just a fact?

'I am a little tired, yes,' Poppy said. 'Somehow it has been a very long day.'

'You'll soon feel livelier,' Lucy said. 'But tell me, how did it go with the Reverend and your son?'

'Oh, Lucy,' Poppy said with a sigh she couldn't repress. 'I think it was a mistake.'

'But how so?'

'When I got home the Reverend had been and gone, the other boy was still there, my son was very angry, and he walked out of the house with that boy on his tail.'

'Eh-eh, there is surely a spirit inside him.'

'If there is, then it is still there. So what good did the Reverend do?'

'You must have faith, Poppy,' Lucy said. 'Remember: God doesn't make mistakes.'

'But all these not-mistakes are very confusing.'

'Praise Jesus, it is a mystery,' Lucy agreed earnestly.

'Praise Him,' said Poppy, forcing down irritation.

'At least the Reverend's visit means that you have seen things as they really are.'

'And how are they, really?'

'Your son has been bewitched by a witch. You have seen that witch, a male witch, who has put an evil spirit, a girlish spirit, into your son. And now that is all out in the open the Reverend can begin the battle. But why did you let your son leave? You should have prayed with him.'

'How could I make him stay? And even if I could, he would not pray with me because he has not accepted Jesus into his heart.'

'Then you must try harder,' Lucy said. 'This is your son's immortal soul we're talking about, Poppy.'

'But I won't win him over by just going on and on,' Poppy said. It was as if she was standing to one side, watching herself. *What is the point of this conversation? That other boy is not a witch. My son is not possessed. Lucy cannot help me. I must speak to the Reverend, call it off.*

'What would your husband say about this?' Lucy was saying. 'When a man is not in the home a boy may – '

'My husband is dead.'

'Eh-enh, I did not know that,' Lucy said, the smile finally coming off her face as she shook her head.

Poppy looked away. What *would* Pacific have said about all this? She had told her son that his father would not have accepted him, but now she thought perhaps she was wrong.

Stanlake had shied from none of the things that made you a man, good or bad. Had he had the chance to make his hunt, that final stage of his initiation into manhood; had he succeeded in it, and she had no reason to think he wouldn't have done, wouldn't Pacific have accepted him, feminine in his manner or not? She didn't doubt Stanlake had the courage the hunt required, and perhaps for the first time she acknowledged that the terrible thing he had done in front of her had taken courage; and that as her husband had knelt there in the dirt, waiting for death, chest out, back straight, he had known it too.

And Cain slew Abel, and Abraham would have slain Isaac, and how could Jesus' tears or Jesus' suffering sweep all that away? But if it did, as she prayed it did, then she should love her son as He would have done. And forgive him?

'Poppy, Lucy – ' It was Mrs Bankole, looking striking in floor-length turquoise and emerald. 'Let's get these cloths put out, enh? Quickly-o.' She clapped her small, plump hands.

Bobbing nods, Poppy and Lucy did as they were told. Still the Reverend had not arrived. Other church members began to come in, stamping their feet and shaking snow from their coats and wraps. Under the guidance of Mrs Ige a television set was wheeled out on a stand and hooked up to a dvd player. A garnet glinting on her forefinger Mrs Ige gestured regally at it with the remote. A blue screen sprang up with a yellow arrow in the top right-hand corner. Then a burst of excited voices and a fuzzy football match that straightaway drew the eyes of the keyboard-player and another, older man who was setting up the drums. Mrs Ige jabbed with the remote a couple more times. The football vanished. Now there appeared a besuited, pink-faced man with parted yellow hair that shone like nylon, standing at a lectern. The man's face was flushed and glistening with perspiration. His front teeth were unnaturally white and oddly bonded together into a single band. Mrs Ige cranked up the volume.

'We here in the United States of America,' the man was saying, 'are proud to stand shoulder-to-shoulder with our brothers and sisters in Christ Jesus in Africa, conjoining in battle in these end times against the forces of sin and darkness that are seeking like a tsunami of sewage to overwhelm those of us who are righteous. Let me be frank, brothers and sisters: it shames me to say it, but we here in the West, we have been lax. We have been weak. We have allowed ourselves to be pushed onto the back foot. The secularists and abortionists and sodomites and feminists and atheists have proclaimed blasphemy a human right, the murder of babies a human right, sodomy and child-molestation a human right. How, brothers and sisters in Christ, how can these wrongs be rights?'

As the dvd spun and the preacher preached, the members of the congregation began at first to murmur, then to call out mm-hms, Yes, Lords, Amens and Praise Hims. Getting in the spirit, the keyboard-player began to add a swirl of uplift to the sermon, and dramatic stings each time the preacher struck the lectern with the palm of his hand.

'You have the chance, my brothers and sisters, to stop these blasphemers, these deviants from gaining a toe-hold in your country, you have the chance to be soldiers for Christ and draw your swords. Throw those tares into the fire! Throw those goats into the fire! Hell, they're all going to burn in the end, why not give 'em a taste of it now?'

Lucy burst out with a feverish, 'Amen!'

'That's why we're asking you to dig deep,' the preacher continued, mopping his face with a neat square of handkerchief, smiling his unnatural smile. 'Give what you can – give everything you can, to this fight, this war as the End of Days rushes upon us like an express train of angels with flaming swords in their hands!'

'Yes, Lord!' someone shouted hoarsely.

'I know times are tight for many of you right now, and I'm not asking you to match the sacrifice Our Lord made for you, for all of us, upon the cross – His life, brothers and sisters! His *life*. And remember Abraham. He was prepared to sacrifice his *only son* because it was what the Lord demanded of him. He had that knife at his son's throat and he was *willing*! All I'm asking for today is just a little money. If it hurts to give – give more! For the Lord will see and weigh your sacrifice. And together we can purge your country of this moral sickness, these abominations, these splinters of sin thrust by the wickedness of men into God's eye!'

Poppy had heard this preacher, or one much the same as him, all of them white and American, several times before. Mrs Ige and Mrs Bankole often had the TV blaring while chores were being done, and they sold the dvds after the services. At first Poppy had wondered why these preachers, these white men who referred to the continent of Africa as a country as if it was the same all over, never demanded money to fight material poverty; never raised their voices for democracy and earthly justice; never railed against financial corruption and political oppression. But then Lucy explained to her that spiritual poverty was the more serious matter, and that since all were equal in Jesus Christ, for the faithful politics was just a distraction from what really mattered.

Along with the dvds Mrs Ige and Mrs Bankole sold a glossy full-colour church calendar. This was the official calendar of the Anointed Joy and Prosperity Mission. It was endorsed by Reverend Obasanjo, though he modestly declined to appear in it. Instead each page featured members of the Ige or Bankole family – at prayer, absorbedly reading the Bible, being happily married with well-groomed children, looking Heavenward in a spiritual fashion against a Photoshopped blue sky and so on. Accompanying each image, usually in white or yellow curlicued lettering, was a wise saying of the Reverend's, something to think about through the month ahead, and a bible verse. The calendars were twelve pounds each, and all profits were reinvested in the church. They sold well: even Lucy had bought one.

Poppy hadn't.

The thought of the collection-basket going round during the service, and the competitive, ostentatious thrusting-in of money as Reverend Obasanjo exhorted the believers to dig deep for the holy war ahead, made her stomach clench.

Yet hadn't the Reverend helped her with her son for free? He had held her family photograph in his strong, scented hands and a look, the strangest look, had come over his face, and he had been moved by compassion. Wasn't he a good man? A blessed man? When she first saw him hadn't she felt at once that she knew him and he knew her?

'These homosexuals with their agenda to seduce your children,' the televangelist was saying, 'they try to tell you it's normal, it's *scientific*. Well, if that's science I don't want nothing to do with science! This' – he held up a white bible embossed with gold – 'This is all the science I need.'

Suddenly unable to catch her breath, Poppy grabbed her coat from its hook and left the room. Perhaps being out in the cold air would help. Certainly getting away from that unending voice would help. She pushed her way through arriving congregants, apologising as she went. A moment later she was outside, gulping the air as anxiety surged through her.

The street was now wholly deserted. The snow was still blowing about, as artificial in the yellow of the neon light as polystyrene snow on a film set. Poppy ached for home, the home that was forever behind her, where only the dead now dwelt. There could be no return. To die now would be an easy thing, for when all social ties are cut, are you not already dead? How strange it was to have survived so much, to have travelled so far, only to find on arrival that the fuel is all used up.

But I have my son. That thought was fierce in her now. I have made mistakes but I can sort them out.

The Reverend's silver Saab turned into the street. It drew up smoothly in front of her. Its tinted windows prevented her from seeing in. A handsome young chauffeur in a dark suit got out and opened the back door for his passenger.

The Reverend emerged. He was wearing a sky-blue suit tonight and had heavy gold chains around his neck, and a large gold cross. Although it was night he wore sunglasses, and he rubbed his nose as if he had hay-fever or a cold.

'Reverend – ' Poppy began.

'Ah, sister. Yes.' Reverend Obasanjo put a disconcerting arm around her shoulders: no man had touched her since Pacific had died. 'Come inside. It is cold out here.' He steered her up the steps and into the building. 'Is your son inside?' Behind them came the double chirrup of the youth locking the Saab. Poppy shook her head.

'Ah.'

'Reverend, what happened today?' she asked quickly, before he could get caught up in greeting other worshippers.

'It went well,' the Reverend said, shaking someone's husband's hand. 'Praise God, there will be a good outcome.'

'Yes, but – ' Poppy was now having to squeeze along the crowded corridor after him. Up ahead organ music was rising in anticipation of his arrival, as if he was a boxer coming to the ring. 'But when I returned home, the jackal was still there.'

'Jackal?'

'The other one. The one who – '

'Ah, yes. You do not need to fear him anymore.'

'But he left with my son.'

'Ah, Mrs Ige. How are you?'

And that was that. They were in the meeting-room. He was taking Mrs Ige's bejewelled hand in his. Poppy had lost her chance. Leaving her behind the Reverend swept through to the back office with Mrs Bankole in hot pursuit. 'Poppy!' Mrs Bankole called over her shoulder, waving a talon at a cardboard box. 'Put more calendars out on the side-table, enh.'

Poppy did as she was told. Perhaps she could speak properly to the Reverend afterwards. But no, he was never alone after a service.

Oh, my husband, my husband, it's your wisdom I need.

Chapter Sixteen

Solid's lounge was in near total darkness: the only light came from a pair of scented candles on the mantelpiece and the firefly tips of joints. The candles had been left behind by some yat who had tried, briefly and unsuccessfully, to domesticate Solid before being sent jeered at on her way. Sweet-scented smoke – twining spirals of cinnamon, orange-blossom and cedarwood – combined with the body-heat of the Crew, the dope-smoke and the heat from the vents in the walls to make the air dense and intimate as flesh. Following Stanlake's instructions they had hung sheets at the uncurtained windows: this was something not meant for outside eyes, and that included peepers with binoculars in neighbouring blocks and police helicopters. Even up on the twelfth floor this was something somehow underground. Once the windows were covered they pushed the furniture back against the walls, clearing a central space for what was to come, though none of them, not even Stanlake, knew what exactly that would be.

On the coffee-table he placed a shallow glazed dish, a kitchen knife, Solid's Wahl clippers, a bag of plain flour, an ashtray overflowing with cigarette-butts, a bottle of vodka with an unbroken seal and, laid out in a row, four unused razor-blades from a box of five. Their careful placement made these discordant items seem surgical, purposive, anticipatory.

As they made their preparations under Stanlake's enigmatic guidance Everil felt, and he knew without exchanging a word or even a glance with the others that they felt it too, a building sense of mystery, of immanence. This was new to them, and it laid bare an unexpected truth: that the cynicism they believed saturated the meat of their brains and the fabric of the souls in which they only barely believed, was, in fact, a surface thing, brittle, less a stain than a lacquer; something that could, as had never occurred to them until that moment, be cleaned or chipped off. To believe your surface was your core, to believe it as strongly as a fact about guns or knives or electricity, and then have that belief held up to you and shown to be false, was a troubling thing. But its corollary – the revelation that you possessed some other unfamiliar, unexpected core – was exciting, almost wonderful. You just needed the tools to get to it. The knife, the clippers, the razor-blades.

The fire-alarm in the hallway, its battery almost but not quite flat, set off by the smoke from the candles and joints and cigarettes, chirruped like some insect of the forest, and that seemed right: part of making the world beyond Solid's now-transformed front room feel remote and othered.

Everil blazed, forcing his crushed lungs to expand to their limit. He had never felt African before. He wondered what in him would respond to what was going to happen in this room tonight, which he knew, whatever else it would be, would be profoundly African. He held the smoke down, felt the chemicals pass through the permeable membranes lining his lungs and enter his bloodstream.

Blood
   Stream
      Flowing flowing
      Time flowing History
        Africa
         Heart

He let the smoke out. Something was spinning inside him bright as a jewel.

Had they been told one thing about Africa at school? If they had, which Everil doubted and certainly didn't remember, it must have been on a day he wasn't there, a day when he was running in the streets. His fault then, for not being there. But still he blamed them, blamed the system that blazoned its indifference to lives like his. Nonetheless he felt ignorant.

African. Yeah, I am an African.

He felt something stir within himself that might be in some way African, and in his mind there was an image: a bird that might be him as a spirit-creature, flying backwards over the ocean at night, and lights on a distant shoreline receding fast. *Back. Going back.*

Going back to go forward. My wings bevelled weird against aerodynamics and nature. Fuck it.

They were now down to their underwear, Everil in black trunks, Pit-Bull in indigo boxers, Solid in white trunks, Stanlake in a lace thong that defied everyday ways of being, that connoted something else beyond. Only Cuts was absent, not yet back from some errand Stanlake had sent him on while the others prepared the room. He had whispered words into Cuts' ear and Cuts had left with gleaming eyes and a strange expression on his face.

After he had gone Stanlake stripped to the waist, crossed to the mirror, and the others watched and blazed as he applied more make-up, staring into his own eyes as he coated his eyelids green and gold, painted his lips crimson, his fingernails turquoise, and dusted his smooth, shiny skull with carnival glitter, becoming what? A spirit?

Stanlake carried a wooden chair to the middle of the room and gestured to Everil to sit. Everil did so, peeling off his vest and shucking off his track-pants as Stanlake plugged Solid's clippers into an extension lead. Stanlake moved the clippers over his lover's skull with buzzing deftness, and the others pretended not to see Everil's erection as it jutted through the cotton-lycra of his trunks. Then Everil stood and Pit-Bull sat, and Stanlake watched as Everil shaved Pit-Bull's head, and Pit-Bull Solid's, and they passed joints round and blazed as they worked, and the air grew sweeter and heavier as they purified themselves in that way, and their skins sheened with sweat, and all of them knew, yes, this was something, and the entire rest of their lives had been no more than a preamble to being in this room, now.

As if it had been long-planned Solid produced a drum from a cupboard, an African drum he had bought from a market stall years ago in an inept attempt to assert a connection with his heritage, an attempt that had brought only confusion and shame and had been quietly put away, now, against all the odds, finally finding its moment. Shyly he began to pat out a rhythm on the stretched cow-hide, and though the drum had not lain for generations in the hut of the ancestors, though it had not been fed with song and the love of hands, or offered blood; though it had been made for tourists and should have been too new a thing for what was now required of it, still it had in it what was necessary. For it was at the beginning of something, the establishment of a new shrine, and Solid sensed that somehow and his confidence grew. As he drummed he looked both younger and older, and Stanlake held the joint to his lips and he dragged on it and his eyes hazed and he drummed faster and harder and the sound filled the room with a density recorded sound, however loud, never does, and charged the air.

To see Solid actually doing something was strange to Everil. Doing, performing, making. Not playing computer-games, smoking, loafing. This was new to all of them.

Stanlake himself, now heavily stoned, was between places and times, now in Solid's lounge, now in the ancestral hut with his Mask brothers, now high on the roadblock with his fellow Beasts, now in the sacred grove in the forest. 'A man does not lie,' he said thickly. 'A man does not cheat. A man does not steal. He keeps his word. He has honour.'

Solid drummed with passion, shining with sweat.

'These are not secrets.' Stanlake raised his hands and began to shake his body to the rhythm, his voice gaining in power as he did so. 'I do not tell you secrets yet.'

He reached into the bag of flour and flung a handful of it over Everil's glistening, freshly-shaved head, then over Pit-Bull's, then Solid's, and there welled up in them feelings they had never had before. Cracking open the vodka he took swigs from it and, as he had seen his father do, blew mists of the hot, clear spirit into the other young men's now-upturned faces, and their closed eyelids trembled. 'Here at the cross-roads the living meet the dead and what do they do? They talk. Here.' With ash from the ashtray he thumbed crosses on their foreheads. 'Here in your heads. Here are your ances-tors. Listen to them.' Scrabbling in the ashtray with his fingers he threw ash on their heaving chests, those shrines of living bones and muscle through which the drum-beat was passing, the only shrines that really matter. 'They are in your heads, in your hearts. I am not telling you a secret. This is not a secret. This is just truth.'

There was a clatter from the hall and a sudden inrush of chilly air as Cuts returned, incongruous, alien in his outdoor coat and woolly hat, carrying under one arm a cardboard box that shifted oddly as he turned and closed the door behind him.

'Good, my brother,' Stanlake said as Cuts handed him the box. 'Thank you.' Solid's drumming slackened as he and the others watched Stanlake lift off the lid. Behind him Cuts quickly removed his hat and coat.

There was a scraping sound inside the box then an eye, round and yellow with a black pupil, appeared at an air-hole. It blinked, then reappeared above the top of the box framed by prickling white feathers and surmounted by a twitching dull-red, fleshy comb, and there was an orange beak. The cockerel's head jerked as it surveyed them in profile, no emotion discernible in its swivelling eye. Stanlake nodded approval and put the lid back on the box, pushing the bird back down inside. He set the box on the coffee-table next to the bowl, the knife, the razor-blades.

'Come,' he said, gesturing to Cuts to take the seat in the middle of the room. Solid's drumming picked up again.

Peeling off his vest Cuts sat: yes, he too would be part of this; needed to be part of it. For in him as in them all was the ache of what seemed like nothing but rejection. Yet he shared with Everil the paradox that Everil himself had only recently been able to acknowledge: that the mother who had rejected him, who had lanced his heart as if it was a boil, had once, beyond his conscious memory, loved him. Briefly as a mayfly, maybe, but she had. And if he could accept that, then he too could love, and what happened in this room tonight seemed tied up with that possibility, the possibility of acceptance and self-acceptance, though he couldn't consciously understand how – wouldn't understand until he saw Everil and Stanlake kiss, and still he couldn't articulate that understanding, could only be struck by his unexpected lack of rage or disgust at such a sight.

Stanlake flicked out the lead and snapped on the clippers. As he began to move them over the brief stubble on Cuts' already close-cropped head Pit-Bull asked, 'Where you get the bird from, fam?'

'Went up Chinatown,' Cuts said, taking the joint Pit-Bull offered him. 'My old man's cash an' carry. Said I needed it for something and he give it me.'

'He arx what you want it for, though?'

'He ain't the type arxes stuff.'

'Still he give it you, though.'

'Yeah. Gratis.'

Cuts blazed. Buzz on, he thought, getting my buzz on. The vibration of the clippers resonated against the bones of his skull as he drew the smoke down, and that, and the rhythm of Solid's drumming passing through his chest, gave him a sense of the transcendent, of which all clubbing, all bluesing, all getting high was the poor relation. Even all fucking that was done outside of love.

Stanlake put down the clippers. 'Clap,' he said, and he began to weave a fresh rhythm through Solid's by patting his hands fast against Cuts' bare chest. Everil and Pit-Bull picked it up and began to move, taking their cues from each other with the easy affinity of brothers. Cuts patted the rhythm on his thigh, moving his head to the base-beat.

'Close your eyes,' Stanlake said. Cuts did so, and Stanlake reached once more into the bag of flour, and Cuts too was libated with flour and then ash from the ashtray, and Solid beat the drum harder and his sides ran with sweat as ash and flour clouded the air. Stanlake blew misted vodka over Cuts' face, then took his hands and Cuts opened his eyes as Stanlake pulled him to his feet, and the four of them danced, taking it in turns to swig from the bottle of vodka and pass it on. And too they took turns to drum when Solid became exhausted, Pit-Bull surprising them by being the strongest and most confident, perhaps because he felt his skin gave him the most to prove, though here in this room there was nothing to prove, only the doing of what needed to be done. Sweat popped on their bodies and ran down their faces, streaking them white and grey, and Stanlake caught their hands and sent them spinning until they staggered, laughing giddily in the blood-warm, breath-dense air.

Then, joint in mouth, he picked up the knife and took the cockerel from the box, holding it firmly by the neck. It tried to kick but its feet were tied together. Stanlake gestured to

Everil to hold the dish ready. Everil did so, only a slight tightness pulling at his face. Stanlake could see that his lover and the others were having to defy their squeamishness in the face of this, a curious, childish squeamishness it seemed to him given their eating of meat, their easy violence towards other human beings; strange that this act, which had been an everyday thing to him, to his mother and father, was most alien to them.

Yet tonight was different for him too. Making a sacrifice was not the same as preparing a meal. Making the offering, feeding the gods, the spirits, the ancestors, released other energies, released into the space that was now a shrine the subtle radiance that is the indefinable difference between a dead and a living thing as a force that could be channelled and used.

Without further delay or any dramatic flourish he drew the blade across the chicken's neck, severing the head entirely, and as the body jerked in his hand hot, bright blood flicked out in erratic spurts onto his face and chest, and onto Everil's face and chest, and Everil didn't flinch, becoming a man then, focusing on catching as much of the blood in the dish as he could, squeamish only when he accidentally stood with his bare foot on the severed head of the chicken where it had fallen to the floor.

Stanlake gestured with the twitching bird towards the others, spattering droplets of blood onto Cuts' and Solid's and Pit-Bull's faces, and their chests heaved. At a further gesture from Stanlake Solid stopped drumming. In the sudden silence the taking in of air now wholly stripped of oxygen and block-solid, it felt, as amber, was difficult, and the boundary between body and environment, self and other, was no longer clear. Stanlake took Solid's hand and drew him forward so he was standing with the others. They fell into line and Stanlake took his place in front of them.

This is the beginning of my reparation, he thought. This is for you, my father, my chance to mend the break as well as I can. To honour what you taught me. To be the man you would want me to be as best as I can.

He put the no longer kicking body of the chicken down on the coffee-table, and next to its soft, feathery mass the knife, which in its sharpness was barely stained. Taking the bowl from Everil he dipped his right forefinger into the shallow slick of blood that Everil had managed to catch and marked a cross on Everil's forehead, and the red covered the grey: life on top of death, the present on top of the past. Ash and blood combined, became a paste: a fusion. Stanlake held the bowl to Everil's lips. Everil took a sip, pushing down, Stanlake could see, a small shudder as he did so, but showing no fear in his eyes, which he at all times kept on Stanlake's.

Moving along the line Stanlake thumbed crosses of blood on the foreheads of Pit-Bull, Solid and Cuts, offering each in turn the bowl to drink from. He felt his father in him as he did this. None of the youths refused to taste the blood as none of his Mask brothers had refused. When that was done Stanlake put the dish to his own lips and drained what remained. The blood was still warm, and tasted of iron with some sweet undercurrent, as if the bird had fed on berries. His lips buzzed, and there was a sudden whiteness in the centre of his brain that radiated outwards, and a rising-up of something. He placed the dish back on the table and picked up one of the razor-blades. He took Everil by the hand.

'Come,' he said. Everil came forward. They stood face-to-face, gazing into each others' eyes, channels now totally open. 'You are my lover,' Stanlake said, and his voice was not loud but it was somehow penetrating. Everil stiffened, and his hand tightened in Stanlake's, but the others didn't respond, too preoccupied perhaps with what their own moment would be, with what would be laid bare in their own hearts. *Like they ain't guess it anyway*, Everil thought. 'And you are my brother. Not my brother in the womb, but my brother as my Mask brothers were brothers, for we became men together. We were welcomed into the tribe of men together, by our fathers, our older brothers, our uncles, our cousins. Today I share with you my ancestors. My father and grandfather, my uncles, my great-grandfather. That line of men going back to the time of men who hunted with the gods in the beginning of things. Do you accept these men as your ancestors, as men who stand shoulder-to-shoulder with your own ancestors who you cannot name, who are lost to you in time and across oceans and through many small-small betrayals, but are still in the meat and blood of you?'

Everil's face was taut, angular in the low light, his narrow chest pushed out, nipples prickling, pupils dilated into radiant black. 'Yes,' he said, his voice hoarse as a lover's.

'This, here, today is a new tribe. It's a new beginning. Do you accept it?'

'Yes,' Everil said, and his voice was choked, and a sudden glitter came into his eyes.

'You called yourself Evill to me. Your name was not a truth.'

'No.'

'I give you first the name of my Mask brother Patrick, who was killed defending my village,' Stanlake said, and with a lack of fear that surprised him, he draw the razor-blade in a diagonal line across Everil's right cheek. 'And then I give you the name of my warrior brother who I loved, who was killed in the forest fighting to be alive because life is fighting. You are Big Gun. Here, now, receive their spirits.' He cut Everil's other cheek. Ruby droplets squeezed out erratically along the lines of the cuts, glinting. 'And now you are a man,' Stanlake said, and he kissed Everil on the mouth.

'Na, blood, I ain't doin' that, though,' Solid said, screwing up his face and shaking his head. 'No homo, blood.'

Stanlake broke off the kiss, leaving scarlet and gold on Everil's lips, and smiled at Solid. 'That is not your story,' he said. 'Come.' And he beckoned Solid to come forward as Everil moved to stand alongside his lover and face the others, a man now looking back at boys.

Pushing out his chest, Solid stepped forward. He let Stanlake take his hand, bracing up as he did so as if the contact gave him courage, or at least charge. Stanlake placed in the ashtray the blade he had used to cut Everil's face and picked up the next one. His eyes were now on Solid's. Solid couldn't sustain the depth of his gaze and looked down. Stanlake swung his hand as if he was a child, the movement metronome-regular, somehow beguiling.

'You have been asleep, my brother. Do you want to wake up?'

'Yes.'

'You have been lost, my brother. Do you want to find

your way and be found?'

'Yes.'

'Forgive those who lost you.'

'How?'

'You do not know what weight they carried: perhaps they too were lost, and if they failed they were only people. Understand that. Feel it and let the love that was in them flow through you. Connect with it and allow yourself to love.'

'I ain't no queer, though,' Solid said thickly.

'Give love to yourself,' Stanlake went on, as though he hadn't spoken. 'Love your friends who are your family and who stand by you here today. Love women. They are not skets and skanks and hos. To be a man is to be able to give love. To have the strength to give love. To be able to receive love.'

And now Solid did look up, and the candlelight flickered across his broad face, and his eyes met Stanlake's and stayed there.

'Your name too is a mask. A block of wood. A burden. I name you for my Mask brother Robert, who I was circumcised with, who I laughed with about girls, and talked to about the future. And I name you for my Beast brother Diamondz, who fought with me in the forest until all our bullets were gone, and who died there with a bullet in his heart. Do you accept these spirits of men? Do you let them in to stand with those ancestors who have always been there in you, whose names you were never told?'

Solid muttered, 'Yeah,' then cleared his throat and said more loudly, 'Yes.' And he didn't flinch as Stanlake drew the razor-blade across first one cheek then the other and said, 'And now you are a man.'

Solid touched his fingertips to his cheek as Stanlake put down the second razor-blade and picked up the third and turned to Pit-Bull. His fingers came away red from the barely-visible slit in his smooth, dark skin and his eyes were wide open and he was in a new place, seeing new things.

Pit-Bull came forward quickly, reaching out to take Stanlake's hand, fearful, Stanlake guessed, no, knew with certainty, that he would be excluded from this because of the lack of melaninin in his skin, though in no other way afraid –

either of pain, or blood, or revelation – and Stanlake saw in his bright, light, eager eyes a love pushed down that was rising now. Perhaps it was only a minute ago, in this room, watching Stanlake and Everil kiss, that this boy had realised he was in love with Everil, in love with his don for all he had fucked as much gash as Solid or Cuts or indeed and paradox-ically Everil himself; this young man who had, perhaps, no interest in the dick or arse of love with a man, or perhaps, unknowingly until this moment, did. Was love what had drawn him to this, as well as hate of where he was from? Had his life been, despite all appearances, a search outwards for love? He had both parents living yet he too was adrift, in need of belonging to something that would hold meaning for him, a beginning that would answer the emptiness within him, in that way the mirror-image of Solid.

'Yes, my brother,' Stanlake said, his eyes on Pit-Bull's, level, undeceiving. 'I will make you a man too. I will name you Blondie, for my brother who died fighting in the war, in the dark, who was called a Beast as we were all called Beasts by our commander, our oga. You live with the name of an animal, so I know you understand what it does to a human being when that is put on you. You are now my brother Blondie, and I give you his spirit, and the spirits of my ancestors and his ancestors who came before, and I welcome you to this.' He cut one of Pit-Bull's cheeks. 'This new tribe.' He cut Pit-Bull's other cheek and the blood beaded instantly. 'I give you a new name. All of us a new name. A name my mother used, and she meant it harshly. But now it is differ-ent. Now we are Jackals. You are Blondie Jackal.' He put his hands on Pit-Bull's head and bent it forward. Pit-Bull's ears were burning hot against his palms. 'And you are a man.' He kissed Pit-Bull on the forehead, sweat and blood and ash sour against his lips. 'A man of this new tribe.'

Stanlake released Pit-Bull's head and Pit-Bull straight-ened, and he was now a soldier standing to attention, chest out, and Stanlake no longer saw his pallor, his otherness: instead he saw Blondie as he had seen him on the roadblock, his Kalash slung across his shoulders, ready for war. Stanlake placed his hand on the smooth flatness between Pit-Bull's curving pectorals, the place where the heart beat close to the bone and was least intercepted by muscle. 'Here is the drum,' he said. 'Always. You too were lost. Now you are found.' Tears started in Pit-Bull's eyes that he quickly palmed away, smearing the blood across his cheeks as he did so.

Now we are four.

Picking up the last razor-blade Stanlake turned to Cuts, the member of the Crew who had been most ambivalent, most resistant to this until Stanlake had tasked him with obtaining the offering; had sent him to his father, and thereby begun in him a restoration of sorts, a falling back into the lines of his own forebears, a facing up to what he had been cut off from, from what had cut him off from himself. 'You brought the sacrifice,' Stanlake said. 'From your father. You repaired that connection. Let the strength of it flow through you like blood, the blood of all fathers.' Cuts' eyes were unrevealing, but his gaze was steady. He would not refuse this. He wanted this. He had no fear. Stanlake drew the blade across Cuts' right cheek. 'I welcome you to my tribe. My ancestors stand next to yours. My comrades are yours. I name you for my Mask brother Matthew, who was killed in my village defending his mother and his sister. His spirit is yours. His spirit is in you. And you too are a fighter. You are Matthew Jackal.' He moved the angled blade over Cuts' other cheek. 'And you are a man.'

Unasked and unexpectedly, Cuts lowered his eyes and inclined his head forward, and Stanlake kissed him on the forehead, and it was a sort of completion. 'Now it is done,' he said.

'But we gotta do something for you, though,' Everil said, blazing and coughing and reaching through the smoke for his inhaler, and his response showed Stanlake that he had achieved something with his improvisations; that his magic had worked and he had succeeded in giving Everil and the others something they needed. They would never speak of what happened here: it would be, as it should, a secret thing between them, and one that was, in any case, not stateable in words. One of the candles guttered and went out, sinking the room a degree further into darkness, and the sheet covering the windows stirred as the wind at the rickety frames made the material swell like a bellows.

Stanlake took a fifth razor-blade from the packet and offered it to Everil. Everil took it reluctantly, a worried look on his face. 'Come,' Stanlake said, tilting his head to offer one cheek. 'Do not drag it and do not cut too deep.' Everil nodded and took a suck on his inhaler. Cuts offered Stanlake the joint for courage, but Stanlake shook his head: he didn't fear this.

'First you was a boy like we was all boys back in the day,' Everil said. 'Then you was a Mask.' He raised the blade to Stanlake's face, resting his little finger for steadiness on Stanlake's left cheekbone. 'Then you was taken from that and made into a Beast.' He drew a light, twitchy line across Stanlake's left cheek, his brow furrowing as he scarred his lover. It was a disconcerting inversion of the knife-work he had done in his life up to this point: when he pulled a blade to menace he didn't need to keep his hand steady. Now he did.

'You was a fighter, you did what you had to, and all of us what's here now get that. Jungle runnings. Then you fucked it off and come here. You give us what you give us. And now you're one of us. Family. For life.'

He cut Stanlake's other cheek. Each slide of the blade Stanlake felt as a cold scratch, more symbolically disquieting than physically painful. And this was a new ritual for the founding of a new tribe, and it was strange and unexpected and even unnatural but not wrong: because here nature did not rule.

'We was the Blows Crew,' Everil said. 'Now we're the Jackals. All a we.'

He put the razor-blade down on the coffee-table next to the others. His hand shook a little as he did so, but the shaking had come only after the event, and did him no discredit. Taking a deep breath he stared into Stanlake's eyes, and his gaze was both a reflection and an interpenetration. Suddenly he hugged Stanlake close, and Stanlake's body was hot and hard against his, and his cheek and ear burned bloody against his lover's, his brother's, and he was more alive than he had ever been.

'Now what, bruv?' Solid asked, brushing the still-beading

blood from his cheeks with the back of his hand, in the moment still but sensing the edging in of the adrenalin drop, the anticlimax, fearing the resurgent existential crisis, the return to what he now saw so nakedly was the oblivious state they had all been in before.

Stanlake broke off the embrace. He felt the hot-cold droplets sliding down his cheeks as Everil moved to stand by his side and their hands linked. 'Now is the hunt,' he said, and once more he was moving out beyond the secrets he had been shown, the things he had been taught; once more he was creating a new way, in a forest not of branches and vines but concrete and railings, one filled not with claws and teeth but knives and broken glass. Unfamiliar to him but becoming less so, and he knew what they would be hunting.

Who.

Their faces were turned towards his, curious, eager, waiting.

'A hunt always begins with a story,' he said.

Chapter Seventeen

Am I wrong in this, Stanlake wondered, as they moved with purpose through the shadows of the rat-run, their feet crunching on the crust of new snow, the soles of their trainers incising logos, leaving hi-tech spoor. I am taking them into danger and for what? My sacrifice. My atonement. The destruction of my enemy. But I need them: I cannot do this without comrades, without brothers. Without my lover. And what am I giving him, giving them?

This. The hunt.

The chance to become men.

That is not nothing and they know it.

Each youth carried with him a blade. 'What about the gat?' Everil asked. Stanlake hadn't wanted to admit that he had got rid of it. Instead he said, and truly, 'It is not a fit weapon for a hunter. It is too – ' he fumbled for the word: 'remote.'

They were dressed in black, black hoodies, trackpants and gloves, and Stanlake painted their faces skull-style in black and white with face-paints he got at the newsagent's, and drew lines down their foreheads and over their freshly-scarred and scabbing cheeks in green and red until to his stoned and accelerated eyes they were, as they would, he believed, be to Makinde too, not the faces of young ragamuffin men off some estate in the U.K. but those of returning warrior spirits: the vengeful dead come back to show that the past cannot be turned off like a television.

They came to a stop in front of one of the lock-ups. Pit-Bull squatted on his haunches and undid a security-bar that had been bolted into the concrete to prevent the garage door being levered up by crowbars. He slid the door up with a clanking metallic flourish to reveal a space part-filled with debris and anonymous boxes in front of which, in a neat row, stood ten new-looking bicycles in different sizes and styles.

He made an expansive gesture. 'Take your pick, yeah.'

They made their choices. Stanlake thought his was pink, though it was hard to tell under the bleaching neon. Everil's was black, with spiky-looking tyres, a mountain-bike, and the others chose mountain-bikes also. They wheeled them out and Pit-Bull pulled the garage door back down and replaced the security-bar. Then they set off, wobbly at first, uneasy on the snow, but gaining confidence and speed as they found it crisp enough to give their tyres purchase. They cycled back along the rat-run, leaving behind them criss-crossing black snake tracks, flicking their hoods up against the CCTV cameras as they hit the up-ramp. They rolled round the disabled access, through the underpass and up the other side. Off the estate there was a bite to the wind. The last dry flecks of snow struck their faces and the streets were empty.

Stanlake alone had ornamented the painted mask of his face with eyeshadow – metallic green – and scarlet on his lips, for of all the Masks, all the Beasts, he was the only one who was here in the realm of the living as himself. His mind went back to the nights the men of the village, transfigured by outline-defying, height-extending costumes of grass and fronds, hugely conical and alien, came whirling through the lanes, not men at all then but spirits of the forest, alarming and unpredictable, radiating soul energies outwards. He felt something of those energies in him tonight, in all of them, his mother's Jackals.

Before they set out he had made them charms, smashing a mirror in Solid's bath, picking out and wrapping the shards in torn-up strips of tee-shirt, knotting them around the forehead of each Jackal, himself last, to turn away harm. Reflect it back.

This will be an end, he thought. After tonight, no more. Broken glass will go in the bin. Make-up will be for beauty, knives for preparing food.

And him and Everil, after tonight?

If they survived this on the various levels they would need to survive it they would be bound together closer than ever, sutured in spirit. And he has seen me as I am and not turned away in disgust. At first I thought that he, and all of them, knew nothing, understood nothing; that their struggle was a delusion, and their pain did not count. But their lives have penetrated mine like the cold of this country has penetrated my bones, and just as they understand me a little now, I too understand them, these starvers among plenty, and I acknowledge the truth of their pain.

And he had put into them spirits that were, perhaps, not the spirits of his dead comrades, of the forest or the ancestors, but were in truth their own spirits that they had denied and shut out, or believed dead or in some other way unreachable. Yes, he had given them that, whatever came.

The pedals jerked under his feet as the chain jumped a gear before catching again. He thought of Chinua, his bag of tools balanced between the handlebars of his bicycle, wobbling along the rutted roads of the district in flip-flops. He himself hadn't cycled for five years.

On the main road the snow had barely settled. Stanlake glanced at his watch. He pedalled faster.

In the oppressive heat of the meeting hall the Reverend was working himself up, mopping his face as he declaimed God's word, rousing up the worshippers who fanned and blotted themselves with handkerchiefs too, the women's bosoms heaving, the men's chests swelling, the keyboard-player swirling and stinging: the call and the response. It was, as it always was, intoxicating, almost overwhelming, and yet tonight Poppy was apart from it, as if behind glass. She clapped her hands and moved her body to the music only because to not clap, to not dance, would, she feared, reveal her in her sin and, as she now realised, her unrepentance.

'Why is it,' the Reverend was asking urgently, 'our young men are so unwilling to respect our young women?'

Cries of 'Tell it, Reverend, tell it!'

'Why are they so reluctant to be providers, protectors, fathers to their children?' The Reverend's hoarse voice was amplified by the speakers that flanked his head to a loudness that was almost painful.

'The parents!' someone called out. 'Sin!' shouted someone else.

'Why don't they want to be gentlemen, enh? I will tell

you. And why do our girls not want to be ladies? Why are they so tough? So coarse in speech and manner? Why are they so afraid to be protected, to be guided? I will tell you! It is these homosexuals. These upside-down, inside-out perverts spreading their confusion. A man cannot be a man with a man. A woman cannot be a woman with a woman. Where is the issue? What can issue forth except venereal diseases? These clothings our young men wear, showing off their backsides and their underpants, these are the designs of homosexuals who want to see such things. Who brainwash. It is *abnormal*!'

The preacher's words cut into Poppy. My son, my only son who wants to make fashions, will not father children, she thought, and if somewhere she knew there were other ways that children could be contrived, she couldn't let in such difficult thoughts, not now, not here, where the preacher's voice beat on her like a bird's wings in an enclosed space. No grandson, no granddaughter. That would have been hard on you too, my husband.

'These people are a cancer, an abomination. Like the goats, like the tares, do as the Bible tells and cast them into the fire!'

The congregation amened and hallelujahed their approval. Poppy thought of Stanlake, head bent over his schoolbooks, quietly studying. She thought of him patiently mending her torn dress. She thought of the jackal's bare, slender arms around him, and wasn't he just a boy too? If her son was bewitched then it was only by love, a bewitchment like the lyrics of old songs on the radio, songs she and Pacific had danced to when they were courting. Why was she robbing him of that? Why was she attempting to condemn his brutalized heart and skin to endless loneliness? For what, exactly? Her hands began to prickle with pins and needles. Wasn't it all when everything was said and done just – spite?

This was agony. This was her Gethsemane.

Everil lent forward over the handlebars of his bike, bracing himself against the wind. Stanlake was just ahead of him, backside high as he pumped his legs. This amazing man, Everil thought.

Solid, Pit-Bull and Cuts followed behind. They were in their stride now: their blood was warm, and their muscles felt good as they pedalled along. The snow meant people were staying off the streets, and the city felt strangely deserted, as if its more than six million inhabitants had been somehow transported elsewhere. Everil hoped that would include those members of rival crews through whose post-codes they were passing, crews as yet unknown because he and the others didn't know where tonight would take them.

A police-car cruised by in the opposite direction. Glancing back Everil saw its brake-lights flare as it slowed to turn and trail them. He caught up with Stanlake. 'The feds, blood,' he said. 'We best vanish, yeah.'

Stanlake nodded and let Everil take the lead: a lifetime in these ends meant he knew every twist and turn of the streets around them. They were partners now, and filled with simplicity.

Everil took the next right and they left the Old Kent Road behind them, heading the wrong way down a one-way street, a first deterrent. Like hunters in the forest they could feel the heat of the greater predator as it stalked them, and they knew that to it they were nothing but feral pests, niggers and wiggers and chiggers on stolen bikes with no lights, perpetrators of crimes both petty and gross, embodiments of future crimes to be put a stop to, perpetual wrongdoers, demonic demonised youth.

Everil slithered to a halt so abruptly that the others, following close behind, almost piled into him. Without dismounting he dragged his bike round onto the pavement and led them down an alley behind some Asian supermarkets that was too narrow for a car. The feds would have to decide whether it was worth the bother of following them on foot, or try to work out where the alley would open up ahead, or give up.

Perhaps there was no crime to link them to tonight.

Like that ever made a difference, Everil thought. My skin is my crime. And my swagger. In the through-pocket of his hoodie the knife lay flat against his belly, warm as a baby.

He remembered the night of the riot, that first night before the clampdown when he had felt – when they had all felt – free; when all doors, all windows had been open and the feds, totally outnumbered, stood by and did nothing, and the postcodes struck a truce and you could go wherever you wanted unmarked. The fires had taken it too far: burning people out of their homes was low. But the shops disgorging all the shit you ever wanted, that had felt like a fine thing, like a compensation, however ephemeral, for everything that had been withheld from them. But even as he had clambered over the windowsill of a J D Sports with three boxes of blatantly-looted trainers under his arm and with his head-scarf knotted round the lower half of his face – not like dem other idiots, so caught up in the wildness of the night they forgot there would be a reckoning – he had tasted an anticipatory bitterness. All those things, all that shit could never fill the hole that ran through him, that ran through them all: it was, all of it, one big lie.

The trainers had been the wrong size. They were still sitting in the bottom of his wardrobe, stacked neatly out of sight at the back: for a while after the riots he had been antsy about trying to sell them, and then he had forgotten about them. Pit-Bull had had to throw a plasma-screen TV over a fence to avoid being busted by the feds on his way home, and had heard it smash as it hit the concrete on the other side.

And then everything had gone back to being exactly the same.

That autumn the African bwoy and his mother had moved onto the estate. Had Everil felt change coming then? Perhaps. And now here it was. But after tonight, what? Him and Stanlake together, yes, that for sure, however, wherever. And the click? But wasn't that already over? Wasn't it ending tonight? The Blows Crew was going – gone; the Jackals were here. But what did that mean? What would their lives be?

He thought of Drilla. Once Drilla had been someone he looked up to. Not as a father-figure but as a projection of a possible future self. A prince of the rubbish-heap, halfway heroic in his bucking of the boot on the black man's neck: one who saw, embodied and defied the lack of value assigned to black male life. And that was all true still, but Drilla was toxic, and did nothing but harm.

Everil rolled his neck, cracking vertebrae. The snow had

stopped now. Let him and the rest think I lost my bottle, he thought. Let 'em think I got stabbed up and lost it. Like I give a fuck. That ain't my life now. His mother came into his mind then, or rather the idea of her, the idea of a mother, and making a mother proud.

How far we must go tonight, though, he wondered. Right now he would die for Stanlake. He would kill for Stanlake. But nothing is without consequence: nothing is got away with. His thigh felt okay so far.

After they had cut through several more back alleys without any sign of pursuit Everil let Stanlake take the lead again, and following him he found that the streets, the alleys, the backsides of the city that he thought he knew so well, were somehow new, or perhaps it was his eyes that were new. His cheeks felt tight and ached where they had been cut, and the icy air stiffened his face and burned and purified his lungs.

'We are nearly there,' Stanlake called over his shoulder. This is good, he thought. Speed, movement, our blood pumping. This keeps us together. It would be the waiting, when their energy and enthusiasm and the effect of the uppers they had taken earlier waned and the cold ate into their bones, that would be hard to manage. I will tell them stories, he thought. I will tell them about the time Makinde tried to give us heart. Following his lead they turned down another alley, coasting.

Stanlake wanted this to be done. He wanted to wear lace and lingerie and be loved. He wanted to be a good son. Cuts had given him the largest and most lethal-looking of the knives, a single solid piece of sharpened steel. Into its undifferentiated handle the name 'Sabatier' had been struck. I did not ask for this, he thought, not any of it. I did not ask the jackals to bother me. I did not ask Makinde to come to my door in his dog-collar with his lying new smooth-smooth face. He could have let it go. He could have kept out of it. And now I cannot.

He didn't want his mother to find out what her pastor was, because wouldn't that one last robbery break her? He would spare her if he could, though he had no idea how. 'We're here,' he said.

They slithered to a stop, threw down their bikes and clustered round the mouth of the alley, peering out at the street beyond. Diagonally across from them was the church, its façade drab and featureless. In front of it sat a silver Saab, its gleaming upper surfaces rendered matte by a dusting of snow. At the top of the steps that led up to the church's entrance stood a broad, burly black man wearing a heavy black overcoat, black glacé shoes and a glistening astrakhan hat. In his ear was an earpiece like a bouncer's at a night-club. They pulled back out of sight.

'Now what, fam?' Everil asked.

'We wait.' Stanlake turned to Solid. 'Diamondz, keep watch.'

Solid nodded and positioned himself in the shadows at the alley's entrance so he could keep an eye on the church doorway without being seen. Before tonight he would have resisted anyone telling him so bluntly what to do: his ego would have been too fragile to just take up a task without kicking off about it. Now the man he was becoming simply did what was needed. The feeling was growing in him – in all of them – that everything in their lives had been for this: those days and nights on the Rock had been a lesson in patience, in endurance, a lesson to be used tonight. Across the street the bouncer clapped his gloved hands together and looked around him with a bored expression. Then he touched his earpiece and muttered something, his breath billowing white. Up above the sky was clearing, and the temperature began to drop. Inside the building the singing rose in both volume and intensity.

Everil sparked up a joint and passed it round. Time passed. Their hands and feet grew cold and their spirits sank.

'This is long,' Cuts said.

'I'm seizing up like a OAP,' Pit-Bull grumbled.

'Okay,' Stanlake said. 'I will tell you a story.'

Pit-Bull and Cuts exchanged a look, but there was, after all, nothing else to do, and Everil's eyes were on them hard; and perhaps in his phrasing Stanlake drew the three of them – and Solid too, for he glanced round from where he was watching – back to some perhaps imagined, once longed-for childhood time of wonder, and to simply listen undistracted to a single voice was a new thing for them.

'I will tell you the story of the dogs' village,' Stanlake said, and he looked at them each in turn, making sure they were attending, that he was their focus. 'Now, the dog is an animal in particular. It lives with us, it is a domestic animal like cows, fowls and pigs. But those we eat, and we don't eat dogs. And when we hunt, the dog comes along to help out. But the dog is a wild animal too, like the other wild animals of the forest, and those animals belong to the ancestors who watch over us.'

'But ain't you kill dem animals when you hunt 'em, though?' Pit-Bull asked.

'Of course you kill them. It isn't a zoo just to be looked at.'

'But don't that like piss off the – ancestors?'

'If they are pleased with us, with our skill and determination, then we are permitted to catch the animals. If not...' Stanlake shrugged.

'So what's the dogs' village, then?' Cuts asked.

'The dog is both with us, and he is with the spirits in the forest. So he is both things, inbetween. My father told me, if you are alive and you wish to find the village of the ancestors, you must pass through the village of the dogs.'

He fell silent then. The others waited. Everil cleared his throat, hawked and spat.

'Well, *and*, bruv?' said Pit-Bull.

'After leaving my friends from the roadblock I walked for many days. At first I thought, 'Go home'. But I don't know the way. I lost heart and I thought, if I cannot find my way home then let me be dead and done like the rest. Let me go to the village of the ancestors. I looked all around me and I didn't have a clue which way to turn. It's not a place like other places: how do you even begin to go there?'

'Through the dogs' village,' Everil and Pit-Bull said together.

'Yes. So with that thought in me I walked some more. I walked and walked and a feeling grew on me. And night came and I came to the dogs' village.' A shudder ran through Stanlake that wasn't just from the cold. Why am I telling this now? But he knew why. To put death in their heads. To release it from mine. Something leaves through the mouth when you tell a story and maybe can't get back in. 'There were no lights in any of the huts of the dogs' village, just moonlight, but it was so bright it cast shadows. And the dogs came out to greet me.'

'Did they like build the village?' Pit-Bull asked.

'Chief,' said Cuts. 'How dogs are gonna build suttin'?' Then he looked at Stanlake. 'They didn't, still?'

'People built the village.'

'Then what, they left?'

'Their spirits left. What stayed behind the dogs came and ate. I saw shapeless things in the shadows. I saw a hand being gnawed like a bundled spider.'

'Did they like try and go for you?' Everil asked.

Stanlake shook his head. 'They had hunted with men, men had fed them scraps from the table, and they still remembered they were part of that. And the spirits watched over me as I walked backwards, keeping my eyes on the eyes of the dogs until I was gone from their sight. I didn't go through their village, so I didn't come to the village of the ancestors. I found another way.'

'So you come home?'

'Yes. I came home.'

His tale told, Stanlake fell silent. 'You ever think you'll go back?' Everil asked, as if just for something to say, but not.

Stanlake shook his head. 'I think this is my home now.' And his eyes met Everil's, and held them.

The singing inside the church stopped. Stanlake joined Solid at the corner, as a moment later did Everil and the others. They watched as people began to emerge from the building. The bite in the air made the worshippers cut gossip and goodbyes short as they hurried off to catch their buses and trains. A short woman bundled up in a heavy coat, fake Ugg boots, a woolly scarf and a tea-cosy hat came out. Stanlake recognised her as someone Poppy worked with but he couldn't remember her name. She bustled off in the direction of the main road.

'Where's your mum, though?' Everil asked in a low voice.

'I don't know,' Stanlake said. 'Maybe she stayed at home.' But he didn't think so: she would have come here. Solid went back up the alley and pissed. No-one came their way: no church member would be reckless enough to use such an unlit and unoverlooked alley for a shortcut, not even on a night like this, when most hoodlums were at home with their X-boxes, and even fiending crackheads were off the streets, or dead and out of it.

The procession of worshippers tailed off without Poppy emerging. The bouncer went in. The musicians came out, hefted their instrument-cases over to a nearby white van, loaded it up, and drove off. More time passed. Everil went for a piss, then Pit-Bull.

The bouncer reappeared at the top of the steps. He was followed by a young man in a smart black suit and no overcoat who looked instantly cold, then two imperious-looking women in headwraps and fur coats. Between the women was a skinny, scared-looking girl of maybe fourteen. Though she wore a duffle coat the girl's legs below her too-short school uniform skirt were bare, and she wore little white socks and inadequate black pumps. Her hair was in two fat plaits. One of the women gripped the girl's arm with bejewelled fingers, holding her in place while she looked around for something or someone.

And then, finally, Makinde emerged in a heavy faun coat. He was smiling, and he exchanged remarks with the women and clapped his gloved hands together as the bouncer padlocked the building behind him.

Poppy must have left earlier.

The bouncer handed Makinde the keys as a minicab drew up behind the Saab. The woman holding onto the girl said something to her in an earnest manner, then released her. The girl stood there submissively, her head lowered. Even from across the road Stanlake could see she was shivering.

The bouncer held the cab-door open for the two fur-coated women. They got in without a backward glance at the girl. The bouncer slammed the door on them and the cab pulled away. The girl kept her eyes on her shoes. The young man beeped the Saab's locks and opened the rear door for the Reverend. Taking her by the arm, Makinde pushed the girl in ahead of him. The young man closed Makinde's door then took his place behind the steering-wheel. The bouncer got in beside him.

Stanlake glanced round at the others as the chauffeur drew his seat-belt across. 'We must be ready,' he said. Hurriedly they disentangled their bikes. Everil passed Stanlake his as the engine of the Saab clicked into life. The chauffeur flicked on his indicator and pulled out. As soon as they could do so without being too obvious, they followed.

This was a gamble, and Stanlake knew it. If Makinde didn't live nearby, if his car could stretch out on the deserted night-roads, he would escape them without even trying. Stanlake guessed he wouldn't live far from his power-base, but even if he was right about that it would still be an endurance test for both him and his Jackals, who were young and tough but smoked and swilled beer and slobbed about deluding themselves that playing video-games was the same as doing things in real life. Even Everil, the leanest, fittest-seeming of the four, was an asthmatic with fucked-up lungs. And there was his wound.

The driver of the Saab was in no hurry, it seemed, and at first the lights were with them, holding it up at every junction. But soon enough it had slid ahead and they couldn't keep up however hard they pedalled. Then, just when they thought it had got away from them altogether, it turned into an all-night petrol station. They caught up and passed it, stopping at the next junction and looking back, relieved to have a minute to catch their breath. Solid hawked and spat, belching repeatedly and almost vomiting, and no-one spoke except to mutter hoarse curses at his own lack of fitness.

All too soon the Saab was passing them again, turning down a side-street that slanted away towards Peckham. They pumped furiously in pursuit. Round a bend and up a steep hillock they raced, sure now that they had failed and it had escaped them, only to find it stuck just the other side behind a bus that had stopped to pick up passengers, double-parking and blocking the way. They slithered to a halt just past the hillock's brow.

By now they had a routine together, falling into single file when there was a chance of being noticed in the car's rear-view mirror, going two or three abreast otherwise, hoods up at all times. Now they hung back, trailing the Saab warily as it crawled along behind the bus, Stanlake leading the way. At the traffic-lights they drew nearer, emboldened. What were they? Only kids on bikes, after all: who would pay them any mind? The lights changed as Stanlake rolled up to the Saab's rear bumper, near enough to reach out and touch it.

Thanks to roadworks they managed to keep up as the car wound its way through Peckham Rye's one-way system. At the edge of Peckham Rye Park, however, it took a left, heading off towards Honor Oak up a long, straight stretch of road that grew swiftly and relentlessly steeper. Once more they were left behind.

'What if we lose it, fam?' Pit-Bull called breathlessly.

'We come another night,' Stanlake called back. 'We come to here, wait, then when he comes we follow him again.'

Solid and Pit-Bull groaned. 'Ah, fam,' Solid moaned, 'that's long, man.'

'A hunt can take many days,' Stanlake said. 'It is not all done and dusted on day one.'

Everil, who was a little way in front and had been leaning forward over his handlebars and staring ahead, looked round and said, 'It did turn in up there. I seen the brake-lights.'

Stanlake nodded. 'We must keep going,' he said, raising his backside and pedalling harder.

'I'm gonna bust a brisket though, blood,' Cuts gasped. The others were now too short of breath to speak. Stanlake knew that if Makinde didn't live on this road then the hunt was over for tonight, perhaps over for good: he was doubtful he could persuade his new comrades to do this again, not for nothing, not without the power of the ritual to heat them, and they were too unused to discipline.

Hearts and stomachs heaving they reached the spot where Everil had seen the Saab turn. To the left was the dark expanse of the park, no side-roads; to the right streets of well-appointed houses ran down towards Dulwich Village. The street Everil had stopped them in front of was long, residential, not a cut-through, and lined with parked cars. At the bottom of it a pair of red lights glowed steadily: a car was double-parked down there. At that distance Stanlake couldn't tell if it was the Saab.

'Let us go down slowly,' he said.

Pushing off with their feet, they let the gentle incline do the work. The streetlights were old-fashioned and weak, and between them were concealing pools of shadow. They free-wheeled for a hundred metres or so. Yes, it was the Saab. Braking softly, they slipped off their bikes and hid behind a conveniently-parked van.

It seemed there had been some sort of argument or debate in the car, because as they peeped cautiously round the van they were in time to see Makinde ill-temperedly push his door open and struggle out with the girl, his hand clamped round her upper arm. He shoved her in the direc-tion of a large detached house. The bouncer got out and followed close behind them. In the still air their feet were crisp on the snow-coated gravel of the drive. Makinde *had* made it big, then, Stanlake thought: he knew enough to know that this street, these houses were all extremely expensive. He wondered how much money Makinde had managed to get out with, how much of what he had said was true.

The three of them disappeared into the house. The chauffeur backed the car into the drive, cut the engine and switched off the lights. Then sat there, an accidental sentinel.

Everil, Stanlake and the others contemplated the house as soldiers would, or burglars. It was three-storeyed and flanked by tall, new, solid-looking fences. One fence had a gate set into it, but the gate was visibly padlocked. On top of the fences shards of glass glinted. Neighbours had equally high brick walls or railings. No easy way through to the back of the house from the front, then, even if the chauffeur hadn't been there, and the drive not brightly lit by a floodlight set into the curve of lawn that glared up exposingly at the façade.

''Llow the front,' Everil said. Stanlake nodded.

'These ain't back-to-backs, though,' Pit-Bull said. 'They got like alleys behind 'em for the bins an' shit. We could try that way.'

'Let us see,' Stanlake said. 'Matthew Jackal, stay here and keep watch. Text Big Gun if anyone comes or goes.'

Cuts nodded. Stanlake and the others wheeled their bikes back up the hill, taking the first right they came to, and soon found themselves looking down a long alley that ran between two rows of back gardens. Green wheelie-bins were placed at regular intervals outside no doubt bolted and padlocked back gates. Fences on both sides were high, ten or even twelve feet, and most were topped with glass shards or coils of razor wire.

'What you reckon?' said Everil.

'See them there?' Solid pointed out small metal boxes that looked down from the fence-tops every few metres. 'Security lights.'

Everil nodded. Motion-sensitive, they would click into life when passed, throwing a revealing spotlight on any putative burglar. 'Anyone count how many houses down?' he asked.

'Fifteen,' said Stanlake.

'If it's got a worser wall we can go over a next one and climb through that way, from the side,' Solid said.

'Each climb's a risk, though,' Pit-Bull said.

'You bottling, though?'

'Just saying.'

'Let us see.'

They rolled down the alley in silence, the only noises the soft sound of their tyres on the snow and the random clicking-on of the security lights as they passed. They'd come on for foxes, though, Everil thought. Plus I reckon people'd get sicka looking out every time they come on pretty quick. Also, and ironically, the high fences would screen them from any curtain-twitcher not on an upper floor.

'Here,' said Stanlake.

Coming to a stop, they looked up. The fence was one of the tallest ones, and new, but there were no glass shards or coils of wire on top of it as there were on those of its neighbours. Above, but too high to catch hold of, the bare black branches of a large tree in the back garden fanned out against a sky that was now clear and pricked with stars. A lone burglar could never have climbed the fence, but Pit-Bull and Solid managed to push first Stanlake and then Everil high up enough to catch hold of the top of it and haul themselves up.

Straddling the fence, Stanlake and Everil took a moment to survey the garden. It was long and dark, and at their end overgrown and largely screened from the house by massed laurel and rhododendron bushes.

Back in the alley Solid and Pit-Bull piled the bikes as out of sight as they could between two wheelie-bins: they didn't want to come out later and find them tiefed, which sounded like a joke, but wouldn't be. Then they were locking hands to wrists with Stanlake and Everil and being hauled up onto the fence. As one they dropped down into the darkness on the other side.

Snow lay lightly there on old, dry leaves and fallen twigs that crackled and popped underfoot. Now they were hunters again, cautious as they pushed their crouching way through the undergrowth, doing their best not to dislodge snow from the brittle branches around them as they worked stealthily forward. Soon they were peering out from the bushes at the more formal garden beyond, and the house.

A broad strip of lawn, blue-white in the starlight, was flanked by overgrown herbaceous borders. On either side were high fences latticed with rotting trellises on which old, woody roses were tethered in thorny arcs. Impossible to climb over discreetly, Everil noted. At the far end of the lawn a short flight of stone steps led up to a balustraded terrace, on which sat a rusting barbeque set and three wrought-iron chairs now cushioned with snow. Old-fashioned French windows gave onto the terrace. Their curtains hadn't been closed, and yellow light spilled out in lozenges across the snow and splayed weakly onto the lawn. To the left was another window, curtained and dark; one light was on in an upstairs room. No lights showed in the upper storeys of the houses on either side.

'What now?' said Everil.

'One of us should go up to the window first and scout.'

'I'll go,' Pit-Bull and Solid said together.

'Whoever goes must step in the flower-beds where the soil is lumpy, so he does not leave eye-catching tracks in the snow. Who is more careful?'

Grudgingly Solid indicated Pit-Bull.

Stanlake nodded and said, 'Step where the snow has not fallen as much as you can.'

Pit-Bull nodded and the others watched as he made his way crabwise along the left-hand herbaceous border, planting his feet as best he could where the leaves above had kept the snow off the black, frozen soil. Avoiding the steps he hung close to the fence, pulling himself up over the balustrade where a mass of dead honeysuckle overhung and shielded it from snow, leaving neither hand- nor foot-prints.

A moment later he was at the corner of the house. Ducking under the curtained window, he slid along the wall as far as the French doors. After a moment's hesitation he peeped in, his hooded head a brief black silhouette against the light within. The room was at that moment unoccupied, it seemed, for he reached for the door-handle and tried it. No joy. He tried again, rattling it a little. Still it wouldn't open. Giving up, he retraced his steps, clambered down over the balustrade and made his way back to where the others were waiting.

'S'locked,' he said. 'But old, though. Like a blade could lever it. But it'd likely make noise, though. Not a lot, probs, but – '

'We gotta get in, still,' Everil said.

'What about the other geezer an' the gal?' asked Solid.

'We can take that fucker,' Pit-Bull said. 'He's a big fucker, but so? We got blades. And heart.'

'True-dat.'

'He ain't part of this, though. Or the gal.'

'We wait for Matthew Jackal to call and tell us the bodyguard has gone,' Stanlake said. 'Then we move.'

'And if they ain't go?'

'We come back another night. Now we have tracked the beast to his lair he can no longer elude us.'

They hunkered down in the bushes. Soon their feet were frozen and their leg-muscles had seized up again. Everil tapped out a cigarette but Stanlake waved a hand to stop him sparking up. 'The flame could be seen from the house and the smoke smelt.'

As Everil grudgingly returned the cigarette to its pack and pocketed his lighter there came a sound – a sharp clack – from the direction of the house. The French windows swung open and Makinde stepped out onto the terrace. He was wearing a short black silk dressing-gown and his bare legs and his face were sheened with sweat. A cigar was in his mouth. From inside the house somewhere the grunts of sex were audible. Yes, Stanlake thought, you have not changed, oga. For all your talk of Jesus Christ and the collar you wear, you are carrying right on.

Makinde cupped his hands and clicked his lighter, a featureless gold block, and puffed on the cigar. He looked out over the garden, a ruler surveying his domain, and for a terrible moment Stanlake was once again the boy who would do anything to please him, to earn the favour of this tall, strong man with his arrogant mouth and his hot-cold eyes. This superior being who had talked so convincingly of the need for revolutionary change, and the need to suppress feelings of mercy in the pursuit of that change, that he had made torture seem righteous; the butchering of prisoners and civilians seem like a duty. Stanlake thought of his father, and felt his face harden.

This hyaena, this snake claims he is a man of God now and perhaps he even believes it, he thought. Perhaps he even thinks God has let him off the hook. And his poison goes on, because my mother believes in him now like I believed in him then.

He spat on the ground.

Makinde shivered. 'Are you done yet?' he called over his shoulder. A male voice replied from inside the house, and though Stanlake couldn't make out what it said, its tone was affirmatory. Makinde grunted and turned to go back in. In the doorway, however, he paused and looked round suspiciously, and his gaze fell with piercing directness on the patch of shadow where Stanlake and the others were crouching.

He can't know we're here, though, Everil thought. But then you don't come through what he come through without you reach that extra level of wariness, still. He thought of the sensitivity of foxes. But this man was a predator, not a scavenger. A top predator, and that could give those hunting him an advantage. Because he was used to being the one with the power, the one who put fear into others. He wasn't used to being afraid. And Everil and the others had lived with fear, of the feds, of youths from other postcodes, since time: they lived inside their fear, turning its sharp edges outwards, and that was another lesson to use tonight.

The voice inside the house said something else. 'Then go and wait in the car,' Makinde said. Giving the garden a final hard-eyed sweep he went back inside, pulling the French windows closed behind him. They heard the lock clack shut, then the curtains were roughly pulled across.

'Like he was looking right at us,' Solid said. 'Like he could see us.'

Everil's mobile buzzed in his pocket. He glanced at it briefly. 'The big fucker's just come out the front.'

'It is time,' Stanlake said.

As one they straightened, shaking cramp and stiffness from their limbs as they emerged from the bushes and came quickly across the lawn. It didn't matter that they were leaving tracks: now it was on. They mounted the steps and crossed the terrace. At the French windows Everil brought out his knife. After listening for sounds in the room beyond, hearing none he stood directly before them and began to work the blade between the wooden frames, probing the snib. Pushing the point with precision, he sprang the lock. There was little sound. They passed inside, Everil first, then Stanlake, then Solid, and lastly Pit-Bull, who carefully closed the door behind him and slid the curtains back into place. By now they had all drawn their knives.

The room was large, high-ceilinged and lamplit. Two outsize sofas of skin-soft brown leather sat at right-angles to each other. Tall gold-framed mirrors hung on the terracotta walls, and over the closed-up fireplace had been set a large, plain gold cross. A black stone coffee-table with crossed tusks for legs sat beneath it on a zebra-skin rug. On the coffee-table was a bible the size of a briefcase. The bible's edges were gilt, and on its scaly black leather cover were traces of powder scraped into lines, and next to them a gold razor-blade. A hypocrite in this too, Stanlake thought. It is good: it makes what I have to do easier.

They passed into the hall. The cream carpet underfoot was thick and spread unbrokenly in all directions and up the stairs. A glance into the dining-room and kitchen and a downstairs toilet told them these rooms were unoccupied. Stanlake crossed to the front door and quietly slid the bolt across and put on the chain. Now even if the others outside had keys they couldn't easily come in.

He led the way upstairs.

Chapter Eighteen

Four doors opened off the unlit landing, of which three were closed. The fourth was ajar, and from it soft peach light spilled out. Everything here was soft, luxurious, clean. Did it really compensate Makinde for what was inside him, Stanlake wondered, or was it futile defiance? We are the return of the buried dirt, he thought. Until you saw my mother you believed you had got away with it. Even now you think I am the stupid fool I was then.

No, not stupid. Manipulated and lied to, fearful and betrayed.

The adrenaline was beginning to surge in him as it was in all of them: the moment was nearing. You thought I would be your creature again. You thought I would be grateful to return to being told what to do at every turn. You are strong, tough. But I too am strong. I too got here. And you will not destroy my new life. You will not destroy my new beginning of love. I will destroy you. And Everil was right, you are the king of lies and bullshit, and I do not think you have this big-man friends you boast of. I think you are the hustler you always were. I think –

He glanced back at Everil, Pit-Bull and Solid, their painted faces white skulls cracked like the wood of old masks, their features stained with make-up and blood and hooded black, their knives out and ready. Feral. That was a word often used, wasn't it, about boys like them? Tonight it was both true and not true: tonight they were Jackals, but they were hunters too, an honourable thing, and this was their completion and his. It was easy to move silently on the thick carpet: an ox could've done it. This was as the ancestors and spirits intended. He crossed to the partly-open door. The others followed. He peeped first through the gap in the hinge, then, seeing little, round the edge of the door itself.

This it seemed was the master bedroom. The cream

carpet continued. The kingsize bed was spread with black silk sheets. Everything else – the bed head and foot, the bedroom furniture, even the wardrobe – was covered with cream leather. On a side table sat a near-empty bottle of whiskey and a cut-crystal tumbler, and by them a blocky steel ashtray. The butt of a cigar rested in one of its four grooved sides. Lines of white powder lay chopped out on a steel mirror next to a gold American Express card that had a frosted edge. Hefty honeyed candles provided the only light in the room, a parody of a romantic atmosphere. The wardrobe doors were open. One side bulged with suits in dry-cleaners' polythene; in the other toning ties hung on a rack as if displayed in a shop, and a stack of new shirts glistened in their plastic wrappers. On the floor by the wardrobe shoes, white, black, brown and cream, sat in a row. Yellow metal buckles glinted. A door off, which was closed, led to an ensuite: from behind it came the sound of a tap being turned and water gushing. On the bed, naked and skinny and scared-looking, was the girl Makinde had brought in earlier. She was so young she made Stanlake think of Florence and her no-breasts. Though she believed she was alone, she held a pillow in front of her.

It was reflected in the mirror on the inside of the open wardrobe-door that he saw her, and at that moment she saw him too, and her eyes widened in alarm at the sight of this garish and menacing figure, black and hunched and skinny and dirty, with the face of a spirit, scraps of night for eyes and a knife in his skeleton-gloved hand. He put a finger to his scarlet, glittering lips and she, sensing – hoping – that this creature meant her no harm, cut off her impulse to cry out. Silently he pointed to the bathroom door and she gave a quick, tense nod. So this was the moment. This was it. Everything slowed and accelerated at the same time. Stanlake, Everil, Pit-Bull and Solid slipped into the room, four black revenants, each with a metal tooth, and it was as if they were at some vertiginous height and starting to plunge down. Hearts heaving they positioned themselves flat against the wall, two on each side of the bathroom door, and the girl watched and they waited. There was the sharp smell of semen in the room, an undertone of iron. Their minds ran faster, faster, their bodies got stiller, stiller. There was another smell, shit.

The toilet flushed and gurgled as piss and crap was sucked away, and above the hum of the extractor fan they heard Makinde's voice, apparently on his mobile. 'My usual fee is double that,' he was saying. 'Yes, double.' A pause. 'Because you will more than double when you pass the plate, that is why, and because I am taking time from my valuable outreaching to help you, so – ' He pulled the bathroom door open, sniffing and rubbing his nose, and the Jackals were out of his sight-line as he stood there in the doorway. Now he was in just black silk boxers, and he tugged at his half-erect cock through the flimsy material. Covering the mouthpiece of the phone he gave the girl a grin and said, 'Ready for round two?' She didn't respond, just lay there frozen, hugging the pillow in front of her budding breasts and near-hairless crotch. 'Get rid of that, enh?' he added, coming into the bedroom and reaching out to tear the pillow away from her. 'What are you hiding for?'

Stanlake stepped forward and raised his knife blade-up below Makinde's jaw. 'Hello, oga,' he said.

Makinde froze. Stanlake could feel his Adam's apple move against the flat of the blade as he swallowed, calculating, Stanlake knew, whether he could jump back and avoid his Beast's blade. But you cannot, oga: the necessary contraction of your muscles to spring will push your jaw down onto my knife and cut your throat. He smelt sweat and cologne. The voice on the mobile, a man's, said, 'Reverend? Reverend Obasanjo, are you there?' Stanlake took the phone from Makinde's hand and, keeping his eyes on Makinde's, said, 'The Reverend is not here,' and ended the call. Then he pocketed the phone.

'Little Gun,' Makinde said hoarsely. The whites of his eyes were coke-reddened and threaded with burst veins. 'I was expecting to see you at church.'

'I thought as you came to my home I would come to yours,' Stanlake said. He stretched his lips and bared his teeth in a lop-sided smile. 'And I brought friends, oga. Old friends. You will remember them.' He felt calm, almost blank, as if he was simply a transmitter for what was going to happen next, the spirits strong in him now. Robert, Matthew, Patrick, this is for you. Diamondz, Blondie, Big Gun, this is for you. My father Pacific, this is for you. 'Big Gun, take his arm.'

At the name Big Gun Makinde started, and then winced as the tiny movement resulted in Stanlake's unyielding blade slitting the skin below his chin. It was a small cut but evidently painful, and the more unnerving to Makinde because he couldn't see how serious it was. Stanlake thought he felt the blade touch the bone of Makinde's jaw.

Hooded head down, Everil took hold of Makinde's left wrist. Makinde tensed at his skeleton-gloved touch, the texture of the glove rough, cold, making him think of bones of the dead, perhaps.

'Blondie Jackal,' Stanlake said, 'take his other arm.'

Pit-Bull did so, his hood hiding his face too, as with his free hand Everil held his knife flat against the rise of Makinde's wood-smooth chest. Makinde tried to resist having his arms pulled back and folded up behind him, but with a knife at his chest, another at his throat, and a third – Solid's – now at his belly, what could he do but yield?

Stanlake raised the blade under Makinde's jaw, forcing him to stretch out his neck or be cut more badly. Makinde's throat lengthened. Veins pulsed. Stanlake knew their names from school: Vena cava. Aorta. Makinde strained his blood-shot eyes from side to side, trying to see the faces of these boys come back from the dead, but all he caught beneath the angled black hoods were flashes of scabrous white paint and bloody, scarified cheeks, and they smelt of soil and snow and leaf-mould.

At a nod from Stanlake the three of them turned Makinde round so his back was to the bed, moving with him as a unit, keeping his arms pushed up behind him and their blades at all times pressed against his now goosebumping skin. The tumescence in his silk boxers had retreated to limp, hidden flesh. 'Sister, give us some room, please,' Stanlake said to the girl as they walked Makinde backwards, and she got up quickly, keeping the pillow in front of her, and watched as they forced him to lie back on the bed.

'Diamondz, something to tie him,' Stanlake said to Solid,

keeping the knife under Makinde's chin ready-ready because he knew that any second now Makinde would realise this was his last chance; that once he was tied up he was done for. Makinde stared up into his face, longing, Stanlake could tell, to wrench his wrist from Everil's grip and punch Stanlake in the head, knock him sideways, spring to his feet, grab up his knife and go on the attack. But Everil and Pit-Bull now pressed their weight down on Makinde's forearms and held their blades against the tangles of veins in his wrists: to attempt such a move would be suicide.

Solid looked about him uncertainly. The girl pointed to the wardrobe. Solid crossed to it and tore a handful of ties from the rack.

'We are your Beasts, oga, back from the dead,' Stanlake said as Solid looped a tie round one of Makinde's ankles, yanked his leg out straight, and tethered it to the bedpost. 'Do you remember us?' Solid moved round the bed and tied off Makinde's other ankle. 'You should have lived quiet-quiet, not started up with these new lies and bullshit.'

Solid passed a tie to Everil. Everil knelt heavily with one knee on Makinde's right forearm and made a slip-knot. He dropped it over Makinde's fist and tightened it round his wrist. Then he pulled Makinde's arm up, intending to tether it to the bedpost above his head. When Makinde resisted Everil dispassionately jabbed him in the bicep with his blade. A line of blood spilled down from the puncture like a red tear. Makinde grunted and stopped resisting. *Oh, truly they are my Beasts*. Pit-Bull copied Everil's knot and tied off Makinde's other wrist, leaving him spreadeagled and unable to move. Only now did Stanlake remove his blade from Makinde's throat, stroking its tip down his jugular. The vein pulsed visibly through its two thin membrane walls, fragile as life, and Stanlake held the knife against it as he straddled Makinde's belly.

'You made us killers, oga,' he said matter-of-factly.

Makinde swallowed. His eyes, hard brown pupils bordered with red stria, glanced calculatingly but uncertainly at the hooded, scarred faces of the boys now leaning over him. 'I made you men,' he said hoarsely. 'You should thank me.'

Stanlake smiled coldly and pushed back his hood to reveal the full effect of his carnival mask, his scarred cheeks. 'It is not the same thing, oga,' he said. 'But you are making us men now, and I thank you for that.'

'Blondie, Diamondz, Big Gun,' Makinde said, pushing into his voice all the suasion he could, his eyes flickering between them. 'My Beasts. My wonderful Beasts. We had good times, enh? Lots of good times. I gave you girls, enh? Girls and guns and drugs and good fucking. And you got away too. You survived. You are here. You are all here.' He forced a smile, his lips stretching wide in a parody of good humour, exposing corrected teeth that were large and straight except for a single jagged canine, a canine that had perhaps been corrected too, but had regressed to lay bare the predator's true nature, that which will always assert itself. Did he at that moment believe they were the hungry spirits of his Beasts returned? If so, was it a true belief, albeit one fuelled by cocaine and whatever other drugs he had been taking? Or was it desperation making him try this tack: humouring the dangerous, unknown mad? Either way, they were here. Either way it was truly a return of the repressed: the inescapability of the vengeful dead lanced through with bright new Christian guilt. And now, in his greatest extremity, this man who believed that he believed in nothing but power, and that he needed do nothing but take and take, found it was not so: he *did* believe. He was in the forest and at the roadblock still: it was inside his head forever and always, waiting. And his Beasts were inside his head forever and always too, and that was their perpetual revenge.

'Little Gun,' he said, sliding his gelid gaze from Stanlake's painted face to Everil's, and who knew what face he saw there now except that surely it wasn't Everil's because he went on, 'Big Gun... Where's your dress, faggot? The one you took from the girl... you and that other faggot, Diamondz...'

'Open him up, blood,' Everil said coolly, though inside he was hot and churning and filled with shrinking dread. 'Do it and let's chip and gone, yeah.'

'My father,' Stanlake began, but the words choked in his throat. His hands prickled cold with wet electricity and his chest felt tight, ribs caging a heart that wanted to expand and burst free, become part of the air and sky, explode with the violence of mortar-shells, shed shrapnel bones like spear-heads and be done.

'You killed your father, Little Gun. But I understand. Let me be a father to you, Little Gun. The father you need.'

Tears were streaming down Stanlake's face now, turning his mascara to black and turquoise claws, making his eyes and his cut cheeks burn as he cried as he had cried that day when his father was kneeling before him in the dust. And this was apt, that this wicked man of pure will who now passed himself off as a preacher should like the devil offer one last misguided temptation. *I have killed my father already, oga. It was only the first time that was hard.* Stanlake pressed his left palm on Makinde's forehead, spider-fingers clamping like a vise to hold Makinde's head in place while he cut his oga's throat. Dead and done. The skin was hot and slick, and he could feel the bone frame beneath. Experience told him that the knife was sharp enough to slice through not just the skin, veins and arteries, not just the sinew and muscle below, but also the gristle of the wind-pipe. If he lent forward and put his weight on it he would be able to force the blade all the way down until it grated on the front of Makinde's spine.

The others wouldn't judge him if he did this, or in their judgement they would find in his favour. Everil would love him no less hotly. This was his faith. He tilted his head back, half-closing his eyes. This was it. This the spirits and the ancestors had given him. My sacrifice. It is now. He felt an inrush of energies, a terrible focus. Beneath him Makinde started to hyperventilate, every muscle in his all-but-naked body straining and twitching, veins squirming vascularly beneath his skin, eyes bulging exopthalmically as his life hurtled towards this climax, this completion. *For the gods will be served.*

'You had better hope there is no hell, oga,' Stanlake said thickly. But at that moment he knew: my father does not require this of me. My Masks, my Beasts, even my Jackals do not require this of me. My father would want me to leave this, get past this, live the life that is left for me. Daddy –

He removed the blade from Makinde's neck and slid off him. Makinde, not understanding, expecting a heartless laugh, a sudden turn, a snaking twist and blow delivered fast, or worse, a change of heart in favour of slow torture, began to gasp short breaths that punched his chest out, hyperventilating. The others stood raised almost on tiptoe, hyped on adrenalin, taut as piano-wire, tall and full of charge as pylons, holding their breaths, waiting. Stanlake bent forward and studied Makinde's contorted face. He reached down and stroked Makinde's forehead.

'Don't worry, oga,' he said. 'I'm not going to kill you tonight.'

Makinde watched him with a terrible uncertainty, trying to master his heaving chest. Surely this was a lie, a wind-up, some final torture? He knew this boy could kill, could do worse than kill; he knew it was not fear that restrained him, neither of the act nor of capture. No-one knew of their connection: he would not be caught. What, then? Makinde had no answer. His eyes strained in their sockets.

'Aren't you going to thank me, oga?'

Dry-mouthed, Makinde forced out a husky reply: 'Thank you, Little Gun. Thank you.'

'We're going to go now,' Stanlake said, and around him the others exhaled. 'Don't try and find us. Don't try your bullying ways. Don't try and be clever. Wherever you go we will find you easy. We're inside your head, oga, and there are many-many of us. So you had better just disappear. But always watch your back, oga. Always check the shadows. You know what we can do because you made us do it.' He turned to Everil. 'Come, Big Gun, we are done here.'

Everil nodded. He and the others put up their knives. Stanlake pulled his hood back up. As one they stepped back from Makinde, then turned and headed for the door. At that moment the girl, who had up until then stood there still as wood, as if to be still was to be invisible and therefore safe, gasped, 'No!'

Stanlake turned and looked at her, standing there naked with just a pillow in front of her. 'Come, sister,' he said, and he held out a hand to her. Still clutching the pillow, she took it.

'My clothes, though,' she said.

He nodded, and she let go of his hand and went to collect

her pale blue cotton panties, skirt, socks, blouse and shoes from where they were scattered on the floor. Suddenly shy, the Jackals looked past her defocusedly as she turned away from them and dressed herself with jerky movements. It took her only a minute, but to them all it felt endless. Once dressed she looked down on Makinde. 'I'm fourteen,' she said thickly. 'I was a virgin.' She hawked and spat in his face. The glob of mucus hit him in the eye. He struggled and tossed his head but he couldn't flick it away.

'You got a coat?' Everil asked the girl as they hurried down the stairs.

'It's in the car, though.'

They left the house the way they had come in, through the back. Everil rang Cuts as they crossed the lawn towards the bushes. 'Mission accomplished, fam,' he said. 'Nah, not that, just – Meet us up the top of the road, yeah.'

They pushed their way through the bushes to the fence, careless now of scattering snow. On this side the fence was cross-beamed for support and easy to climb, though still they helped pull each other – and the girl – up and over the top. Once back in the alley they took up their bikes.

'Ride wit me, yeah,' Solid said to the girl. 'Come sit on the handlebars.' She looked at him doubtfully. Her thin arms were hugged tight around her, and she was already shaking with the cold. After contemplating her for a long moment he peeled off his hoodie and offered it to her. She hesitated, then took it and put it on. His bare arms goosebumped: he was only wearing a vest underneath. 'You'll be alright, though,' he said, looking strange with his painted, scarred face, in just a vest on a snowy night. She gave him the twitch of a smile.

Cuts was waiting for them on the corner. 'We best get off road soon as, yeah,' Everil said, conscious as ever of their stolen bikes and blatant knives, their visibility on this empty street as a pack of mischief-making hoodies. They headed back up to the main road, Solid wobbling awkwardly with the girl on his handlebars, her bare legs splayed out, vulnerable.

Now they weren't having to follow the car it was easier: they could choose their pace, cut through parks, ride on pavements, go the wrong way through one-way systems.

They kept moving but didn't hurry: it was all done now. Their adrenalin levels were falling, and they took it easy, maintaining just enough of a pace to keep their muscles warm. All of them were light-headed, and each in his way felt oddly purified. New lives, undefined but somehow enticing, lay before them.

Stanlake was travelling in spirits. On a dirt road, in torn khaki and diamante, Big Gun, Diamondz and Blondie saluted as he passed by them by. Somehow he was moving above the ground, as if in one of the rebel trucks but no longer in contact with anything physical: flying. They smiled sadly as they touched their fingers to their foreheads in salute and sent him on his way. Then he was dancing with Patrick and Matthew and Robert in the village square, laughing and clinking bottles of beer, and from somewhere behind and above him his father was watching: seeing that against all the odds his son had made his hunt, and done it well. And with the soldier-boys, who now scrambled up behind him laughing, the village boys and his father, were Everil, Pit-Bull, Solid and Cuts, finally belonging to something: to this company of men, this new shrine. And the road ran through Stanlake, and the village square was in his heart and the Beasts and the Jackals were dancing there too, all of them together, and he knew he would never be alone again.

'So where we going, then, fam?' Everil asked as they neared the Old Kent Road.

'To my drum. Home.'

'It done, yeah?'

'Yes.'

'You reckon he'll pull something, though?'

'No. Because he wants to live. Back in the war I think he did not care much. None of us did, and it made us strong. But today, in his nice-nice house with the admiration of others, he values his life. I saw it in him and he knows it makes him weak. He does not have fool-fool people around him who want to die for him, not like the old days, just sharp-type people who want money and will desert him when it stops coming. And he does not know who or what you are. He only knows I called you by the names of ghosts of boys that he betrayed.'

'So what now?'

'I need my mother to meet this girl. And I want her to meet you too.'

Everil pulled a face. 'But she has met me, though.'

'You as you are now. And the rest of my new comrades. And the girl – I need my mother to know what her preacher is. But please, Big Gun, don't tell her *who* he is. Back then, that day, she never saw his face. All she needs to know is he is a bad man who should not be in our lives. And this girl can help us get rid of him for good.'

They returned the bikes to Pit-Bull's lock-up and made their way to Stanlake's block. By now their fingers were numb, their feet throbbed icily and their lower backs and thigh-muscles burned. Everill's wound pulsed and Solid, bare-armed in his scoop-neck vest, was shuddering with cold. It was gone one a.m.

In the lift Everil kissed Stanlake on the mouth, and their lips were cold at first, but there was a heat behind them that built rapidly. The others looked sideways much as they had done when the girl was getting dressed, and, as with that, the obliqueness came from feelings more of shyness than what they would have been before: revulsion. The girl watched more directly but said nothing. This was, after all, no more strange than the other things that had happened tonight, and it did her no harm, was perhaps even a protection.

The lift-doors opened and they got out. Stanlake's mind was both blank and whirling as he slid his key into the front door of his flat. Before he had a chance to turn it the door was pulled open from within, and almost as if she had been shoved Poppy flung herself into her son's arms and hugged him close. She smelt of cocoa-butter and cinnamon and onions, and her soft, bare arms were strong and encompass-ing. Tears squeezed from her closed eyes. 'I'm sorry,' she said breathlessly. 'I'm so sorry.'

'I too,' he whispered. 'I too.' And the others watched, unashamedly this time, as mother and son embraced, and their eyes glistened. After a while Stanlake and Poppy released each other. 'Mummy,' he said. 'These are my friends. This is Everil.' Everil took off a glove and offered

Poppy his hand and she took it and her fingers were warm
and his were cold, and she looked at him, but now with
neither fear nor resentment. Cuts stood next to him.

'This is Cuts,' Everil said.

'Clarence,' Cuts corrected him. 'My name's Clarence.'

'Clarence.' Poppy nodded, taking his hand briefly. 'I am
Poppy, Stanlake's mother.'

Stanlake turned to Solid. 'Zachariah,' Solid said. Then,
looking down, he muttered, 'I'm sorry, like. Like, about
before. Like how we, um – ' He looked to the others, who
nodded sheepish agreement.

'Yes,' Poppy said. She took his hand and held it, and he
looked up at her and his eyes were afraid and his expression
was boyish, and there she was, this African mother, and she
had seen him and said yes, and touched him.

And Pit-Bull introduced himself as Shaun, and it was as
if the masks of paint and blood they still wore, and as if the
night they had gone through had freed them from their old
selves and permitted them to move at once both backwards
and forwards in their lives. Poppy now turned to the girl,
who had been hanging back awkwardly, and her expression
changed to one of concern. 'But I think I know you,' she said.
The girl looked frightened: was this somehow after all a trap?
'From church, enh? What is your name?'

'Berta,' the girl said, avoiding Poppy's eyes, plucking at
her short skirt, trying to cover her bare legs.

'Let's go inside,' Stanlake said. 'You can see she is cold.'

'Come in please,' Poppy said, stepping back to let them
enter, first her son and – yes, she could think this word now
– his boyfriend, then Berta, then Solid, Pit-Bull and Cuts.
They bundled through into the warmth of the kitchen.

As well as the usual kitchen things and a map of Africa
on the wall there was, on a shelf, a framed photograph
flanked by lit candles. Someone who knew that photograph
would have remembered how just the day before there had
been a crack running across its surface. The glass had been
replaced, and the father's smiling face was no longer obscured. The candles – scented, with bits of orange peel in
them – gave a soft, aromatic glow. And the Jackals looked at
what was clearly an altar in a room that was now not only a

kitchen but also a shrine, and saw a smiling Stanlake and his mother and father, and only Berta saw and did not understand all that that meant; and yet she sensed that here was the resolution of something as Stanlake reached out and touched the perfect glass with the tips of his fingers.

Poppy squeezed round her son and his guests to fill the kettle and make them tea. Stanlake and Everil shared a mug, as did Solid and Berta, and then there was just one mug left, and Poppy passed it to Cuts, but he insisted she keep it for herself, and he and Pit-Bull drank tea awkwardly from tumblers, having to set them down between sips to avoid burning their fingers until it occurred to Pit-Bull to put one of his gloves back on. And there was cheerful, abstracted talk about the night's events – the concrete avoided due to Poppy's presence – and brag about fitness and stamina. The evasion made Poppy feel like a little girl again, envying the men their hunt and their men's secrets. But she wasn't a little girl, she was a mother, and her son had come back to her, and she smiled.

Everil said suddenly, 'Shouldn't there be like a feast though?' and at that they all realised how hungry they were.

'But everywhere's closed though,' said Solid. 'Nando's, Mickey D's, KFC.'

'So we cook,' Stanlake said.

'How though?' asked Solid, looking around. 'Dere ain't no microwave.'

'The stove,' Stanlake said, unable to push down a smile.

'But what, though?' asked Pit-Bull.

'The chicken.'

'But you can't just cook that, though, fam,' Pit-Bull said. 'It's got feathers and feet and shit.'

'I will pluck it and gut it,' Stanlake said.

'Cheese an' bread, fam.'

'You're funny, my brother,' Stanlake said. 'Don't be afraid.'

'I ain't *afraid*, fam,' Pit-Bull grumbled. 'Just, it's...' He shrugged and tailed off, blushing.

Stanlake turned to Cuts. 'Matthew Jackal, will you get our chicken?'

Cuts nodded. Poppy saw him to the door and let him out.

In the kitchen they fell quiet, sipping their tea, young and radiant and finally and proudly part of the tribe of men. Eventually Pit-Bull said, 'Maybe we oughtta like wash our faces, is it?'

Stanlake nodded and pointed him to the bathroom. Everil and Solid followed, peeling off their hoodies as they went. While they were washing Stanlake said to Poppy, 'Mummy, you need to talk with this girl. Don't be afraid,' he said to Berta. 'Just tell her the truth about the Reverend.'

Berta nodded, understanding that this was the price of her protection, and she let Poppy lead her from the kitchen to her bedroom. Poppy clicked on the bedside lamp and they sat side by side on the mattress and talked quietly, hand-in-hand, and in a little while Berta was letting the tears fall while Poppy watched her with gentle eyes in which tears started too.

Some time later a rattle came at the front door and it was Cuts with the chicken in a carrier-bag. By then the others had washed their faces and Berta and Poppy had dried their eyes. Cuts handed the chicken to Stanlake and went and scrubbed his face while Poppy dug out onions, peppers and sweet potatoes, and put palm-oil and spices in the pan.

After removing his war-paint Stanlake cleansed and moisturised then reapplied eyeshadow, mascara and a little lip-gloss. Rebuilding his free, feminine self, he changed into a navel-revealing and figure-hugging vest, slipped on the white lace thong and wrapped cloth round his hips sarong-style. Everil kept him company in the bedroom while he changed, lolling on the bed and watching his lover's trans-formation with evident pleasure, then caught Stanlake's hand in his and pulled Stanlake down, rolling on top of him as Stanlake squealed and pretended resistance.

Solid and Pit-Bull sat sipping tea in the kitchen and listened to soft words and laughter coming from Stanlake's room, and stifled sobs from Poppy's.

'What you wanna do, fam,' Solid asked Pit-Bull, 'like, now? I mean like, with your life?'

'I dunno, blood,' Pit-Bull said. 'I know this, though: I ain't wanna go backwards. I ain't like where we was. And believe, you can't stand still in life.'

Solid nodded. Then, his thoughts going in another direction, he asked, 'It bother you, though? E being – like that?'

'I'da thought it would,' Pit-Bull shrugged. 'But it don't, though, somehow. I mean, not like I'd do none a dat, no way, blood. No homo, blah blah. But still, though, it ain't bother me like it's spose to. You?'

Solid shook his head. 'Cos it's just him,' he said. 'Just them.' He took out a cigarette and went to light it, but didn't: it didn't seem respectful.

'You like dat gal,' Pit-Bull said.

'She aiight. Too young, but she got some heart, you know?'

Their conversation was ended by Cuts' returning with the chicken, and soon the kitchen was bustling with activity. The sights and smells of cooking were unfamiliar to Everil, Solid, Cuts and Pit-Bull, like something out of a storybook. They pulled faces as Stanlake briskly plucked the chicken, and bent over and mimed vomiting when he deftly drew its guts and wrapped them in newspaper. Solid chased a squealing Berta out of the room with one of the severed chicken-feet, and she laughed, and he laughed too.

Under Poppy's guidance Cuts carefully sliced a pepper. His movements with the blade were tentative, and he narrowly avoided cutting a finger as it skidded on the flexible curve of the pepper's bell. Behind him the rice-pan steamed and bubbled. Everil did better with peeling the sweet potato, some long-ago memory resurfacing of being at an aunt's house and getting roped in to help with the meal.   Aunt Esther. It had been what, seven years since he had seen her. Ah, no: there had been the funeral. But that had been all fake sentiment, all business. No real faces that day. Pit-Bull cut a courgette into too-fat slices, and then had laboriously to go back and bisect each over-chunky slice without cutting his fingers in the process.

It was a haphazard meal, and Poppy found it hard to let the boys fumble and stumble so inefficiently through their chores. But she managed it, helped perhaps by the presence of Berta, with whom she could in some small way conspire in enjoying the young men's ineptitude – though truth to tell

Berta was equally bereft of domestic skills. It was three a.m. by the time they sat down – or leant where they stood – to eat. By then they were out of talk, each alone with his thoughts and yet companionable.

In the end Poppy didn't go to bed at all that night. She let Berta take her mattress. The others she left in Stanlake's room, her son and Everil in the bed, Cuts, Solid and Pit-Bull on the floor, on and under the few blankets and sheets she had to spare. Once all was quiet she stacked the plates in the sink, washed her face, changed and got ready for work.

The edges of the sky were pearling as she closed the front door behind her. Her eyes were twitchy and sharp with tiredness. Lucy would be waiting for her at the bus-stop wondering why she had left service so abruptly the night before.

Today she would have much to tell her.

Chapter Nineteen

The days and weeks and months passed. The scars on the boys' cheeks healed, became faint. The Anointed Joy and Prosperity Mission was rocked by scandal as one underage girl after another came forward to tell of abuse by the Reverend and some of his associates under the guise of 'spiritual guidance sessions', both at the church and at his 'million pound' Honor Oak home. Mrs Ige and Mrs Bankole made a joint statement to local journalists saying that the girls must surely be possessed by evil spirits to make such wicked and dishonest claims, and that they and the other congregants were 'one thousand percent behind' their pastor. Despite their vote of confidence Reverend Obasanjo nonetheless felt obliged to step down from a leadership role in the church. His successor, Reverend Agbaje, who arrived as a new broom, lacked charisma and was generally felt to be a disappointment, though out of loyalty Lucy kept going. Poppy didn't. She would find another church, she said to Lucy, but right now she wasn't in a hurry. Relations between the two had cooled since Poppy told Lucy that with God's help she was doing her best to accept her son's homosexuality, even allowing his boyfriend to stay over.

So it was that Poppy didn't hear about it when the Reverend was arrested for identity fraud. Being in the U.K. illegally was only the start of his troubles, as it turned out: once his true identity had been uncovered he was exposed as a wanted international war criminal, and remanded to Brixton Prison until extradition could be arranged for him to stand trial for his activities. Stanlake managed to keep the local paper from his mother the week the story was reported. If Lucy saw it she kept quiet about it.

Since the night they had gone to the Reverend's house Stanlake and Everil moved in the world more fearlessly, and the future opened for them like a flower. Stanlake continued his studies and started to look at fashion courses. Everil dropped out of dealing, letting it be assumed that after almost being killed by Stats he had lost his nerve. No longer part of the game, he found that he didn't care much about losing the respect of the other players. He cared a little, of course, because he was a man and had a man's pride, but only a little.

Solid took over as boss of the Crew, but not with much appetite. The longing for a wider world was in him too, and the endless hours of hanging around in the underpass waiting for punters no longer excited him – or any of them. He began to look for apprentice work as a garage mechanic. In the evenings he drummed. Pit-Bull, in a surprise left turn, began volunteering at a nearby youth centre, helping other young people with their reading and writing. Cuts started to work part-time in his father's warehouse in Chinatown, enjoying the novel thrill, the rootedness of a pay-packet.

It was the year they became men.

One Saturday afternoon, when the spring sunshine was warming the air, the blossom was thick on the branches and the new leaves were bright, Everil arranged to meet Stanlake at the top of Brixton Hill. He cycled there, feeling fit and looking toned in a black mesh vest, a black leather baseball-cap high on his shaven, headscarfed head. Old-skool hi-top Nikes were on his feet, and he wore baggy black shorts that at the back were pushed down below his butt, which was itself sheathed in enticing skin-tight grey lycra. On his fingers were gold sovereign rings, and his mother's gold chain was around his neck. A carrier-bag with things in it hung from one handlebar of the bike. He checked his phone and nodded to himself: he was on time.

A bus drew up at the stop, the doors opened and Stanlake stepped down. Today he was all in blue: a tight turquoise halter-top, denim short-shorts that showed off his shaved, smoothly-muscled mocha legs, knock-off Camel tractor boots, bold blue eye-shadow, and on his shaved head was a blue silk headscarf. Around his neck and wrists on leather thongs were cowries. Glimpsed fleetingly, despite his flat chest and narrow hips, he could be taken for a pretty girl. By the second glance he was past and gone, and so he moved through the world, avoiding harassment as best he could. His fearlessness was some insulation; his boldness, small though he was, an intimidation that in the main offset the challenge wound up in his appearance.

He had friends at school now. Mostly girls who were intrigued by this pretty African boy who wore make-up, who made performing femininity an embodiment of freedom and not a burdensome capitulation in the unending battle to score a man. Around the girls orbited the boys who were seeking their attention, and the smarter ones soon learned that accepting the androgynous sun at the girls' centre was shorthand for, 'I'm not a jerk, I'm mature, sophisticated.' Trevone nicknamed Stanlake Boyoncé, and the name made Stanlake laugh, and he didn't disavow it. Some of the boys he even helped with their studies, if warily, and only ever on school grounds. And the nights of knives and nightmares faded and took their proper place in the past, and were replaced by nights of kisses and caresses. And when the nightmares did come Everil was there to hold him.

With barely a glance about them Stanlake and Everil kissed hello, forcing casualness, forcing parity. *Because fuck the world if they don't get it.* Stanlake lifted himself up onto Everil's bike, wedged his hips between the handlebars and lent back into Everil. Framed by his lover's arms he let himself be pedalled slowly along. Things clinked in the carrier-bag that swung from the left handlebar each time Everil bumped it with his knee. Their way was flat for a while, then they rolled down a gentle hill and the breeze was warm and there was a fragrance in the air.

After a while the road rose again. It quickly grew steeper and they wobbled to a stop, Everil holding the bike steady so Stanlake could more easily wriggle out from between the handlebars and dismount. This was Gypsy Hill, and they wheeled the bike up it at an easy pace. A short way on they came to a parade of local shops and restaurants. The area felt prosperous but was also racially diverse. Above, the sky was a pale blue, scudded with clouds.

'Where are we?' Stanlake asked.

'Crystal Palace.'

'Is there a palace?' Stanlake knew often there wasn't:

there were no elephants at Elephant & Castle; there was no castle.

'There used to be. Like two hundred years ago or summink.'

'And was it made of crystals?'

'Or summink. Glass. Like the biggest greenhouse ever. It burned down, though.'

'Why here?'

'Cos my mum useda bring me here when I was a kid,' Everil said. 'Well, that's some of it.'

They came to the brow of a hill that on its far side fell away steeply and looked out across a large park. The park covered half the hillside and spread out over the level ground at the hill's foot, and was dense with trees. Beyond it residential streets ran away in endless order. Hand in hand Everil and Stanlake entered the park, passing under a stone arch into an ornamental garden transected by gravel paths. On a sloping oval of lawn a group of young white people were sitting chatting. Someone out of sight was playing a guitar softly. Everil and Stanlake followed one of the paths down into the trees.

'What is the other part?' Stanlake asked, picking up on the last thing Everil had said some minutes before.

'I'll show you.'

They came to the bottom of the hill. Beyond the trees was a small lake round which a path ran. In the middle of the lake was an island from which tall rocks and narrow trees rose.

'Look.'

Stanlake looked. At first he saw nothing out of the ordinary. Then on top of one of the rocks he noticed perched the carving of a creature, slate-coloured, with spread, featureless wings. A dinosaur, he thought, though it didn't quite look like the dinosaurs in films or on television. Something about the quirkiness of its appearance made him smile. Pterodactyl, he remembered: that was its name. Soon he began to notice others. Something large and scaly and four-legged the colour of dull jade, with a small horn on its nose and a half-humorous look in its eye, loomed in the bushes. Near the pond's edge an exopthalmic ichthyosaurus plashed in an implausibly shallow pool. Mostly grey and muted blue, the creatures were oddly charming. As he looked at them Everil's hand tightened in his.

'My mum used to read me this book,' Everil said. 'Back before she was permanently fucked up. It was like my favourite. It was about how the dinosaurs were after it got dark. This boy what lives next to the park sneaks in and sees 'em come to life.'

'What do they do when they come to life?' Stanlake asked. 'Hunt?'

'Nah, they just – they just got these secret lives no-one knows about.' Everil looked round at Stanlake. 'I guess it said something to me, you know? Even back then, even before I knew I – Anyway,' his voice caught. 'Anyway, this is the place.'

'The place?'

From the carrier-bag Everil produced a burnished metal canister. It gleamed dully in the sunlight. A breeze sprang up, stirring the branches above their heads and setting the leaves dancing. Somewhere a dog began to bark joyously and a woman's voice called. Everil passed Stanlake the bag, which was still weighty with other things, and unscrewed the top of the urn. He looked around. No-one was nearby. The wind was moving out across the water, and there was a dazzle of sunlight caught on its tremulous surface. Everil held the urn out at arm's length and tilted it. Ash began to slide out. As it fell it was carried away, darkening as it touched the surface of the water, then vanishing below. Everil tilted the urn more and the ash ran faster. A few heavier bits dropped with small splashes into the water at their feet, bone fragments that reminded him – reminded them both – that this was actual as well as symbolic: that this had been his mother's body. And then the urn was empty.

'Goodbye, Mum,' Everil said in a choked voice. He took a breath. Then he screwed the lid back onto the urn. Stanlake held the carrier-bag open, and Everil put the urn back in it. He found Stanlake's hand again and they stood that way for a while, hand in hand, looking out across the small lake, hearts beating.

'What else did you bring?' Stanlake asked.

'Champagne. But it don't seem right, though.'

'My father taught me that we pour a drink for the one who is gone. We offer it to the ground. To the spirit realm.'

Everil took the bottle out of the bag. Moët Chandon. It had been chilled, and its sides were slick and sweaty with condensation. He peeled off the foil and untwisted the wire that caged the cork. With both thumbs he popped it, and the cork flew out over the water and sat bobbing there, its metal top glinting. Someone somewhere unseen laughed at the distinctiveness of the sound. Uncertain what to do next, Everil passed the bottle to Stanlake.

'For Annette,' Stanlake said. 'We honour the mother of Everil for giving him life and passing on what lessons she learned and what love she had to give. We thank her, and ask her to give him what help and wisdom she can, and we honour her.' He tipped a foamy splash of the champagne onto the ground. As it soaked away he took a swig from the bottle and passed it to Everil, who took a swig too, then wiped his mouth.

'I wanna say this is for Stanlake's dad,' Everil said, raising his voice as if there was an audience of spirits out there beyond the water that he was addressing, as perhaps there was and always had been. 'This is for Pacific. Cos if he ain't been there then this – man – what I love, he ain't be here either. I know you had to go through what you had to go through, and that was bad. But if you ain't, if my man here didn't – do what he did, you'd of all died. You give it up so that ain't happen. So thanks, yeah. I owe you. And – that's it.'

And he made his libation, and he turned to Stanlake and, resonating with the past and with eyes on the future, they kissed.

The End

Also available from Team Angelica Publishing

Out now:

'Reasons to Live' by Rikki Beadle-Blair
'What I Learned Today' by Rikki Beadle-Blair
'Colour Scheme' by John R Gordon
'Faggamuffin' by John R Gordon
'Fairytales for Lost Children' by Diriye Osman

Forthcoming:

'Black & Gay in the UK' – an anthology
'Tiny Pieces of Skull' by Roz Kaveney